TRINITY'S LEGACY

P.A. Vasey

Copyright © 2019 P.A.Vasey
All rights reserved.

All characters and events in this novel are fictitious and any resemblance to real persons, living or dead, is purely coincidental.

This novel is dedicated to my wife Andrea, who indulged me in what started out as a bit of fun but soon became another of my obsessions outside of work (the other being cycling). My daughters, Rachael and Lauren read the drafts and gave me encouragement and feedback, but because they weren't completely unbiased (!) structural analysis and critical reading of the manuscript was by Kate O'Donnell at *Linecreative*.

"Two possibilities exist: either we are alone in the Universe, or we are not. Both are equally terrifying."

- Arthur C. Clarke

PROLOGUE

The Chief Resident didn't look at me but just pointed down the corridor in the general direction of the patient bays. She was writing an entry in a chart as her pager went off and the phone by her elbow started ringing. She had the stiff-backed posture of a soldier, and her unlined face was calm and collected as she picked up the phone with one hand while looking at the number on her pager. I saw her smile in that cold and distant way that professionals do as she took another call and started the process of admitting another patient.

"Mommy, can I stay here and play with the big computer?"

My five-year-old daughter, Kelly, cannot yet see the world through my eyes, and generally I am good with that. But occasionally, as a single parent, I need to bring her to work, to my world, where the darkness and suffering happens. However, hanging onto my arm, iPad in hand, all she could see was a big TV with a flashing screen saver of some Marvel movie character floating in the sky, lightning bolts raining down on some helpless adversary.

The Resident, a doctor called Meiko I'd met a few times in the ER, glanced at me and put her pen down. She gave a wink to Kelly and patted the chair next to her. Kelly looked up at me and I nodded assent so with a little squeal, she jumped up into the chair and pulled it closer to the desk. Meiko smoothed Kelly's curly blonde hair out of her eyes and gave her the mouse to play with as she continued to take her telephone call.

I smiled a 'thanks' and picked up the thin manila file she'd pushed towards me and flicked it open to the ER page that detailed the admission notes and the reason for my visit, as the Oncology Fellow. The entry was brief, but informative: The patient was male, mid-seventies, brought in by ambulance paramedics after a 911 call from a local grocery store. Apparently he'd been found unconscious behind one of the fruit and vegetable aisles. There were a couple of blood results attached, but nothing diagnostic or particularly informative. I noted that a brain scan had been ordered and Meiko had written: *'Likely intracerebral event, CVA or tumor, refer to Internal Medicine and Oncology.'*

"When's he having the CT scan?" I said to Meiko, who was still on the phone. She held up a finger in the universal gesture of 'hang on a sec', and swapped the phone to her other ear. Then continued her conversation, ignoring me.

I got the hint.

I kissed Kelly on the forehead, barely getting an acknowledgement, and headed towards bay number three. I walked past nurses and porters running between patients carrying charts, x-rays, sample bottles, syringes, drugs and everything needed to keep the chaos from becoming madness. There was the constant rush of footfalls, squeaking trolley wheels, telephones ringing, monitors beeping and pinging, and I found myself longing for my office, where I'd been ensconced for the past couple of hours in companionable silence with Kelly, reviewing my own charts for tomorrow's morning rounds.

The curtains around bay three were drawn, and so I pulled them open and stepped through. Lying on the trolley was a young tattooed black man, draped in gold chains, dressed in a tracksuit and wearing Nike hi-tops. He was holding his abdomen, where a surgical pad and dressing had been applied, and which was oozing crimson. He seemed not to be in pain, and had a dreamy opiate-imbibed look to his eyes. The name above his bed written in precise sharpie was 'Jayden Washington'. Three similarly attired males, and one female, who looked very pregnant, surrounded him.

Seeing me, one of the guys gave a low whistle, and nudged his injured pal who gave me a sly grin. Now they were all checking me out, eyes doing that up and down thing. I was instantly regretting putting on my black tights and knee-high leather boots this morning, which were all the fashion in Chicago that winter, although I had assumed the white lab coat and stethoscope would offset any fashion faux pas.

"Hey doc, been waitin' ages," slurred Jayden. He had a round face and one of those sharply cut goatees. He was a good fifty pounds overweight for his height, which I guessed was about five feet nothing given the way his Nikes weren't touching the footrest.

"I'm not your doctor," I said. "Wrong bay."

"Yo can be my doctor any day, know what I'm sayin'," chimed in another of his buddies, followed by a round of snickering and a fist bump. The girl gave him a thin-lipped stare and turned to me, hands on her hips.

"You going to fix him?" she snapped.

I shook my head. "Your doctor'll be along in a minute. I'll let her know."

"Hurry along then," she said.

I sighed and mouthed "dicks", before turning on my heel and leaving through the curtain. I peered at the chart again, and tried my luck in bay two.

Jackpot.

Well, sort of.

Lying on the bed was a man beaten down first by old age and then by some sort of neurological catastrophe. His withered face was drooping on the right side, and drool was tracking down his chin pooling at the root of his neck. Ill-kept iron-grey hair was lank and pallid; his eyes were open and a milky blue with early cataract formation. He was long and thin, stick-like arms poked out from underneath a T-shirt bearing the logo from the zombie show 'The Walking Dead'.

The irony didn't escape me.

I popped the chart on the side table and said, "Hello, anybody there?" There was no response so I grasped his hand and squeezed, repeating the question. His hand felt cool and rubbery, wiry tendons palpable under thin skin. I stood back to get a better look at him, and someone nudged me from behind the curtain.

"Excuse me," I said, and moved away a little, assuming I'd just backed into a visitor standing outside the curtain. There was a swishing noise as whomever it was tried to find the slash entry, and then a face appeared. Followed by a gun.

I backed up as the gun's owner entered the bay. He was young, seventeen or so, his collection of gang tattoos with spidery designs and Latin writing curling up around his neck. His eyes were staring and watery, his mouth pulled down in a sneer, a thin film of sweat on his moustache.

He took a quick look at the man on the bed and then pointed the gun at me.

"Where's Jayden?"

The weapon was twitching, but from where he was standing, he wouldn't have any problem with his aim. The hole at the end of the barrel looked three feet wide.

"Jayden who?" I said, raising my eyebrows.

He jutted his chin at me, mouth curling downwards. "You don't want to be fuckin' with me."

There was more swishing, this time from behind the curtain on the opposite side of John Doe. Three of Jayden's buddies stepped through, and squared off across the bed at the man with the gun. He bared yellowed teeth, turning the gun sideways gangsta style and pointed it at the three newcomers. His eyes were narrowed, and there was a cool hatred there. He'd have no problem pulling the trigger, if he hadn't already. I guessed he was coming to finish the job on Jayden.

"This is a hospital," I said, while moving to the foot of the bed and out of the firing line. "You can't bring guns here."

"Yeah Tyler, get the fuck out," scowled one of Jayden's entourage, very helpfully.

I flicked a glance at him. "You guys need to leave, too." I could see a fairly obvious bulge under his sweatshirt. He was packing and therefore probably the others were too. I kept my hands in the pockets of my white coat, mainly to keep any of them from getting too excited, but also so I could press the emergency button on my phone.

"Did you hear what she said, asshole?" Jaden's buddy hissed ominously.

Tyler's eyes turned towards me, and the gun followed in a sweeping arc. Immediately, the others drew weapons from jackets and pant pockets, and all of a sudden the situation had gone from one angry guy with a gun to the OK Corral. Big glistening black 45s wagged in the air, twisting and pointing like in the movies. I inched backwards towards the edge of the curtain, which was tantalizingly half open. In the distance I could hear the tannoy announcing 'CODE BLACK', and the patter of running feet approaching.

There was no sound in our bay. John Doe lay oblivious to everything, and none of the gunmen were talking. If stares could kill, everyone would already be dead. I held a hand up towards Tyler, the seventeen-year-old child with a hand cannon.

"Hey, Tyler. Look at me. It's not too late. Just leave. Police are on their way."

I could see it in his eyes. The fast blinking. Jerking left and right. He was looking for a way out. Anger had segued into fear, trapped in a nightmare of his own making.

I breathed in, and licked some moisture onto my suddenly-dry lips. "Tyler. Sometimes it takes courage to back off, live to fight another day, you know?"

At that moment the curtain behind him twitched and billowed and my daughter ran in, laughing and waving her iPad looking for me. I screamed her name and hurled myself towards her, arms outstretched, heart hammering, and all the guns seemed to go off at once. The sound was like a million thunderclaps, cracking the air as if the very fabric of the atmosphere was being ripped apart. Something hot seared the side of my head above my right ear, and I tumbled onto the floor, everything spinning and churning like a washing machine.

Booted feet stepped over me and the gunshots continued, and I was being kicked and stepped on as more people entered the bay. I turned my head sideways and vomited, acid burning the inside of my mouth. I tried to pull myself up onto my elbows but someone yelled "stay down!" and I found that this was all I could do anyway. My eyes fluttered, and I lay there, hot and coppery-smelling blood trickling down the side of my face and dripping onto the floor. I stared at the droplets forming into a puddle, wondering who's it was, and if it was mine, and why there was no pain.

Then, arms grabbed me from behind and I was being pulled out of the bay.

I had glimpses of blue and black police uniforms swarming around the bed, and of white-coated figures swarming over bodies on the ground. Track suited, adult bodies, bleeding and gasping and limbs twitching.

And one little girl, lying on her side, head turned towards me, eyes open.

DAY 1

CHAPTER ONE
Six months later
Indian Springs Hospital and Medical Centre, Nevada

I entered the empty doctors' office, the early morning sun squeezing through half-closed blinds, probing and casting zebra-like patterns into the darkened corners. It was a small functional space, with worn but comfortable lazy-boys lining the wall facing the window under which was a desk groaning from the weight of an idling computer monitor, abandoned coffee cups, and reams of half-completed paperwork. A wall clock looked balefully down. A variety of coloured theatre scrubs and a few stethoscopes draped over hangers decorated another wall. A dartboard sporting the face of Donald Trump occupied another. A pot of coffee bubbled on a low table. A single door with an inlaid window obscured by more blinds was covered with notices and flyers.

I poured a cup of coffee, and took a sip, savouring the smooth bitterness and the hit I always got from the stewed sludge in the bottom of the pot. I flopped down into one of the recliners, and closed my eyes. The ward outside was bustling with morning activity, nurses and orderlies walking up and down doing their jobs, chatting and laughing. There was the usual hospital smell of disinfectant, and a pleasant waft of toast and coffee coming from one of the rooms next to the kitchen. The intermittent beeping and pinging of cardiac monitors could just be heard from the central station.

It was relaxing, soporific even. I felt myself drifting off.

As usual my thoughts gravitated to Chicago, and my daughter. I couldn't properly visualize her any more. She was like a ghost. What had once been my whole life and existence was now a memory, a shadow lingering in the depths of my mind, slowly but inexorably becoming more insubstantial. My mind called out to her, but the connection was missing, and in its place was a numb paraesthesia, an empty place, hollowed out by grief. Sometimes, the shell was filled with tears and burst open like a crack in the side of a dam. More often these days, I felt nothing, or I didn't know how, or what, to feel.

The rising crescendo wails of an approaching emergency vehicle broke into my reverie, and I pulled myself up to peer out of the window. An ambulance swerved into the parking zone, gravel crunching and tyres screeching.

I went through to the ER where a receptionist speaking into a phone and two nurses flicking idly through magazines occupied the front desk. As would have been usual for the time of day, the wait area was empty of patients. The receptionist was a heavyset woman called Carlie, who noticed me and smiled whilst cradling the phone on her ear. I held my hands palms up, mouthing, "What's going on?"

Carlie shrugged back and spoke into the phone, sarcasm dripping and looking at me with lidded eyes, "Yeah, we can hear you now guys, thanks for the heads-up."

She put the phone on its cradle, and pointed to the entryway as a trolley crashed through the heavy plastic doors, guided by two paramedics. One was holding an IV line and steering the trolley with his free hand, while the other was pushing from the rear, oxygen bagging the occupant of the trolley. Two men in their early twenties, dressed in jeans and T-shirts followed, stopping to look around the reception area like deer caught in headlights.

I put my coffee down on the bench, and gestured for the paramedics to take the patient into one of the three empty medical bays. I moved over to the left side of the trolley and through the oxygen mask got a glimpse of a white Caucasian male in his forties with black hair, and a greyish-white appearance to his skin. The paramedics had him in a supportive neck brace. His eyes were closed.

I recognised the lead paramedic, a stocky blond guy called Jeff. "Hi, what've we got?" I said, all business.

Jeff looked up and smiled. "Good to see we've got the big-city hot-shot on today. Dr Morgan, how you doing? This guy was hit by a truck, couple of clicks on 95 just east of Mercury."

I flicked a glance over at the two men, still standing in the middle of the ER front entry. "Their truck?"

"Yep. Apparently just wandering down the I-95, pitch dark. Truck ran straight through him. Made quite a dent in the hood."

I nodded and waved a hand in their direction. "Hey, you guys. Get over here. Tell me what happened?"

The larger of the two sidled over; his companion hung back but kept his eyes on the patient on the trolley.

"What's your name?" I said.

"Bob. Bob Westwood." He reached out for a shake but I was snapping on gloves and hands in a silent 'don't touch' kind of way. He moved a bit closer to the trolley, peering at the figure under the blanket. I coughed and he shifted his gaze back to me. "Yeah, so it was early. One-ish I reckon. Me and my brother here were driving down the highway when this guy appeared directly in front of us, just walking down the centreline, cool, as you like. Carrying no lights, nothin'. We wuz goin' fifty-sixty or so but I braked hard, and pulled the wheel over to the left, tried to cross into the opposite lane. Didn't make it."

"So was it a glancing hit, maybe just the edge of the truck?"

He shook his head. "Here's the weird thing. I swear I saw him raise a hand towards us and suddenly the brake wouldn't work and the steering wheel kinda became disconnected from the wheels. Hit him full on. He bounced off the hood, cartwheeled into the windscreen, shot over the roof and back down the road like a rag doll. We zigzagged down the highway for fifty yards or so before the brakes came back on.

I killed the engine and my brother and I just kinda stared at each other in shock."

I imagined the truck's engine idling, smoke settling as they turned the ignition off and the sounds of the desert starting to impose. Frogs and crickets chattering in a nearby water hole. A not-so-distant coyote howling plaintively just above the sound of wind through the bushes and the scouring of wind-borne sand across the road.

You know the sort of thing.

I blinked to clear the image and turned to Jeff who was continuing to bag the patient, squeezing the rubber balloon, pushing oxygenated air into the patient's lungs.

"Do we have a name?"

"No name, no ID," he said.

I dismissed Bob with a wave and he wandered back over to the reception to join his brother. I turned back to the trolley and pulled my stethoscope out of my pocket.

"What's his status?"

The other paramedic, a balding younger guy I hadn't met before, looked up, shook his head. "Not sure. Can't get a reading on his oxygen sats, but he isn't cyanosed. Auto-reader gave a figure of sixty-six per cent on six litres oxygen, but that can't be right so we've disconnected it. I can't find a pulse, and he's got no blood pressure. He doesn't appear to be spontaneously breathing."

"So he's dead then?" I said.

"Theoretically yes, but he keeps moving. Look…"

He nodded at Jeff who stopped his ventilatory efforts with the mask and removed it. The patient twisted his neck, as if stretching and yawning.

I frowned. "Clearly not dead."

"I know, right?" said Jeff. "I've been bagging him at twenty per minute without any spontaneous respiratory effort. Yet he still shows signs of life."

"Maybe it's all instinct," I mused softly to myself, "and he's brain dead."

The other paramedic shrugged. "He's got a temperature. A *smoking* forty-two degrees."

I put my hand on the patient's forehead, expecting to feel the heat of a fevered brow. I recoiled and looked at the paramedic. "Really? He feels cold. Clammy, even."

"Weird, isn't it? And there's more. I can't get a response to pain stimuli. I got his GCS at 3; all 1 for EMV; his pupils are really, really big, but they're equal and they don't react to light stimulus."

"That's not good," I said, quietly.

All 1 for EMV meant the lowest score for eye, motor or verbal response; evidence pointing towards coma and possible brainstem damage. I hooked him up to a cardiac monitor, applying sticky pads to his feet, arms and chest. I switched on the machine, and watched as the lines appeared. Flat. No cardiac electrical activity.

"We've struggled to get intravenous access," said Jeff at the head of the gurney. He pointed to the IV running into the forearm. "I don't even think that's in a vein. His skin's so tough, I couldn't get no back-flow of blood."

I looped my stethoscope around my neck, and pulled the sheet down to get a good look at the patient. He was tall, with his feet hanging over the edge of the gurney. A head taller than most people I would consider tall. He didn't look lanky though, as there was bulk to him, in all the right places. He had a full head of blue-black hair, cut short and GI-like. He had strong arched brows and thick eyelashes and his face was chiselled with cut cheekbones and an aquiline nose. He was striking up close, but his pale skin and thin lips made me hesitate in calling him handsome.

"Doc," said Jeff, bringing me back to earth. "What do you make of the wetsuit?"

I saw that the paramedics had cut open his clothes to gain IV access, but I hadn't registered what he'd been wearing. I took a second to re-appraise this fact. "What was he doing wearing this in the desert?"

The second paramedic shook his head and grinned. "Fancy dress party?"

I gave him flat eyes. "Right."

He shrugged. "Why not? Maybe from the Base, out on pass, at a wild party? Coulda got drunk, and his buddies left him behind as a prank. You know those guys can party."

He smiled knowingly at me and I felt my cheeks burning.

Small town.

I pulled some scissors out of the top pocket of my scrubs, and started cutting away the rest of the wetsuit. I carefully peeled away the neoprene top and started my examination. I worked methodically over his upper body, feeling for abnormalities, swellings and deformations consistent with fracturing or internal bleeding. Everything seemed structurally normal. I once again noted that he was toned with very well defined musculature but interestingly he had no body hair. I tried to pull up a section of his forearm skin between my fingers, but nothing moved. It felt like leather. Or rubber. Anything but what normal skin should feel like.

"So… no signs of bruising over abdomen and chest wall," I was talking to myself. "Upper limbs appear intact." I stood back, hands on the side of the trolley and give a perplexed look. "Skin coloration definitely a little pale and waxy. The skin tone is tight, very tight …"

Jeff was standing back, watching, chin in hand. I looked up and caught his eye. He raised his eyebrows and blew out his cheeks.

"Doc, there's not a bruise or a scratch anywhere. I can't see any blemishes either, can you? No moles, birthmarks, nothing."

I nodded slowly, and pushed the earpieces of my stethoscope into place and listened to the man's chest. I could just hear a faint low noise, which I took to be heart sounds, very slow. I then placed the stethoscope on the abdomen, held it there for half a minute, then moved it around and listened again. I looked up at the paramedics, worried, and placed a hand on the abdominal wall. It was solid, like a board.

"I can't hear any bowel sounds," I said. "I suppose the impact might've produced a traumatic ileus, shutting down his bowels."

Or he could simply be bleeding out.

I pulled a pair of scissors from my pocket, and eased them between the skin and the wetsuit. I started cutting, expecting a tough job because of the thick rubber but the scissors sliced through the material like paper. Methodically I cut lines from the ankles to waist, and removed the leggings.

"Must be the cheapest wetsuit in the world," cracked the other paramedic.

I ignored him and ran my hands over the patient's legs, checking for broken bones. Everything looked structurally intact. There was no sign of injury to his legs or pelvis. I looked up, brow furrowed.

"There're no cuts or bleeding. Isn't that a little strange?"

They both nodded in agreement.

I stood back. "He must be one tough son of a bitch."

"I'll tell you something else," said Jeff. "When we lifted him onto the stretcher, he weighed almost nothing. Like a child. Can't be more than ninety pounds."

I looked up sharply. "That doesn't fit. Look how tall he is. And he certainly isn't emaciated."

"I guess. Maybe he has hollow bones," he said with a smile.

I gave him a sarcastic half smile back. The nurses were hanging around the bay so I decided to get them busy.

"Hayley, try and get some basic blood work off please. Can we get a full haematology profile, random chemistry including magnesium and glucose, blood gases, oh and a toxicology and alcohol screen? Carlie, you call the radiologist in, lets get a CAT series of his head, neck, chest and abdomen. I also need him catheterised to culture his urine. And culture his blood as well."

The nurses started moving, jolted into action. I got out my phone and took a quick picture of the patient, pulling the oxygen mask down for a better view. The plastic covers on the ER main doors slapped, and my colleague for the morning shift Clem Reynolds pushed through wearing Nike running gear and holding a Starbucks cup. He had a fringe of grey-white hair around his balding, mottled scalp but his face was free of lines and his eyes sparkled with youthful vigour. He took in the situation with a glance, and went straight to the opposite side of the couch, checking the patient out.

"Interesting start to the day?" he said, a twinkle in his eye.

Clem was an ex-military surgeon in his early 60s who did ER work in his spare time from being Indian Springs' only general practitioner. He was well liked and respected locally, and I'd appreciated the support and collegiality he'd offered to me when I arrived. I had stayed with Clem and his wife for two months while I was getting my act together and finding my feet. I can't imagine how hard I must have been to live with, but Clem never complained.

I gestured to the man on the trolley. "Do you recognise him? Maybe one of the GI Joes from the Base?"

Reynolds was gently turning the man's head side to side. "Never seen this guy before. Where was he found?"

"He was taking a stroll down the middle of the I-95 just a few miles east of Mercury. Those guys hit him." I pointed to Westwood and his brother, who were watching proceedings, wide-eyed.

"We tried to avoid him, but ..." Westwood stuttered.

"You guys still here?" I said. "You need to check in at the counter over there".

When they had shuffled away I turned to Reynolds. "Better get the police to talk with them. Something's not right. The paramedics said the hood was all bashed in from the impact. This guy shows no obvious sign of injury."

Reynolds nodded, and then leaned over the patient and put his mouth close to his ear. "Hello, can you hear me? You're in a hospital. Can you hear me?"

There was no reply, so he placed a knuckle over the man's sternum and dug it in back and forward with a twisting movement. The man stirred, his neck now arching backwards and upwards.

Jeff looked up, "that's an improvement."

Suddenly, the man's eyes flickered open, and the cardiac monitor came to life. Red and yellow lines started spasming and jerking across the screen before settling into a nice steady rhythm of eighty beats per minute. The oxygen saturation reading flicked to ninety-nine per cent. I stared unbelievingly at the monitor. All the parameters were now normalising. The automatic blood pressure cuff was activating and flashed up a healthy 120/65 reading.

"What can I say, I'm a good doctor," said Reynolds, a wry smile creasing his features.

I fished in my white coat pocket and brought out an ophthalmoscope. I pulled down the patient's right eyelid and shone the ophthalmoscope's light at the pupil. There was no light reaction, the pupil staying large and fixed. I leaned closer, winding the focus wheel down on the scope and attempted to bring the retina at the back of the eye into view. The optic disc came into focus and I could see numerous grey/black lines arcing concentrically away from where the optic nerve should be. I was about to examine the edges of the retina when there was a brief pulse of phosphorescent light that spun counter-clockwise along the lines, disappearing into the edge of the disc.

I straightened. "That's ... that's very interesting."

Clem looked up. "What?"

I turned the ophthalmoscope around in my hand as if I had never seen one before. I looked up at Clem and held it out to him. "Take a look."

He took the scope and leaned down to examine the man's other eye. After a minute or so looked up, disbelief etched on his face. "Is that ... electricity?"

He moved around to the left side of the trolley, and examined the other eye in the same deliberate way. He then handed the ophthalmoscope back to me, stood back, and wiped his mouth with the back of his hand. "Unusual pigmentation of the retina, don't you think?"

"I don't know what to think. I've never seen anything like that," I said.

I hadn't. It was so abnormal it made no sense at all.

Jeff had put the oxygen mask back over the patient's mouth, and re-started bagging him. He looked up at me, and then over at Reynolds. "Are you guys going to do anything to help this guy?"

Clem was jolted out of his daze. "Yes, absolutely. Kate, whatever that was, it'll have to wait. You said his abdomen's rigid and there aren't any bowel sounds. He must have some internal injury so maybe he's bleeding internally. Do you think we should prep him for emergency surgery?"

I laid a hand on the prostrate figure's abdomen and nodded absently. I looked into the man's face. "Sure, but let's get some scans first."

CHAPTER TWO
Indian Springs Hospital and Medical Centre, Nevada

One floor up, and adjacent to the surgical suite, I waited with Clem and the radiologist Pete Navarro for the images from the CT scanner to appear on the monitors. The radiographer was in the scan room next door with the patient, attempting to find a vein to cannulate after Jeff's needle had tissued soon after arrival in the CT suite. I looked through the leaded glass that separated the reporting room and scanning area, and gave the radiographer a hesitant, questioning thumbs up. Although he was masked, I could see that the expression in his eyes and his body posture indicated that he was still struggling with the IV. Our eyes met, and he replied with a negative downward gesture of his own thumb.

"No-go for intravenous contrast then," I sighed, looking at Clem. "We'll need to make do with non-contrast images."

"Did we get the blood work off?" he said.

"No. We can't find any veins. Probably all shut down, despite that Bp reading. I'm probably going to have to put a central line in, or do a cut-down."

Navarro grunted unconcernedly from the centre console chair. He was a fit looking thirty-something ex-airforce corporal with a buzz cut and a non-regulation moustache. I'd heard that medicine had been his second career, and that he'd left the military under a bit of a cloud. He seemed well suited to radiology given his obsessive-compulsive tendencies and poor people skills. Being in a dark room most of your working day looking at x-rays and scans, dictating reports and not needing to speak to actual humans would not have appealed to most people, but he seemed right at home.

"Don't worry," he said. "We'll get all the information we need from the non-contrast scan. I'll dial the gain up and increase the number and intensity of the slices." He smiled proudly. "This is cutting edge shit we got here, you know."

Navarro was both proud and protective of his equipment, and given the almost unlimited budget the US Airforce had to work with, he had been able to receive next generation upgrades to the scanning equipment whenever he asked.

"We can also put him through the fMRI machine," he grinned, "although its a shame he didn't have his accident next week, 'cos the new FDG-PET would've been ready."

I raised my eyebrows at Clem, and gave Navarro a blank stare. "Yeah, lucky for him I guess…"

Clem was now perusing the scan pictures that were starting to be downloaded onto the large LED monitors on the desk. I leaned in to watch as he used the mouse to enhance and flick between images. He switched to the quad screen tool and pulled up multiple sequences of brain, chest/abdomen, pelvis, and what was quaintly called the 'frog view' by medics in remembrance of animal dissection in student days. He then focussed on the brain, and as the images came into high resolution.

I turned to Navarro. "Well, what am I looking at?"

He shrugged. "Anything particular you're interested in?"

I leaned over him to get a better look. "Well, he was hit by a truck at high speed. Is there anything broken, signs of internal injury, you know, that sort of thing?"

Navarro pursed his lips and grabbed the mouse out of Clem's hand to take control of it. He enlarged the images and scrolled backwards and forwards in order to view sections from the front to the rear of the body. There was a faint blurring on the edges of the screen, like an interference pattern, and I pointed this out, but he waved me off.

"Yeah I know, I'm trying to adjust. Something's not calibrated right."

A kind of afterimage shimmered into view, an outline of a human body, hollowed out with no internal organs, flickering back and forward between normal anatomical structures like an old cinema reel.

"The contrast must be too high," he muttered. "The HUD number on bone windows is off the scale." He started jabbing at the keyboard, making the software algorithms subtly alter the appearance of the tissues, both solid and liquid. I couldn't see any significant changes manifesting on the screen.

"Speak English?" I said.

Navarro didn't look up, and continued to flick between dials. "Well, according to this, bone density is ten, maybe twenty times the upper limit of normal. Like concrete." He adjusted another dial with his mouse and the numbers running up the side of the screen spun downwards. "Oh, that's better. More like it."

The images on the monitors stabilised and became recognisable body parts again, sectioned horizontally by the CT scanner.

Reynolds pointed at the brain images. "What about his head? Any injury? Looks healthy and undamaged to me."

Navarro ignored him and continued to scroll through the images, enlarging sections here and there, adjusting contrast and windows to delineate and define soft tissue structures, bones, lung parenchyma. I was racking my brain for diseases and conditions that could fit with what was going on. Diagnostic medicine was all about interpreting signs and symptoms as clues in a mystery, and using pattern recognition to arrive at an answer. Nothing appeared to be forthcoming.

Navarro enlarged a section of the spinal cord from the cervical region to the upper thoracic and toggled between the soft tissue view and bone view. He then stopped abruptly and put both hands on his chin, staring at the screen.

"What?" I said.

He was shaking his head and when he looked up and there was a slightly mad glint to his eyes. He flicked his chin at the screen where he had frozen the last image.

"This is the most anatomically perfect scan I've ever seen. Every organ and every structure looks like it was drawn from Gray's Anatomy. There're no abnormalities anywhere. No cysts, no anatomical variants - nothing."

"That can't be right," I said. "The driver of the pickup said they hit him full on doing fifty clicks, so he should be broken into little pieces."

Reynolds stood up and stretched. He was still in his running kit. "It's a puzzle to be sure."

I noticed movement out of the corner of my eye and saw the radiographer in the scan room waving his hand frantically in a motion for us to come in. He pointed wordlessly at the cardiac monitor that had been silently displaying the patient's vital signs. I could see a number of flat lines and flashing red numbers indicating a drop in blood pressure and heart rate.

"Shit," I said. "Looks like he's in trouble again."

I ran out of the reporting room, followed closely by Reynolds. A brief glance at the monitor confirmed a situation requiring urgent action. Clem put his stethoscope on the patient's abdomen, and shook his head, indicating no bowel sounds. The abdominal wall was still rigid to touch. I pulled my ophthalmoscope out and gazed into the man's eyes again, and tested his pupils for reflexes.

Clem reached out and touched my arm, "Kate, I think he needs surgery. A diagnostic laparotomy at least."

I picked up my mobile phone and started dialling but then I stopped, thinking hard. "Clem, what if there's progressive cerebral oedema, and we just aren't seeing it yet on the scans. Fluid squashing his brain could explain this presentation. A head injury from the impact, brief neurological improvement, then he deteriorates… it would fit."

I started moving the man's limbs around, checking for neurological damage and indicators of normal neurological function. Clem looked nervously at the monitors, seeing a sea of red numbers. "Kate, we need to do something, now."

I continued to pedantically evaluate the man's neurological status. Something wasn't right with this whole picture. Clem shook my arm again, but I gritted my teeth.

"He's been in a car accident Clem, and he's unconscious. That's our most pressing problem. We need a central IV line to give him steroids, diuretics, and anything else to keep him alive. But we'll need to do this quickly, and in the operating theatre."

The monitors continued to show agonal-looking traces and unrecordable blood pressure readings. I called through to Navarro. "Pete, can you rustle up the porters to get him taken through to theatre."

Navarro nodded and picked up the phone. I turned to Reynolds, "Clem, you go scrub up while I see what I can do to stabilise him."

Reynolds gave a sigh of resignation. "Right. See you in five". He took off down the corridor in the direction of the changing room.

Navarro pointed at the monitor. "Look, we're getting that afterimage again. I don't think we can rely on these scans to tell us what's going on."

"OK, so much for your fancy scanners then," I said.

Navarro gave me a 'fuck you' look that I ignored.

I helped the radiographer unhook the monitoring machines from the patient and together we started manoeuvring the trolley towards the door. Silently, and without warning, all the lights went out in the scanning room. At the same time, the displays on the monitors and recording devices scattered around the room went dark. The reporting room behind the window where Navarro was watching was also plunged into darkness, and there was a loud decrescendo electronic burble as the CT scanner powered down. As my eyes struggled to dark-adjust I could just make out Navarro getting up from his station and coming through to us. He bumped into the doorframe, cursing. "Power's gone out across the board. Why hasn't the emergency generator kicked in?"

I had no answer for that. "Get the front of the trolley Pete, let's see if we can still push him through to the OR."

As I took hold of the bed I heard a new voice, calm and relaxed, toneless, echoing around my head.

That will not be necessary.

The voice was male, but not Navarro's. I looked around the room, squinting, trying to see into the corners, identify the source. I shook my head to clear it.

"Who's there?"

Navarro's voice answered, "Just me Kate, who else?"

"No, there's someone else here, didn't you hear him? Clem, is that you?"

There was silence. Then the radiographer piped up. "There's no-one here Dr Morgan. There's only one way in."

I looked down at the figure on the trolley, but couldn't make out anything other than a prostrate form lying under the blanket. "Was that you?" I whispered.

Without warning, the lights came back on and the computer terminals and scanner started to reboot noisily. As my vision adjusted to the new lighting, I saw that the man on the trolley was no longer unconscious, and was staring up at me. There was a hint of green phosphorescence coming from his eyes, and then his pupils constricted, shutting it out.

Yes, Kate. Thank you for trying to help me.

The soundless words reverberated around inside my head, and an unwelcome shiver ran down my spine, like a bolt of electricity.

CHAPTER THREE
Indian Springs Hospital and Medical Centre

I stopped in front of the patient's hospital room and turned to the police officer that had insisted on coming with me. He was an overweight Latino with a moustache that would have looked awkward on Yosemite Sam. Not for the first time I wondered what the dress code was for cops in this town. He went to open the door and I gestured for him to wait up.

"I need to speak with him first. When I'm happy that he can give an interview I'll give you a shout. Okay?"

He nodded reluctantly and leaned back against the wall, taking out his cell phone. I gently pushed the door open and entered, closing it behind me. The room was an airy, magnolia-coloured space eight yards square with a large double window facing the desert and overlooking the airbase and its two main runways. There was a low three-seater couch under the window, and a cupboard built into the sidewall surrounded by various shelves that housed a few figurines and other items designed to make the room less clinical. A single hospital bed was adjacent to the right hand wall, braced on one side by a bank of monitors and on the other by a table sporting a jug of water and two glasses. There was a solitary vase with a bunch of pink and red flowers on a shelf by the window, presumably left by a previous occupant of the room. People take flowers into hospital rooms because, despite all the technology and medicine, there's something in our humanity that requires natural beauty as part of the healing 'process'. Otherwise aren't we just carbon-based machines getting fixed up, tuned and serviced?

The man's face in was in near-profile, sitting upright in the bed. His skin was lighter than mine by a few tones, his high cheekbones accentuating angular drawn-in cheeks and his thin mouth. His nose seemed smaller in proportion than it should be now that he was sitting up. There were no lines around his eyes, but I could make out thin grooves tracking down the sides of his mouth from his nose. His short hair was catching some of the sunlight from the window, and glistened bluish-black without a hint of grey. His age was hard to pick; in the ER I had figured forty-something, but now I wasn't so sure.

He slowly turned his head towards me but made no other acknowledgement of my presence. I moved to the side of the bed and picked up the clipboard. I made a note that there were no red lights or muted warning alarms on the machine and scribbled down the readings from the cardiac monitor which was giving off a steady beep every two seconds or so. I stopped writing and took a breath.

"Hello. How are you feeling?"

He met my gaze and blinked a few times before moving his mouth slowly. At first no sound emerged, but then as I leaned forward he spoke, initially in a whisper, but then with increased volume. "I am … better."

I smiled and stood up straighter. "That's good, I'm glad to hear it. You gave everyone a bit of a fright earlier. Do you remember much about what happened?"

He continued to stare directly at me, which was starting to get unnerving. I wished he would blink more frequently. It was a bit reptilian.

"Well, how about you give me your name?" I said, attempting to break the ice.

"My name is Adam," he said, the words coming out slowly and deliberate, as if he wasn't sure and was testing the name to see if it fitted.

"Adam, what? Can you remember your full name?"

He turned his head back to the window, looking out at the clear blue sky and scorched earth of the airfield. A twin engine jet fighter was cranking up to speed, preparing for take-off on the runway a couple of hundred yards away.

"I remember walking down a road," he began, slowly. "I remember a vehicle approaching."

I looked up from the chart, nodded encouragingly. "Yes, a truck hit you, full on. You were out cold for quite some time. Do you have any pain?"

He looked up at the ceiling, a slight tilt to his head. "No. There is no pain."

"You've been very lucky. You don't appear to have suffered any injuries." I tried a sympathetic smile, "Amazingly so, in fact."

"I died," he said, so softly that I couldn't be sure I had heard him correctly.

I felt a strange unease creep over me, a chill in the air like someone had opened a window to let a winter breeze get in. The hairs on the back of my neck tugged erect and I had to make a conscious effort not to hug myself.

"What d'you mean?"

He turned to look at me again, and I found it hard to keep looking at him, so intense was his gaze.

"You are in danger."

I shook my head, and briefly closed my eyes. There was a pressure in my temples, like the first signs of a migraine. And then I heard the other voice, this one inside my head.

I must leave this place. Do not try and stop me.

What the hell was happening? Why was I hearing voices?

I looked at him. "Was that you inside my head?"

"Yes," he replied out loud, matter of factly. Then the voice within spoke again, more urgently.

I must leave. Before anyone is harmed.

He suddenly reached out and grabbed my wrist. There was a wave of nausea and my head seemed weightless as if I was going to pass out. My body felt like it had been plunged into ice-cold water and everything seemed to pixelate and spin before me.

I was suddenly standing on a cliff edge in an underground space, in some sort of oval cavern with dark furrowed walls curving smoothly down to a creviced floor, and the walls above arching up a hundred feet or more to the open sky. In the near distance and illuminating the cavern was a spherical object the size of a basketball floating three or four yards above the floor. It was pulsing silently and rhythmically cycling through the colours of the rainbow. The immediate volume of air surrounding it appeared hazy and the surrounding cave walls were out of focus and blurred as if seen through a mirage. I saw my own breath frosting in the semi-darkness.

Adam was standing between the sphere and me. He looked different. His hair was longer and he had a couple of days' growth of a dark beard. He had tanned crow's feet around his eyes, which crinkled as he smiled at me. For some reason, I felt very afraid.

"Adam, wait," I heard myself saying. Strangely, it was not my voice.

At first he appeared not to hear, and didn't respond. Then he looked back, a puzzled expression on his face. "It's so cold, Gabe," he said. "Can you feel the tingling in the air?"

I put a hand up to shield my eyes from the light, which was becoming more intense and silvery. At that instant the sphere rapidly compressed and contracted to the size of a golf ball before surging to become a fluorescent pink and red freckled orb a yard in diameter. I became aware of an increase in the static charge over my skin as the temperature fell further.

Adam continued to walk slowly towards the globe, one hand shielding his eyes, the other arm raised as if in greeting.

"Wait, what are you doing?" I shouted, again in another voice. Male, high pitched, a bit whiny.

He was now almost directly under the sphere. I tried to move, but my legs wouldn't take me forward. There was a pressure building around my head and shoulders, as if the atmosphere had thickened and gravity had been augmented. I crumpled to my knees, my legs unable to support my weight. Adam was now standing upright directly under the sphere, gingerly reaching up to touch it. I felt a terrible foreboding that I couldn't explain. My mouth felt dry, my stomach turning and twisting, nausea bubbling to the surface.

"Adam, move away!" I managed, my voice cracking.

He again looked back towards me and some part of my brain registered that he didn't appear affected by the pressure wave, and that the blinding light didn't seem to bother him. There was another oscillation and the globe expanded so that his face was now only a foot or so below the sphere.

"It's ... beautiful," I heard him say.

I felt dizzy, my head was spinning and acid was starting to tickle my larynx. I tried to say something, to call out again, but greyness was speckling the edges of my vision. He turned and gave a half-smile. There was sadness in his voice, a tinge of melancholy.

"It's going to be okay Gabe," he said. "You don't need to worry about me."

I wondered who Gabe was, but then the sphere contracted and surged outwards, completely enveloping him. I was crushed by a pressure wave of searing intensity and toppled over hitting my head on the rocky cavern floor. The last thing I saw was the roiling surface of the globe, an ocean of orange, yellow and red waves, inexorably expanding towards me before exploding in a burst of blinding white light, and a kaleidoscope of stars and galaxies.

I forced my eyes to open, and I was sitting on the hospital bed. A fog wrapped around my brain like a blanket and I felt like I'd been held underwater and just come up for air. Adam was next to me, and had his arm around my shoulders. He was still holding my hand. I looked into his eyes and again there was a brief flash of phosphorescent green from behind the pupils.

"What did I just see?" I said, a quiver in my voice.

I am not sure yet. But it is important.

I hesitated. "What happened to you?"

Before he could answer, there was a knock on the door and the cop who'd been waiting outside entered. He coughed into his fist and moved towards the bed with a lopsided smile as he took in the fact that doctor and patient were sitting on the bed and the patient had his arm around the doctor.

"Sorry to interrupt, Dr Morgan." He raised an eyebrow, pulled out his notebook and flipped it open while licking his fingers theatrically. I got up from the bed, somewhat awkwardly, and Adam's eyes followed me.

"My name is Officer Ramirez," the policeman said, looking at Adam. "You were involved in an accident along I-95 today. I have witness statements that you were walking down the middle of the highway just after midnight. Do you have any recollection of those events?"

Adam's eyes flicked over to Ramirez and he regarded him silently. Ramirez met his stare and held it. "Sir? I'm asking if you remember what happened?"

There was another long pause, then a slight nod. "Yes."

Ramirez smiled. "Can you tell me about it?"

Adam continued to stare, but said nothing further.

Ramirez pursed his lips. Sighing, he pulled out his phone, and held it up, activating the flash. "Okay, well first I'll just take a picture, run it through our databases. Look straight into the lens please."

Adam held up his hand and shook his head. "No. I do not think so."

Ramirez frowned. "Sir, I was being polite. I'm going to take your photograph now, so please put your hand down." A puzzled expression appeared on his face as his fingers tippy tapped over the screen. "Hmm, none of the buttons are working."

At that moment Adam swung his legs over the side of the bed and stood up, still connected to the panel by monitor wires. He was wearing a hospital gown which was buttoned up the back and even in his bare feet he towered over the cop. Ramirez took a big step back, one hand now resting on his holstered gun.

I had a bad feeling about this, so I reached out and gently touched Adam's arm. "It's OK, they're just trying to help you. Let's get you back into bed."

He looked down at me, expressionless.

I must leave this place.

The voice in my head again. What was going on?

Ramirez put his notebook back in his pocket and moved forward, entering Adam's personal space. He reached out and firmly took hold of Adam's wrist.

"Sir, I think you should do as the good doctor said, get back into bed and let us do our job."

Adam flat-palmed Ramirez directly on the sternum.

There was no warning, and the speed and violence of the act gave the cop no chance to react. He flew across the room like a swatted fly and crashed into the wall, his head leaving a bloody indentation half way up, before he slid to the ground.

I screamed and instinctively jerked backwards into the monitor, knocking a couple of glasses over along with all the charts. Adam briefly glanced at me and then strode over to the fallen cop, snapping the cables and wires connecting him to the monitors. Unhappy-sounding bleeps and pings started coming from the equipment, and the readings became random and meaningless. He knelt down and felt for a pulse and rested his head on Ramirez' chest. He then gently turned him over and laid him in the recovery position so that secretions or blood would not block his larynx.

He stood up and waved a dismissive hand at the machines, which went instantly silent. "He will survive," he said to me, "but he needs urgent medical attention."

With that, he strode out of the room, gown flapping, broken wires trailing behind him. A cold shiver trickled down my neck and the hairs stood up as the micropapillaries of my follicles reacted to the adrenaline coursing through my veins.

His voice, calm and toneless, echoed around my head.

You are all in danger.

CHAPTER FOUR
Indian Springs Hospital and Medical Centre

The door was half open so I knocked softly and entered without waiting for an answer. Reynolds was sitting behind his desk, fingers steepled, deep in thought. He looked at me through lidded eyes, opened a drawer and pulled out a bottle of Jack Daniels and two shot glasses. "Close the door, Kate. Pull up a chair."

I shook my head.

Reynolds frowned. "The police are here. We've only got five minutes or so. We need to get our story straight."

My eyes narrowed but I said nothing. He looked at me, a hangdog expression on his face.

"He assaulted a cop, Kate. A cop who's now a patient here with a fractured sternum and a significant pulmonary contusion."

I walked over to the window, and peered out through the slatted blinds. Reynolds' office was on the second floor, with a view of the car park and the suburbs of downtown Indian Springs. Streetlights were flickering epileptically, and shopfront neon signs were beginning to fluoresce.

"What are we going to tell them?" I said without turning. "I mean, what sort of story are you thinking of? I've spent the last hour trawling though his scans trying to make sense of it all and I tell you Clem, I'm out of ideas."

Reynolds arranged the shot glasses on his desk, and moved them around absentmindedly as if he was going perform a magic trick. "Kate, he's almost certainly a sick man. Possibly dying somewhere."

I gave a heavy sigh. "We both looked at the same images. Those CT scans were perfectly normal. How can that be…?"

"He put a police officer into hospital," he interrupted, choosing to ignore what I'd said. "They're going to find him and they're going to throw the book at him. From a medicolegal perspective, we should say - let's see - that we found some kind of brain abnormality. I think it's not a stretch to say that when he woke up he was confused. Then, he became agitated, and hence the violent act towards that officer. That's not uncommon with brain injuries as you well know."

I turned back to the window, puzzled and frustrated. I'd been trying to find some kind of coherent explanation, but this wasn't it. It wasn't even close. "Clem, stop just there." I said. "You remember those strange lights on his retina? We both saw those."

He didn't answer, so I took a deep breath and decided to dive in. "Clem, he spoke to me… in my mind. Like some - some fucking form of telepathy." I stopped, and wondered how much I could say to Clem without him thinking that I was flaky.

He pursed his lips, and reached over to pour himself a generous shot of Jack. He wiggled his eyebrows invitingly, but I shook my head. He sniffed it and took a little sip, before downing the glass in a single gulp and sat back in the chair, looking up at the ceiling, seemingly fascinated by the cracks in the emulsion.

"Clem…?" I pleaded.

He put the glass down and swivelled to face me. "Kate, Dr Navarro has forwarded those scans to a colleague in Vegas. A neuro-radiologist. Until we know what's going on, I respectfully suggest that the police have no right to our speculations. We owe them facts."

"What facts might they be?" I said, folding my arms.

Reynolds started counting with his fingers. "One, we were prepping him for an emergency operation to evaluate his neurological situation."

"Which you argued against," I pointed out.

"Two, he regained consciousness and so the operation was abandoned. Three, he became aggressive and assaulted a police officer and his doctor…"

"That's not quite right though, is it Clem?"

"... *And* his doctor. Four, subsequently leaving the hospital without medical consent. End of story."

"End of story? We've no idea where he is. Don't we have a duty of care, for fuck's sake? It's entirely possible that he could be lying in an alleyway somewhere, having seizures, anything…"

"Kate, Indian Springs is a small town. He'll be found soon enough. Telling the police he was hit by a truck will've given them enough reason to expedite the search." He poured another shot of bourbon, shrugging, "I mean, how far can he go wearing a hospital gown?"

I knew Clem was right about that, and the fact that our duty of care actually ended when he kind of self discharged. But I wasn't going to let this go and was about to reply when there was a knock on the door. Reynolds grimaced and rolled his eyes before indicating that I should open it. I did, and facing me were two uniformed police officers.

I recognised Sheriff Woods of course. A sandy-haired middle-aged man, huge in every way, wide and tall. The doorway wasn't made for people like him, and he kind of turned sideways to pass through. He was that guy who had to get two airline seats in coach just to stop other passengers giving him a hard time. He was also the opposite of the fat and jolly stereotype. In my previous encounters with him he'd always been a miserable and ornery bastard, but a straight shooter. A no-bullshit kind of guy. I realised now why Reynolds wanted to play this as easy as possible.

The other officer, a female, was new to me. Her red hair was braided under her hat, and her bony, angular features gave her a hard-faced look. There was something in the way she held herself, as if unsure of where her limbs should be.

"Dr Morgan, always a pleasure," said Woods, removing his hat. He smiled past me at Reynolds, cold-eyed, "Clem, nice to see you."

Reynolds was standing up and shuffling around his desk having hurriedly secreted the bourbon and glasses back in the drawer. "Hello Doug. Please come in."

Woods walked up to the desk and pulled out a seat, gesturing for his companion to take the other one. He introduced her as Officer Chatfield, on secondment from Pahrump, the largest town in Nye County, fifty miles south of Indian Springs. He squeezed into the chair opposite Reynolds, which creaked ominously, pulled a notebook and pen from his back pocket and opened at a blank page. He looked at me and gave another slight smile.

"Thanks for meeting with us," he said. "Hopefully this won't take too long."

"How can we help, sheriff?" I said.

He leaned in, brows furrowed. "How can you help ... let's see now. I've got a man down in this here facility, put there by one of your patients who is now AWOL. Am I doing well so far?"

"You know that's the case, Doug," said Reynolds, a placating look on his face. "As I said on the phone, the patient was almost certainly suffering from concussion following his accident. I think he was confused, probably disorientated."

He glanced at me. I shrugged, "Happens a lot."

"Well, we'd certainly like to find him for everybody's sake," said Woods. "Do you have a name for him yet?"

Reynolds shook his head. "Adam something. That's as much as we got from him. I don't think he could remember. There was no ID on him. We tried to get a photograph but that was when he crazied out and made his exit."

Woods' eyebrows went up. "Don't you think that's a little suspicious? Like he had something to hide?"

"He did appear confused," I said. "He awoke very abruptly after being unconscious for a good few hours. I think maybe the whole situation threw him, what with the cop and all the questioning."

Woods nodded slowly, staring at me. "Did you talk to him?"

I started chewing my nail, then stopped self-consciously. I went round the corner of the desk and perched there. I

34

looked down briefly at Reynolds who gave a slight shake of his head. I turned to Woods, "I'm afraid that could be perceived as falling within the realms of patient-doctor confidentiality."

He leaned back in the chair and steepled his fingers giving Reynolds and I a withering look. "Doctors, really? Is this the game we're going to play? Your patient isn't charged with any crime - yet. I'm merely looking for information that might help me locate him and hopefully return him safely to your care for further treatment."

I tried to look conciliatory. "Look, Sheriff Woods, he really didn't say much at all. Just that he needed to leave."

Woods coughed into his hand, and put down his notebook. "Alright then, let's start with a description? Or is that against medical ethics, too?"

"Doug, we'll give you anything you need to find this poor fellow," Reynolds interrupted. "It's just that there isn't much to tell."

I got up off the desk and started pacing, while Woods flipped open a notebook. He licked the end of his pen. "Dr Morgan, how about we start with his appearance? Perhaps how he was dressed when he was brought in to your emergency room?"

"That was the weirdest thing," said Reynolds before I could reply. "He was wearing a wetsuit. You know, one of those neoprene things people go diving in…"

Woods looked over at his companion and gave her a look that I couldn't decipher. He screwed the top back on his pen and placed it next to his notebook on the desk. The two cops pushed back their chairs and stood up.

"Is that it?" said Reynolds, puzzled.

Woods was staring at me. He looked grim. "Not by a long shot, Clem. Dr Morgan, I need you to come to the station with me. Someone you need to meet."

CHAPTER FIVE
Nye County Sheriff's Office, Pahrump

I drained my second cup of stewed police coffee in as many hours and sat back in a very uncomfortable (purposefully, I was sure) plastic chair. I glanced up at the one-way mirror dominating the far wall and shot daggers at whoever was watching me. The lighting was oppressively stark and intrusive, emanating from a single UV strip bisecting the ceiling. The room was painted an insipid shade of lime green and a single door with a peephole slider comprised the far wall. There was a sickly sweet odour of sweat that was partially masked by disinfectant, and for a moment I wondered whether it was coming from me. I lifted my armpit up to my nose just as the door opened.

Woods entered, carrying a manila folder and mug of coffee with "*World's Best Dad*" emblazoned on it. He flopped into the chair opposite and took a sip from the mug before looking up. "You want more coffee? Pot's still hot."

I felt my irritation building, augmented by the caffeine taking over my bloodstream. I leaned forward and tried to look intimidating. "I've been gone from the hospital over three hours now, drinking your shitty coffee. So, remind me why I'm here?"

Woods gave me a stony-eyed look, and said nothing. I sat back and seethed. "Am I under arrest or something? I mean, what the fuck?"

The door opened a second time and Officer Chatfield entered, accompanied by a thin, balding man in his fifties, all dishevelled hair and a scraggly salt and pepper beard. Chatfield sauntered over to the windowed wall and nonchalantly leaned back against it, looking at me with barely disguised boredom. The man remained by the door checking out the room, and his eyes alighted on me after a few seconds.

"Who's this?" I said to Woods.

The Beard continued to look nervously around and I noticed he was wearing a Nye County Sheriff's Office cape on top of what looked like a diver's wetsuit. He glanced over at Woods who gestured for him to sit down next to him, which he did somewhat reluctantly.

Woods continued with his poker face, and nodded at me. "Dr Morgan, meet Professor Gabriel Connor from the University of Las Vegas. Palaeontology department, right Professor?"

The Beard granted me a half smile and nodded a greeting. Woods placed the folder on the desk between us, licked his right index finger, and started deliberately turning through the pages. I glimpsed photographs of Connor along with copies of his university degrees, driving licence, and what looked like lists of cell phone numbers.

Connor looked uncomfortable and had started squirming in his chair. "Look, what have I done other than, what, trespassing through a deserted old military testing site? Nothing but big holes in floor of the desert."

He had a high-pitched voice, and spoke very fast. A muscle twitched at the corner of his eye, and he folded his arms tightly across his chest.

Woods stopped flicking through the file and looked up. He sat back and the chair creaked ominously. He glanced over at Chatfield, who continued to silently eyeball Connor.

"Tell me again what you were doing in a prohibited radioactive area, Professor Connor," said Woods.

Connor sighed dramatically. "I told you already. I was looking for new cave systems to explore. Part of my academic research. I wandered off the trail, and got lost."

"And that's why you dialled 911?"

"Yes, I panicked at first but then I killed the call when I realised I was okay."

Woods seemed to consider this. He leaned forward and put his mobile phone on the table. He pressed a button and tinny voices came out of the speaker.

"Hello, this is the emergency service. We've been trying to contact you. Are you in need of assistance please?"

Connor closed his eyes and I saw him take a deep breath as he heard his own voice.

"Hello, thank you. No, we're okay; I must have dialled 911 by mistake. All good. False alarm. Thank you again."

There was a brief hesitation on the other end before the operator's voice came back more insistently. *"Please give your name and the nature of your emergency."*

Connor's voice sounded flustered, *"I'm good thanks. It was a mistake. We don't need any assistance."*

The operator was having none of it. *"State Police vehicles are within two minutes of your location, please stand by."*

Woods killed the playback and knotted his eyebrows at Connor. "'We'. Sounds plural don't it? I'll ask you again - were you on your own, Professor?"

"Yes. I was."

Woods stared unblinkingly at him and I could tell Connor found it hard to keep eye contact but stared back anyway. I'd read somewhere that if you averted your gaze it would suggest duplicity, and perhaps give away the fabrication or falsehood that you were developing. After what seemed like an interminably long minute Woods languidly nodded then continued his perusal of the folder. He stopped at a page that contained a black and white CCTV photo. I squinted, trying to make out what it was showing but it was grey and blurry as well as being upside down.

Woods looked up at Connor like a predator homing in on its prey. "What happened down in the crater?"

Connor swallowed, and I watched him as he ran his tongue around his teeth trying to lubricate his mouth. I would have felt sorry for him, if I wasn't so pissed.

"I was clumsy," he began. "I fell backwards and hit my head on some rocks. I blacked out for I don't know maybe five maybe ten minutes. When I woke up I was disorientated and so I called 911. But then I killed the call and decided to head back up. When I got to the surface I saw the missed calls and you guys were already heading in. That's it, really." He tried a smile, looking at Woods and then at me. He tapped his fingers on the desktop, a nervous gesture. "Actually I should thank you for coming so quickly in case I was in trouble. Did you triangulate the call like they do in those movies?"

Woods' lips pouted, like he was mulling this over, and there was an awkward silence in the room. I'd had enough and stood up, glaring down at him. "I'm sorry Sheriff but I fail to see what relevance this has for me?"

Woods raised a finger and picked up his cell phone and speed dialled a number. He sat back and looked at Connor again, seemingly revelling in the uncomfortable silence. He pointed at my chair, indicating that I should sit down, but I ignored him and folded my arms. After a few seconds the phone was connected. I could hear a deep male voice at the other end talking slowly and continuously but I couldn't make out what he was saying. This went on for a couple of minutes while Woods' face remained impassive as he stared at Connor. There was a gap in the monologue and then Woods said with eyebrows furrowed, "Are you sure?"

There was more talking, to which Woods nodded a few times and then hung up. He regarded Connor again silently for what seemed an eternity before sitting back and folding his arms. "Now Professor, I'm going to ask you again. Were you alone today?"

Gabriel was overtly perspiring now, and not just because of the wetsuit. He glanced over at me, but I gave him nothing. "I think I've answered that question," he stammered.

"Not to my satisfaction, you haven't," said Woods, shaking his head. He leaned forward. "I've just spoken to the team onsite at the crater. They recovered two large and very heavy duffle bags stuffed with *two* sets of diving equipment from the floor of the cavern."

I could see Connor thinking fast, the cogs ticking over and the mechanism chugging to come up with another lie. "So what? I've been down there before. I left that other bag there last time for backup. Also, I was hoping to be joined by a friend, but he backed out at the last minute".

Woods glanced up at Chatfield, who was now listening intently, and then lazily brought his gaze back to Connor. "So this isn't your first trespassing offence, is that what you're telling me? Thought you said you just got lost?"

"Look, there were no *'Do Not Trespass'* signs. Just signs about the radiation."

"Didn't you think that was warning enough, professor? You being a man of science and all?"

"There was no significant radiation contaminating that particular crater. I had a Geiger counter. I'm not stupid."

"So what's with the wetsuit? I mean, you're in the middle of the desert."

I was watching this exchange like a spectator at Wimbledon. Connor swallowed, and shook his head in an exasperated fashion. "I thought I'd seen water down there on my initial scouting trip. Underwater cave systems often have water you know, and this was a deep, man-made hole in the ground. By definition it's an unexplored cave system. I was certain it'd dip below the water table. Underground caves like that often have streams and significant bodies of water. Catnip to explorers like me."

"Isn't that sort of thing dangerous on your own?" said Woods, arching an eyebrow.

Connor shook his head. "The guy who was going to come with me was an expert cave-diver."

Woods looked up, interested. He turned the page on the file and hovered his pen, looking up expectantly. "Can you give me this gentleman's name, please?"

Connor swallowed nervously, seemingly weighing up what to say. I could feel my heart rate picking up, and I stared at him as he shuffled in his chair, clearly mulling over his answer. "His name is Adam Benedict. He was - is - an old friend from my college days. He lives in San Francisco. I'm sorry but I don't know the address. I hadn't seen him for many years but we'd kept in touch via texting and email. I'd heard on the TV that there'd recently been a family tragedy. His wife had been murdered, you see. Breaking and entering while she was sleeping and he was overseas on business. I felt sorry for him, so I asked if he wanted to join me on this trip. Thought it might help, y'know?"

My mind was racing. The vision Adam had put into my head came flooding back. The cavern and the globe of light with Adam walking towards it. The name he kept calling as he looked back at me.

Gabe.

Connor was there, with Adam, in the cavern. He saw Adam disappear. I wondered why he wasn't coming clean with the police, but then I knew if I called him on it, I'd have to explain how I knew, and to be honest I wasn't ready to unload the telepathy and the dream like experiences yet. I had a professional reputation to try and preserve. Or at least that's what I told myself.

Woods tapped his pen on the table. "So this Adam Benedict won't mind if we give him a call to check out this part of the story?"

"He never returned my last message," said Connor quickly, rubbing his sweating palms together. "But I'm sure he won't mind. If you can track him down of course. I think he travels overseas a lot so presumably that's why he didn't get back to me." He smiled at Woods, apparently pleased with himself but it sounded unconvincing, even to me. He scribbled a cell phone number on a piece of paper and slid it to Woods who took it without looking.

"Can you describe this guy?" said Woods.

Connor nodded. "I might have some photos back in my office. I'd be happy to go and look them out for you."

Woods shook his head. "Later. How about a description for now?"

Connor looked at the ceiling, squinted as if he was trying to recall details. "He's very tall, about six-seven. Built like a swimmer. Toned, I guess you'd call it. Muscles like ropes."

"White guy?" said Woods.

"Yes, very white actually…" Gabriel tried a nervous laugh. "For an outdoorsy type he isn't very tanned. Last I saw him he'd grown a bit of a beard and let his hair grow out. He generally had short black hair, crew cut, you know like one of those army types."

Woods continued to scribble in his notebook. "Does he have family?"

"He was an only child, I remember that. As I said, he'd lost his wife recently. Cora - that was her name. He also has a daughter from a previous relationship, but he doesn't see her much. Name of Amy. We certainly didn't talk about her."

"What about a job?"

Connor continued to look thoughtfully at the ceiling strip. He tapped his bottom lip as he tried to give the impression of digging deep to get information. I wasn't fooled, and I doubted whether Woods was, either.

"No, I don't think he has one. He got quite an inheritance when his parents passed away, and he married well. His wife was the breadwinner. Quite the successful businesswoman, she was. She indulged his cave-diving hobbies, kept him sweet, y'know? He was also a pretty successful athlete. A National Ironman champion, if I recall. Very fit."

Woods put the pen down and looked directly at Connor without blinking. "So, just to be clear Professor - this Adam guy had a rich wife who was murdered, right? Presumably he benefited from this, financially? Was he a suspect?"

Connor sat back in the chair and sighed theatrically. "Look, as I said, he is really just an old college buddy. We were close back in the day, but that was a long time ago."

Woods finally broke off his stare and stood up, hitched up his pants and walked over to the far wall to stand next to Chatfield. She pushed herself off the wall and coughed. "A person fitting this description was brought in to the 'Springs ER earlier today. He was hit by a pickup truck walking along Mercury last night. Pretty grim by all accounts."

Woods raised his eyebrows at me. "But then he kind of 'self-discharged' himself from hospital, ain't that right, doc?"

I now understood why I was here. Connor was definitely lying about Adam not being with him. They were both wearing the same scuba diving kit. Woods wanted me to make the connection. I was about to say so, when to my surprise Woods gestured to the door. "All right Professor, I guess we're done here for now. You can go."

Connor pushed up out of his chair, relief etched over his face.

Woods gave a feral grin, "But please don't leave the area. We're not finished yet."

Chatfield opened the door and waved Connor through. He glanced furtively in my direction as he shuffled out. After he'd left I turned to Woods and opened my hands.

"So that's it? You bring me all this way, and for what?"

Woods simply smirked and walked over to the door. "Like I said, we're not finished yet. But you can go for now."

Then I was being escorted out of the room, fuming.

CHAPTER SIX
I-95 Interstate, Nevada

I barrelled down the empty highway, the powerful twin halogen headlights of my Jeep Cherokee illuminating the road for a hundred yards before becoming impotent in the face of the deep velvet blackness of the desert night. There was an occasional coruscating moon peeping grudgingly from behind fishnet clouds, and spider-shaped shadows of Joshua trees flashed in the peripheral zone of the beams. The radio was silent and the only sounds in the cab were the hum of the tyres on the tarmac and the wind whistling past the boxy corners of the vehicle. My eyes kept getting drawn to the mesmeric flicker of the centre road markings as they disappeared beneath the hood, and I tried not to picture a tall figure appearing out of no-where, dead ahead with no time to get out of the way.

Shaking my head to clear it, I glanced at the clock. I couldn't believe it was only eight-thirty. The caffeine hadn't worn off yet and my mind was buzzing. The police interview had slightly unnerved me, but not as much as my encounter with Adam Benedict. I could still hear his voice in my subconsciousness and bouncing around inside my head. The complete weirdness of that notwithstanding, it was clear that something extra-ordinary had happened to him - but what? I couldn't figure it out. Woods was closemouthed as a clam at the end of the interview and had dismissed me just like he had Connor.

I pulled into my space at the front of the hospital, only a short walk to the side door that leads into the ER doctors' office. Thankfully the room was empty, meaning Clem had gone home presumably having decided to take calls from the comfort of his armchair and TV. The coffee machine was still lit, and despite my already over-caffeinated blood I lifted the jug up to my nose and savoured the aroma.

"Mmmm ... fresh coffee. Mind if I have a cup of that?"

I jumped, nearly spilling the pot, and saw Gabriel Connor peeking around the door, an apologetic look on his grizzled face. He'd put on some tortoiseshell glasses that actually made him look semi-professorial until he shuffled into the room still wearing the wetsuit and a pair of scuffed white tennis shoes. He saw me looking and shrugged.

"Yes, I know, but I didn't have time to change. Einstein wore odd socks you know. Sometimes, no socks..."

"You followed me here?" I said, putting a menacing tone in my voice.

"Sorry, yes," he said. "I think we need to talk."

He seemed hesitant, definitely nervous. I thought about it for a few moments but then shrugged and waved him in. He looked harmless enough. He closed the door behind him and I poured us both a cup of black coffee. We sat down on a couple of the recliners along the wall, and I flipped the footrest up and kicked off my shoes. I brought the cup to my lips and the strong aroma of over-stewed beans filled my nose. I thought I was going to start getting palpitations. Connor was looking at his cup but not drinking. I decided to say nothing, and let him lead. After all, he'd come to me.

"Dr Morgan," he began slowly, "did you talk with Adam?"

"Yes," I said. "Briefly."

I wasn't sure whether I wanted to share anything with him at this time, but he seemed a geeky kind of guy and I didn't get any odd vibes from him. Not that my instincts were always accurate.

"Was he - okay? I mean, did he seem, I don't know how to put this... normal to you?"

I leaned further back in the chair and stretched. I could feel a headache coming on. I carefully placed the mug on the armrest and closed my eyes, fighting a yawn. "Professor, you've come all this way to tell me something. Why don't you just get to it?"

He seemed to consider this for a moment, as there was a long pause, followed by a resigned sigh. "Yes, you're right.

Okay, well it was a few days ago. Adam was burying his wife. I was late - as usual - I got there just as the last of the mourners' limos were pulling away. This was in Colma, just outside San Francisco." He raised his eyebrows at me. "You know Colma, right?"

I shook my head. Never been to 'Frisco.

He grinned. "Most of Colma's land is dedicated to cemeteries. Apparently the population of the dead outnumbers the living by over a thousand to one." He took a loud slurp of his coffee. "Hence the name: 'The City of the Silent'".

"Are you trying to be an asshole?" I said.

"Once a professor, always a professor ..."

"Maybe you could move it along a bit?"

"Yes. Of course. Anyway, I'd just flown in from Vegas that morning. I'd heard about Cora on the news a day or so before. Couldn't believe it."

"What happened?"

"You need to understand," he said, leaning towards me for emphasis, "we'd kinda lost touch, I'd moved from Chicago to take up a position as Professor of Palaeontology at the University. Tenure. Big deal for me." He looked away, embarrassed. "Not that this matters of course. I could see that Adam was in a bad place. Cora's family are - well - just awful, awful people. And then there's his daughter, Amy. Didn't even come to the funeral or the wake. I mean, she wasn't actually Cora's child, and she and Cora weren't close, but I thought she would've been there to support Adam. After all, she was murdered..."

I was about to say something, but my voice caught, and emotions entombed and locked away broke the surface like zombie hands poking through a grave. The face of my own daughter flashed before me, lying on a gurney, pale and lifeless, a scrape of blood on her eyebrow and a smudge of dirt on her cheek. Nausea swirled around my empty stomach and a surge of profound sadness covered me like a wet blanket. The pain was still deep, and I closed my eyes and blinked back the tears I had vowed I would not shed again.

"Adam had returned from South America," Connor was saying. "Flown in from Santiago. As his aircraft taxied to the gate he'd texted Cora. There wasn't any response to his texts and she wasn't there to meet him at the gate as they'd arranged. He'd caught a cab but when he arrived home he found the front door wide open and the lights in the house were out. They still think it was a home invasion gone wrong. The police blamed smack-heads looking for cash to score a hit. They think she'd been followed... maybe the junkies saw that she was alone... the security cameras weren't working properly..."

He stopped talking and took another loud slurp of coffee. I thought about Adam finding his dead wife in that scenario. All those treasured memories suddenly trashed from the mind, replaced with evil, darkness and despair. Sorrow would be his new status quo, sadness his new best friend. I had often wondered when sadness would leave after such an event, and what emotion would replace it. I'd been working on that question for the last six months and hadn't gotten an answer. My insides felt as raw now as they did that night in the Chicago ER.

"So how did this end up in a trip to a radioactive crater?" I managed to say, rubbing the sleep from my eyes and hoping he wouldn't notice.

Connor's mouth twitched, and he shrugged in a 'what can you do?' kind of way. "I'd been planning an expedition to visit some new dig sites for my students. Uncharted caves and underground systems, that sort of thing. Adam had been and done many things in his life, and for the last couple of years he'd been a professional cave-diver. Recently he'd been to the Peruvian Andes where he and a couple of locals had spent three weeks mapping and exploring new underground aquifers."

I knew that cave diving was a dangerous pastime, having watched documentaries on Nat Geo. Squeezing through tight and claustrophobic underground spaces to get into pitch-dark flooded caves. But when you get there, you could be floating through some of the last lost worlds on the planet.

Connor continued, almost reading my mind. "I've been in caves that ranged from huge liquid aquamarine chambers cut with shafts of sunlight, to sinkholes boasting gardens of silent fallen trees." He paused and pursed his lips. "The fact is, Adam was lost. The empty house, the loss of his soul mate, a senseless murder – or so the police had concluded. I could sense his growing despondency. I could see the early signs of depression."

"So you asked him to come on a holiday with you. To 'get over' the murder of his wife?"

Gabriel looked at me, and a twinkle appeared in his eyes. "Caves never before explored or catalogued. Guaranteed."

I frowned. "In Nevada? The nuclear graveyard?"

He looked at me strangely. "It's not what you think."

CHAPTER SEVEN
Indian Springs Hospital and Medical Centre

A month before, and on a whim, Connor had taken a tour of the Nevada Test Site, a one and a half thousand square mile patch of desert where the United States military had undertaken most of their post-WWII atomic bomb tests. The bus tour had taken two hours during which Connor and a dozen other tourists had been driven past roped-off areas and huge mounds of desert and craters moulded by the fierce atomic explosions of cold war paranoia. Cameras, mobile phones and videos were banned, and the guide had talked almost non-stop about nuclear detonations that vaporised solid bedrock forming massive underground chambers subsequently poisoned with radioactive rubble.

Connor had been fascinated and saw the potential for exploration and finding new fossil records in the man-made caves, as there were very few virgin sites for palaeontologists to explore in mainland US. It seemed that the only problem was the residual radioactivity, which should have been a deal-breaker. But the security seemed very light; the assumption being that the threat of ongoing radioactive contamination would deter visitors.

Like the good academic he was, Connor did his research.

Over the next three months he'd driven around the site at night armed with a map, a list of the nuclear tests from the Internet, a Geiger counter and night vision goggles. The bomb-testing area was criss-crossed by three hundred miles of paved roads and twice that amount of unpaved dirt tracks so he was able to steer clear of the four seemingly abandoned heliports and airstrips that also inhabited the site. He'd evaluated the larger craters from the surface noting their size, apparent depth, and the amount of local radioactivity. He'd decided that while there was higher than normal background radiation, there were no really dangerous areas - provided that he didn't spend a long time there. Some of the craters appeared to be more contaminated at the edges, suggesting that below the surface there would be higher and therefore more dangerous levels of radiation.

One particular crater appeared to be unique. On the surface it seemed morphologically similar to all the others, but the radiation signal at the edge was no higher than ambient background level. Connor consulted his records and read that the underground detonation there took place in 1953. There were eyewitness accounts describing the mushroom cloud and the detonation blowing out a circular chamber in the desert floor which then collapsed forming multiple canyons and tunnels. Satellite images showed that the crater resembled one of the meteor strikes on the moon he'd seen photographed by the Apollo missions. It was approximately 50 yards across, making it one of the medium-sized holes pockmarking the desert floor like acne on a teenager's face. Connor had shone his torch down the precipice into the inky blackness and was unable to see the bottom. However, during an early morning scouting trip he thought he saw something shimmering, as if the light was being reflected from a water surface.

"So you went there the next day?" I asked. "After Cora Benedict's wake?"

Connor nodded. "I laid out my plan that night over a bottle of scotch. Adam was keen to go, but a bit concerned about the radiation risk - despite the data I'd collected, and shared with him."

"But you still went." I said.

"Of course."

He passed over his mobile phone, opened at a photograph of the Nevada desert hazing, shimmering and presenting a vista of bleached scrubland dotted with cactus plants, parched bushes and cadaverous trees. There was a highway in the background, arrowing into ancient mountains that had deeply coalescent shadows raggedly scarring their sides. The sky was panoramically cobalt, the sun in ascension, and a few wispy clouds stretched thinly across the upper reaches. I flicked to the next photo, which was of a road sign. It had serious-looking writing framed by a radiation tri-foil in black and yellow, and was acting like a sentry to the desolate wasteland behind.

It read: *DANGER, HIGH RADIATION AREA.*

Connor grinned. "I know. The sign's just overkill. They want you to turn back. There's no significant radiation where we were heading. I told Adam there was nothing to worry about. The Government's had that place bubble-wrapped for twenty-five years."

I handed the phone back and he reached down and unzipped a small rucksack by his feet, bringing out a portable two-piece Geiger counter. He flicked it on and it began to register ambient ionisation events. Sporadic and irregular clicks of normal background radioactivity could be heard.

"We had this with us at all times. What you're hearing now is the same as we heard in that desert. Nada." He shook his head and put the counter back in his bag. "Government continues to put those signs up, scaring folks away."

I looked at him across the top of my coffee, and said what had been bothering me. "You know, I still find it hard to believe you thought there'd be water down there."

He raised his eyebrows and shrugged. "I was pretty sure that there'd be streams and pools and so on, given the depth of the explosions and the water table in that area. Any sufficiently deep hole should have filled with water by now." He paused, and then smiled across at me. "Did you know that the Mayans thought underwater cave systems represented 'portals to the underworld'?"

I frowned. "My recollection of South American history is hazy at best, but I do remember that that they also thought sacrificing children to their gods would bring them luck."

Connor seemed to shrink into himself a little, hiding behind his cup. He glanced sideways at me.

"I thought that crater was safe."

"Caverns formed by nuclear explosions," I said.

"I know," he said, quietly.

"Are you going to tell me what happened down there?"

He put his cup down and looked straight ahead. If I'd ever seen a thousand yard stare, there it was.

"It took us two hours to climb down to the floor of the cavern. The walls were good for handholds and pegs. It wasn't the hollowed-out circular cavity we were expecting at all. The rock falls and roof collapses had produced random stairways of boulders that spiked upwards into the main chamber. We found a few sizeable cracks in the floor that opened out into other passageways, so I decided to descend one of them. It was hard getting down there but Adam was up top feeding me lengths of rope and keeping me from going too fast. We'd thrown glow-sticks down first and these'd come to rest in another space below the passageway. As I descended, the intensity of the glow seemed to be decreasing rather than increasing, and the crevice was narrowing just below the point where I was hanging. Adam thought it was going to be too tight, but I was convinced I could get through."

He paused to take another sip of what must have been cold coffee because he grimaced and lowered the cup to the floor. I looked at my watch and saw that it was nearly eleven. I got out of my chair and walked across the room to look out of the window. There was a diffuse orangey light in the distance from across the highway where the town outskirts began, but all was quiet.

"Did you get through the gap?" I asked without turning.

His chair squeaked as he got up and joined me at the window. I could smell his sweat, oozing through the pores of the wetsuit. He stood close to me and I moved back slightly so that he got the hint.

"No," he said. "I had to turn back. I started to climb up but the light from Adam's helmet torch was blinding me so I asked him to turn it off. But when he did, instead of the darkness I was expecting, Adam was kinda framed by a halo of light. The air was charged with some sort of static electricity, like what you get before a thunderstorm hits, and the temperature in the cavern just plummeted. I can remember the hairs rising on the back of my neck, despite the sweat leaking down from under my helmet. I asked Adam to look behind him as I thought that maybe someone had followed us down." His voice had dropped to a whisper, and I was struggling to hear him. He looked even more uncertain, as if he didn't know how exactly to proceed with his story.

"Was there?" I whispered. "Was there someone there?"

Connor sighed deeply and gave an involuntary shudder. "Adam looked down at me - and here's the thing - he had this strange expression on his face. He looked puzzled but his eyes were wide and staring. I remember him calling, something like 'Fuck, this is seriously weird you need to come up and take a look at this' and then he walked away from the edge and out of sight."

"That's it?" I said.

Connor looked away and I knew he was lying.

"By the time I'd gotten up out of crevice he was gone."

CHAPTER EIGHT
Joey Malone's Sports Bar and Grill, Indian Springs

An hour later, close to midnight, I sat hunched on a leather-backed stool at Joey Malone's Bar and Diner, a Kraken rum and coke in front of me. Joey's had a low convex ceiling with mood lighting and dark wooden beams. Pennants and signed football jerseys bedecked the walls between booths that were occupied by some GIs tucking into burgers and fries. The bar was a long straight counter with a dozen or more rickety stools facing ten wall-mounted TVs, all silently showing sports or news programs with subtitles ticker-taping along the bottom. Behind it was an Aladdin's cave of drinks, the backlighting illuminating the alcohol in inviting golden colours. Joey Malone's was a regular haunt of mine - although usually only at weekends, I liked to think. At this time on a Friday night the bar was about half empty and the non-smoking rules were relaxed. A couple of guys along the bar had lit up, smoke twisting in an artistic way forming curls in the gloom, illuminated by the bar lights and flashes from the TV jukebox. Bowie's 'Starman' was playing. Bowie was crooning on Mick Ronson's shoulder something about how the Starman would like to meet us but thinks he'd blow our mind.

I'd changed out of my scrubs and was wearing jeans and a t-shirt topped off with a net cardigan. My hair was pinned back and up into one of those bunches that other women seem to do so effortlessly and yet still look as if they could be going to the opera. I'd not yet mastered that particular skill. I popped out a compact and flipped the mirrored cap open. My eyes looked bloodshot, with bags the size of coal sacks dragging them down. I pursed my lips, and wondered if I should pop on some lipstick, but then I thought better of it.

The sole bartender tonight, Harry Gibson, ambled towards me absentmindedly cleaning a beer glass. He wiggled his eyebrows and put a clean tumbler in front of me.

"Bad day, Kate? This is a late one even for you."

I took an appreciative sniff of the Kraken in my current glass and downed it in one, letting the spicy liquid coat the inside of my mouth before swallowing. I closed my eyes and let out a deep breath.

"Harry, you've no idea," I said, putting the glass down heavily on the counter. "I'm just glad you never close."

"You still look gorgeous, Kate," said Harry. He'd seen my weary look as I put the mirror back in my purse. "If you need to unload, you know that's what we barmen do best."

I gave him a tired smile. I needed my bed, but I wanted one last drink as I tried to wrap my head around all the stuff that had happened. There was so much that made no sense. I prided myself in my medical skills, but the experience with Adam in the hospital had left me with more questions than answers. Did I really hear his voice in my head? Wouldn't that make me crazier than him? And then there was the vision, if that's what it was, of Adam in the cavern, and then Connor's story, which only made things more confusing. And why was Connor in trouble? It sounded like the police just had him for trespassing, so I couldn't imagine he'd be up for more than a token fine. He was scared, and not of the police.

I shook my glass, and Harry got the hint and added a couple of fingers of rum and some cubes of ice. I swirled it around and gave him a silent toast before taking a large slug. Out of the corner of my eye I caught movement and as the door opened three uniformed soldiers entered and rolled over to the bar. I could hear them laughing and talking loudly, and there was a high five in there somewhere. They looked over to Harry and leaned on the bar, waving.

"It'll need to wait," I said to Harry. You've got more customers."

"Don't go away," he said with a wagging finger, and took off in their direction.

I knocked back another mouthful of the rum, and shook my head to clear it. I couldn't accept that I'd heard his voice in my head, because that would make me - well – insane. I now regretted that I'd mentioned this little fact to Clem because he'd either ignored it or dismissed it out of hand. Either one was bad for me. But something wasn't right. Something was off-kilter about the whole thing.

I finished the rest of the rum and looked down the bar at Harry who was serving the soldier boys a round of beer. They were talking very loudly and by their body language were clearly very drunk. I began to look away but the one nearest caught my eye and raised his hand, waving me over.

"Hey there Blondie, come and join us!"

Fuck, just what I needed.

His friends were now looking over as well and also started to make noises and gestures designed to encourage me over. I could see Harry attempting to pacify them and trying not to disturb any of his other patrons, who really couldn't have given a shit anyway. I shook my head and raised the glass to them as a kind of toast. "Thanks guys but I'm heading home after this one."

Unfortunately they didn't get the hint. Egged on by his friends, the soldier who'd caught my eye shuffled out of his barstool and staggered over. He slouched against the bar and looked me up and down with lidded eyes. The smell of stale beer and cigarettes caused me to wince. His badge said Private Delacruz, and I put out a hand in the universal gesture of 'back the fuck off'.

"Look, *private*, I'm just having a quick drink and then I'm going home. It was a long day at the hospital."

His eyes widened and he leaned in, his beery breath causing me to turn my head away. "So, you're that doctor?" He shouted over to his buddies, "I've scored with the hot doc-tor!"

There was some further cheering and a high five. I sighed inwardly and closed my eyes. I figured I knew how this would go down. Within a few weeks of arriving at Indian Springs, word had gotten around the Base about the new young female doctor at the hospital. Given what I'd just gone through in Chicago, I tried to keep myself to myself, maintain a standoffish kind of posture, which wasn't a stretch to be honest. I'd erected walls around myself so high, and I was so emotionally drained, that all I wanted to do after work was sleep or drink. Then after a couple of months and a particularly late night at Joey's I got involved with one of the soldiers from Creech - a Military Policeman no less. Big, handsome, confident... you name it, he was it. I fell for him, but the relationship didn't last more than a few weeks. He was posted out of country at 24 hours notice but not without leaving his buddies a full account of our time together.

I was quite famous for all the wrong reasons in the military part of town.

I took another drink as Delacruz' two compadres, both in their early twenties, shambled over. Buffed up young marines full of beer and testosterone, starting the weekend as they meant to continue. Delacruz leaned in again and put his hand on my arm.

"Come on, lemme buy you a drink. It's just polite."

Before I could reply, my saviour Harry appeared.

"Guys, the night is young. Go and finish your drinks back over there, and leave the lady alone."

One of the soldiers, an enormous mountain of a man with bad acne and a broken nose, squeezed in between Delacruz and me. He stuck out his tongue and propping both elbows on the bar and invading my personal space even more. His breath was stale and garlic-infused. I wondered if I would pass out.

"Jeez, Harry we just want to say hello. She looks lonely."

On the other side, Delacruz leered at me. "We can be very entertaining, you'd better believe it, hey?"

His buddies roared approvingly and 'hi-five'd' each other again. There was some fist-bumping as well.

I glanced at Harry, and raised my eyebrows warningly. He got the hint.

"Guys," said Harry sternly. "I'm going to have to ask you to move down the bar and leave the lady alone. Don't make me call the MPs now. That would mess with everyone's night, wouldn't it?"

Reluctantly and with somewhat petulant looks at Harry the three soldiers wandered back to their barstools where their drinks were waiting. They cast unapologetic looks back at me but then lost interest, as there was a touchdown in one of the games on the screen.

"Thanks," I said as Harry ambled back over. "Normally I couldn't give a shit but I just don't need this tonight."

He smiled. "Hey, all good. They're just kids. You need a bit of space, right? Long day and all." He poured yet another Kraken into my glass, and I swilled the brown liquid around the glass, chinking the ice cubes. "You waiting for anyone?" he asked, with a sympathetic smile.

I shook my head. "Nah. Gimme a few minutes and I'll be out of here."

He nodded, and moved off to serve another customer. I took out my cell phone and flicked through the photos until I came across the picture I'd taken of Adam Benedict in the ER. The quality was poor but he was clearly identifiable and I wondered why I hadn't given it to the police. That would've been the sensible thing to do.

I was about to dial the number Sherriff Woods had given me, just as Harry appeared again. He leaned forward, conspiratorially.

"Kate, this guy says he knows you?" He indicated with his chin down the bar in the opposite direction to the soldiers. "Seems more like your type?"

I turned and peered down the bar. Sitting a couple of barstools along and looking up at the TV screens was a darkhaired man dressed in ill-fitting hospital scrubs, croc overshoes and a white coat buttoned uncomfortably all the way up. There was a stethoscope draped around his neck.

He turned to face me and his voice exploded in my head.
Hello Kate.

I jerked upright and stared into the face of the man from the hospital. His unblinking eyes bored into mine and I got a rush of vertigo as if I was suddenly standing on a cliff-edge. A cold flush made its way up my scalp and the hairs on the back of my neck stood up. I pushed back the barstool and leaned on the bar for support, my legs shaking.

"How the fuck can I hear you in my head?" I asked, a tremor in my voice.

"I can explain," he replied, softly. His voice was deep, and accent-less. "I mean you no harm."

"Really?" I said. "What about that 'you're all in danger' stuff? Oh, and the policeman you put in hospital?"

He looked back up at the TV screen. There was a basketball game going on. It was the final seconds of the final quarter and the scores were tied. Muted cheers could be heard from the soldiers at the other end of the bar. Led Zeppelin's 'Immigrant Song' had replaced Bowie. Harry had always been a 70's fan.

"I will explain, but first I need somewhere to stay."

I couldn't believe he was asking me this. I laughed. "Well there's a hotel two blocks down the street."

"I have no money. No cards. No … ID."

"Not my problem," I said.

He nodded slowly, and continued to watch the game. I slid along the bar and squeezed into the barstool next to him. He didn't look away from the TV. His hands were on the bar, long fingers interlocked. He looked awkward in the barstool, as if sitting was unnatural. An image of Praying Mantis, popped up into my head, somewhat unnervingly.

"You know, I'm sure the police would be happy to put you up," I suggested, somewhat snarkily.

He looked away from the screen and smiled at me, although the movement appeared awkward and forced. His eyes were big and dark in the half-light, his face angular with deep shadows reflecting the light from the glassware and whisky bottles.

"I cannot be in custody. I have … there are things I must do. Things that I - I need you to help me with."

"Me? How can I be of help? I don't know you."

You already know so much

His words bounced around my brain, his lips not moving. My head was starting to hurt and I wished the Kraken was still in front of me. I squeezed my eyes closed and realised I was bunching my hands into fists, my nails digging in painfully. I opened them slowly and tried to calm down, tried to suppress the tremors.

"Stop doing that telepathy thing," I ground out between gritted teeth.

What was I saying? Telepathy… for fuck's sake, I was a doctor, trained in evidence-based medicine and science. Telepathy was in the realm of bullshit-pseudo-science.

He reached out and gently took hold of my hand.

"Kate, I have looked into your mind. I know you. Your past, and your present."

My past? I was starting to get angry.

"Really, such as?"

He looked over me, his head at an angle as if deciding what to say.

"Your father was stationed at Creech Air Force Base from the late 1960s, flying training missions in B25 bombers. When you were five years old there was an acrimonious divorce and your mother secured full custody and moved you to Chicago. Your father paid generous support but your mother was strict and rarely granted him access. The last time that you saw him was at your graduation ceremony at Chicago City Hall."

I shook my head. "Much of that's common knowledge. You could've spoken with Clem Reynolds or fucking Googled me."

He nodded, and then continued. His face had taken on guileless, sympathetic appearance that I found strangely unnerving. A pounding started in my ears, jungle drums threatening to obscure his softly spoken voice. His grip on my hand increased slightly and he leaned forward, dark eyes boring into mine.

"Your daughter was killed in the Chicago Memorial Emergency Room. You were asked to see a patient and had brought her with you because you had no child minder. A gangland turf battle spilled over and a random bullet punctured her lung and transected her spine. You were also hit, but the police pulled you to safety. Kelly died at the scene."

I felt my eyes moistening and I stared at him wordlessly. My heart felt like it was gripped in an ice-cold vice, the blood pumping out of it cold and listless. I was unable to speak, my mouth as dry as sandpaper.

"You tried to contact your father, but a stranger picked up the phone and told you that he, too, had died a few months previously, after a short battle with cancer."

I could feel tears trickling down the side of my face. He reached up and delicately wiped them away with his fingertips. As he touched me I could feel new emotions washing into my consciousness, just as my feelings were about to take me to a dark place.

"What are you doing?" I managed.

"Let me help you," he said.

Somehow - how, I don't know - I understood that he was coaxing my liver cells to manufacture anxiolytic proteins that he then pushed into my blood stream and through the blood-brain barrier. I could feel them washing through my cerebral cortex, easing the fear and the sorrow, like a broom sweeping decayed leaves and twigs into the gutter and off the road.

I looked up at him blinking through eyes full of tears.

"What are you?"

He didn't answer, and was surveying the bar, taking in the soldiers, Harry, the other customers. The music had stopped and the background cheering from one of the games was also muted. There was the clacking of cutlery from the booths and the low hum of bar conversation. All seemed normal, ordinary people, doing regular things.

"Everyone is in danger," he said quietly.

"What do you mean?" I whispered.

"I will explain, but not here."

I looked down at my hand, seeing how small and fragile it looked in his grip. I pulled it away, testing to see if he would let go. He did.

"Am I in danger from you?" I said, holding my breath.

He smiled again, more convincing this time.

"No."

I came to a decision. "All right then, let's get out of here."

I took his hand, and we hustled out the back. The bar was on the corner of 1st and 2nd street, on the north side of the Veterans Memorial Highway. We exited through a side door onto 2nd and I looked around us. The streets were empty of life and shadowy, with the only light coming from the bar windows. There was a red Dodge pickup parked a couple of yards away. No traffic noise was evident despite the close proximity of the highway. Directly across from the bar was a small public park, and beyond that a pedestrian bridge crossed the highway leading to a patchwork of suburbs that spread out for a dozen blocks or more.

I could smell Joey Malone's kitchen, meaty and oily and inviting, and I realised I'd not eaten since breakfast. My stomach grumbled loudly. I pointed to the bridge. "I live over there, it's a fifteen minute walk. Are you up to it?"

He nodded. "Yes. Of course."

At that moment, the door behind us crashed open and disgorged Private Delacruz and his companions. They stumbled out onto the sidewalk, beer bottles in hand, and saw us straight away. Acne Mountain laughed and pointed at me.

"You left without saying 'bye!"

His voice was even more slurred than before and he moved away from the door towards Adam, who was standing on the edge of the sidewalk. He seemed to be sizing Adam up, and then sniffed the air disdainfully. "Who the fuck are you then?"

The other two soldiers moved either side of us, stopping on the road in a semicircle facing the bar, trapping us on the sidewalk. I turned to Delacruz and raised my hands. "This is an old friend of mine from the hospital. We go way back…"

"Bullshit, doc," he said. "I ain't never seen him 'round here before today."

Acne Mountain was now aggressively checking Adam out, feet apart, rocking forward and backwards. I turned to Adam and whispered, "These fuckers are drunk. We should go back to the bar, where it's safer…"

Adam looked at me and for a brief instant I felt a wave of reassurance being pushed into my mind. A mental arm around my shoulders assuring me that everything was going to be okay. But as quickly as this feeling washed over me I sensed something else, something bubbling under the surface. Something malevolent and pernicious. Something becoming excited by the mere thought of violence. I saw Adam kind of shake his head as if trying to clear it, and then his voice floated into my thoughts.

It is too late.

The three soldiers had all moved closer. Acne Mountain was smacking his lips, not taking his eyes off Adam.

"I can fix this," I said under my breath, looking sideways at Adam. "Let's get them all back inside the bar before you get your ass kicked."

A flicker of green phosphorescence transited between his eyes. His thoughts pushed into my brain, resonating and soothing.

Do not be afraid.

Acne Mountain was now right in his face. He and Adam were about the same height, but the difference in physiology was staggering. The soldier looked like he could wrestle a bear, and snap Adam in half like a twig. The other soldiers had not moved, and Delacruz was looking at me with a confident, evil grin on his face.

I heard Adam wordlessly speak to me.

Events are in motion.

In that microsecond between standoff and violence, I saw Acne Mountain's eyes flick from Adam to me. His face showed no fear, just a smirk. Without looking he reached out and pushed Adam in the chest, the sort of move most drunken street fights start with. There was no reaction from Adam; no movement at all. Acne looked surprised but regrouped instantly, stepping forward and swung a haymaker into Adam's face. It never landed. In a move too fast for my eyes to follow, Adam swayed to the left in a fluid motion and caught hold of Acne Mountain's fist in his own hand.

Adam briefly glanced in my direction and closed his eyes.

Kate, this is for your own safety.

"What…?" I began, and then my throat closed up. I was paralysed. Petrified like stone. I tried to breathe, but my chest muscles would not expand my lungs. Spots started to appear in front of my eyes, and I could feel my heart hammering away in protest. Then my legs lurched and I found myself involuntarily walking backwards, only stopping when my backside touched the fender of the red Dodge. The soldiers surrounding Adam were also frozen like mannequins. Delacruz had been winding up to hit Adam with his bottle, and the beer was now comically dripping into his hair from the upended bottle. Acne was clutching his hand with his other one, and his face creased with pain. The other soldier had backed off a few feet, and was staring at Adam with eyes like dinner plates.

Adam looked over at me, blinked, and the paralysis dissipated. I took a huge breath in, sucking air as far down to the bottom of my burning lungs as I could. Then a high-pitched whine tore at my ears and they popped like I'd been shooting up an elevator. My hearing became muted, like I'd suddenly put earplugs in, or stuck my head underwater. The soldiers were holding their heads, faces locked in rictus agony. Delacruz with his mouth open in a silent scream. Acne shaking, blood beginning to trickle from his ears. Delacruz looked over at me and yelled something but the noise continued and I couldn't make out his words.

Slowly, the screaming subsided and the pressure in my head eased off. I felt nauseous and acid flowed up from my stomach. I brought my hand up to cover my mouth but then fell forward onto my knees and proceeded to vomit a mixture of bile and dark rum onto the sidewalk. I felt Adam's hands take hold of me and gently pull me to my feet. He walked me to the passenger seat of the Dodge, and I slumped forward, breathing heavily, still feeling the urge to vomit. The driver's door opened and Adam got in, eyes ablaze with an emerald glow. The truck's engine roared to life and it's headlights exploded, flooding the street in stark white radiance. I could see the three soldiers lying motionless, with pools of black liquid tracking from their heads into the gutters.

"Are they dead?" I stammered.

He didn't reply, and the truck engaged reverse gear and backed off a couple of yards before doing a fast U-turn over the opposite kerb and accelerated down the street. I noticed in a surreal way that Adam didn't have his hands on the wheel and hadn't touched the gearstick. The truck screeched to a stop at the T-junction and turned into 1st street.

"Where are we going?" I said, finding my voice.

"To your home," he said, looking almost apologetic. The green glow was slowly subsiding from his eyes.

"No. No no no no…" I went to open the door but the lock clicked down before I could touch it.

"Kate. I mean you no harm. Please believe me."

The truck drove itself to the end of 1st street and turned onto North Frontage Road, and towards I-95. In a hundred yards or so it took the exit ramp and accelerated to match the speed of an 18-wheeler, heading west.

"We will take the next exit and loop back into the town," he said. "It should only take ten minutes to get to your address."

"How do you know where I live?" I asked, and it sounded sullen and piqued even to me.

I was sure he raised an eyebrow before answering. "Your thoughts are not closed to me." He then tried a smile, which wasn't a bad effort. "I am sorry."

I sat back in the seat. Took a deep breath. "Are they dead? The soldiers."

There was an unreadable expression on his face. "I do not know for sure."

I felt sick again. He looked at me, and his brows furrowed a little. "Kate, they were about to initiate unprovoked violence. On a stranger. You know what they could have done to you."

I swallowed, my anger bubbling up, "I've had to deal with that sort of shit all my life and I've always been able to talk my way out of it. And the bar was just there. We could've gone inside, easily."

He gave what I thought was a sigh, "I acted in self defence. And I acted to protect you. I had no control over my response."

"What do you mean, you weren't in control?" I said, my mind racing.

"I will try and explain later, but first we must get to your house, and I must change out of these clothes." He looked at me and this time there was definitely a raised eyebrow. "I believe Major Richard Jackson, US Military Police, left some clothes at your home when he was unexpectedly posted to Europe three months ago."

CHAPTER NINE
Indian Springs, Nevada

The drive took fifteen minutes and neither of us had spoken further. We left I-95 and turned into the suburbs where the properties thinned out. The roads and houses languished in almost complete darkness, and Adam extinguished the Dodge's headlights as it turned into McFarland Avenue and followed the road south for a couple of miles to Betty Ridge Court.

We pulled up outside my house, a single-storey property set back from the road thirty yards or more and accessed by a gravel driveway on the right leading to my garage. There was no garden, just desert-y scrubland and a rash of cactus plants leading to a door that looked bleached grey and black in the moonlight.

Adam turned to face me and switched the engine off. "I believe this is your home."

Did I detect a note of disapproval? I fished in my handbag and brought out a remote key that I used to open the garage. "I know it's not much, but I wasn't planning on staying here for ever."

"Do you own a car?" He was looking up the driveway to the garage, which was empty.

"Thought you could read my mind?" I said, somewhat huffily.

"I am able to access your thoughts at will, but I can choose not to. I decided to allow you some... privacy"

I sighed. "My Jeep's back at the hospital."

"Then we need to hide this vehicle," he said. "It would be considered 'stolen'."

"Put it in the garage for now - but it can't stay there. I'm pretty well known in that bar. It won't take them long to figure out where we've gone."

He nodded and the Dodge came to life again. He guided it into the garage and I remote-closed the door behind us. I led him through a side door to the kitchen. Lights came on automatically, and I threw the keys into a bowl on a side-table and walked over to the fridge. I brought out a half-full bottle of wine, grabbed a glass from the draining board and held it up, aware that my hands were shaking. "Well I'm going to have another drink. Join me?"

He'd entered the kitchen and was looking around the room, taking everything in, slowly and deliberately. "Where is your dog?"

"How did you … never mind." This mind-reading thing would take some getting used to. I grabbed a bag of peanuts off the shelf, one of my staples after a long day in the ER. "He's with a neighbour. She takes him three days a week when I'm on day shifts. Walks him, stuff like that. I'm supposed to pick him up in the morning."

He walked into the hallway and I followed, pointing to another adjoining door. "My bedroom and the wardrobe is in there, go help yourself."

Without a word, he walked through to the bedroom leaving me in the kitchen holding the bottle, glass and a large back of salted nuts. I went through to the sitting area that I'd fitted out with a large screen plasma and a 3-piece leather suite. I collapsed into the sofa, reached for the remote and turned on the TV. It auto-tuned into a game show, and I dialled the sound down until it was just audible. I poured some wine into the glass and set the bottle down on a small coffee table. After taking a large swallow, I ripped open the peanuts and popped a handful in my mouth. Chewing, I reached for my handbag and upended it onto the sofa discharging the usual female handbag detritus. I rummaged through the pile of handkerchiefs, lipsticks and pens, becoming more frantic as I realised my phone wasn't there. I'd left it in the bar.

Fuck.

I put my head in my hands and started rocking backwards and forwards, the fog of fatigue and alcohol preventing me from thinking straight. Out of the corner of my eye I saw Adam standing in the doorway. He was dressed in desert combat military BDUs and untied black army boots. He tightened the belt on the trousers, and the whole ensemble came together quite well. The arms were a little short in the sleeves, as were the trousers, but tucked into the boots it would pass muster. He sat down in the chair facing me and tied the laces, clumsily but effectively. He seemed to be concentrating hard on getting the knots right, and at times his fingers seemed to get trapped in the twine. When he was finished he looked around the lounge. Through his eyes I could see the sparse decorations and the lack of personal items. There were no pictures on the side tables, no vases, no jars with fresh flowers.

"Have you just moved in?" he said, straight-faced.

I took another large swallow of the wine and said nothing.

"You are correct, we cannot stay here," he said. "The authorities will make the connection. They will be here soon. First thing in the morning, if not tonight."

I finished the glass and refilled it with the rest of the contents from the wine bottle. There was a not unpleasant fuzzy feeling now permeating my mind as the alcohol took the edge off the day's events. I offered him the bag of nuts, and when he ignored me I shovelled another handful into my mouth. He was looking at the TV, which was showing a family hugging each other and dancing around ecstatically while a game show host smiled beatifically in the background. The volume was muted, and I could imagine the blandness of the audience's applause and the clichéd music swelling up to make sure we understood how fabulous life was going to be for the family from now on.

The caption underneath read: *total prize won $1000*.

"Is this your life, Kate?" He said in a quiet voice.

"You think you know my life?" I growled. I avoided his stare, and wondered if he could hear the pain in my words, feel the emotion seeping out, perceive the invisible scars that I'd hidden from everyone.

"I know that you are unhappy here."

I took another drink. "Thought you weren't going to read my mind? Or is that only when it suits you?"

His face was in half shadow, his cheekbones prominent and gaunt. He leaned forward a couple of inches, crossing his arms on his knees. "I know that this town is not what you were expecting," he said. "I know that you only came here because your father was based here, and that you grew up here. You wanted to re-connect with good memories."

It was true; the pain was not going away. There were nights when I closed my eyes and tried to sleep and all I could see was Kelly being lowered into a shallow grave, screaming soundlessly at faceless mourners in black standing above. Then there were the mornings I woke up wishing I too was dead and buried, in some afterlife I didn't believe in, holding my baby daughter again. Tears welled up in my eyes and I brushed them away. I stared at the wine, absently tracing my finger on the condensation clouding the glass.

"Did you find what you were looking for?" Adam said, almost in a whisper.

I looked at him, sitting there on my couch. He remained still, like a waxwork figure, his hands on his knees and his head at a slight angle like a dog listening quizzically to his master. I gave a wet smile. "I ... I thought coming here would be a good thing, but... I was ... I had to get out of Chicago."

"Would you like to talk about Chicago?"

"What's there to talk about? You can't change the past, only the future."

"The past informs the present, and therefore will change the future."

He leaned back in the sofa, almost relaxing, but as poker-faced as ever. I took another drink and closed my eyes. My stomach was in knots, tightening like an old fishermen's rope.

"Work was all consuming, long shifts and then long hours studying. I'd seen less and less of my dad since the divorce, and he never visited. My mom and I became very close." My voice caught in my throat and my mouth became dry. I hugged myself tightly. "Without her, I could never have brought up my daughter."

Adam said nothing but his eyes had never left mine. I could feel my face start to crumple. "When she died, it was just me and Kelly."

He closed his eyes and my mind was instantly flooded with images from my life, a waterfall of people and places in glorious Technicolor. Then the images coalesced into recognisable narratives. Chicago. The one night stands, usually at the end of a particularly difficult and depressing shift, and always ending with a guilt-ridden departure in the mornings or sometimes in the early hours. Nightly drinking alone in my apartment and falling asleep in front of the TV dressed in the day's bloodstained scrubs. The torrid and intense affair with one of the senior surgeons in a Chicago hospital; a relationship predicated on his moods and whims and when he could sneak away from his wife. The vow to leave him there and then, but the shifts continuing, the work intensifying, and the stresses of trying to be the 'other woman' becoming overwhelming. The morning I sat on the toilet after a bout of vomiting, staring in shock and horror at the faint blue line on the plastic pen, a simple and clinical way of telling me that my whole life was going to change. The confrontation with the surgeon, his anger when I said I wanted to keep the baby. His insulting offers to 'pay for the abortion' or to pay for me to leave Chicago.

And then a flash-forward to the Emergency Room. Me screaming hysterically as the emergency response team tried and failed to save the life of the only family I had left.

"Two months later you moved here," said Adam. "The town where you were brought up, but had never returned."

I drank the last of the wine and shakily put the glass down on the edge of the table. "Well that brings us up to date then. No more deep, dark, dirty secrets left."

But as I said it there was a nagging feeling, a sensation that I was missing something. I chewed at the inside of my cheek. "There's something you've not told me. Something you've kept from me isn't there. About my past. My past … here, in Indian Springs?"

Would you like me to open those memories to you?

His unspoken words floated and swirled inside my head, teasing and tormenting. I closed my eyes and scrunched up my face, rubbing my fists into the sockets.

I can do it. Would you like me to?

Would I?

I looked up. "Yes."

He nodded imperceptibly, closed his eyes for a second and then looked straight at me, and then right through me. I felt light-headed and intoxicated and took in a huge shuddering breath as my mind filled with long forgotten images of people and places. It was as if I had suddenly acquired the master key to a memory palace with multiple hidden and locked rooms. The images were alive and I could smell and taste and live the memories like they were happening in real time.

I saw my father and mother laughing and playing with me in a park just outside the airbase. I was on a swing and they were both pushing me. My father looked handsome in his air force uniform, his dark hair and moustache trimmed and tidy. My mother, blonde hair tied up in a bow, was smoking a cigarette. The sky was deep blue and I could see wispy contrails interlocking in the stratosphere.

I was then sitting on my father's knee in the cockpit of a military jet as he pointed out various switches and dials and I gurgled nonsense and tried to lick the side of his face.

I was then sitting on the floor of a playgroup with four other children, watching a black and white TV while making figures out of play-doh.

I was then in my bedroom locked in a cot and screaming at the top of my little lungs while I watched my father beat my mother to a bloody pulp.

"I am sorry," I heard Adam say.

I closed my eyes and the tears came again, but this time they were welcome. They spilled down my face, salty drops falling from my chin and drenching my shirt. I was trembling and couldn't stop. Sobs punched through, ripping through my muscles and bones as the walls came tumbling down. I became aware of a hand on my shoulder as Adam silently moved over and sat next to me. I sobbed into his chest and felt him holding me, rocking me slowly as my tears soaked his chest. I pulled away, my lashes heavy with water, howls of misery coming in waves, broken apart by short pauses for recovering breaths.

After a time, when there was nothing left and I was spent, I crumpled back into the sofa. I sniffed loudly and wiped my nose with my sleeve. Adam handed me a paper cloth from the mess out of my handbag, and I used it to blow my nose.

"I am very sorry," he said again.

I nodded, and folded the handkerchief in my palm before absent-mindedly starting to tease it apart, layer-by-layer. "My mother told me you know, when I was older, but I never believed her because I couldn't remember it ever happening." I took another sip of the wine then sat back, looking at him through watery eyes.

"They are repressed memories," he said. "A safety mechanism your brain uses, to protect you."

I felt my heart rate slowing and my breathing coming back to normal. The pain was still there, the emotions still raw. "That's some trick," I said. "How do you do that?"

"I do not know." He held his hands out, palms up and looked sadly at them.

Without thinking, I took hold of one of his hands. I marvelled at the coolness of the skin, the rubbery texture, and for the first time I noticed the lack of fingerprints. I turned it over and felt for a pulse. There wasn't one. Time stopped.

Pieces of the puzzle finally dropped into place. But the big picture still eluded me.

"What are you?" I asked.

"Cogito ergo sum," he replied with an enigmatic smile.

"'I think, therefore I am'. Yes, I get that, but what are you? Are you human?" I pictured the scans, the lack of injuries. "Are you alive?"

"I am Adam Benedict." He tapped his head. "At least inside here."

I took a deep breath. "But who is Adam Benedict, really?"

"Are you sure you want to know?"

I nodded, unhesitatingly, if only to move things away from me, and my emotions.

Without changing expression he reached up and brushed a lock of hair behind my ears. Immediately my mind was flooded with images, smells, and sounds. Memories so vivid that I felt I was physically present.

His memories.

I could detect a faint metallic smell in the air, and hear the distant sirens of police vehicles. I was standing in an expensively and stylishly furnished living room facing a huge bay window overlooking a large expanse of water. Dawn was breaking outside, and twinkling lights from ships and boats and larger islands a mile or so further out could be seen. Just visible within a rolling bank of morning mist was a red suspension bridge.

"San Francisco?" I said.

He just nodded.

The scene continued. My field of vision moved and sprays of blood came into view, obscenely splattered against a magnolia-coloured wall. Randomly upturned furniture could be seen, in addition to a cracked mirror and bottles and wine glasses littering the floor. More smears of blood tracked diagonally up the mirror from what I surmised was an arterial spray. I felt a deep sense of foreboding as I entered a bedroom dominated by a huge four-poster. Another open door lead to an ensuite and I could make out another pool of blood which had merged with a dark brown rug and spread across what had been self-coloured carpet. There was more blood on the sheets and pillows, and a few splashes on the wall by a bedside lamp leaning at an angle against the corner of the headboard. A drawer on the bedside cabinet was open, and inside I could just see the handle of a pistol.

Lying by the bed was a semi-naked woman. Her skull had been crushed from behind and the impact had made a dent that was filled by matted hair and congealed blood. As my perspective changed I could see that the woman's eyes, open and lifeless, were staring at the wall. Her mangled lip and obviously broken nose were caked in dried blood, cracked and blackened. One of her hands appeared to be reaching out to the drawer, and her other arm was twisted beneath her body. There were stab wounds on her torso, but the bleeding there seemed to have stopped quickly. My medical mind worked out that the fatal wound, the blow to the head, had come fairly soon after she had been stabbed.

The scene's perspective changed again and I was now kneeling next to her. A hand reached out to stroke her hair and I heard a male voice sobbing, an awful groaning, guttural sound. I felt myself sit back on the bed, and in the mirror on the wall opposite I saw the image of a distraught Adam Benedict, tears rolling down his face as he contemplated the body of his murdered wife.

"Her name was Cora," he said quietly.

The vision faded and Adam's face swam into view, now back in my living room. His head dropped and I pulled his hand to my face and held it there with both of my own. I looked into his eyes, blue and wide, expecting tears but there were none to see.

"Two damaged people, are we not?" he said.

I nodded silently. I sensed that he was one blow away from breaking. I was intimately familiar with the path he was on, the road to a destination where there was no going back, no redemption.

It was time to step up. Maybe for both of us.

"I heard you have a daughter?" I said, as gently as I could.

He nodded slowly, and a rueful smile played across his lips. "Yes, but we ... wait..." He stopped and stood up, his head turning to the window. "We are about to have a visitor."

He walked over and opened a couple of the blinds with his fingers. I could see the glimmer of car headlights playing over his face. I jumped up, straightened my shirt, and joined him at the window. "I don't get visitors."

A car crawled down the street, before stopping outside my house. It was a taxi, white phone decals and an advertisement just visible on the side. It's internal light went on as the passenger paid for his fare before opening the near side door and getting out. He reached in the back seat and pulled out a large duffle bag that he slung over his shoulder. He turned to face the house.

I brought a hand up to my mouth. "Fuck. That's Richard. What's he doing here? He's supposed to be in Berlin."

Adam closed the blinds and looked down at me. "Perhaps it is more than a co-incidence, given recent events?"

I felt a mild panic rising. "What are we going to do?"

"Nothing," he replied. "Do not answer the door. Presumably he will then leave."

I shook my head. "No, no ... he has a key. I gave him it before he left. I'm a fucking idiot."

Adam moved away from the window, closing the blinds. "He must not find me here. It would create a problem."

I thought fast. "Okay, here's what we'll do. You go hide in the garage. I'll pretend to be in bed and when he comes in I'll get rid of him."

Adam raised his eyebrows.

"I'll get rid of him. I promise," I said, pleading.

He grudgingly nodded, and went back through the kitchen into the garage, closing the door behind him. I ran through into the bedroom and tore my clothes off, leaving them littered around the room. I pulled on my pyjamas and jumped into the bed just as I heard the key turning in the front door.

CHAPTER TEN
1355 Betty Ridge Court, Indian Springs, Nevada

I quickly turned the bedroom light off, pulled the sheets up to my chin and closed my eyelids just enough so that I could see and maintain the appearance of sleep. I could hear him walking on the creaky floorboards in the living room, unzipping the duffle bag and then going into the kitchen and opening my fridge. There was a tinkle of glassware followed by the sound of spurting water from my leaky faucet and then the bedroom door cracked open and his face peered through. I could see him looking around the darkened room and registering my shape under the sheets. He opened the door fully and stood there framed in the light from the lounge, holding a glass of whisky. He was wearing a white T-shirt and black jeans, his sandy hair short and spiky.

He looked good.

I remembered when I first saw him with his shirt off for an army medical, and how he took my breath away with his sculpted, tanned body. Despite my emotional walls and professional attitude (or so I thought) he asked for my number and called the next day. The relationship was physical and intensely passionate, on my part at least. I used him and he was almost always at my beck and call, always in my bedroom. We never dated, or were seen in public, which made everything work for me as I was settling into my new home and town. However, the day he left for Berlin I discovered he'd been two-timing me with at least two other women, one of whom was a nurse at the ER.

He tiptoed toward my side of the bed and so I waited until he was right next to me and then jerked upright and screamed. I pretended to scrabble for the sidelight, and eventually flicked it on.

"Richard! What the fuck are you doing here?" I shouted, trying to sound frightened and incensed at the same time.

He sat down on the bed next to me and a wide grin split his face. His confident eyes looked me up and down, stopping at the undone buttons on the front of my pyjamas.

I pulled the sheet up to my chest. "I thought you were in Germany?"

"Got back tonight," he replied with a shrug. "In to JFK, then the last flight out into McCarran. Came straight here."

I crinkled my nose and my mouth turned sour. "Why on earth would you do that?"

"I missed you. I been thinking about you a lot while I been over there."

I snorted, and now the indignation was real. "You missed me? After what you did? And not a single fucking call or text in three months!"

He looked hurt, and gave a theatrical-sounding sigh. "Look, I had to go dark. Not by choice, but I was working with the Bundespolizel. I can't really talk about it, but it involves a couple of GIs and some inappropriate governmental interactions, so to speak."

He looked expectantly, clearly waiting for me to ask for more details of his top-secret mission. At this moment in time I couldn't give two fucks. I shook my head and folded my arms. "How'd you get in?"

He attempted a sheepish look and started stroking my arm in an affectionate way, but one that now made my skin crawl. "I still got the key you gave me," he said, giving the mega wattage smile again.

He must have seen the dark look I was giving him, so he cracked another half smile and tried to look petulant. "I didn't mean to hurt you, Kate. You know, when I left. I just wasn't sure where we was going. We never said anything about being exclusive, either. You acted pretty cold at times." He shrugged, "It was hard to figure you out."

I pushed his hand away and shook my head vigorously. The nerve of the guy. "Bullshit, Major Jackson. You were having a great fucking time. All your buddies said so."

He held his hands palms out in a conciliatory gesture. "Now Kate, there may have been some talk in the mess, and I may have said a few things, but babe, it was *all* complimentary."

He leered at me and wiggled his eyebrows. I remembered that Adam was a few yards away in the garage, and no doubt listening in. I tried to slow my breathing, and figure out what I needed to do in order to get rid of him. Maybe I could just offer him a second chance, another time, and that'll placate him. But... he did turn up on my doorstep in the middle of the night, so that spoke volumes about his intentions, didn't it? The presumptuous asshole. As if I was that kind of girl. Wait ... I had been that kind of girl when we'd met. Shit, what to do...

"You got company?" I heard him say, interrupting my thoughts.

He was looking over towards the window, his eyes narrowing. Peering past his shoulder, I saw the scrubs, white coat and crocs that Adam had deposited there earlier.

Shit.

Richard regarded me coolly and his voice dropped a semitone. "So who does all this belong to then? Those shoes ain't your size."

I thought fast, decided to go with, "Richard, it's really none of your fucking business now, is it?"

He stood up and theatrically pulled the blankets off me and peered underneath. "Where's he hiding? Not there." He turned around, surveilling the room, "Maybe under the bed?"

I was about to reply when Adam pushed his voice into my head.

This is not working. You must get him to leave or I will intervene.

I stood up, resplendent in my pyjamas, and realised how unthreatening I must look. I hurriedly fastened up the top buttons on my top and kneeled on the bed staring at Richard. "I need you to leave. Now. And give me back my key."

He pursed his lips and continued to scope the room. He moved to the bedroom door so I jumped off the bed and pushed a finger into his chest. My heart was hammering away, and I felt a heady mixture of apprehension and anger.

"I said, I need you to *leave*."

He looked down at me and tilted his head sideways. I glared back, daring him to argue but hoping that he wouldn't. I didn't fear him, but I realised that I was worried about what would happen if Adam emerged and confronted him. I knew Richard was capable of defending himself, but with a jolt I recognised that I was terrified of what Adam might or could do to him.

You are right to be afraid. This will not end well.

I nodded to myself and put a hand on Richard's arm. "Please," I whispered, putting a pleading note into my voice. "Just go. We can talk later. I promise I'll call you in the morning."

He glanced up and watched the fan blades spinning lazily and softly overhead. I wondered what he was thinking about but then he looked down at me and shrugged. "Alright, maybe I should go."

My relief was palpable and I lowered my head, exhaling audibly. He turned and ambled slowly out of the bedroom into the kitchen. I followed behind, furtively looking at the door through to the garage that thankfully remained closed. Richard abruptly stopped in the centre of the room and glanced back over his shoulder. "I'll need a lift back to Creech."

"My car's at the hospital," I replied quickly, "Let me call you a cab."

He pursed his lips, regarding me through lidded eyes. I tried to keep his stare. It was hard and with a sinking feeling I realised that in his job he would've faced better liars than me. He arched an eyebrow, and I saw him glance at the door through to the garage. I shook my head, hoping he wouldn't do what I thought he was going to do, but he was already thinking it. He reached over and yanked the door open. Adam stood on the entrance mat and stared blankly at Richard, hands relaxed by his sides.

"Well now," said Richard. "What do we have here?"

Adam looked over at me, and I knew what he was going to say.

He cannot know I was here.

Indeed. I pulled on Richard's arm again. "Can't you just leave? We don't want any trouble."

He folded his arms across his broad chest and regarded Adam with a smug look. "We don't want any trouble, do we?" He glanced back at me and cracked a humourless smile. "Hey, aren't those my clothes? Having a fancy dress party were you? Playing doctors and soldiers?"

I looked at Adam, a sinking feeling coming over me. "He doesn't have to get hurt," I said. "We can talk to him."

Richard raised his eyebrows in feigned astonishment. He laughed again, turning his attention back to Adam. "She says I don't have to get hurt. Are you going to hurt me?"

"You may be hurt," Adam replied, matter of factly. "I am very sorry."

Richard had unfolded his arms, and was now staring belligerently at Adam. I was thinking furiously what I could do to defuse the tension. Was there an olive branch I could offer Richard, some lie that would make him back down? I didn't know what to do. I'd never known Richard to back down from a confrontation. Came with the job, I guessed. Military Police had to deal with errant soldiers all the time. Couldn't be seen to be weak.

"Richard…" I began,

He ignored me and tapped Adam's chest. "Those are my clothes. Take 'em off and then you can leave."

Adam met the stare without blinking and didn't respond. Richard looked at me and winked, a confident grin cracking his face. "Can you believe this guy? You did tell him about me, right? I mean, what I do for a living?"

Almost in a whisper, I said, "Richard, please, just go."

Adam looked at me and sadly shook his head. "Major Jackson cannot leave now. He has seen us."

With that he stepped forward and put himself within a few inches of Richard's face. Richard didn't flinch or back away, clearly relaxed and confident in his ability. He was about six inches shorter than Adam, but was much more solidly built.

I could also see that he had an M9 Beretta tucked in the back waistband of his jeans.

"Take off that uniform," Richard said, lowering his voice to a growl. "Now."

"Richard, can we sit down and talk about this?" I tried one last time. "It's not what it seems."

His gaze had not left Adam's face. "We can sit down when your boyfriend here has gotten out of my fucking uniform."

I inched forward and reached out to touch Adam's arm. Adam broke the staring contest and glanced at me.

"Can't you just ... wipe his mind?" I pleaded.

He seemed to be considering this, but then Richard grabbed his wrist and tried to twist it behind his back in what I knew was a classical restraining manoeuvre. Unfortunately for Richard the arm would not bend, and remained rigid, like a pipe. He then went for a judo throw by putting a leg behind Adam and pulling the front of his shirt. Again, nothing happened. I watched horrified as he then went for a head-butt, coiling his neck backwards like a cobra and snapping it forwards aiming for the bridge of Adam's nose. A split second before impact, Adam lowered his chin and the head-butt connected solidly with his forehead. Richard grunted in pain and staggered backwards, grasping for support on the kitchen counter, his legs looking like rubber.

"Let it go, Richard!" I shouted.

His face mottled crimson, his eyes popped, his tree-trunk neck straining, he put his head down and charged with both arms out to grab Adam in a bear hug. As he slammed into him, Adam placed a hand on his neck, and effortlessly pushed him to the ground like a tonne weight had been dropped from a great height. He crashed to the floor and rolled over onto his back looking completely discombobulated. Adam stood over him, and to my horror his eyes were glowing phosphorescent green. An unpleasant smile flickered across his face.

"Is that all you have?" I heard him say, in a strange high pitched, almost whispery voice.

Not Adam's voice.

Not Adam.

To my horror Richard shook his head as his fuse relit and simmered and fizzed like a firework before launching. He exploded with unrestrained fury and went for the gun nestling in the small of his back. He drew it insanely quickly, and pointed it at Adam's face. I rushed forward, arms outstretched, shouting, but Adam's hand flashed out in a blur sending the gun spinning through the door into the lounge. Richard cried out in agony, clutching his hand, fingers splayed out at unnatural angles. He scrabbled backwards into the wall, his feet slipping on the kitchen floor and knocking a chair over. He tried to pull himself upright but Adam planted a boot on his chest and leaned in. Richard tried to push the leg away but Adam pressed harder and I could hear what sounded like ribs cracking and his breathing became ragged and jerky.

My foot touched something and I looked down to see the Beretta. I had a brain snap and picked it up and shakily pointed it at Adam. "Let him go," I screamed.

What the fuck was I thinking?

His head turned towards me, hard staring green eyes that never blinked. I sensed my mind opening to him, and waited for the familiar sensation of his thoughts coming through. But what I sensed was completely different. I felt like I'd been dipped in an ice bath, and everything good and positive was sucked out of my head. The urge to look behind me, the feeling of some ancient evil sneaking up on me, was overwhelming. A high-pitched wail exploded inside my head and I screamed and dropped the gun. I sank to the floor, head in hands as the pain intensified, lancing through my temples. I found myself curling up into a ball and rolling over on my side like a foetus. Then as suddenly as it had started the sound was gone and the pain melted away, almost as if I had been given a morphine shot. When I opened my eyes I saw that Adam had picked up the Beretta and was examining it, like a child with a new toy. He took hold of it in both hands and snapped it in two, almost effortlessly. Bullets and pieces of bent and broken metal and mechanism spilled out onto the floor. He flicked a wrist almost contemptuously, and the remains flew across the room, skidding to a stop at Richard's feet.

I struggled to get up using the kitchen top counter as support and leaned back, my heart thudding and my vision swimming and blurred. Richard was still clutching his ribs and making no attempt to pick up the mangled piece of metal that used to be his firearm. Adam looked at me again, and instantly something started to probe my mind. An inquisitive and glacially analytical consciousness infiltrated my brain, contemptuously pushing past any mental barriers I may have erected, seeing deep into my psyche. I felt cold and frightened in a primeval sort of way, like an antelope on the savannah aware that death was approaching, and that it was soon going to be ripped apart and eaten alive.

He squatted down next to Richard, who raised his hands into fists, but then his eyes glazed over and he slid sideways to the ground. He felt for the pulse at Richard's neck. The green glow was receding from his eyes and with it, the malevolent presence I had felt. Richard was now snoring quite peacefully, and Adam turned him onto his side.

"What've you done?" I asked, horrified.

He stood up and looked over at me. I was a bit wobbly and felt nauseous, but my head was clearing. He nodded towards the front door.

"We must go now, before the authorities arrive."

I shook my head. "What's going on? You - you were different."

He put a hand on my arm. "Please Kate, come with me. I will explain later."

I found myself being swallowed up by his eyes. Black pools of emptiness surrounded by a rim of glorious pale blue. Then I was inside his head once more. I saw his wife, Cora, vivid and alive, full of happiness and love. I felt his anguish that he had never gotten to tell her he loved her one last time. Didn't get to hold her before she slipped away. Didn't get to look into her eyes before she died. I thought of my own daughter, but no matter how hard I tried, I still couldn't fully see her face, like a newspaper exposed to sunlight, a ship leaving harbour into a foggy sea. The only clear vision that emerged was the one I had been trying so hard to forget; her lifeless body on the morgue slab. In despair, I pressed my forehead against the door and tried to slow my breathing. An ocean of grief threatened to overwhelm and drown me.

Adam reached out and gently touched my shoulder. "Please," he said, and there was an almost pleading tone to his voice. "I ... need you. I cannot do this alone."

I blinked as a wave of dizziness assailed me. The presence was there, in his head, watching and observing. I could sense a power struggle taking place, a contest with only one winner, the ultimate prize being Adam's very soul. Then the visions disappeared, like crackling embers leaving a campfire and reaching for the darkness and emptiness of the night sky.

I realised I couldn't abandon him.

Wouldn't.

"We'll need to get you into some other clothes rather than the army gear. You might as well take his civvies?"

He nodded and quickly shed the BDUs and dressed in Richard's jeans and t-shirt. He kept the desert army boots on, and laced them up. I went through Richard's duffle bag and found a black denim jacket. I gave a shrug and threw it at Adam. "I bought this for Richard, you might as well have it."

"Thank you," he said. "Would you like to change as well?"

I smiled, looking down at my PJs. "Give me two minutes. Mind telling me where we're going?"

Before he could answer there was a loud knock on the front door. The kind of knock associated with law enforcement.

"Police, open up."

I saw a flash of green in Adam's eyes. He looked sadly at me and I heard his voice in my head.

I am sorry.

I cannot be taken into custody.

The room started spinning and the last thing I remembered was Adam lowering me gently to the ground.

DAY 2

CHAPTER ELEVEN
Highway 15, California

In my dream, I was somewhere else.
Someone else. I was Adam.
Observer and participant in his memories.
I knew now that he had died an agonising and final death, and had welcomed it.
But then he didn't die.
His consciousness, his very self, had been downloaded, patterned, and retained. His thoughts bobbed like flotsam on a tide of sentience, purposeless and directionless. Embryonic, primitive neurological connections grasped and stretched as words, basic syntax structures and language patterns surfaced from reformed memory architecture. Neural networks came together in a new alignment of organic and synthetic circuitry. Electrochemical switches were integrated with organic tissue, enhancing the transmission of data and information.
Like a computer, it seemed like he was being plugged in, rebooted, and was gradually coming back 'on-line'. His visual cortex was re-established, and a wall of luminous dense clouds of dust and globules of plasma swam into view. Slowly but progressively these coalesced into recognisable images of faces, places and events both familiar and unfamiliar. The setting sun, scarlet and transitioning to obsidian, under a star-speckled heaven. Storm clouds gathering in a gunmetal sky, torrential rain pouring down in icy sheets, claps of thunder and lightning forks savaging the atmosphere. Running feet and damp-smelling air over unpaved paths awash with mud, streams and swollen rivers. A little girl, reaching up with stubby arms and fingers. A beautiful vivacious woman sleeping under pristine white sheets, dark hair splayed over a pillow, a half smile on her lips.
I knew this was Cora Benedict.

I could now sense an array of unsophisticated emotions. Despair, despondency, misery, and many more.

Then he spoke, but not to me.

Where am I?

Subliminally, inexorably, something approached. Shapeless and silent, like an unwelcome stranger at night. A presence, preternaturally evil, ice-cold, and ancient. Like the vacuum between the stars.

There was a tickling of neural pathways and a converging of consciousnesses. Communication was being established. I was overwhelmed by a crushing claustrophobia. The new mind was frighteningly and unfathomably different and…

Non-human.

Whatever it was, it was analysing Adam's newly emerging language and thought patterns, sublimating words and sentences in order to communicate with him. Thoughts, which were initially meaningless and lacking in syntax and context, became rapidly clearer. The words, when they came, were considered, deliberate, and devoid of emotion.

[How did you get here?]

It seemed everywhere, internal and external. A detached and glacial intelligence. I could feel Adam trying to push it away, but it advanced with almost contemptuous ease.

Where am I?

[Where do you think you are?]

I have no idea.

Images began to materialise out of the plasma fog, flickering on and off like an old movie. Blue cloudless skies over red-tinged desert plains surrounded by Granite Mountains with snow-capped peaks. Human faces, all colours and shapes, swimming in and out of focus. Children playing in an autumn-gold park. Aquatic life flowing effortlessly in an aquamarine subterranean ocean. A spinning orb, a kaleidoscope of colours painting the sides of a dark cavern. A skeletal house overlooking the sea. An empty grave on a rainy, windswept hill. The face of Adam Benedict staring emotionlessly out of a blood-spattered bathroom mirror.

The alien spoke, anticipating the question.

[Yes, that was you]

The tendrils of recognition were achingly close, and I felt Adam's frustration. But at the moment, recognition and understanding were like ships passing in the night.

I can't remember my name.

[You will]

An oval shadow sublimated into view, shifting grey-black and emerging from a darkness backlit by red mist. A rapacious face, lupine with reptilian green orbs for eyes, materialised into existence. There was a boreal penetrating gaze and a predatory awareness. The impression of being looked over by a creature at the top of the food chain.

What are you?

The reply was both physical and subconscious.

[This is how we were]

I don't understand.

[We were once like you, corporeal beings.]

The face drifted in and out of focus but two green points of light relentlessly and unwaveringly stared at me. There was a gleam of pearl-white and jagged teeth, feral and terrifying. A hint of a huge multi-limbed crab-like body behind, luminous cerulean in colour. Then the features started to change like a melting ice statue, and a humanoid face started to take shape. Remodelling of bone and musculature occurred at a dramatic rate, until the face staring back at me was Caucasian with gaunt high cheekbones and short-cropped black hair. It had strikingly blue lifeless eyes. Showroom dummy eyes. They blinked slowly and the mouth opened as if to yawn as the head tipped backward. The features contorted and twisted briefly as if in pain, but then relaxed and settled into a neutral pose. Green phosphorescence flickered briefly behind the pupils, and then was gone. The simulacrum in front of me started spinning. A feeling of being stretched like butter spread too thinly over sliced bread washed over me.

Darkness consumed me once again.

CHAPTER TWELVE
Highway 15, California

The crackle of tyres on gravel woke me from a deep sleep. The dream had been surreal and unsettling. I opened my eyes only to immediately close them as the sun burnt its way through to my retinae leaving bright wavy yellow lines that bobbed and danced. Disorientated, I squinted into the light and saw that I was in the passenger seat of a car bumping and lurching along an uneven road. Adam was driving, and he glanced my way briefly and turned the wheel a hard right. He was manoeuvring the vehicle down a narrow path towards a group of buildings coming into view around a corner lined with manicured bushes and small trees. I was scrunched up against the passenger door, and now that I was awake I felt stiff and uncomfortable. I cracked my neck and stretched, suppressing a yawn. My stomach rumbled.

"Are you hungry?" he said. "You have missed breakfast."

I nodded, my eyes still getting used to the brightness.

He pointed, "There is a restaurant up ahead."

I squinted through the front windshield as we approached a dilapidated-looking diner with a few dusty pickup trucks parked outside. Next to it were a couple of souvenir shops and a gas station. A family with four children were heading into the diner.

"Where are we?" I said, stretching again.

We pulled into a parking bay in front of the main entrance and he killed the ignition. "Just outside the town of Barstow."

I was puzzled. "Never heard of it. How long've we been driving?"

He looked at me, his blue eyes wide and guileless. "About eight hours. We are now in California."

My eyes were sticky so I rubbed them, feeling the matter cracking and sprinkling off the lashes.

"I let you sleep," he said. "I thought you needed it."

"I had a strange dream." I said, looking at him sideways. "At least I think it was a dream."

The fog in my head was clearing and with a start I noticed I was wearing jeans, sneakers and a grey UCLA sweatshirt. Last I remembered, I was in my P-Js. I looked at Adam and raised an accusatory eyebrow.

"I'm not sure I want to know, but how did I get into these clothes?"

"I changed you into something more appropriate for travelling," he said. Was it my imagination or did the corner of his lip twitch? "I promise I did not look."

I fixed him with what I considered my best death stare. "Not remotely funny."

He nodded in seeming agreement, and the shadow of the smile on his face vanished. He turned back to look out the window towards the diner and started to open his door.

"You owe me some answers," I said. "Now, before we go any further."

"I am not certain that you will like what I have to say," he intoned solemnly. "But I will tell you what I can."

I was about to reply when there was a flash behind my eyes and my head spun like I'd been sucker punched. An after-image of the nightmarish crab-like creature from the dream appeared, and then faded away into a grey mist. My vision cleared and I was back in the car, and Adam was staring at me with a concerned look on his face. I waved him off and we exited the vehicle, which I noticed was the Dodge from last night. We walked into the diner and were shown to a booth that had a view of the car park. We took opposite seats, our knees touching. The diner wasn't busy and there were no other customers in the adjoining window booths. TVs playing daytime talk shows were hung along the walls in between square pictures of plastic-looking food. I grabbed a menu from its holder on the wall and flicked through it. Five pages of food, some of it still actually on the menu itself. I scratched at some of the caked-on organic matter with my nail and it sloughed off like dandruff.

"All day breakfast then?" I said, looking up with a smile.

"I am not hungry."

He was staring out of the window, chin in hands, elbows on the table.

"Fine, well you won't mind if I do then," I said. I caught the eye of a waitress who sauntered over with a bored look on her face. She was a thin young woman, her lank mousy hair falling in frayed ribbons about her faded t-shirt. In her hand were a small writing pad, and a biro. She was perspiring significantly despite the air-conditioning. I smiled at her and asked what she recommended.

"Eggs is good," she said. "Still time for the breakfast special. Ten bucks, all you can eat."

She gestured to the panels above the cash till, where pictures of breads, toast, rolls, and troughs of bacon, sausages and artificial-looking eggs were displayed. I rubbed my hands together and gave a bright and breezy smile. "Alright then, eggs it is. Eggs, hash browns and some bacon. Extra crispy."

She wrote this down, and turned to Adam. "Something for you sir?"

"He's fine. Just coffee," I said, with a dismissive wave.

When she'd left I folded my arms and sat back in the sofa. I watched him, silhouetted in the window, scrutinising the parked vehicles out front. "Selecting our next ride?" I said, tongue in cheek.

"Yes, however it is going to be difficult. The owners will undoubtedly report the theft immediately. I am reviewing other options."

I nodded, and then leaned forward conspiratorially. "How about you just do a Jedi mind trick on the owners? Or hey, just do it to everyone in here?"

He stared blankly back, apparently weighing this suggestion up. "That is certainly one of the other options."

"I was kidding, but you really could do that?"

"Yes."

I regarded him coolly. "So, what exactly are you, Adam Benedict?"

He lowered his head and brought his hands together, intertwining fingers on the tabletop. He looked like a supplicant, praying at an altar.

"I am not sure what I am," he began. "I know I used to be a human being."

"Used to be? So what happened to you?" I asked. Part of me didn't want to press this conversation, but the dream kept coming back to me. I wanted to pretend it was all in my mind but here I was, in a diner, with a guy who should be dead.

"Fragments of memory are coming back to me. My mind is a jigsaw puzzle with many missing pieces. I remember being in a dark place. There was a bright light. Pain. Suffering. Then - nothing. Then… I was somewhere else."

"I spoke with a Gabriel Connor. Friend of yours. He said the two of you went into a crater in the Nevada desert. Do you remember?"

His eyes seemed to glaze over and his head dipped a fraction more. There was a long silence, and I could almost sense the cogs working overtime to retrieve the memory.

"Yes, I think it is coming back to me. I was in the crater. More of a cave, actually. With Gabriel."

My heartbeat picked up and an unsettling anxiety came over me. I took a drink of water from the table and wondered if Adam would notice the slight shake to my hand.

"What's the last thing you do remember?" I ventured.

He looked back out of the window. "A ball of light. Silence. Pain. A constricting band of pressure around my temple that worsened as I opened my eyes. I remember seeing the edge of the crater high above, and a glimpse of a blue cloudless sky. I can see shafts of light playing on a rock wall that is covered with metal carabineers and pitons. There are a couple of ropes and a temporary ladder. I remember being entranced by dust motes floating on light beams, making their way down to the cavern floor."

He paused, and I said nothing, waiting for him to continue.

"Then the light consumed me," he said, "and the crater was no longer there."

I leaned forward, tentatively probing. "Gabriel said you vanished. Disappeared. Where did you go?"

He looked straight through me and it felt like the temperature in the diner had dropped by fifty degrees. "I died. Then I was resurrected."

I stared back at him, and time seemed to slow down as the rest of the diner faded into the background like that scene in 'Jaws' when the camera zooms in on Roy Schneider's face. "By whom?" I asked as calmly as I could.

"I do not know. But I know that I was dead, and then I was not." He looked up at me and his eyes looked haunted. "I remember being glad that I had died, and angry that I had been saved."

"Sounds like a religious experience to me," I said trying to lighten the mood. "Did you meet God?"

He shook his head; maybe it was too early for humour. "No, I do not think so. But I believe I was sent back."

"Who sent you back? More to the point, why?"

He reached over to my coffee cup and absentmindedly turned it so that the handle was facing me. "My cognitive and memory functions are still suboptimal. I cannot answer that."

"You're sounding like a computer," I said. I'd noticed his speech pattern was stilted and that he didn't use contractions. I sensed he was being evasive, and the dream continued to play in the back of my mind. I couldn't shake the sensation of coming 'online', of being rebooted.

"I do not feel myself," he continued in a monotone as if to confirm my observation. "Something has happened to me. Something unusual. My mind is not completely my own."

"Like when we were back at my house?" I said.

He nodded, and I felt that chill again, that subconscious primeval feeling of being threatened and in danger. I wondered when or if I should mention the dream, or whether he was already reading my mind. He sat back and looked around the diner, taking in the families, truck-drivers, tourists, locals minding their own business and contemplating their own day-to-day issues and problems. Seemed so normal to me. Life just going on day by day.

I suppressed a shiver and decided to address the elephant in the room.

"That wasn't you back at my house was it?"

He closed his eyes briefly and then looked directly at me. The blueness was temporarily replaced by an emerald flash, and then reverted to blue.

There it was.

Hiding in plain sight.

The alien.

"Something has come back with me," he said. "You have felt it."

Ice continued to drizzle between my shoulder blades. I closed my eyes and concentrated on what I had felt during that event.

"Yes. When you'd been fighting Richard there was an almost feral pleasure at the violence being perpetrated. Something 'inhuman' was watching and enjoying the experience."

"You mentioned a dream," he said. "In the car?"

"When I was dreaming I think I had 'access' - if that's the right word - to your memories. I was there when you met … it. When you were being - what's the right phrase – reborn. Remade, is that a better way of putting it? I think I could see and hear it. Whoever, or whatever, it is."

He was looking intently at me, hanging on my every word. I was about to ask him what he remembered about the experience when the waitress arrived with a plate stuffed with eggs, browns and bacon all covered in icing sugar and a layer of syrup. It smelled divine. I was soon tucking in, realising that I was starving and had not eaten for over twelve hours. In between mouthfuls I looked up at Adam who'd resumed his visual survey of the car park.

"Can I talk with it?" I said, hesitatingly.

"Kate, I cannot summon it at will," he replied somewhat snippily.

I took a slurp of coffee. "So what happened with the police back at my house? I mean, all I can remember is the knock on the door."

"I do not know," he said without looking at me. "My immediate memory of it has been erased."

I stopped mid-fork. "Erased. Again with the computer-speak. Why would your mind be erased?"

"I do not know."

I resumed eating, stuffing another huge portion of bacon into my mouth and dribbling syrup down my chin. I picked up the napkin I dabbed a couple of spots.

"You have missed a bit," he said.

Self-consciously, I wiped the whole of my chin clean and finished the coffee. I looked at him again, noted the smoothness of his face, the lack of lines or defects, the perfect symmetry of his eyes, the jet-black hair with no streaks of grey. He looked like a waxwork model, not quite real but scarily lifelike. He stared back unblinking and once again I became very unsettled. I saw the showroom dummy eyes again. Blank. Dead eyes.

"Are you inside my head now?" I said.

"No."

"But you can do this at any time?"

"Yes, and much more."

"Such as?"

"My mind is able to reach far beyond the confines of its physical structure. I am able to control external organic neural pathways."

"Mind control? That's what you did to me outside Joey's?"

"Yes. But not only organic pathways. At this moment I can access all five billion pages of the world-wide-web just by thinking of it. One zettabyte of data. I can interact with any electronic system and change it's programming without any physical contact."

"But you're still human, right?" I said.

"I am not sure what I am any more. The mechanics of my musculoskeletal system have been significantly enhanced. Watch."

He leaned back and put his arm along the couch, grasping the solid metal rail along the top cushion. Without changing expression he clenched his fist and the metal just warped and flattened as if it was plasticine. He looked at me and a muscle seemed to twitch at the side of his mouth.

"I do not know why, or how, I have these abilities."

I took a deep breath. "There has to be a reason. You said that your memory had been 'wiped', so isn't there any way you can access those 'files'?" I tapped my index finger on my temple for effect. "Like you did for me?"

He looked back out of the window. "There is something that keeps coming up."

"Go on," I said, leaning forward.

"There is a place called the SETI Institute. Have you heard of it?"

"My father used to talk about it. It's where they search the skies for signs of ET, and little green men."

"Yes. Scientists based at SETI have been looking for alien life in the Universe since the mid 1980s. However, more recently they have been sending messages out to the stars. They call it 'Active SETI'."

"Are you saying that we succeeded in contacting an alien race?"

He nodded slowly, his eyes closed. "I believe so. Indirectly, perhaps."

I could see a brief flickering of phosphorescence behind the eyes as if an internal conversation was taking place. Which was probably not far from the truth.

"Active SETI was heavily criticised in the press and by many in the scientific community because of the risk of revealing the location of the Earth to non-friendly alien civilisations. The fact that it would take thousands or millions of years for any signals to reach other galaxies was the mitigating factor. So the program went ahead and humanity sent out an invitation."

I shook my head at the hubris of the scientists involved. "I may've seen too many sci-fi movies, but these aliens aren't likely to be 'friends of the earth' are they?" I made the air bunny ears.

"I cannot say for certain, but I do not believe so. It is statistically probable that most alien races will be millions of years more advanced than us. They would have evolved in completely different ways as well."

"But maybe in better ways? Better morality?" I leaned forwards. "I mean, maybe they outgrew all the supernatural beliefs and in-group fighting that's going on here?"

"Speculation."

"I know, but there's a chance isn't there?"

He gave a slight smile. "What I cannot understand is this - interstellar distances are immense between galaxies. It is highly unlikely that a signal could have reached another galaxy in this timeframe. Active SETI was doomed to fail."

"Well that's good, isn't it? For us, I mean."

"Yes and no."

"Why no?"

"If the signal *was* somehow intercepted by a much more advanced alien race, *and* they have a means to get here, I do not believe that humanity would survive."

"But we have nuclear weapons," I said somewhat glibly.

"Humanity has had nuclear technology for less than a hundred years. Imagine a civilisation that has had a thousand years of further development. A million years. We would be completely inconsequential."

"Here's a thought - maybe your purpose is to facilitate the arrival of a friendly alien civilisation. As a messenger maybe, or some sort of scout."

He looked up and raised an eyebrow. "A harbinger? They do not always bode well for what follows…"

He stopped abruptly, and peered over my shoulder. I turned to check out what he was watching and saw that the

TV on the counter was tuned to a news channel. On the screen was a picture of Adam, enlarged using digital enhancements from the photo I had taken in the ER. The caption tickertaped along the bottom:

BREAKING NEWS: SUSPECT IN QUADRUPLE COP HOMICIDE IN NEVADA ON THE LOOSE. ADAM BENEDICT IS CONSIDERED EXTREMELY DANGEROUS. DO NOT APPROACH.

Adam stood up and awkwardly shuffled along the table to exit the booth. The waitress had stopped serving and was watching the TV, as were the other patrons in the diner. It wouldn't take them long to recognise Adam.
"Time to go," he said
I remained seated, my heart pounding. "Did you kill those policemen at my house?"
He glanced back at the TV, and lowered his head.
"I do not remember. But it is very likely."

CHAPTER THIRTEEN
Brentwood Heights, CA

The rest of the drive took a couple of hours, Adam saying little, and to be honest I needed time to think. He didn't exactly tell me where we were going, just that it was in Los Angeles. The City of Angels seemed like an ironic destination to me, as I was now convinced that there was a demon in his head. I was furiously trying to reconcile everything that had happened with the fact that I'd agreed to go with him. Willingly. The police and god-knows who else were looking for us, and despite what he said about his memory lapses, it sounded like he'd definitely been responsible for the deaths of those police officers. I'd seen him threatened and what he was capable of. But something inside me knew that it wasn't Adam Benedict that had killed them. The person I had connected with was scared, confused, trying to come to terms with the death of his wife and whatever had happened to him - and had asked for my help. It scared the shit out of me that whatever else was co-habiting might take control again, and turn on me. I found myself shaking my head. Did I know what the fuck was I doing?

Adam turned the Dodge into a well-tendered street in the suburb of Brentwood Heights. We pulled up front of a circular driveway that led to a Mediterranean-styled mansion with a metal entry gate flanked by red-bricked pillars. Tall shrubs, squared off and flat-topped, surrounded the gardens on either side. Well-tended conifers and palm trees were visible both sides of the house, and a silver Porsche 911 Targa was parked just on the curve of the driveway. The afternoon sun cast elongated shadows through the gate, and some of the more sheltered streetlights were starting to twinkle.

Adam got out and beckoned me to do the same. I stayed resolutely put.

"It's time to tell me why we're here," I said.

There was no response so I fixed my lips in a tight grimace, locked the door and folded my arms. A minor act of defiance. He leaned in to look at me through the open driver's side window. There was a flicker of green behind his eyes and the door lock clicked open.

"Party tricks," I murmured, shaking my head.

A large silver BMW with blacked out windows cruised round the corner, not slowing down. There was a quiet drone from a helicopter somewhere beyond the tree line. Sirens could be heard from the distant freeway.

"Law enforcement will almost certainly have the details of this vehicle by now," he said, leaning in to my window.

I gave a dismissive shrug, and decided to play hardball. "Good. Maybe when they get here you'll tell them what's going on? Clearly this is a 'need to know' kinda thing?"

He looked at me, an unreadable expression on his face. "Kate, we do not have time for this."

"Then tell me why we're here?"

An exasperated expression crossed his features and he nodded towards the house beyond the gates. "I am looking for someone. A piece of the puzzle. I believe he lives here."

"They won't let you in," I said. "You're a stranger, and this is Los Angeles. A very, very upscale part of it. Not going to happen."

"We will see," he said, opening the door and gesturing for me to get out.

I sighed and swung my legs onto the sidewalk, standing up to stretch and shake out the cramp. The sun was still warm and pleasant and the surroundings were so 'Beverly Hills' that I closed my eyes just to remind myself of the surrealism. When I re-opened them, he was just standing watching me, no expression on his face. I tried to feel into his mind and decipher his emotions, as I'd been able to do previously, but this time there was nothing. He'd locked me out.

"I've been thinking about what happened to those police officers," I said. "You claim that you don't remember? I really find that hard to believe."

He glanced down at the pavement for a moment, before re-appraising me. Maybe he was deciding what part of the truth to tell me. I had no way of knowing.

"You may not believe this," he said, "but I truly cannot remember what happened."

"Is this something to do with your alien room-mate?"

There, I'd said it.

Alien.

He looked grim. "I think so. There is selective memory suppression. I do not seem to be able to stop it taking over, although I am working on it."

"Maybe you should try harder," I said.

He nodded, even though I'd said it as a joke. "I believe it knows I am not comfortable with its actions. However, I also believe it needs me to be complicit in whatever it intends to do. There appears to be some form of symbiosis involved."

"Symbiosis?"

"Yes. A relationship between organisms that live closely together. One organism benefits while the other is neither harmed nor helped."

"Wait up," I said. "It needs you to be complicit in murder so it benefits," I said. "What happens if you don't comply?"

He looked at me opaquely, and there was an uncomfortable silence. After a few seconds he walked over to the entry gate and took hold of one of the bars, giving it a little shake. Dust was agitated free and a few cracks appeared on the paintwork where the bar joined the concrete.

"We going to break in?" I said, only slightly rhetorically.

He pointed to a chrome burnished plaque on the left hand pillar bearing the name 'Lindstrom' in Latin-styled lettering. "I am hoping we do not need to."

"Old friend of yours?" I said.

"We have never met."

"So, tell me why we're here?" I asked again.

"Corey Lindstrom is the only progeny of Professor Augustine Lindstrom."

He resumed his survey of the house and gardens. I folded my arms, none the wiser.

"And he is?"

"A famous scientist. An important piece of the puzzle."

"When did you figure this out?" I got into his face but he leaned past me and pressed the intercom button.

"Perhaps you should do the talking at this point," he suggested with a smile.

"You're joking. What, so *I* get to ask if they'll let us in?"

The smile stayed in place and he folded his arms. "They may be more receptive to a female stranger."

I was about to protest when the intercom chimed. Taking a deep breath I squinted into the camera and leaned in towards the microphone I assumed was behind the grille. I cleared my throat.

"Uh, yes, hello. I was wondering if I could speak to a Mr Corey Lindstrom."

There was a pause, then a curt female voice answered, "Doctor Lindstrom is not available. Can I ask who is calling please?"

I looked back at Adam, and I suddenly felt mildly vertiginous as his mind opened and I could sense his emotions and thoughts pouring into me. He flicked his chin towards the camera.

Lindstrom is definitely inside the building, along with two other individuals.

I nodded and leaned back in to the intercom, looking directly into the lens.

"We're students from UCLA. We're doing a research project and we were told that Dr Lindstrom, maybe, would be able to help us out. It'd be fantastic, really. We're on a super tight deadline."

I grimaced back up at Adam, who raised his eyebrows but remained poker-faced.

I must speak with him. Face-to-Face. It is very important.

There was static from the intercom and then the voice replied, somewhat stuffily, "How did you get this address? We aren't listed, you know."

I mentally crossed my fingers. "Yes, but we found out that Dr Lindstrom's father, Professor Augustine Lindstrom, was the head guy of the project we're studying. So we'd love to pick Dr Lindstrom's brains, even if only for half an hour?"

The static hissed, and I thought the woman had gone. Adam's words floated into my subconsciousness.

Tell her we want to talk about Trinity Deus.

"Trinity Deus?" I said, puzzled.

A man's voice came over the intercom, deep and throaty, a big man's voice. Indignant and curious at the same time.

"What did you say? Who are you people?"

"Dr Lindstrom, is that you?" I said, injecting some excitement into my voice. "My colleague and I have so much to ask you. Please, we'd be no trouble at all. It would help us so much in our research. Quarter of an hour, max."

I looked up at Adam who dipped his head in approval.

That is Lindstrom. He is looking at you through the CCTV camera. He likes what he sees. He is deciding whether to let you in.

I straightened, and gave a happy smile into the camera, pushing my hair behind my ears. I considered fluttering my eyelashes but stopped myself. I mean, I hadn't bathed or cleaned my teeth for over forty-eight hours. I probably looked like a vagrant.

"Okay, but I don't have long," came Lindstrom's voice. There was a solid sounding clunk, and the gate unlocked and slowly swung open.

"Thank you," I gushed, and turned to Adam who nodded approvingly again.

I led the way up the driveway, which was bordered by beautifully manicured grass and expensively tendered shrubbery. I admired the 911 and ran a finger across the hood as we approached the front door, which was opened by a portly middle-aged man wearing golf shorts and a pink polo shirt. He had a neatly trimmed salt and pepper beard and was sporting a huge Omega SeaMaster watch. Peeking out from behind his shoulder was a similarly aged woman with platinum blonde hair dressed in a tracksuit and gold-tinted running shoes.

I held out my hand, which he hesitatingly took and held with a damp grip. "Doctor Lindstrom I presume? Thank you so much for this," I said, and almost curtseyed. "I'm Kate, and this is Adam."

Adam nodded, but didn't reach out for a shake. Lindstrom smiled and beckoned us inside the hallway.

"Yes, well you caught me at a good time. Just back from the golf course. My one day off from the hospital."

He introduced his wife as Holly, and we followed him through the hallway, Holly trailing a few steps behind.

"I'm amazed you've heard of 'Trinity Deus'," he said, looking back at us over his shoulder. "That's not common knowledge at all. I knew you were serious when I heard you say that."

We walked through a large atrium, two storeys high and framed with paintings and photographs. Hung from the ceiling was a huge art nouveau brass chandelier. At the end of the atrium was a polished wooden staircase leading down to a lower level and another archway opening on to a large sitting room with impressive floor to ceiling windows. A lap pool and an expansive entertaining deck could be seen outside. Lindstrom led us up another winding staircase to an open plan dining area and a lounge filled with expensive white leather sofas. Everything backed onto a kitchen space, which looked like it came unpainted straight out of a German car factory. Behind a floating counter I caught the eye of a young Hispanic woman in a maid's outfit, busily slicing freshly baked bread. She looked up, but didn't smile or acknowledge the Lindstroms or us.

"Lovely place you have here," I said to Holly, who had caught up at this point.

"Thanks," said Lindstrom, speaking for her. "We like it."

Holly wandered off and sat down on one of the couches. I watched the maid bringing her a large glass of brown liquid, which was either iced tea or something alcoholic. I thought I knew which.

I turned back to Lindstrom, "You mentioned a hospital - what sort of doctor are you?"

"I'm a hepatobiliary surgeon. Liver transplants, that sort of thing."

He puffed up his chest and I smiled but didn't ask any other questions, which seemed to irritate him a little. He led us to the dining table where we all sat down. His fingers brushed against my arm as he guided me into a chair, lingering more than I would have liked. He grinned at me, showing perfectly maintained white teeth, before moving away. My flesh crawled again and I remembered how I felt when Richard had touched me back at the house. Lindstrom poured himself a drink from an antique globe-shaped cabinet in the corner of the room, and returned to the table with what looked like a large whisky. He took a sip before sitting down and then seemed to remember his manners.

"Would you like a tea, coffee or an alcoholic beverage? I can have Maria make something for you?"

Adam shook his head. "No, thank you Dr Lindstrom. We do not want to take up more of your time than is necessary."

He nodded, and sat down next to me. "Well, okay then, let's get started. How can I help you?"

"We need to see all documents and journals from your father's work, with particular reference to the 1950's atomic weapon development program in the Nevada Desert."

I guessed that Adam's small talk circuit had been disconnected. Lindstrom coughed and whiskey dribbled down his chin. He wiped his mouth with the back of his wrist and frowned at Adam.

"My father passed away more than fifty years ago. Those documents are almost certainly in the Government's archives."

"That is not correct," said Adam. "When Augustine Lindstrom left the Government to set up his private company he took his research with him."

Lindstrom was now staring at Adam, a look of bewilderment on his face. "That was classified as I recall. How do you know all this?"

Adam's expression did not change. "The group of scientists calling themselves 'Trinity Deus" were led by your father. There was a particular project he was working on, one that the Government and US military regarded as a failure. It is specifically that project's documentation which I need to see."

Lindstrom put the whisky glass down noisily and shook his head. "I think your research is a bit inaccurate, son. There aren't any of those documents left."

Adam said nothing, but I saw a glimmer of emerald phosphorescence behind his eyes. Lindstrom hadn't noticed anything and had turned in his chair to look at me. He gave a wide smile.

"Now, is there anything else I can help you with, dear?" He looked me up and down without any sense of shame and actually licked his lips.

Adam said, "Dr Lindstrom, I have access to government archives and electronic databases from around the world."

"Oh, well you can't believe everything you read," Lindstrom said without turning.

Adam continued, "I am aware that you keep boxes of your father's work in your basement panic room."

At this, Lindstrom stood up, no longer the friendly host. He pointed at Adam, his finger shaking slightly.

"How could you possibly know that? Who are you people?"

Adam remained seated, his fingers now steepled. "Nevertheless, it is a fact. Please now show us the way."

Lindstrom was bristling. "I'd like you to get the fuck out of my house now."

I saw another brief flicker of green behind Adam's eyes and suddenly Lindstrom's face went slack. Without another word he turned and starting walking towards the stairs. I watched him go and gave Adam a quizzical look. He gave a slight smile and stood up, gesturing that we should follow Lindstrom.

I noticed that Lindstrom's wife and maid were frozen like mannequins in a shop window. "Do not worry, they are unharmed," said Adam, glancing back at me. "It is just a temporary paralysis so they do not activate any alarms or call law enforcement."

"Why didn't you just do this as soon as we got in?" I said, annoyed. "And more importantly, couldn't you have done this to those drunk soldiers? And the police at my house?"

I stared at him, seeing the green light flicker behind the pupils. I couldn't sense his mood, his thoughts. His mind was still closed.

"Adam," I said, quietly. "Is that still you in there?"

The green light faded again and he blinked. His head twitched almost imperceptibly, as if something internal was resetting, or rebooting.

"Yes, I am here. Please follow Dr Lindstrom."

We went down two flights of stairs to where Lindstrom was standing motionless in front of a solid-looking door with a key code entry system. As we approached, Lindstrom's fingers stabbed at the pad and the lock clicked loudly accompanied by the whirr of cogs and gears as metal cylinders were electronically moved and turned. He pushed the door inward and lights automatically activated, revealing a generously sized room about eight yards square. On one wall above an antique desk covered in books and papers was a LCD screen showing various external angles of the house. A couple of bookcases filled with leather-bound volumes and boxes of journals and magazines occupied another wall. The facing wall harboured a low couch, a couple of recliners and a fridge set into the wall itself. Elliptical air-conditioning ducts in the roof started to crank up, blowing cold dusty air.

I walked into the centre of the room and the door swung closed behind me. It clunked solidly and there was a prickly heat sort of sensation in my head, and a sudden clarity of thought as if I'd woken up from an anaesthetic or surfaced from a dive. I watched Lindstrom walk over to the bookcase in the far corner and start rummaging around in a box. I glanced at Adam who seemed unsettled, his neck twitching and a puzzled expression on his face. He looked back at me and I expected to hear his voice in my head but nothing happened.

He touched Lindstrom on the shoulder. "Doctor, what is the composition of this room?"

"The walls are lead lined and integrated with electronic countermeasures," Lindstrom answered in a slurred voice. He then swayed and put a hand against the bookcase to steady himself. He shook his head and looked around the room as if seeing it for the first time. When he saw us his eyes widened.

"How did you two get in here?"

Adam ignored him and looked at me, a puzzled expression coming over his features. "Kate, I cannot access your thoughts, or his. The room has an EMF blocking system."

"A what?" I asked.

"You folks are going no-where," Lindstrom said from the other side of the room, his voice now clear and unaffected. There was a loud ratcheting noise as he chambered a round into the shotgun he was holding and pointing straight at Adam. "I've activated the distress alarm and the police are on their way. ETA less than ten minutes." He pointed to the couch with the gun. "Now both of you sit down and let's wait for the Cavalry."

I backed slowly into the door, aware that Adam had not moved. Lindstrom remained behind the couch, the shotgun pointing unwaveringly at Adam's chest. Adam was on the other side of the room and still shaking his head slowly as if to clear it. There was movement on the TV monitor and I glanced up to see an LAPD patrol car pull up to the main gate. Four armed officers exited the car and another vehicle nudged in behind, more officers disembarking at speed. They efficiently de-armed the main gate and moved quickly along the driveway towards the front entrance.

I quietly backed up until I touched the door, feeling behind for the handle. Lindstrom's gaze flicked over to me and he gestured again with his gun, indicating the two recliners.

"I told you to sit down," he said through gritted teeth. "Cement your asses to those chairs, and don't let me see any sudden moves. This is my house, and I will defend it."

But then to my horror, Adam rushed Lindstrom. He had to travel six yards to reach him. Lindstrom's finger had to travel less than half an inch to pull the trigger. I did the math, closed my eyes and put my hands over my ears. The shotgun went off with a deafening bang, amplified by the confined space and acoustics. I blinked and saw Adam jerk violently backwards and bounce off the wall.

Lindstrom chambered another round, but Adam had already recovered his balance and rushed him again. He backhanded Lindstrom, the blow landing squarely on the side of his head. Lindstrom cartwheeled sideways over the couch and fell in a tangled mess on the floor. Adam walked over to him and lifted him off the floor by his neck, his eyes lolling back in their sockets, blood starting to trickle out of the side of his mouth. Adam threw him onto one of the lazy-boys like a rag doll and backhanded him again, causing his head to snap to the side. Lindstrom immediately lost consciousness but to my horror Adam seized him around the throat and began to squeeze.

I was flattened against the door, and saw the shotgun lying on the carpet a foot away from me so I dived for it and gathered it up. Without thinking what I was doing I chambered a round, the ratcheting noisy and reverberating around the room. Adam turned swiftly and stared at me with bright green eyes and a vicious look on his face. His lips pulled back in a feral snarl and he dropped Lindstrom and rushed towards me. Instinctively, and I guess with basic survival instinct kicking in, I fired the shotgun point blank. He jerked backwards as if pulled by wires and crashed into the wall by the TV monitors. He slid to the floor, his legs crumpling, eyes closed. The room echoed with the thunderclap of the discharge and gun smoke started to fill the room. I took a few steps toward him, my heart pounding with adrenaline and nearly bursting out of my chest.

"Adam...?" I said softly.

His eyes snapped open and he started to get up and I screamed and kept firing and firing until the weapon clicked empty. The room was now completely opaque with gun smoke and my ears were ringing like Big Ben.

Then the lights in the panic room went out.

CHAPTER FOURTEEN
Brentwood Heights, CA

With my ears still ringing from the blasts, and my nose full of acrid gunpowder smoke, I hesitatingly moved towards Adam. He was lying on his side, eyes closed, and not moving. The front of his white t-shirt looked to be a ragged mess, and the skin underneath looked blackened and ruined. Weirdly, there was no blood.

I could just make out Lindstrom twitching and stretching on the recliner so I figured he was still alive. Keeping the shotgun trained on Adam I tried to see what was happening on the TV screens. I squinted through the smoke that was starting to drift downwards to layer the room like a winter mist. On one of the monitors I could just see the front atrium door and three LAPD officers, guns drawn, looking in. At that moment a voice came through a speaker underneath the screen. It was crackly but audible. There was a microphone next to the speaker so I picked it up and pressed a little red button on the stem.

"This is Dr. Morgan," I whispered as loud as I dared. "I'm inside the panic room."

One of the police officers, a well-built man with a buzz cut and wrap-around Oakley sunglasses could be seen talking into a walkie-talkie. He looked directly at me through what I assumed was a security camera above the front door.

"We heard the shots," he said. "Where's the perp?"

I glanced over at Adam who hadn't moved. "He's here with me."

I still had the shotgun pointed on him but I realised it was empty so I put it on the counter by the speaker. My hands were remarkably steady, considering everything.

"We have two casualties," I heard myself saying. "Lindstrom is down, and Adam Benedict has been shot. Multiple times."

The officer nodded and pulled his radio from his belt with his other hand. He spoke quickly into it and I heard him say, "Captain, we have a GSW." There was static, and I could see him watching me through the camera again while he spoke with his superior. He was saying, "I've got Dr Morgan on the intercom, sir. Situation seems under control. Need the code for the panic room ASAP."

I closed my eyes, feeling the tension and adrenaline leaking out of my system. I sank to my haunches and leaned back against the wall, blowing out my cheeks. On the monitor I could see the scene further up the road from the house. There was now a yellow and black barrier manned by a half dozen LAPD officers and squad cars parked diagonally and blocking entry from adjoining streets. A trim and dapper looking African-American man wearing a dark suit and tie could be seen leaning on a black limousine and talking into a phone. Despite the fading light he was still wearing sunglasses. He raised a hand towards the camera and waved. A new voice crackled from the speaker.

"Dr Morgan," he said, "I'm Special Agent Lawrence Mackie with the FBI. It's a real pleasure to hear from you. Are you alright?"

The other monitor showed a view of the Lindstrom house surrounded by at least six police vehicles. A dozen or more officers with high-powered rifles were taking position behind the cars or fanning out along the street.

"Dr Morgan? Are you there?" Mackie's voice crackled. "It's OK now, we'll be in soon. You're safe."

I glanced over at Adam, who remained statue-like lying on his side. Regret washed over me like the gentle breakers on a shallow beach. Each wave sent a tingle of ice down my spine. I still couldn't see any blood, even as the smoke was settling. I moved closer. The front of his chest was in darkness, blackened and tattered, but there was definitely no blood.

I keyed the microphone and took a deep breath. "The perp ... Adam ... he's been shot."

"So you said," replied Mackie. "Emergency crews are on here on standby."

The microphone quivered in my hand, the shakes starting now. "He took multiple shotgun blasts in the chest at point blank range. Through the heart."

Mackie looked nonplussed, and shrugged. "Then he'll be dead already and this'll all be over in the next few minutes."

I had a bad feeling about this but I couldn't explain why. I glanced over at Adam and in the dim light from the screens I saw his hand twitch. I jerked backwards toward the speaker again and grabbed the mike. "No, you don't understand. I don't think he's dead. He's not ..." I stopped, wondering what I could say that wouldn't elicit a derisory laugh from Agent Mackie.

Mackie could be seen shaking his head. "Then the shots must have missed his heart but at that range there'll have been some serious tissue damage. He's not going to survive."

Behind him I could see that neighbours were starting to come out of their houses and gravitate towards the police lines. A TV news van had just arrived and was disgorging a pretty brunette reporter with her camera crew. I could just about hear the thrum of rotor blades through the speaker. Or maybe it was so close it was coming through the walls.

Mackie spoke again, clearly trying to maintain my interest and morale. "OJ and Nicole used to live in this area you know. Had a condo not far from here. Made Brentwood infamous."

"This could be bigger," I said.

Mackie pointed at the increasing crowd and the TV crew. "See those vultures gathering? We can't wait any longer. Let's get you out of there. We'll talk when it's all over."

I almost bit the microphone. "Agent Mackie, you don't know what you're dealing with here. I need to speak with someone in charge."

He smiled crookedly. "Well that's me at the moment. Dr Morgan, there's an APB out on him for killing police officers. The FBI wants to apprehend him more than any fugitive I've ever been involved with. Hell, my Boss is even flying over to be here at the sharp end."

I closed my eyes, feeling panic rising again. I grabbed the microphone and stared directly into the camera, willing Mackie to understand. "There're things about Adam Benedict that you don't know. Things I don't know how to say over this line. Things you need to see to believe. To understand. Please, I need to talk with your superiors. Before this goes any further."

Mackie was about to reply when I saw another officer run over to him, holding a radio. He grabbed it, listened intently before nodding and handing it back. I glanced at Adam again, and could just about make out a twinkling green light through the lids of his closed eyes. His neck was twitching and both hands were moving, his fingers stretching.

I gripped the intercom tightly. "Listen to me," I implored. "People are going to die. You don't understand who he is… what he is."

"Then tell me who or what he is, Dr Morgan?"

"I can't!" I shouted. "Please, just …"

"Well, I guess we'll have to find out the hard way," Mackie interrupted. "SWAT's gone in. It'll all be over in the next few minutes."

CHAPTER FIFTEEN
Brentwood Heights, CA

Like a zombie in a B-movie, Adam slowly got to his feet and fixed his glowing green eyes on me. The lights in the panic room abruptly came back up and through the thinning smoke I could see the ruined t-shirt and shotgun impacts on his chest and stomach. I could just discern a ragged hole in the skin about twelve inches wide and abstractly I noted a dull bluish tinge to the underlying tissue. I watched as he tapped the wound, using two fingers, and I heard a dull metallic noise, like body armour or a metal carapace. He looked up at me again, still scowling, but then his face abruptly changed, and all emotion faded from it, as if a tranquilliser dart had hit him.

"Adam?" I said, tentatively.

He ignored me and walked over to Corey Lindstrom, who was whimpering and had a slack look to one side of his face. There was a swelling on his jaw and his nose looked broken, blackened rivers of blood running down both sides of his mouth. Adam stepped over him and walked to the wall behind the bookcase. He reached out a hand and gently caressed it almost like you would stroke a horse. He dipped his head and put an ear to the wall, listening for something. He looked sideways at me and gave a half smile. The green light had gone from his eyes, and he looked less, well, scary. He continued to run his hands over the surface of the wall.

"There is a network of electronic nodules behind the inner plasterboard layer and in front of the lead lining," he said. "I can feel the impulses and waveforms of the electronics as they are transmitted between the nodes." He stopped with the caresses and stood back. "I have isolated the wave modulation of the room's EMF jamming system."

Suddenly, as if a switch had been pressed, I was back inside his head, following his thoughts and seeing things as he was, in real time. It was incredible. His neural transmission and processing was lightning fast, like a computer chip with multiple input and afferent signals being dealt with simultaneously. The volume of data being processed was overwhelming and I was drowning in information.

He crossed to the bookshelf, scanned it briefly and picked up a box from the bottom shelf labelled 'Vienna, 1965'. He carried it over to the table and sorted through books, photo albums and journals until he came across a particular grey notebook, one inch thick and bound with elastic and string. He snapped the bands off and flicked the first page open. I could just see crude pencil sketches of electronic devices surrounded by labels and handwritten scientific formulae. He turned the page having apparently committed it to memory and proceeded to flick through the rest of the journal, reaching the last page and closing the book ten seconds later.

"Adam," I said, tentatively, trying not to think about the fact that I'd just shot him multiple times in the chest with a shotgun. "What's going on?"

His head snapped up and I caught movement out of the corner of my eye. The monitors showed dozens of LAPD officers armed with handguns and assault rifles taking up positions around the house and gardens. Adam noticed this too and waved a hand, enhancing a screen here and there, zooming in on surrounding paths, garden walls, and side-roads, seemingly noting the composition of the force being assembled against him. Then without warning the alien's voice lanced into my head, penetrating my thoughts and pushing everything else to the periphery.

[We must leave now]

The alien was talking to him and it felt like I was hiding round a corner, silently eavesdropping. Adam walked back to Lindstrom, who was trying to staunch the flow of blood coming from his nose with the bottom of his shirt. With his senses no longer impaired, Adam could see through the damaged bone and connective tissue under the impact site on Lindstrom's skull. There was a subdural haematoma starting to flood the tissues of his frontal lobe, a process that would undoubtedly kill him if he didn't get help very soon. Adam looked back at me and I gave him a concerned look, but again I heard the searing voice of the alien.

[We do not have time for this. We must leave]

Adam shook his head.

He must get medical assistance or he will die. I can stabilise him.

He constructed a neural command that he transmitted to Lindstrom, shutting down the conscious part of his brain. Another neural command slowed his heart rate by selectively increasing the vagal nerve amplitude and enhancing the parasympathetic neural pathways. Lindstrom slumped over and folded into the couch. Adam manoeuvred his feet into a semi-recumbent position and turned his head ensuring the airway was patent. As he was doing this, I could sense that the internal dialogue and battle of wills was still raging. He closed his eyes, addressing the alien.

This will slow the bleeding. I will inform the police, in order that medical staff can treat him.

The alien's reply was contemptuous, and cold.

[His fate is irrelevant. We must leave now]

Adam accessed the screens again, switching to the view outside the panic room door. Six LAPD officers were crouched on the staircase while two more were working on the electronic keypad using some kind of handheld device. He addressed the alien again.

Allow me to limit casualties. Ultimately, this will be beneficial to us.

I took a deep breath and moved to Adam's side. I set my face to neutral, or what I hoped was a kind of casual indifference. Inside, the fear was again coursing through my veins, and I concentrated with all my being to prevent it showing. I hoped he wasn't reading my mind, and that the alien really was unable to hear me.

"Adam," I said. "Tell me what I can do to help you."

Abruptly, the alien's presence seemed to vanish, and he turned to me. His face appeared pale and waxy, and the strain was showing.

Come with me.

"Why me?"

I need you... to help me. You are part of this now.

Doubt shot through me like an arrow, perforating my organs and blasting out the other side leaving a ragged hole. Then doubt became worry, its roots twisting and burrowing deeply, worming their way into my psyche.

"I'm scared," I said, my voice cracking.

He reached out and touched the side of my face. His mind opened, and again I could feel the anxiolytic proteins flowing out of my liver into my bloodstream, slowing my heart rate and relaxing me.

"That's not fair," I said.

Remember I said that everyone is in danger? I can prevent it.

"What if you can't? I said, swallowing hard.

Then everyone will die.

We watched the screen that showed the police officers pouring into the house above us, and down the stairs to the panic room door. They were carrying fearsome black weapons, and wearing black uniforms and body armour and helmets.

Adam mentally reached into the door's electronics and scrambled the keypad, causing it to short out and overheat. On the screen, police officers could be seen jumping back as it started to smoke. He walked over to the panic room door and sent an override command to the lock. The cylinders tumbled, and the heavy door swung open inwardly. He turned to me and put a hand on my shoulder.

Cover your ears and nose. I will protect you. My neurological abilities are still partially affected by the countermeasures, so this will be a physical defence. Stay close.

I put my hands over my ears and screwed up my eyes just in time because a few seconds later two flash-bang grenades rolled through the open door and exploded in a paroxysm of noise and smoke. Suddenly I was seeing through Adam's eyes as if I was wearing night-vision goggles. Noxious yellow smoke was pouring out from the canisters and the density of the gas in the room was now soup-like. My nose was filling with fumes and I started to cough and splutter. I could just about hear the whup-whup of rotor blades through the open door as the police helicopter arrived on station overhead.

The first SWAT officer crabbed awkwardly into the room, gun first. Blinded by the dense smoke billowing through the small room, he couldn't see Adam standing calmly by the side of the door. A few seconds later the SWAT officer was in the middle of the room, followed by two others who had moved left and right in flanking positions. They were wearing tactical vests and ballistic helmets, their Perspex eye protectors lifted up and over their heads as they breathed through gas masks. The leading SWAT was swinging his gun in a lazy arc, ready to shoot. Adam grasped the gun and the front of the guy's ballistic vest in one movement and threw him into his colleagues who tumbled like bowling pins and crashed into the back wall. Another SWAT officer rushed through the door shotgun first but Adam slammed him against the doorjamb, denting the Kevlar shell of his helmet, and bounced him back through into the corridor like a pinball. He picked up the shotgun and, wielding it like a baseball bat, followed the disarmed police officers through the door and up the staircase. I sneaked a peak around the jam and watched him swatting policeman left and right with huge kinetic swings. In less than three seconds it was all over.

I ducked back in and looked for a place to hide but Adam appeared in front of me and so I backed nervously against the wall. I was about to say something when he shook his head at me and knelt down beside one of the unconscious officers. He pulled the radio from the ballistic vest and spoke calmly and without inflection into it.

"There are injured officers in here but there are no fatalities. However, Mr Corey Lindstrom has a subdural haematoma and requires urgent medical attention." More footsteps and urgent voices could be heard at the top of the stairs and there was the sound of gun slides being racked. Adam flicked the radio on again. "I am leaving now, with Dr Morgan. You must withdraw your forces. I may not be responsible for what happens if you try to stop me."

He dropped the radio and picked the shotgun up. He seemed to be studying it, and once again I was inside his head. A specifications database was overlaid onto his visual fields describing the gun as a *Benelli M4, gas operated semi-automatic 12-gauge shotgun, 6+1 magazine capacity.* He knelt by the unconscious police officer and removed the handgun from his belt holster. This time the overlay read *Glock 21, .45 calibre, 13 round capacity.* Checking the load in the Glock, he glanced down at me.

Kate, listen to my instructions and follow my thoughts. I will keep you safe.

"Safe from who?" I said. "The SWAT guys won't harm me. They want you."

He nodded absently and flicked the safety off both weapons. "I will keep you safe."

Taking my hand, he pulled me up the stairs. At the top of the first level he turned and gave me a benevolent smile.

"'The weak can never forgive. Forgiveness is the attribute of the strong'."

My eyebrows popped up – he'd just quoted Ghandi at me. Was he letting me know it was okay I'd shot him multiple times with a shotgun? I almost laughed out loud.

As we climbed, I could see him analysing the number and composition of the waiting SWAT and LAPD, mapping their positions out to one hundred yards on a 3D grid in his visual field. He logged where every patrol car, law enforcement agent, and type of weapon was, and where all the civilians were corralled. At the top of the staircase he turned and I heard his voice again.

Stay behind me.

He stepped out of the staircase in full view of the police officers hunkered down outside the entrance lobby. Before they could react he fired three one-handed shots from the

Benelli. The officers were blown backwards by the close range impact of the shotgun bullets that blew apart their ballistic vests, knocking the wind out of them, breaking sternum bones and ribs but not penetrating vital organs. He pulled on my hand and we set off running as fast as I could keep up. My heart was hammering and I was looking all around me but realised that I had no idea of the plan. I decided that the easiest thing to do, to survive, was to do exactly what he said and go where he took me.

We got to the front door and without breaking stride he kicked it completely off its hinges and sent it sailing into a low hedge where two kneeling SWAT were hiding and taking cover. The heavy door, made of thick oak and lined with strip metal, ripped through the foliage taking the police officers with it. We ran parallel to the house toward the rear patio and garden. In his 3D overlay I could see two groups of four LAPD around the back of the house carrying rifles and sidling up along the rear wall in a slow moving line. As we cleared the corner he brought the shotgun up and fired at the nearest officer, who took the impact squarely on her vest. The huge kinetic energy of the round at close range blew her backwards into the SWAT team lining up behind her. All four were knocked to the ground in an ungainly pile of bodies. As they tried to push off each other and reach for their weapons I sensed Adam reach out and scramble their cognitive processes with a simple diversion of neuronal activity. Their eyes closed and they crumpled like marionettes having their strings cut.

He glanced at me and gave a half smile.

That worked. I am now fully functional.

A bullet whistled past my shoulder and was followed by two more as another four-man SWAT finally got their act together.

"They're shooting at us!" I yelled, incensed.

He swiftly brought the Glock to bear and fired eight shots in four rapid groups of two, every bullet hitting dead centre of their ballistic vests. The impact from the heavy slugs knocked each officer over, either unconscious or down and out of the fight. No fatalities. The precision of his shooting was uncanny. He looked over his shoulder at me, knowing what I was thinking.

No one will die here today.

I nodded, looking up. The noise from the police helicopter was increasing and I saw that it was now only twenty yards or so directly overhead. A virtual schematic swam into my vision; *Bell 206 Jet Ranger*. One of the LAPD's workhorse air support division choppers. I could also sense the three minds in the helicopter, the pilot and two police officers, and somehow I knew that each was carrying a rifle with a sniper scope. I could hear one of the snipers taking orders from a superior officer to shoot-to-kill.

Adam reached out and took control of the LAPD pilot's mind. The helicopter yawed violently, throwing the passengers against the sides of the craft with only their seat belts keeping them from falling out. He then sent the craft into a controlled spin and it dramatically lost altitude. A few yards above the lawn, he made it nose up, and set it down. It did so in protest, rotors spinning rapidly and whipping up the bushes and trees with a gale force wind.

He grabbed my hand again and his eyes burned into mine.

Run.

We ran to the helicopter and he pulled the pilot's door off its hinges, throwing it away from the rotor blades. He ripped the belts off from the seats and threw all of the crew out of the open door onto the grass. The pilot was reaching for her gun but Adam jumped into the cockpit, grabbed her by the jacket lapel and tossed her through the open door where she cartwheeled to join the others on the lawn.

He held out a hand to me.

Get in and buckle up.

I did as I was told.

He was scanning the cockpit instruments. The fuel gauge was at 85%. The schematic for the Bell appeared again, and he pulled up specifications and performance. It had a stated cruising speed of 100 knots and a range of 430 miles with a full tank. He did a calculation for the distance to a place called Mountain View, California, and cranked up the rotor rate before lifting off vertically to clear the tree line. My stomach felt like it had relocated to my pelvis, and I gripped the side of the door with white knuckled fingers. He kicked the power up and we surged forward at a rate of climb that took us out of sight of the house and war zone in mere seconds. It felt giddy, like a rollercoaster ride.

I saw that the other helicopter, the TV news one, was hovering just above the tree line and turning to follow us. Adam sent a neural signal to the pilot, temporarily paralysing him. The helicopter jerked and spun, losing height and crashing into the trees, rolling over on it's side, rotors chewing up the manicured turf. I watched the dazed pilot and the cameraman climbing out of the stricken craft, seemingly unhurt. Adam pushed our speed up to 120 knots, and dropped the nose so that we were flying at an altitude of one hundred feet. The helicopter skipped over buildings and power lines with yards to spare. My visual fields were overlaid with GPS mapping of routes, building structures and police positions. He was processing incoming radio messages and filtering out white noise to separate the police bands.

I grabbed a headset and shouted into the microphone. "They'll be able to follow you. This won't be the only chopper in the air."

His face was serenely impassive, and he looked out the window, and around the skies.

The police and FBI communications are now in disarray. They are unable to track us.

I sat back in the cockpit and watched the roads and houses and trees flying past. I kept quiet, wrapping my arms around myself to keep warm as the turbulent airflow buffeted around the door less cabin. I thought about the events of the last few minutes. I knew that he was flying the helicopter without consciously thinking about it. He had complete control over it and was able to process hundreds, maybe thousands, of other tasks at the same time. I glanced again at the hole in his shirt and saw that the break in the skin had gathered together and seemed to be healing in real time as I watched.

I estimate we will be there in 2.1 hours, however the fuel may run out 6 minutes beforehand. I suggest we put down outside the town, in a covered location.

He was talking to the alien. The Jet Ranger was now cruising steadily at one hundred knots, hugging the coastline at an altitude of fifty feet. He monitored every one of the craft's systems constantly and his neural interfaces adjusted the yaw and thrust according to his commands. The fuel gauge now read just below half full, and he had the radio constantly cycling through all the military and law enforcement frequencies, processing all the information simultaneously as it came through. The shoreline whipped past, silvery in the moonlight. I could make out a few small craft bobbing up and down in the bay, and two bigger craft with parties underway on their upper decks lit up like Christmas trees. There was a gentle onshore tide lapping against the deserted beaches. A few single-track roads ran parallel to the sea with a main highway lit up by yellow blotches further inland.

"Adam," I yelled into the wind. "Where are we going?"

We banked to follow the highway northwards, and there was an increase in radio chatter from a US Navy carrier out at sea, forty-five miles from our current position. He pulled up images and maps from GPS and satellite data and sent out an active pulse of radar in the direction of the carrier. There was an instant return, showing the approach of two aircraft vectoring in on our position at a high velocity. He turned the helicopter landward, heading for the highway and pulling high G-forces.

"They have sent two jet aircraft to intercept us. The aircraft are F-16N fighters carrying six AIM-9 Sidewinder heat-seeking short-range air-to-air missiles and two radar guided AIM-7 Sparrow medium range AAMs. They will be within our visual range in a matter of minutes."

I was about to reply when the alien cut in.

[We do not need to avoid these aircraft. Destroy them.]

He continued to power the helicopter inland, going lower than before, skimming the dunes and fields at head-height. I clung onto the seat for dear life. His voice sounded in my head again, but he was talking with the alien.

We must put down and find cover. I cannot avoid these aircraft. They are fast and highly manoeuvrable fighters. I am unable to lock on to them.

There was a dismissive, almost contemptuous wash of emotion and then:

[You have not yet learned the full extent of your abilities. There is no threat]

Through Adam's senses I picked up two new heat signatures peeling off from the lead F-16 and exponentially outpacing the aircraft. I realised that they'd fired two missiles. He pulled up a schematic of the AIM-9 sidewinder, focusing on the detonation mechanism, guidance systems and speed.

"We can't outrun them, can we?" I shouted nervously.

"No, not at a closing velocity of Mach 2. We have five seconds before the missiles hit."

He hit the gas and violently pulled up on the stick. The helicopter stalled, dumping all forward velocity and bringing it round to face the incoming missiles. His internal display showed that the missiles' guidance systems had semi-active radar homing and they were now locked on. I felt him reach out and send an electronic self destruct message to the warheads IR proximity fuses. At a range of one thousand yards, both missiles exploded and fragmented into the bay, producing a shimmering light fantastic on the tranquil waters.

The alien seemed pleased.

[Good. Now destroy the aircraft]

I sensed Adam's discomfort, but he again accessed a forward display, overlaying with GPS data and satellite feeds. The two F-16s were now vectoring to do a strafing run using their 20mm Vulcan cannons. Their afterburners had kicked in and their forward velocity was just over six hundred knots and they were descending at 50,000 feet per minute. Our helicopter was now hovering motionless a few feet above the highway, a sitting target for the F16s.

The alien spoke to Adam, contemptuously and dismissive.

[Arm their own missiles, activate their proximity fuses, and blow them out of the sky]

I saw Adam shake his head.

The pilots will not have time to eject, and will die. There is another way. Once they are within range I will enter their systems and deactivate their flight controls. They will lose control but have time to eject.

[We will be in range of their weapons by then]

No. I can do this.

I sensed Adam prepare the necessary neuronal pattern formulation that would disable the jets, and he set the helicopter down on the highway. He idled the rotors, quickly looking up and down the road, checking there were no approaching vehicles. He looked at me briefly, but said nothing. The alien spoke, still seemingly unaware of my physical presence.

[They are trying to kill you]

He didn't reply. The two F-16s were now only seconds away from a firing solution that would tear the helicopter to pieces. He reached out again, sending viciously disruptive neural pulses at the speed of light directly into the electronic brains of the fighter jets. I saw their fly-by-wire flight control system fail, and all input from the stick and rudder controls was lost. Both aircraft started to yaw and pitch uncontrollably while continuing their rapid descent. One pilot ejected from his cockpit in an explosion of glass, the chair being blown backwards and away to safety from the fatally wounded aircraft that was now tumbling into the bay.

Adam switched his perception to the other aircraft that was still screaming towards the ground, the pilot having not ejected. I sensed him enter the pilot's mind, and I saw the pilot struggling with the controls, but not panicking. I saw him firing his cannon, flames stuttering from the nose of the F16. A hailstorm of 20mm shells began to track towards us, gouging waterspouts in the ocean. The pilot then switched the gun to automatic, hoping for a lucky shot, and activated his ejector seat.

With a flash of insight, I realised that our helicopter was almost certainly going to be hit by some of the rounds. I grabbed for my seatbelt buckle, but as I was struggling with it Adam ripped it off the frame and without any preamble pushed me out of the cockpit door. I hit the ground hard, rolling across the highway and stopping as I hit the soft grass of the embankment. The subsonic rounds arrived en masse, and stitched a linear pattern across the highway, the grass bank, and finally into the Jet Ranger. The rotors disintegrated and the fuel tank ignited in an incandescent fireball. A few seconds later and a hundred yards further up the highway the pilotless F-16 smashed into the tarmac, exploding in a paroxysm of jet fuel and white hot metal.

I shakily got to my feet and took in the scene, raising a hand to block out the brightness of the flames. As my eyes adjusted to the darkness, I looked past the two conflagrations and into the distance where a couple of vehicles were approaching from the south. No red and blue flashing lights yet, but that wouldn't be long. I turned and took a few steps towards the helicopter, stumbling and nearly losing my balance as my leg gave way from a lancing pain. The Jet Ranger was now a ball of flame, black smoke drifting inland.

"Adam?" I called.

There was no way anyone could have survived the fireball, was there? I peered into the flaming cockpit but was unable to get closer because of the heat. I stumbled backwards and sat down heavily on the side of the highway. My clothes were torn and covered in grime, and I ached all over. In the distance I could hear the first of multiple sirens getting progressively louder.

I tried to focus my mind, tried to sense Adam's presence.

Nothing.

DAY 3

CHAPTER SIXTEEN
Deer Ridge Golf Course, Brentwood, CA

I slumped into a leather-backed Chesterfield-styled armchair and took in the views of the valley and Mt Diablo in the distance. The sun was appearing over the ridge behind the tree line, and the sky was a kaleidoscopic swirl of oranges and golds, deepening shadows in the bunkers and lightening the green of the fairways that wound and undulated into the foothills of the mountain range. Silhouettes of birds could be seen, dipping behind the trees. An FBI helicopter was parked on the 18th green, blades rotating languorously, the morning sun reflecting off its windows. A couple of golf buggies were making their way back towards the clubhouse, their elderly occupants unaware that their private country club had just been commandeered by the FBI and that they would need to make alternative plans for the day's activities.

Last night I'd been taken to a local Holiday Inn by a couple of uncommunicative police officers, bundled into a suite and given a complementary overnight pack from a bemused concierge. I was told to get some sleep and that I would be 'debriefed' in the morning, by whom I had no idea. I asked about Adam, but the officers just shrugged and gave the impression that such information was either above their pay grade or of little interest. I considered stamping my feet and making a scene, but I was so tired I decided to go with the flow and crash. I fell asleep almost the instant my head hit the pillows, and woke six hours later with the same welcome screen on the TV and the curtains wide open. I had just showered and gotten back into the same clothes (which not unpleasantly smelled of charcoal and wood smoke) when two different police officers called and escorted me into a squad car. They lured me with coffee and an almond croissant, so it was a no-brainer.

Now that I was in the club's luxurious private members' bar & grill, I had been left to my own devices. The surroundings were very old-world old-money country club and smelled of stale cigars. It was a semicircular space with a flagstone tile floor and about a dozen two-seater couches facing each other across low-set mahogany tables. Larger tables for dinner were scattered around the room, flowers on each table. A dark wood bar with green leather inlays and studded with bronze fasteners was set back away from the bay windows. There were no televisions behind the bar, but lots of rare Scottish single malts, Kentucky bourbons, Caribbean rums and Eastern Bloc vodkas. The bartenders and servers had been dismissed and four LAPD officers stood to attention outside, preventing anyone from entering.

Locked in and bored, I decided to check out the bar and found a bottle of Kraken. Rummaging around under the counter I pulled out a tall glass and filled it with ice and poured myself three fingers worth of rum. Adding some lime I swirled the glass, let the ice cool down the rum, lifted the glass in an imaginary toast, and downed it in one. It only temporarily bothered me that I was drinking alcohol at six o'clock in the morning, but I figured this was going to be an interesting day and I was a little nervous about what was going to happen.

As the spicy liquid trickled down my throat the glass doors burst open and a group of serious-looking people arrived. I assumed they were FBI or secret service or some other government agency as they all wore the same suits and had curly plastic dangling from behind their ears. They fanned out around the room taking corner positions. The doors squeaked open again and more people entered the bar. A white-haired man in a grey suit caught my eye and regarded me with a stern look. His pockmarked skin contrasted sharply with the crispness of his perfectly tailored suit, I reckoned bought from Saville Row or some other bespoke London shop. He walked with a slight stoop, yet moved swiftly across the diner floor towards me, accompanied by three others, clearly his subordinates. They were all in their thirties, wearing dark suits and with lanyards around their necks.

I decided to pointedly ignore everyone, and refilled my glass with Kraken before heading over to one of the window settees. I sunk back into the soft leather and leaned back to admire the view of the rising sun. My eyes drifted to the tree line where the sky was pink and the sharp prongs of the bare trees seemed to have ripped a hole in the clouds. It was like they were inflicting a wound on the sky and the colours of the day were bleeding out. Sequin-silver stars, like the glowing embers of a dying fire, winked down at me from the firmament. I closed my eyes and took a deep breath, the warmth from the sun and the rum starting to relax me.

"May we join you?" came a low voice behind me.

I nodded, saying nothing, playing it cool. The white-haired man took the seat opposite and regarded me through lidded eyes. He gave a crinkly smile. "You've probably figured out we're from the FBI," he said, deadpan.

I raised my eyebrows, duh.

"My name's William Hubert, I'm the Director of the FBI Science and Technology Branch, Operational Division."

The alcohol was starting to kick in, and I felt a little buzz of confidence. However, the adrenaline rush of the last couple of days had left me mentally exhausted.

"Nice title, I'm impressed." I said in a tone that suggested anything but. "Bet it's hard to fit all that on a nameplate."

Hubert cracked another lopsided grin and looked sideways as the others joined us on the sofas and pulled up chairs. A dark-haired woman with flawless ebony skin gave me a slight smile and opened up a large laptop on the desk between us. Hubert nodded at her. "This is Colleen Stillman, she's my second-in-command. Practically runs the department."

Stillman looked up briefly, smiled again, and resumed booting up her computer. Hubert pointed to the other two, a man and a woman, who had sat down opposite.

"These folks, they're both from NASA, here in an advisory capacity."

I took another slug from my glass, crunching ice, and pointedly looked out of the window. "NASA rocket scientists? All for little old me."

There was a commotion at the dining room entrance, and another man entered, flashing his badge aggressively at the goons on the door. He was wearing ripped jeans and Nike hi-tops and a T-shirt featuring Darth Vader sporting funky white sunglasses. This was in complete contrast to the rest of his appearance, which was of a portly middle-aged scientist with a hairline receding rapidly toward a patch of sparse sandy growth at the back. He was wearing round-rimmed glasses, which he took off and started cleaning on his T-shirt as he headed our way.

Hubert leaned over and winked at me. "The Star Wars fan here is Dr Michael Holland from FBI Operational Technology. He works for me."

Holland sat down next to Hubert and gave me a quick smile. I settled back into the couch, crossing my legs. I was feeling a weird mixture of anger and apprehension, but I guessed I maybe had more to gain from this than they did.

Hubert reached into his jacket pocket and produced a brown envelope, which he placed unopened onto the table. I looked at it, arched an eyebrow, but didn't move to pick it up.

"Dr Morgan," he said, the humour now missing from his eyes, "We're here to talk about Adam Benedict of course. But first I need to fill you in on some background details. Colleen, are we connected yet?"

Stillman glanced up and nodded. "Yes sir, I have the pilots now. On screen are Major James Powers and Captain Lyle Hunter."

She slid the laptop into a position on the end of the table so everyone could see the screen. I could make out two uniformed USAF personnel sitting behind a whiteboard that was covered in hand-drawn graphics and maps.

Without looking up Hubert said, "Gentlemen, welcome and thanks for waiting." He looked at me, pointing at the screen. "On the left is Major Powers who's the commanding officer of Reaper Squadron, based out of Creech. Next to him is Captain Hunter who I believe has just come off a twelve hour shift flying a Predator drone over Afghanistan, which may explain the bags under his eyes."

The airmen nodded wordlessly. Hubert sat back in his chair, giving off the air of a man bored with proceedings. "Two days ago Captain Hunter photographed something unusual. Captain, would you care to elaborate?"

Hunter cleared his throat and glanced sideways at his superior officer who nodded wordlessly. "Yes sir. At 0825 hours on October 21 I was test-piloting a prototype drone over the Nevada desert. This drone developed some technical difficulties requiring me to return it to base." He turned and pointed at one of the maps behind him, which was overlaid by red lines and co-ordinates. "At 0845 hours my IR detector registered a magnitude five flare from the ground directly perpendicular to my aircraft, which was at that time at an altitude of forty-five thousand feet. The camera was automatically engaged and took a series of photographs which I've downloaded and sent to you as requested."

Stillman clicked a few keys on the laptop and the airmen were reduced to a secondary window as the screen changed to photographs of a grey desert pockmarked by depressions and craters resembling the dimples on a golf ball.

Hubert looked back at me. "These were taken 36.79 degrees north, 115.9 degrees west, co-ordinates in the Nevada desert. More specifically, these co-ordinates are for Area 5 in the Nevada National Security Site, otherwise and previously known as the 'Nevada Test Site'."

"I know what that is," I said. The Nevada Test Site area began thirty kilometres or so west of Indian Springs. I took another sip of my rum. "It's where the atomic bomb testing was carried out during the Cold War."

Stillman scrolled through more images, stopping at one that displayed a monochrome desert floor pockmarked by multiple craters and indentations. A single-track road could just be made out in the bottom right corner and there was a white vehicle parked next to a rock formation at the start of the incline to the crater.

"This is the first digital image of the sequence," said Hubert. "The crater at this location measures about forty-five yards in diameter. Colleen, run the sequence please."

Stillman brought up a checkerboard of about twenty images, each time-stamped and showing the same crater at half-second intervals. From the sixth photo onwards there appeared an expanding luminescence which started just off-centre and by the end of the sequence had enveloped the whole aperture of the crater.

"Major Powers, would you like to comment?" said Hubert.

Powers spoke up from off-screen. "Yes sir, we analysed these data from the drone camera, which has a thermo graphic, infra-red and multi-spectral targeting system. The maximum luminosity was recorded as twenty thousand lux. There was no radiation spike, no thermal signature, and apart from background static no noise was picked up."

I gave Hubert a withering look. "It's a while since I did physics. Can somebody translate into English?"

The guy with the Star-Wars t-shirt leaned forward, scratched his nose, and looked at me intently. Despite his appearance, his eyes were fiercely intelligent.

"Twenty thousand lux is difficult to look at," he said with a twitch of his lip. "At midday the sun is producing around one hundred thousand lux."

"A bomb, then?" I suggested with a shrug.

He shook his head and smiled patiently. "Can't be a bomb because there's no heat or noise."

I looked at the laptop screen again. The sequence scrolled onward, the luminescence fading and collapsing until there was no sign of it and the crater looked exactly the same as at the start.

Hubert coughed. "Major, Captain, thank you for joining us. That'll be all for now."

Stillman cut the feed and the window went blank. Hubert looked at me and tilted his head, saying nothing more, waiting for my response. I knew where this was going but I decided to play coy and ignorant for a while longer.

"Well this is all very interesting," I said, affecting a nonchalance I didn't feel.

Hubert sat back and folded his arms, his eyes narrowing. Stillman shot me an expression that suggested she knew I was stalling. I didn't care because I wanted them to lay it all on the line for me. Hubert seemed to realise this and wagged a finger in the direction of the laptop.

"When I received those images from Major Power, I had all comms traffic from that area flagged and directed to me. Within a few hours we'd intercepted a 911 call from exactly those co-ordinates. Local law enforcement was going to ignore it because the caller hung up. Colleen here was on the ball and got them to follow it through, also getting a couple of our agents to tag along. They were there within two hours, almost the same time as the local patrol."

Stillman leaned forward, hands on knees. "Our team found some guy climbing out of the crater. A Professor of palaeontology called Gabriel Connor. He said he was alone, but the evidence we found indicates otherwise. According to the agents on site he was fairly evasive, to say the least."

She let this hang in the air and the rest of the gang looked at me, waiting. Hubert folded his arms, giving a smug look.

"But of course you know all this, don't you Dr Morgan?"

I took a deep breath. Time to share.

"Sure, okay. The local PD, guy called Woods, is the sheriff. Took me to Pahrump where I met Connor. I heard his story."

Hubert remained impassive. "I believe he gave testimony that he was alone in the crater."

I said nothing. I wasn't sure I was ready to talk about the subsequent conversation I'd had with Connor in my office. Not until I got some answers from these guys. Stillman leaned in and her dark eyes bored into mine. I tried to hold her stare, but I blinked first. She gave a little smile of victory. The bad cop-good cop routine?

The good cop, Hubert leaned in again. "What can you tell us about Adam Benedict, Dr Morgan?"

I folded my arms. "You first."

Hubert looked at me strangely for a second before pursing his lips and tapping the table in front of me. "Fair enough. Would you be so kind as to look inside that envelope?"

I was starting to feel trapped and nervous. I thought about refusing but things were moving fast, and I really needed to get my head around all of this. I picked up the envelope and made a show of turning it around a few times before using my nail to tear the seam and tip the contents onto the table.

Photographs.

The top-most one was the picture I'd taken on my phone of Adam at the hospital. The others were screenshots of his CT scans, blown up in high resolution. I picked up the brain scan and once again marvelled at the symmetry and the sheer 'normality' of it.

I shrugged, "So what?"

Stillman reached forward and tapped a purple fingernail on the scan. "We obtained these from the radiologist, your Dr Navarro. He sent them to a colleague in Vegas, who saw sense and forwarded them to us."

"Okay, well then you'll know that there's nothing abnormal to see on these images," I countered.

"Dr Navarro was concerned about an interference pattern which he couldn't explain, or correct for," said Holland. "By all accounts, Navarro is a bit OCD. Lucky for us, it turned out. He was concerned that he'd calibrated the scanners wrongly or that maybe there was a fault in his highly expensive government-owned equipment."

I picked up another photograph, an aerial shot of the crater we had just seen on the laptop. A time-lapse that showed a sequence of increasingly bright lights emanating from within it, similar to the images we'd just reviewed on the laptop. I flicked it back onto the table. Stillman glanced at

Holland who picked it up and holding it up in front of me, he pointed to the light emanating from the centre of the crater.

"This anomaly - for want of a better word - exhibits a periodicity approximating twenty four hours and lasts for less than five minutes."

"Anomaly?" I said, eyebrows raised.

He looked at me with an even stranger intensity before taking his glasses off and cleaning them on his T-shirt again. Clearly a nervous tic.

"We've spent the last week analysing this photograph using the most advanced technology we have. We're still no further forwards as to its nature."

Hubert unfolded his arms and leaned in. "But it isn't a naturally occurring phenomenon, that's for sure."

I reached for the Kraken, but Hubert gently stopped me with his hand. "Kate, I don't know what Adam Benedict has told you, but he isn't who he says he is."

Stillman closed her laptop and looked at me. "You're the most important person in this room now. You've spent time in his presence, in his company. This is … unprecedented."

I was feeling dizzy and it wasn't just the Kraken. I looked out of the window at the lightening sky and blinked as the sun poked around the curtains.

"Kate, Adam Benedict was in this very crater when the anomaly appeared," said Hubert. "Connor lied to the police, of that I'm sure. A few days later Adam Benedict - or something resembling him - was brought into your Emergency Room."

He deliberately reached into an inside pocket and brought out a second brown envelope. He tipped out another stack of photographs and fanned them out on the table, face up. I picked up the topmost photograph. On it was an x-ray of a human figure. The external shape was that of a male, but the internal structure was wrong. There was an outer layer a couple of millimetres thick but no inner layer. No bones or organs or any recognisable human anatomy at all. In the middle of the chest was a sphere roughly the size of a golf ball, with dozens of small protuberances on its surface. There were thin gossamer-like filaments emanating from it, spreading out in all directions, connecting everything. I could just make out the vague outline of eyes and a mouth, but where the brain should be was a rhomboid-shaped object a couple of inches in diameter, free-floating in the cranium. More filaments from the sphere could be seen extending up to it and wrapping it in concentric circles.

I looked up. "I don't understand. This isn't ... a human being."

Hubert sat back and crossed his knees. "That is your Adam Benedict. The scans you saw were deliberately distorted and altered."

"By who?"

"By him. We don't know how, but I presume in the same way that your monitors were tricked into displaying apparently normal vital statistics."

I stared at the photograph. "No, that isn't possible. I've spoken with him, been with him. I've felt him... sensed his emotions. Something's happened to him, yes, but... he's not this ... machine."

"How do you know?" said Stillman earnestly. "You'd never met Adam Benedict before. How do you know that was he? Have you heard of the Turing Test?"

I put my head in my hands and ran my fingers through my hair. Despite the shower, I could still smell cordite and gunpowder on my fingers and my nails were cracked. The edges of my hands were all scraped and bruised and I brought them up in front of my eyes and turned them slowly. Fingerprints, veins, bones, tendons. Human accoutrements. I looked up and saw that they were all waiting for my reply. I felt overwhelmed and tears started to well up in my eyes.

"Yes I have heard of the Turing Test, and no I wasn't speaking with an A.I. - Adam is a human being. We shared... memories. He opened my mind to hidden places. Traumatic memories that I'd suppressed." Tears were flowing now and I brushed them away with my sleeve. The floodgates had opened and the words poured out. "He let me in to his head, and I felt his emotions, his sorrow and his anguish. He'd found his wife murdered. It was real. I can't prove it to you, but I just know it was real." I hugged my knees and buried my head, rocking slowly backward and forward.

"I believe you," I heard Hubert say softly.

Stillman reached over and gave me a handkerchief. I accepted it gratefully and blew my nose loudly.

There was a pause and then Hubert said, "Kate, you need to understand - that isn't Adam Benedict. It may be his mind, his consciousness, but it sure isn't his body."

I jerked upright as realisation dawned. "Oh my God."

"What?" said Hubert.

I looked around at them all, wide-eyed. "I don't think he knows exactly what he is. He told me he was 'saved' … as he put it. Restored back to life. He thinks he's still human, more or less, not a machine!"

Holland sat back and interlaced his fingers behind his head. "Who does he think 'saved' him?"

I stared blankly out of the window and I caught my reflection, pale and drawn. I took a deep breath and plunged in. "He said he died and was brought back to life by aliens."

Stillman raised her eyebrows and sneaked a sideways glance at Hubert who was staring at me, an intense expression on his face.

"One of them has come back with him," I continued. "It's in his head. No, in that machine." I pointed at the photograph.

A weird smile appeared on Holland's face. "So this alien - it controls him?"

I nodded slowly. "I think it's trying to - there's definitely a conflict going on in there."

"Why is he here?" asked Hubert. "Why was he sent back? What else do you know?"

I shook my head. "I don't think he knows what he's doing here. During our last conversation, he was wondering whether he was some kind of envoy, or intermediary. Like

John the Baptist, you know, clearing the way for Jesus Christ and all that …"

"Great analogy," said Holland, sarcastically. He shot a look at Hubert. "The herald of the apocalypse. Wait until the evangelists hear about this."

Hubert ignored him. "Are there any more aliens here? Is it just the one?"

"I don't know." I took a deep breath. "What I do know is that Adam said that we are all 'in danger'."

Holland looked pointedly at Hubert. "That anomaly - whatever it is - is the key. We need to figure it out, learn how it works."

"What are we going to do about Adam?" I asked. "I mean, do we even know if he survived the helicopter crash?"

"We have to assume that he did indeed survive," said Holland gravely.

CHAPTER SEVENTEEN
Deer Ridge

Hubert twisted in his chair and flicked the blinds down behind me. Shadows darkened and criss-crossed the room and lights automatically came on around the bar. Holland had wandered over and was looking for a drink, and the two NASA employees were on their mobile phones, texting or Facebooking, I had no idea. Hubert settled back into the couch in front of me and took his jacket off. I was expecting a shoulder holster at least, but was disappointed to see his pants held up by yellow and blue stripy braces. He saw me looking and gave a smile as if to say 'I'm the director of the FBI I can wear what the fuck I like'. He started to roll up his sleeves, and turned to Stillman who was back tap-tapping into the laptop.

"Colleen, we need to bring Dr Morgan completely up to date with what we know about the crater." I frowned at him but before I could speak he continued, "Kate, you need to be fully in the loop with all aspects of this, especially if you're coming along for the ride."

"Who says I want to?" I challenged.

But I was definitely on board. For a billion reasons.

Stillman turned the laptop my way. She clicked onto a file that opened up a set of photographs of atomic explosions, some black and white but mostly colour, dating from the 1950's onwards. She minimised it to the corner of the screen and pulled up a file. She started scrolling through pages of data all green background and black words and numbers arranged into dates and columns, until she found the one she wanted. She reached out and froze the screen, and pointed with her pen, tapping the screen. "There. That one."

I squinted, wishing I'd brought my reading glasses. Holland returned, drink in hand, and took his glasses out from his shirt pocket where they had been precariously hanging from a button. He pushed them up his nose and sat down next to me. I looked covetingly at them for a second, and then turned back to the laptop.

The heading at the top of the screen read:

PROJECT PLOUGHSHARE

There followed two pages of data columns. I scanned through them for a few seconds, but soon got lost in the river of information. I looked at Stillman and raised my eyebrows. "So, what am I looking for?"

She pointed at the screen. "Each column contains the data from every nuclear test at this site between 1952 and 1971. They were all done as part of a program called Project Ploughshare."

"Strange name."

"Not really. Ploughshare was the US governmental term for the development of nuclear explosives for peaceful construction purposes. It was the program to develop what they called Peaceful Nuclear Explosions or 'PNEs'."

Holland leaned back and put his hands behind his head. "Peaceful uses of the atomic bomb... almost an oxymoron."

Hubert nodded wryly, saying nothing.

Stillman continued, "Well, according to the official record this involved rock blasting, mining, making tunnels - that sort of thing. Says here there were thirty tests in this area over the course of a decade or so, but by then the environmentalists were getting antsy and the number of high profile demonstrations snowballed which eventually closed the program."

"I remember that," I said. "There was a lot of bad publicity, and that NASA astronomer guy took part."

"Yes, Carl Sagan," said Stillman.

I nodded. "So, which of these tests produced our crater?"

Stillman scrolled down the page until she stopped at a line:

STORAX/SEDAN:
NTS/shaft/crater/1450ft/Classified/100Kt

"This is our baby. An underground detonation from 1953. The depth of the blast was almost one and half thousand feet under the desert floor, and it was designed to produce a large cavern that could then be evaluated for tunnelling viability. Tunnelling through mountains, I guess." She highlighted the right hand column with the mouse. "The yield was about one hundred kilotons of TNT. That's more than ten times the energy produced by the Hiroshima A-bomb."

Hubert looked at me. "Kate, what's odd about all of this is the absence of any eyewitness reporting of this detonation –"

"–And yet there are pages and pages of accounts documenting the other ones," finished Stillman. "Most versions talk about explosions blowing the top off the shaft, and producing a cap which often collapsed, producing a crater or cavern."

She relinquished the mouse somewhat reluctantly, and I double-clicked pictures of the detonations and their aftermath. Nuclear fireballs and hellish mushroom clouds spiralling into the stratosphere of a clear blue Nevada sky. Craters, difficult to size accurately as there were no surrounding trees or other vegetation to give it some scale. Groups of observers dressed in Army fatigues staring into the distance without any radiation protection or goggles.

"The Department of Energy estimated that more than three hundred megacuries of radioactivity remained in the local environment at the end of the nineties when they stopped testing," said Holland. "This is one of the most radioactively contaminated locations in the United States. But according to the team on site, this particular crater isn't radioactive at all."

"I don't understand," I said. "How can there be no radioactivity?"

Holland lowered his chin and wiggled his eyebrows at me, "There is this 'classified' section…"

Hubert's eyes hooded. "What's classified appears to be the actual type of atomic weapon used," he said. "You know, plutonium, or whatever."

"And that information is provided for all the other tests, but not for this one," said Holland. "So, basically we've no idea what produced this particular crater." He took a large drink of what smelled like brandy.

"Shit," I said looking alarmed. "Isn't that kind of an important starting point?"

Hubert looked pointedly at Holland. "So Mike, I want this to be your priority. Get another team on site at the crater, A-SAP. You're the point man. Security, electronics and detectors. Whatever you need. Set up mobile office and labs. Once you're active, start round the clock surveillance of the crater and the cavern."

Holland nodded, stood up and downed the rest of his drink. Hubert turned to Stillman. "Colleen, that site is to be isolated and sealed off. Get local PD to assist."

"Roger that." She pulled out her mobile and started tapping out numbers, but Hubert hadn't finished. "We need to get the specs for the bomb that produced that crater. I want you to find out if any of the scientific team involved are still active. Or even alive. Contact whoever's currently the chief of the Nuclear Regulatory Commission, and use my clearance. Don't take any shit either. This is all pre-1980 so it'll certainly come under the Freedom of Information Act. Then get more Agents to Indian Springs and personally link up with Holland and his team on site. Report back to me when you're there."

"Hang on," I said, a light bulb going off in my head. "When we were in Lindstrom's house. Adam said, and I quote: 'Corey Lindstrom is the only progeny of Augustine Lindstrom'. That's it!" I sat back with the air of Hercule Poirot, having just solved a murder. "He was looking for a bunch of files. We need to look up Augustine Lindstrom." I squeezed my eyes closed and forced myself to think. The pieces were there and I just needed to fit them together but my thoughts were sluggish, and I felt like I was treading through treacle.

Stillman looked at Hubert, puzzled. "I don't remember seeing that name in the database."

"Must have been classified, or deleted," said Hubert. "So that's where you can start looking. Kate, is there anything else you can tell us?"

"He mentioned SETI," I said, slowly, looking up.

"SETI?" said Holland. "What can he want with that place?"

"Adam said SETI's 'welcome from earth' message was received by the aliens." I shook my head, "Or at least I think that's what he meant."

"So what?" said Holland with a dismissive wave of his hand. "Is he going to use the transmitter to contact the other aliens? Give them directions?"

I looked up. "I think that's exactly what he's going to do."

Holland pulled a face. "I don't think that would work. The distances involved are too vast."

"But we should assume that's a possibility," Stillman interrupted. "We need to evaluate all leads, right?"

I smiled at her, grateful for the support. Hubert called over to the NASA scientists. "I want you two to go back to Lindstrom's house and secure all those diaries and notes. Then make sure you get them to the crater where Dr Holland will be setting up his team. Get to it."

The scientists nodded, and stood up in sync with Holland.

Hubert checked his watch and looked at Stillman, then Holland. "If we're right, we've got twenty hours or so before the anomaly appears again. Alert the local PD at SETI and get everyone out of bed and lock that place down. Tonight."

Holland started to walk away, but stopped and turned. "If he survived the crash, we have to assume that Adam Benedict - or the alien - now has access to these data."

Hubert looked grim. "I know. But SETI is about four hundred miles from where the helicopter went down. If he's heading there, it's going to take him some time. I'll put out an APB so the Highway Patrol can ID him if he steals a car."

Stillman sat back down and turned to Hubert. "We should fly to SETI, check out the transmitter. Mike's team can lock down the crater."

Hubert contemplated this for a second and then nodded. Holland turned on his heel and almost sprinted out of the dining room.

I leaned back in my chair, and picked up the photo of Adam. He looked so human, so normal on the outside. On the inside, anything but human. I slowly shook my head and flicked the photo back onto the table. All right, so inside he was a mass of what – transistors and electronics? What were any of us inside, other than an organic soup of tubes and fluids and ugliness? Wasn't it our mind, our consciousness, which makes us human?

I touched Hubert's arm. "Adam's the key to this. He's still one of us. We need him on our side. I know what I felt from him, and it was real. He's still human."

"Maybe at first," said Stillman.

I looked at her. "What do you mean?"

She glanced sideways at Hubert who looked at me through lidded eyes. "Why do you think there were so many LAPD and SWAT at that house, Kate, and how did they get there so fast? A routine panic alarm was set off and half the county's emergency response teams arrive within a few minutes?"

I hadn't thought about it but in retrospect, he was right. "You knew that Adam Benedict was there, didn't you?"

"Yes. When the local police and paramedics arrived to clean up the mess outside the bar where he assaulted those soldiers, one of the paramedics ID'd him from the night in your emergency room. The barman gave the police officers your address."

I stared at him silently.

"Sheriff Woods sent a MP, and four police officers to your house that night, Kate."

I closed my eyes. So it hadn't been a coincidence that Richard Jackson had turned up on my doorstep. I should have known. I was about to say so, when Stillman leaned forwards and put a hand on my knee.

"Those four policemen were killed, Kate. Murdered. Their bodies were ripped apart. They never had a chance to discharge their firearms."

I felt numb. "Adam told me his memory of that event had been wiped."

Stillman gave a snort, and Hubert also looked at me disbelievingly. There was an uneasy silence, and then he stood up and pulled out his cell phone. He punched a few numbers and spoke tersely into it before snapping it off again. He shrugged back into his jacket and made for the door.

"The jet's waiting. Let's go"

CHAPTER EIGHTEEN
Airborne, Heading for Mountain View, CA

The FBI's Gulfstream jet cruised at thirty thousand feet at just over five hundred miles per hour with no discernible turbulence and minimal noise from its two rear mounted jet engines. I leaned back and looked out the window, seeing the full moon and a couple of wispy clouds in the inky blackness of the sky. All that was left of the day was a chalky mauve sky, and even as I watched that faded into a stygian darkness as the stars took over the heavens. I tried to pick out a constellation or two, but the reflections from within the cabin were too bright.

I was sitting in a comfortable leather recliner opposite Hubert, who was tapping away at a computer touchscreen on his knee. On the other side of the aircraft sat Colleen Stillman, in front of another large touchscreen display and keyboard. She appeared engrossed in moving objects and icons around various locations on an electronic map. There was a polished wooden table between us on which were scattered the photos and scans of Adam Benedict.

Or whatever he was now.

I'd been served a cup of piping hot tea by an agent now doubling up as flight crew, who had then disappeared to the back of the aircraft where two other agents were camped. It was a peculiar brew, sweet and herby, and I pictured dipping a couple of biscuits in and watching them melt before eating. I took a sip, savouring its sweetness, and closed my eyes.

"Memories," I murmured.

"Excuse me?"

My eyes flicked open to see Hubert appraising me with a raised eyebrow. I took another drink before replying.

"I was thinking of how Adam pushed his thoughts into my mind. He'd wanted me to feel his emotions - confusion, apprehension, fear and loneliness – and see the world through his eyes. He'd wanted me to experience his memories, to make me understand that he was still a human being, with a traumatic past and an even more traumatic present. And then he'd opened up my memory vault, which'd been locked down for decades. The memories he showed me - I'd suppressed them for almost all of my adult life – were basically of my father beating the shit out of my mother."

Hubert closed his laptop and folded his hands on the lid. "Did you ask Adam to release these memories?"

"Yes. And that's the thing. He was quite apologetic and I really felt that he was sad for me. He tried to comfort me. This from a man who had recently discovered the body of his murdered wife, a man who had also died in an inexplicable event and somehow had been revived, or whatever we want to call it. Despite all that, he wanted to be there for me. He wanted to comfort me… he… he knew about my daughter. My mother…"

Hubert just nodded, and waited patiently for me to continue. I felt the tears stinging my eyes, and I subconsciously started wringing my hands, scratching the dirt under my nails. Suddenly, and uncontrollably, grief surged through me and my breathing increased, ragged and jerky as if my diaphragm was twitching from an electrical current. I buried my head in my hands and I could picture the tiny grave, the grey skies and constant drizzle, feel the cold wind. I'm kneeling in mud, sobbing and wailing while everyone's trying to comfort me, a mixture of sympathy and horror on their faces.

"For months afterwards I was empty of hope. I struggled to fill the void with anything meaningful or worthwhile. Then the drinking started, and there was no one to tell me to lay off, to tell me that I'd had enough. I left the Chicago ER but that meant days alone in my apartment, with the bottle for company, and believe me it wasn't a good friend."

I felt a hand on my knee and saw that Stillman had left her seat and was squatting next to me. She wrapped her arms around me and I cried, the kind of desolate, ferocious sobbing that only death and loss can produce. I have no idea how long I cried, but eventually the shuddering of my shoulders calmed down and Stillman released me but remained by my side. She handed me a bunch of napkins and I dabbed my puffy eyes dry, and wiped away the snot that had dribbled down over my lips and chin. I looked over at Hubert and he gave me a kindly smile.

Stillman reached over and picked up the radiograph of the Adam-shaped receptacle for Adam's consciousness and the mind of a predatory, homicidal alien.

"Adam's in there," she said. "Trapped, and with God-knows what alien creature calling the shots. He's alone, trying to reconnect with his own memories, his own past, and trying to figure out how he fits in the world."

Hubert looked earnestly at me. "Your companionship, the connection you made, might have been an attempt to retain his disappearing humanity."

I felt a gnawing hole growing in my stomach. "And with me gone, he's lost that. He has nothing to relate to."

The rest of the flight took place in relative silence as Hubert and Stillman tip-tapped on their screens and I dozed on and off. After about half an hour or so, there was a change in the engine noise, and we started to descend. Hubert closed down his laptop and put it away in a steel briefcase. He gestured to one of the agents who brought him a glass of water garnished with a lemon, which he sniffed before sipping. He noticed me watching him and smiled, leaning back in his chair.

"Kate, have you heard of the Fermi paradox?"

"No," I said, but I was very glad of the change of subject.

He had his fingers steepled and was now looking over my head like a schoolmaster about to deliver a lecture. "Fermi was a physicist who made a compelling argument that we - humans - are probably alone in the universe. The argument goes that there are billions of stars in the galaxy, many much older than earth and many with a high probability of having earth-like planets. If some of these planets developed intelligent life, and then if interstellar travel was developed by just one such intelligent species, then the galaxy could have been - and should have been - traversed and colonised in about a million years or so."

"So, hence the paradox," Stillman chipped in. "Where are all the aliens? We should have been visited by them many times over."

"Indeed," said Hubert. "Their absence could mean that extra-terrestrial life is extremely rare. NASA has been listening to the void between the stars for years and there've been no signals detected. It's awfully quiet out there."

"And yet they're here," I said softly.

Hubert leaned forward and looked intently at me. "One answer to the Fermi paradox may be that our preconceptions of the ubiquity of intelligence in the galaxy is wrong. Perhaps some restriction imposed by astrophysics and biology makes life very rare, and that the rise of advanced intelligence is only a recent event."

"Recent in cosmic terms, of course," finished Stillman.

"Perhaps," said Hubert, "we're at the beginning of history. What if humanity and these aliens are the only two intelligent civilisations that have arisen in the universe so far? In separate galaxies, far removed from each other. So Fermi's paradox is solved, at least for their galaxy because they not only traversed it, they colonised it."

"Think how advanced they must be," said Stillman in an awed voice. "The abilities and technologies they must have mastered over the millennia. Humanity is just starting out on this journey."

I thought about the sheer 'alien-ness' of the alien mind, and wondered how they must view humanity. Perhaps as we view ants or other bugs. Certainly not with any respect or concern for our wellbeing.

"This should never have happened," I said. "These aliens and humanity should never have met. Our respective civilisations should've been simply too far apart for any communication, let alone to make physical contact."

Hubert nodded, his fingers re-steepling. "So how does SETI fit in? I mean, how on earth did that message get through to them?"

I thought about it. "The 'anomaly'. What if it's some kind of communication hub?"

"An interstellar 'router' of sorts?" threw in Stillman. "We could use it to talk to them. Think what we could learn from them."

I felt a headache beginning. "I didn't get the feeling they would be interested in a lecture. Why should they? We're nothing to them. Just apes with brains. To them, we're pond scum. Bacteria. Dust."

"Apes with nuclear weapons," said Stillman, arching an eyebrow. "We can defend ourselves."

"Are you sure about that?" I countered.

"Whatever Adam is," Hubert said, "and if he has survived, our priority is to stop him contacting the other aliens."

"What if that means we have to kill him?" said Stillman to no one in particular.

"What if you can't?" I said softly.

We landed at a private airstrip and were greeted by a long line of black limousines, US Army vehicles and SWAT trucks. Half an hour later we all pulled up at the main frontage of the SETI Institute on North Bernardo Drive. With precision arrogance, the army rolled their trucks over the lawns and shrubs surrounding the tall glass main entrance. Stillman jumped out of the first truck, a boxy black armoured leviathan, and waved the other vehicles into pre-arranged positions around the grounds. Heavily armed police disembarked and started setting up road blocks and fortified positions behind trees and grassy verges illuminated by red and blue flashes and the orange glow from the Institute's own soft night lights.

Our black Lincoln town car snaked around the SWAT trucks, and pulled to a stop by the entrance. We jumped out, Hubert talking on his phone, and were immediately accosted by a man clearly brimming with indignation and anger. He couldn't be more than sixty or so, but walked with a cane, his right leg dragging after him. I'd seen eighty-year olds in a rehab ward walk better than him. His face was all pale and sickly, with no prominent bones and no chin to speak of. An equally irate petite brunette in her forties wearing a white lab coat ran over to us. She had porcelain skin that was ashen, almost anaemic, and there was a cold sweat on her forehead and cheeks. Her lab coat was monogrammed with the name *Dr Marianne Rogers, Senior Astronomer, SETI*. She bounced on her feet and started wagging a finger in Hubert's direction.

"There are over one hundred scientists still working inside, many in the middle of very valuable and delicate research projects. They can't just leave."

Hubert pointed to the main entrance. "If your colleagues won't leave under their own steam, we'll clear the building ourselves, room by room."

She seemed to physically deflate. Her tone changed, and she no longer sounded as belligerent. I also noticed she had tear-stained cheeks, and her mascara was starting to smear.

"Dr Holland said that this might be our own fault?"

Hubert gave a slight smile. "Indirectly, perhaps. It seems that your 'hello from earth' signal did reach another galaxy. We just don't know how."

"It was a bad idea in the first place," I piped up, folding my arms.

Rogers looked at me and wrinkled her nose. "Who's this?"

"This is Dr Morgan, she's an advisor to the FBI." Hubert replied, straight-faced. He then turned on his heel and set off at a brisk walk towards the Institute. I dropped in step with him, and Rogers hustled to keep up. Inside, we walked past entrance desks, a gift shop, and a small cafeteria on our way to a bank of elevators next to a glass doorway in front of the Carl Sagan Centre. I stopped and looked in, cupping my eyes on the glass. I could just make out a stage with a lectern and a rising bank of seats set back like an amphitheatre.

"I understand you were instrumental in setting up 'Active SETI', Dr Rogers?" I asked without turning.

"The discovery of extra-terrestrial civilisations is the crux of our mission, of course," she replied, looking downcast and quite miserable. "That's what every scientist here is dedicated to. Active SETI was an initiative to send out a peaceful message, a way of announcing to the galactic community 'we're here'."

I turned and raised my eyebrows. "The galactic community? Sounds like you've been watching too many Star Trek episodes. Perhaps you should've kept quiet until humanity was ready?"

She folded her arms and gave me a challenging stare. "When would we have been judged 'ready', Dr Morgan? And by whom?"

Hubert leaned in. "Kate is correct, and now the survival of our species may be on the line."

Roger's face dropped. Hubert grasped her arm and led her down the corridor. "Doctor, I'm aware that you can control the radio signalling from the control room in the basement. You need to take us there and shut it down, permanently."

She looked dismayed. "Permanently?"

Hubert nodded. "It's the only way. Yes, or no?"

Rogers took a deep breath. "The transmission is sent via the Allen Telescope Array at Hat Creek, just North of here," she said. "It's taken fifteen years to fine tune and design the interface and matrix to ready that message for transmission."

We rode the car down two floors and arrived at a large windowless room containing the most sophisticated computers and electronica that I'd ever seen. Rogers gestured towards a piece of freestanding equipment sitting unattended but festooned with lights and plasma displays. Around it were a number of mobile chairs and wireless keypads on wheeled tables.

"That's the controller of the ATA," she said. "It links to all the data readers and diagnostic equipment in this room."

"How long to shut it down?" asked Hubert. "Not fifteen years, I hope."

She sighed. "A couple of hours. Less if I'm left alone."

"Excellent, then I suggest you get started."

We turned to leave. There was a 'ping' and the elevator doors opened revealing half a dozen or more SWAT officers, carrying large leather bags and suitcases. The leading officer nodded at Hubert who nodded back, a silent look passing between them.

Rogers caught the look, and turned to him. "What are these police officers doing here?"

Hubert gave her a sober look. "'Plan B'. You've two hours, doctor. Make it work."

As the officers filed past, Hubert put a hand out to stop the doors from closing and beckoned me to join him in the elevator. I squeezed in and he pressed the button.

"What're we doing now?" I said.

"We're not staying," said Hubert. "I've a feeling we're going to need some leverage with Adam. You and I are going to Las Vegas."

"What's in Vegas?" I said.

"Adam Benedict's daughter."

"What? You found Amy?"

"Yes. She's been located. The local sheriff and Professor Connor are en route. We'll meet them there."

DAY 4

CHAPTER NINETEEN
Wynn Hotel, Las Vegas, Nevada

The flight to Vegas took less than forty minutes. The sky was a velvet black and the Nevada desert underneath us completely invisible, but as we approached the city, colours exploded onto my retina. Blues, greens and yellows were inlaid onto the obsidian canvas, so resembling a huge illuminated computer chip that I was expecting to see an *Intel* logo somewhere. Then what looked like an electric monopoly board with hotels and pyramids and an Eiffel Tower came into view, and as we descended these became towering works of bad-taste art. I could make out thousands of people meandering up the main strip, bisected by wall-to-wall headlights and taillights.

We glided into McCarran at around 1am, where another motorcade awaited us. After an LVPD-escorted fifteen-minute drive, our black Crown Vic screeched around the 180-degree entrance into the drop-off zone of the Wynn Hotel and pulled up in front of a set of gaudy gilt-edged doors. A lanky concierge dressed in a military style outfit and a top hat approached and opened the near passenger door. He was abruptly waved off by a couple of FBI agents who had disembarked from a second car that had tailgated in behind us. Hubert and I jumped out and we were hustled through the lobby behind an arrowhead of agents parting the crowds like Moses at the Red Sea. The fine marble floor shone like polished glass and every step echoed dramatically. A chandelier hung from the ornately decorated ceiling, casting rainbow lighting effects around the walls. Hotel guests stared at us as we moved swiftly past the long granite-topped check-in desks towards the bank of elevators on the far wall. Agents stood in flanking positions as we waited for the elevator car to arrive, politely prohibiting other guests from accompanying us. Even at this late hour, the lobby was teeming with high rollers, hangers-on, tourists and locals streaming in and out of the basement level casino via other similarly gaudy escalators at the end of the lobby.

I was clutching a bag with 'FBI MEDIC' stencilled on the side, and had been officially co-opted into the federal government during the descent into McCarran. Having had to do the raised right hand thing and solemnly swear the oath in front of Hubert and Stillman, I questioned whether this made me a 'Special Agent'. Hubert had given me one of those looks that suggested 'nice try'.

A real Special Agent spoke into his cuff microphone and turned to Hubert, saying, "Room 1890, sir. Sheriff Woods will meet us outside."

Hubert nodded, and the car arrived. We squeezed in and an agent pressed the 18th floor button. Seventies disco music piped through at a volume just loud enough to be intrusive, and the car lurched slightly before accelerating upwards smoothly and silently. My ears popped after a few seconds, and I swallowed to clear them. Hubert appeared to be checking his phone messages, so I tapped him on the arm.

"I thought we'd be meeting at a police station?"

He looked up, and shook his head. "Woods called and said to meet here. Some… problem."

The elevator slowed to a standstill and the doors whooshed open in a way that reminded me of Star Trek. The irony didn't escape me. We got out into a long, dark, red corridor, which made me think of that scene in The Shining when the elevator opened and an ocean of blood poured out. Nothing about this gave me good vibes. Halfway down were two police officers flanking one of the suites. As we approached, one of them leaned back and knocked softly, and the door opened almost immediately. Woods and Connor emerged, and Woods gestured for us all to move down the corridor a few yards. The agents took up positions at both sides of the room, all sunglasses and gun-shaped bulges in their identical black jackets.

Connor furtively glanced at me and gave me a small smile. "Hello Kate, nice to see you again."

I wasn't sure how to reply with Woods standing right there, but Hubert let me know he understood. "Kate, Professor Connor has seen fit to come clean with law enforcement and FBI, isn't that right, Gabriel?"

Connor coughed nervously into his hand, and nodded.

"Alright," said Hubert. "We're all up to speed then. Is she inside?"

Woods moved closer and spoke, almost sotto voce. "She is, but she's not in a particularly good state."

"Meaning what, exactly?" said Hubert.

Woods looked grim. "Meaning, she's drunk. And also probably stoned."

"Is she able to hold a conversation?" I asked.

"She was able to hold a conversation with the undercover vice cop who busted her trying to pick him up in the casino."

"I don't think I'm liking what I'm hearing," said Hubert, in an ominous tone.

Connor gave a nonchalant shrug. "I think she'll be okay. As I told Sheriff Woods on the way over, she knows me. I know her. Let me see what I can get out of her?"

I asked, "How well do you really know her?"

Connor smiled. "I've known her since she was a little girl. Remember, Adam Benedict and I were close friends after college. I knew her mother too, Francesca Banks."

Hubert had earlier given me the rest of the bio. Francesca Banks and Adam had met at college, and were together for a couple of years. They split up, but not before Francesca fell pregnant with Amy. Adam hooked up with Cora much later.

I frowned. "Was Adam close to Amy?"

Connor grimaced. "Francesca was a complete bitch to Adam when she found out about him and Cora. Tried to poison Amy towards him. Still tried to get lots of financial support, mind. She found that Cora came from money, and so of course she tried to screw Adam for more child support.

But then Francesca herself got married to some rich real estate broker who became Amy's legal guardian."

"How often did Adam get to see Amy after this happened?" I asked.

"Hardly at all."

Hubert sighed heavily. "I'm not sure this is going to help."

Connor held up a hand. "It might, hear me out. Francesca died from cancer when Amy was about sixteen and so Amy had gotten back in touch with him. Adam told me that she'd been in trouble - alcohol, drugs, that sort of thing - and he'd tried to help her. That was years ago, however."

I looked at the door to the room, guarded by the police. "What are we going to tell Amy about her father now?"

Connor pursed his lips. "We can't tell her the truth. She won't believe us for a start."

Hubert digested this. "Okay, let me do the talking. Let's go see her."

Connor nodded, reluctantly it seemed, and Hubert gestured for the policeman to open the door. We entered into a big, brash suite containing a kitchenette, bathroom and shower area that led into a main living area. There, a huge king bed dominated, all pure-white, Egyptian cotton sheets, facing a large plasma TV and a desk/chair combo in front of bay windows which were closed with blackout blinds. A sprawling leather sofa occupied the other wall, covered with gaudy striped cushions. The TV was on but muted, a CNN reporter talking animatedly to the camera in front of what looked like a bombed-out Middle Eastern village.

Lying face down on the bed, snoring peacefully, was a young blonde woman dressed in fishnet tights, a miniskirt and a lacy bra. There were bruises along her arms, which were thin and wiry, and I could see the top of a tattooed dragon on her left hip. A police officer was perched on the edge of the bed next to her, holding her hand.

Hubert knelt down by her side and pulled one of her eyelids back, revealing a pinpoint pupil in bloodshot eyes. She stirred but didn't wake up. He looked up at me, eyebrows raised, and shook his head..

"Narcotised," I said. "She's recently had a hit."

He moved back and let me sit on the side of the bed. I opened my Medikit and turned the girl's arm over while feeling for a vein in the antecubital fossa. Finding one, I got a cannula set out of the bag and put a butterfly into the vein, fixing it in place with steristrips. I rummaged through the bag and pulled out a small brown vial, which I tapped with my finger a couple of times before breaking the seal and drawing its contents into a thin syringe. I removed the needle, screwed the syringe to the cannula and slowly injected the full amount into the girl's arm. Even before the syringe had fully deposited its load into the circulation, she took a massive raggedy breath and her eyes opened, pupils now super-sized. She started flailing around but I'd already grabbed her by the shoulders and waved the police officer to hold her down.

"You used adrenaline?" asked a fascinated Hubert.

I shook my head. "Naloxone. It's an opiate antagonist. Blocks the effect of the heroin and actually reverses it's effect. It acts very quickly, as you can see. It can be dangerous, but I figured she was young enough to handle it."

Amy was now staring around the room and giving a good impression of a deer caught in headlights. I released one hand from her shoulder, brushed the hair out of her eyes, and gently caressed her forehead. "It's okay Amy, there's nothing to worry about. My name's Kate. I'm a doctor. You're safe."

The girl closed her eyes for a second and licked her lips. The hint of a tongue piercing glistened in the darkness of a mouth framed with black-smeared lipstick. She took in the other occupants of the room - the police officer standing by the bed, the uniformed Sheriff by the TV, Hubert, and Gabriel Connor.

"Gabe? Is that you?" she slurred, the words coming out as if through treacle. "What the fuck you doing here?"

Connor was about to speak but Hubert waved him off before he could reply. He stepped in front of Connor and fixed her with a piercing stare.

"Amy, my name is William Hubert and I'm with the FBI. We need to ask you some questions." He flashed his badge in front of her face.

She screwed up her eyes and made a show of not reading it. "I'm not stupid, this is Vegas. Check out the next room, you'll see the same thing happening."

Connor leaned in. "Amy, this is about your father. He's in big trouble."

Hubert looked up sharply, and Amy caught the stare between them. Her eyes narrowed and she turned to Hubert. "What sort of trouble?"

"The sort that involves national security," said Hubert, glaring at Connor.

"What's in it for me?" said Amy.

Hubert sighed and shook his head. "Well, you won't go to prison, for a start."

Amy wriggled further up the bed so she was sitting facing everyone. She straightened her bra/top and pushed her hair back from her eyes, where it had flopped down. I noticed the high cheekbones and the aquiline nose. Her slender body was like a Victoria Secret model, her eyes, blue like the sea, were rimmed with thick mascara. She was quite beautiful, and had Adam's DNA written all over her.

"What's he gotten himself into?" she said.

Hubert looked at me and nodded, which I took as tacit instruction to lead the conversation. "When did you last see him?" I said, somewhat evasively.

She looked upwards and to the right. I'd read somewhere that this meant the person was lying. Or was it upwards and to the left?

"Six months ago, more or less," she said. "He came to see me here in Vegas. We spent the weekend together. Went on a helicopter ride out to the Canyon. It was great. He's a good father."

I saw Hubert glance at Connor who shook his head fiercely. Something about this wasn't gelling.

"Amy, how old are you?" I said.

"Twenty-four."

"How long have you been a hooker?"

'None of your business."

"Does your father know?"

Amy paused. "Yes. But he doesn't judge me."

Connor looked at Hubert who nodded his assent. He sat down on the bed and folded his arms.

"Amy, I was with your father recently and he didn't talk about you. We talked about anything and everything, but not you. I find that strange."

Amy's face darkened. "I don't know Gabe, he never talked about you neither, and I've not fucking seen you for years."

Connor winced, and then took a deep breath. "Did you know Cora had died?"

A shrug. "Sure."

"Were you at the funeral?"

Another look upwards and to the right. "Sure. Why wouldn't I be?"

Well, there was the lie, but something else wasn't right and I couldn't put my finger on it. Hubert stood up and walked over to the window. He pulled back the drapes and stared down at the glitzy lights of the Strip, pulsating neon and LED, the heartbeat of another city that never slept.

"Amy, you need to come with us," he said.

She crossed her arms. "Are you going to tell me what sort of trouble my father is in?"

"Not yet. And this is non-negotiable. Grab the rest of your gear." His phone trilled, and he pulled it out of his jacket pocket and listened. He acknowledged it curtly and looked at me. "That was Holland. At the crater. He's found something. Wants us to go there."

I looked up sharply, "Adam?"

Amy glanced warily between Hubert and me. Then she smiled slyly, "He's missing, right? So what's the big deal?"

I ignored her and strode over to join Hubert at the window. He leaned in and spoke softly. "I'm not sure she's going to be much help, but whatever, we'll keep her here under lockdown, just in case."

"You sure you know what you're doing?" I asked

He looked at me, sighed, and slowly shook his head. "Do any of us?"

CHAPTER TWENTY
Nevada Test Site

I grabbed the chance for a quick sleep in the adjoining room and woke up a few hours later feeling refreshed but hungry. The minibar was well stocked so I set about devouring every chocolate bar and packet of potato chips that I could find. It was still dark outside, but my watch said five am so I spent five minutes reading the instructions on the coffee percolator before firing it up. It was bubbling away when there was a knock on the door and Stillman poked her head in.

"How you doing?"

I gave her a little smile. "Yeah, I'm doing OK. But I'm worried. Has anyone heard about Adam?"

Stillman shook her head. "Nothing. And that worries me too. Maybe he didn't survive the helicopter. Prelim crash reports didn't show any organic remains, just burnt twisted metal and plastic. Hubert reckons he's dead."

My eyebrows furrowed, so I flicked the TV on, and tuned to CNN. The anchor was giving a summary of the state wide weather reports, before promising to go live to Paris where there had been rioting overnight. There had been a brief mention of the helicopter accident before I went to bed, but it had been a very vague, non-story, with no details. I threw the remote on the bed and leaned on the tabletop cradling my coffee mug.

"He's not dead, I'm sure of that. But what's he up to?"

Stillman pursed her lips and nodded agreement. "Wish we knew. Obviously best case scenario is that he didn't survive. Sorry. But we've got to work with what we have. SETI is locked down, and Amy's here, safe and sound."

"So it's the crater for us, then," I said.

"For you," she replied. "I'm babysitting Amy."

The UH-60 Black Hawk of the FBI Tactical Helicopter Unit touched down with an accompanying dust storm of biblical proportions. Its four bladed main rotor continued to spin as I scuttled out along with Hubert and two agents, our heads bowed as we sought to avoid decapitation. Mike Holland waited a safe distance back, his shirt pulled up over his mouth and nose in an attempt to minimise inhaling a significant proportion of the desert floor. Behind him were a silver-sided van and a black Lincoln town car, both with drivers ensconced in their seats, windows closed, air conditioning cranked up to the maximum. As we approached, Holland was waved off by Hubert who pointed to the car, covering his ears from the rotor noise. Holland opened the back door of the Lincoln for us and then ran round to the passenger door to slide in. The other agents got into the van behind and the convoy pulled away at speed, kicking up more dust and obscuring the view of the helicopter powering up and lurching into the sky on it's return journey to Creech.

Holland turned in his seat to us, his face slick with perspiration, dust and unconcealed excitement. "How was your flight in?"

Hubert looked out of the window, wiping his forehead with a handkerchief. "Shitty. The G-5 was unavailable, so we flew that bird from McCarran." He turned to stare at Holland. "It better be worth it, Mike."

Holland's face split with a grin so wide his face looked cracked in two. "This is the best day of my entire life, sir. You are not going to believe what we've discovered."

Hubert nodded, non-plussed. "Well I hope this year's science budget has been well spent then."

The Lincoln suddenly made a hard right and climbed up a dirt road towards a group of modular mobile offices and trailers huddled together at the top of the rise. Behind these I could make out what looked like a couple of portable generators and another three FBI vans with satellite dishes on their roofs linked by thick wires and cables and a perimeter fence of poles hammered into the dirt and tied together by fabric tape. FBI agents wearing ballistic vests and big black guns were hanging around the fence watching us arrive.

I teased Holland, "I see you've gone for the low key approach."

He pulled a face. "You've been with the FBI, what, less than twelve hours? This is how things get done."

The vehicles stopped at the tape and Holland directed us towards the nearest trailer, a fifty-foot long modular unit with three side windows and two doors connected by a ramp to the ground. Another agent was standing guard by the foot of the stairs and he nodded to Holland and walked us up the ramp to the door. The interior was dark and I squinted to get my eyes dark-adjusted at the same time shivering with the sudden drop in temperature. Facing me was an Aladdin's cave of electronic equipment and video monitors, all noisily bleeping and squawking. There were screens everywhere, dozens of wireless keyboards, racks of buzzing and humming hard drives, fans and power strips. Duct-taped cables were laid haphazardly across the floor connecting to a long desk manned by three techs dressed in lab coats and sporting FBI lanyards. The smell of ozone and stale coffee permeated the atmosphere. Soft classical music piped from somewhere in the ceiling.

With the door closed, Holland beckoned one of the lab technicians over. "Jo, can you access the video as we discussed on this monitor here, and bring up the feed from the Chinese detector as well."

Hubert was pulling his jacket back on, frosted breath coming from his mouth. I flipped my hoodie up. We pulled over a couple of chairs, and Holland sat in the middle but sideways with one arm on the desk supporting the bank of monitors. A tech was flicking switches and making seemingly random adjustments to a piece of hardware linked to three desktop computers. The screen came to life, showing a picture of a subterranean rocky floor illuminated by spotlights. Dotted around the floor were various pieces of equipment linked by cables and running to a spot out of sight of the cameras. There was a timer/clock at the bottom right of the screen, which read *8:42:33AM:PDT*. The adjacent monitor was displaying pulsing red and yellow lights and numbers, overlaying a blue and black kaleidoscope whorl pulsing in and out hypnotically every few seconds.

"All right," said Holland, rubbing his hands together. "We triangulated all our detectors last night at the bottom of the crater. Video, IR, EMS, everything, and had it all plugged in and running at around four am. I was planning to run some validation scans and algorithms this morning, after a couple of hours in the sack." He clicked on a mouse button and the timer on the screen started to run. He smiled, and pointed at the video monitor. "But then it happened."

For a minute nothing changed on the screen, but then a sphere of white light appeared out of nowhere above the cavern floor. It was on a level with the spotlights, about fifteen feet or so in the air, and seemed to be approximately the size of a baseball. The timer ticked over for another minute, then two.

"Is that it?" I said.

"Wait," said Holland.

As the timer flicked to 8:45 the sphere grew in size and intensity, swelling to the size of a basketball. It started to cycle through the colours of the spectrum, shimmering and glistening, at times looking transparent and watery, then crimson and fiery like a red giant sun. Over the course of the next two minutes or so it pulsed larger and larger, increasing in intensity and size, until I found it hard to look at the screen. Then, as suddenly as it had appeared, it was gone, vanishing into its own central point as if sucked down a plughole.

Holland looked more excited than a pre-schooler given a puppy for Christmas. He swivelled his chair so that he was facing another keyboard in front of the monitor with the whirling pattern. He deftly made a few keystrokes and the whirling stopped, and a column of numbers and symbols started scrolling down the side of the screen.

"This is the feed from the Chongqing detector. It was developed in China a decade or so ago, and refined and improved by a couple of ex-Harvard geniuses at NASA. There's one in orbit in the International Space Station, and we've got the other one."

"What does it detect?" I asked.

"Gravitational waves."

Hubert looked puzzled. "What are they?"

Holland was beaming. "Ripples in the curvature of space-time. Massless and very hard to detect because when they reach the earth they usually have small amplitude and an almost infinitesimally small volume. Detectors have to be extremely sensitive, and usually other sources of white noise overwhelm the signal."

"What produces them?" I was racking my brain to remember physics lessons. Twenty years and a lot of water under the bridge since then.

"Spinning objects in space," said Holland. "Binary black holes, rotating supernovae, revolving neutron stars, those kind of things. Gravitational waves carry energy away from them. Astronomy has been revolutionised by the finding of these waves. They're giving us incredible insights into the workings of the universe. New ways to observe and quantify the very early universe, which isn't possible with conventional astronomy."

"Save the lecture for another time Mike, and get to the point," interrupted Hubert, giving him a stony look.

Holland sat back. He pointed to the screen with the frozen whirling pattern and with a mouse click set the image running. "This is a two dimensional representation of the gravitational waves generated by that object. We're seeing the effect of a polarised wave on a ring of inert particles in the detector. These waves are travelling at the speed of light and oscillating roughly once every two seconds, with a wavelength of about five hundred thousand kilometres." He turned back and pointed to the picture of the rocky cavern floor, which now was missing a couple of spotlights but otherwise looked undisturbed. "By evaluating red shifting and blue shifting, and analysing the absorption, re-emission and refraction of the waves, we can say without doubt that these waves came from that sphere."

Hubert shook his head. "How can that be possible? There's no way there's a black hole or supernova in that cavern. Has to be a measurement error, doesn't it? You said yourself that you hadn't had time to calibrate the detector."

Holland raised his hands in surrender. "I know, but there it is. We've been cross checking the algorithms for the last couple of hours. The data are real. These are quantum fluctuations."

"Quantum fluctuations?" I said. "Fuck, Dr Holland, you'd make a shitty science teacher."

"Well you know what they say," he replied with a smirk. "'If you think you understand quantum theory, you don't understand quantum theory'." He leaned over and activated another monitor sitting directly above the one displaying the cavern floor. He turned to the technician again, "Jo, if you would be so kind… replay at one third speed please."

The technician's fingers flew over another keyboard and the screen lit up with an image of the sphere at almost its maximum size. It appeared as a hellish orange-red colour, it's surface rippling with auroral beauty. She started the clock running and we had to look away as the sphere changed to an incandescent pure white light before contracting and condensing into nothingness.

"Rewind, and stop at t-minus half a second before it starts to deflate," said Holland.

The image slowly reversed, and a white light appeared to grow out of nothingness, mushrooming into to a sphere almost the diameter of the cavern itself. The instant before it transitioned from white to blazing crimson there was a flicker of what appeared to be a watery, glass like refraction pattern.

"Stop there," he said, moving closer to stare at the picture.

I noticed that the other lab technicians in the room had stopped their activities and had gathered around to watch. On the screen was an obsidian globe, dotted with pinpricks of light and gaseous opacities.

"Are they... stars?" I said, leaning in.

Holland nodded energetically. "Stars, but not our stars. This is the exact co-ordinate in space that the anomaly is vectored towards. It's a galaxy millions of light years away, almost at the edge of the observable universe. By using the HUBBLE Space Telescope and vectoring the line of sight from the portal's opening with the sky directly above the crater, we've identified a cluster of optically dark point sources just outside the Milky Way's galactic plane. Nothing anywhere in the sky resembles this, and so initially we thought it was just a molecular cloud, or an unmapped stellar nursery filled with protostars." There was a tinge of awe in his voice now, and you could have heard a pin drop. "We've complete databases of the night sky around our planet because Hubble and other telescopes have been cataloguing these for decades. I asked the mainframe to identify the systems and constellations you can see here, and they came up blank. Those aren't our stars."

"Not our stars," I repeated.

Hubert sat back. "Could this be an Einstein-Rosen bridge? A wormhole?"

"Yes, I believe so."

There was a knock on the door and one of the agents opened it bringing in a welcome, warm dusty breeze. I could make out the sound of a helicopter, approaching fast.

The agent addressed Holland. "She's here, sir."

Holland nodded. "Excellent, I'll be out in a sec."

Hubert arched his eyebrows. "Expecting guests, are we?"

"I didn't have time to tell you sir, but you're going to want to meet her. I really had to twist her arm to come here you know."

I looked at them both, head moving back and forwards like at a tennis match. "Who's coming?"

"Someone who might just have the answers we need," said Holland with a big, shit-eating grin.

CHAPTER TWENTY-ONE
Nevada Test Site

I watched from the edge of the security fence as two soldiers helped an elderly woman, wrapped in a tan shawl to protect her from the dust storm, down from the Black Hawk. They gently supported her arms and walked her over to the Humvee, where Mike Holland was holding open the door. I suppressed a laugh as she irritatedly pushed them away and made her way up the hill to our office, Holland in tow. The occasional strand of once golden hair was still visible through the lifeless grey mane that limply framed her ageing face. She regarded me with piercing clear blue-grey eyes deeply set into a leathery face sculptured by wrinkles and painted with age spots. I held out a hand, which she took and gave a firm no-nonsense shake.

"Professor Cohen, nice to meet you," I said.

"Retired Professor," she shot back, adding, "and very happily retired. The knock on the door at two in the morning brought back unpleasant memories."

Holland had caught up and leaned in. "I'm sorry Professor, but I hope it was impressed upon you the urgency and seriousness of this situation?"

She snorted derisively. "You lot like your secrecy, don't you. No, the exact nature of why I was kicked out of my very comfortable bed, whisked to a private airfield, and flown here, wherever here is …"

"Nevada," I said, smiling.

"Nevada, then. Well, it was not explained to my satisfaction, no."

We headed up the path towards one of the larger trailers, allowing Cohen to dictate the pace. She was surprisingly fast; I was expecting a wonky gait due to arthritic joints and failing eyesight but she was as quick a mountain goat up the hill. As we approached, Holland ran around her and opened the door, beaming like a school kid eager to please. I followed a few steps behind and watched her as she strode in, head held high, and took in her surroundings. There was a conference table in the centre of the room, with a multi-view television monitor on the wall behind flashing various news reports, tactical maps and a CCTV picture of the inside of the crater. Hubert was sitting at the table with a dozen or so other men and women.

"Professor Cohen," he said, standing up and gesturing to the empty chair next to him. "Thank you for coming. Please sit down. I'm William Hubert. You've met my colleague, Dr Morgan, and obviously you know Dr Holland."

Cohen nodded, a quick bird-like gesture.

"We're from the FBI," Hubert continued, "specifically the Science and Technology Branch."

She said nothing and looked around the room at the others around the table. Hubert smiled and made the introductions. "Mike Holland is our senior scientist and over there is his number two, Sonya Davis. Sitting next to her are Diane Lynch and Michael Sandoval, both from NASA. Everyone, this is Lauren Cohen, recently retired Emeritus Professor of Theoretical Physics at UCLA."

I pulled out the chair next to Hubert, and Cohen sat, drawing the shawl tight around her shoulders. She coughed a phlegmy cough.

"Alright, so we know who everyone is now. What's going on and why am I here?"

Hubert laughed, "Straight to the point, I've heard that about you." He hesitated, "Is it okay that I call you Lauren?"

Cohen was in the process of balancing her spectacles on her bony nose. "It's my name, isn't it?" she replied, somewhat haughtily. "Why don't we dispense with the pleasantries and get on with this? I see we're in Nevada, and I certainly know this particular location, although it's been a few years - no, decades - since I was last here."

Hubert nodded, looking across the table at Holland who was tapping out notes on a tablet computer. "Okay, let's get to it. Dr Holland, please proceed."

Holland pointed at one of the monitors where a black and white photograph of a young woman, wearing a white lab coat, goggles on her head, clipboard in hand, was looking directly at the photographer. Behind her was a computer the size and shape of an upturned mattress, and a half dozen or so scientists standing and posing for the photograph. I squinted up at the picture, which was grainy and low-def.

Hubert pointed at the screen. "This is you, Lauren? From 1953, I believe."

"Yes, that's me," said Cohen. "So what? I worked on the atomic program, you all know that. I left soon afterwards to pursue an academic career. It's all in my file."

Hubert glanced over at Holland, who changed the picture to a series of columns and data. "Professor, you worked on all these tests. We've information on all of them, except this one."

STORAX/SEDAN:
*NTS/shaft/crater/1450ft/**Classified**/100Kt*

Cohen looked at the highlighted text. "Yes, I remember that one very well. Still classified is it?"

"What can you tell us about this test?" said Hubert.

She sat back in her chair, closing her eyes. "I'd like a cup of tea please. Darjeeling if possible."

Hubert flicked his head towards the agent standing by the door who promptly left the room. I looked at Holland who just shrugged. Cohen slowly opened her eyes, lizard-like.

"You need to understand the context here," she began. "We'd just come into possession of a hydrogen bomb. The ten-megaton detonation of 'Ivy Mike' in the Pacific the previous year was groundbreaking. Awe-inspiring. The government was pushing all sorts of money into developing these things, and so were the Soviets. It was the start of the arms race and well, there could be only one winner. Or so we thought."

"But this wasn't a hydrogen bomb was it? Not in Nevada." said Holland.

"No, of course not, stupid." Her voice took on the timbre of a schoolmistress and she looked at me with a prim smile. "You must understand, 'Ivy Mike' weighed eighty tons. Eighty tons! It produced a huge bang, sure, but it was a dirty explosion, and from a non-portable delivery system. It wasn't going to be feasible for limited warfare, and would not be a deterrent to a very mobile Soviet army occupying vast swathes of civilian-dense land over a Europe-wide battlefield."

I got it. "So why weren't you just developing better hydrogen bombs then? Why was the focus on atom bombs?"

"I'll tell you why. But first, you need to know the difference between an atom bomb and a hydrogen bomb. You do know that don't you?"

"I'm a medical doctor. Pretend I know nothing?"

She harrumphed. "Well in simple terms, atomic bombs derive their explosive power from fission of heavy unstable nuclei belonging to very exotic nuclear materials, such as isotopes of uranium and plutonium." She paused and looked at the faces of the people around the table, checking that she hadn't lost them. All seemed well, so she continued. "Hydrogen bombs on the other hand, are fusion devices. They're very complicated structures incorporating uranium shielding, plutonium, and fusion fuels such as liquid deuterium. But at the heart of any H-bomb there's a fission device used to start the process of fusion… a small A-bomb, by any other name. The weapons we were developing were boosted by a mixture of deuterium and tritium in their core, which actually undergoes a very small yield fusion reaction to produce enormous numbers of neutrons."

"So, okay then, an A-bomb kicks off a H-bomb," I said.

Cohen nodded and spread her hands expansively. "Yes, but in an uncontrolled fashion and producing enormous amounts of energy, enough to lay waste to entire continents. So our remit was to finesse the technology and produce smaller, portable atomic weapons with controllable payloads."

I narrowed my eyes. "So basically you just started scaling down the bombs to make them portable for the battlefield?"

Cohen shook her head, and tried to make the movement non-patronising. "No, other labs were working on that. We went in a different direction. We were evaluating newly discovered isotopes for the reactions. We discovered a novel and highly energetic reaction that released a phenomenal amount of neutrons, unprecedented at the time. We thought that if we could establish a way to confine this burst of neutrons there was the potential for a controlled release of a massive amount of clean energy."

She paused for effect and the room was silent, with all the scientists listening with rapt attention. "We figured out a way of controlling the amount of energy released by varying the amount of reaction going on in the core. Lindstrom called it a 'quad stage self-replicating fission-fusion hybrid'. It was unique, beautiful in concept, using highly reactive isotopes found at the far end of the periodic table."

Hubert nodded again to Holland, who brought up another photograph, this time of a group of scientists standing together behind a rectangular shaped device, the size of a large briefcase.

"Do you recognise any of these men, Lauren?"

"Of course. I'm retired, not senile. That's Lindstrom at the front, always the narcissist and hogging the limelight. He was the leader of our group. That's me on the far right. Stuck on the end, as usual. The fat one is Hershel Duggan, an experimental physicist from Harvard. The other is Eddy Fincher, a brilliant theoretical physicist from Los Alamos. Lindstrom took all the credit, but we did most of the grunt work at Los Alamos. We called our group 'Trinity Deus', you know, after the first nuclear detonation at Trinity, New Mexico in 1945."

She paused, lost in thought. The agent re-appeared with a cup of tea and placed it in front of Cohen who nodded her thanks. Hubert leaned forward in his chair, and tapped his fingers on the desk.

"Lauren, this is important. You need to tell us what went on that day. In 1953."

Cohen slowly opened her eyes. "I remember calling through to Lindstrom, on the red phone. I was about a mile away from the detonation site in a recording booth situated in a trench, protected from the blast, or at least so we thought. The dials started to register huge spikes of ground movement amplitude. We had cameras around the entry port shooting multiple angles and set back in concentric rings to catch everything. But what I saw made no sense. It was the opposite of an explosion - some form of implosion, maybe. Everything was being sucked down into what looked like a giant sinkhole. And I mean everything - rocks, soil, and all our equipment. I used some choice language over the phone, I can tell you. I told Gus to shut it down, shut the reaction down instantly before we were all sucked in. Thankfully he did, and the reaction stopped. The cameras showed the crater, but there was no sign of a nuclear explosion."

"So what happened then?" asked Hubert.

Cohen shrugged. "Gus fronted the cameras and reporters. Told them that this was a prototype of a radically different type of atomic weapon, and like all new designs and technologies they don't always go according to plan. Then he exited, stage left. The official line was that it was a dud. The detonation yielded only around a hundred kilotons of TNT, despite the fact that we had programmed it for five hundred. So much for the controlled regulation of the payload that Gus had spruiked to the press."

"But it wasn't a dud, was it?" I said, quietly.

Cohen sighed, and sat back in her chair. "Everything was shut down by the government. Gus left the Los Alamos laboratory soon afterwards, taking the research program with him to a private lab in LA. He was very disgruntled by the way the government and military mothballed and ceased to fund his research. They called the project a failure, and of course the stakes were so high, what with the Russians gaining ground rapidly with their own atomic program."

"Did you stay in contact with him after he left?"

Cohen smiled. "For a while. We got married, you know."

Hubert raised his eyebrows, and looked across the table at Stillman, who briefly shook her head in ignorance of this fact.

"Lauren, did you follow his work at all?" asked Holland. "I mean, were you part of his research team in LA?"

"No. Our marriage lasted only six months. I'd diversified my own career anyway, got more into education, lecturing, that sort of thing. We hardly saw each other. And he'd ruined things, of course."

"What do you mean?" asked Hubert.

"Well the bastard had gotten me pregnant."

A ripple of laughter went around the table.

Cohen smiled grimly, nodding. "We had a son, Corey. I brought him up on my own. Hard times."

Her expression became sorrowful, and tears welled up in her eyes. Holland reached over with a handkerchief, which she gratefully took.

I was deep in thought.

Corey Lindstrom.

The son.

"What happened to those records from the bomb tests?" I asked slowly.

Cohen looked me in the eye, and there was a kind of wistfulness to her stare. "When he died, I was sent all his log entries and diaries. We hadn't spoken for years, so I was really annoyed having to take delivery of what was mostly clutter and rubbish. After all, he hadn't published anything of note and had become quite the capitalist in his private practice. I kept a few notebooks from our Los Alamos days. Notebooks containing formulae, diagrams and so on. For old times sake, more than anything."

"Do you still have them?" asked Hubert, glancing across the table at me.

"No, I kept them locked in a case for decades, and when I had a spring-clean a couple of years ago, I gave them away. To Corey."

Hubert and I shared a look of resignation. He sat back in his chair.

"We've already confiscated the contents of Lindstrom's office and that panic room. We'll get those notebooks sent here, so that Holland and Lauren can look them over. Maybe we can catch a break."

"It's too late, isn't it?" I said, my eyes darting around the table. "Adam and the alien already have the formula."

"We don't know that," said Hubert. I noticed bags under his eyes, but they were still incredibly clear and focussed. "That's why we need Lauren to see what exactly was in those notebooks. Meantime, we'll head back to SETI first thing in the morning. General Baker is flying in and I've got to brief him and his staff before we leave."

There was general nodding and shuffling of papers around the table as people stood up to leave. Hubert waved a hand to me. "Kate, I'd like you to sit in on that meeting too."

I took a deep breath. "I guess so, but I really don't seem to be contributing that much."

Hubert shook his head. "On the contrary Kate, I believe that you're the most important person in this room."

He left me standing there and moved to join Cohen who was now engrossed in conversation with Holland and the other NASA scientists. I didn't seem to have a job to do, and hadn't been invited to hang around, despite being so important. I decided to take a walk, and pushed open the door of the office. The air was warm and musty with hints of petroleum, wood smoke and oil. I looked up into the darkening sky and to the south, just above the dune, I could see a swarm of small black dots with larger black dots hanging underneath.

Chinook Transport helicopters. Dozens of them.

DAY 5

CHAPTER TWENTY-TWO
Ground Zero, Nevada Test Site

My phone alarm buzzed quietly but insistently, bringing me out from what had been a disturbed sleep. I reached across from the bunk bed to the chair where my phone was vibrating and picked it up.

Four-thirty. In the morning.

There was no one else in the little office I had been allocated, just the bed, a couple of chairs and a small desk. I swung the blanket off and heaved my legs down, my feet jumping a little feeling the cold of the linoleum. Bright lights could be seen moving around outside the closed blinds, and I could hear (as I had all night) the distant sounds of earthmoving equipment, helicopters coming and going, and the shouting of soldiers getting and receiving orders.

There was a port-a-loo in the next room, and after I'd done a little pee I helped myself to a travel toothbrush and gave my mouth a thorough clean. I splashed cold water over my face and pulled my hair back into a ponytail using a couple of ties from my sweatshirt pocket. I wished there was a mirror, but then perhaps it was a good thing there wasn't. I doubted I'd like what I saw.

I pulled my sneakers back on and stepped outside. Further up the hill the crater was now illuminated by intense arc lighting and appeared almost unrecognisable from just yesterday. A metallic canopy the size of a tennis court was being delicately lowered by four industrial cranes, slotting onto buttresses made out of desert rock and concrete. Wire fences and military vehicles encircled the site like layers of an onion. Interspersed between the barriers were pieces of military equipment the size of large wheeled lawnmowers, adorned with aerials and weaponry and hard-wired to generators set further back on the main campus.

I set off at a brisk climb, squeezing through partially erected security fences. Dozens of army vehicles were making their way up the single-track road toward a roped-off parking area on the northern aspect of the crater. Army troopers in full desert BDUs and FBI agents in flak jackets were milling around a large 18-wheeler unloading more pieces of mobile artillery. Four hulking battle tanks were stationed further down the slope, their guns and secondary armaments pointing down the hill towards the access roads. HUMVEEs sporting machine guns were off-roading at various locations around the site, moving soldiers and technicians between different emplacements and outbuildings.

I approached a low-set tan-coloured portable office and pressed the security pass I'd been given on the door pad. There was a flickering of LCD lights and it clicked open. I took a last look around the site and entered, closing the door behind me. The noise of the construction work and diesel engines muted significantly. Inside, the rest of the team were already in the makeshift conference room sitting around a long table, tablet computers open and tapping away. At the far end were four military personnel sitting upright and stiff in that way soldiers do, even when at ease. I recognised the drone pilot Major Powers, sitting next to Holland. Hubert was in conversation with an army officer, a trim figure the low side of sixty with a silver buzz cut and razor sharp cheekbones to match. He had crow's feet tan lines at the corner of his eyes, which were as grey as his hair. He seemed small and I absently wondered whether he'd met the height requirements as a young marine. But he was as muscular as any soldier I'd seen, and I guessed he'd be the soldier you prayed would be at your side when the fighting began, the soldier who would have your back, and who would fight when all was lost.

"Dr Morgan," said Hubert as I sat down next to him, "This is Lieutenant General Shane Baker. He's tasked with the security of the crater."

Baker actually ignored the introduction and started to scroll through his cell phone. I caught a glimpse of graphs of stocks and shares. I leaned in and said, "So you're in charge of this massive show of force being assembled here?"

He looked up and gave me a steely glare before resuming his browsing. "We've all got our orders, doctor."

I looked at Hubert as if to say 'what the fuck's his problem?' but Hubert's mouth just twitched and he shook his head. I suppressed a yawn and poured myself a glass of water as Holland stood up and edged along the table to stand in front of the big screen. He coughed into his fist for attention and leaned awkwardly on the backrest of a chair in the middle of the table. There was a sudden quietness in the room, and I felt a tingle in my spine and at the back of my neck.

"Good morning everyone and thank you for coming at this early hour," Holland began. He pointed to the biggest screen inlaid into the main display, and a technician changed the image to the picture I'd taken of Adam Benedict on the hospital gurney. "As you all know, this is an unparalleled moment in the history of our species. Humanity is no longer alone in the universe. This is not a human being. It is a facsimile of a man previously known as Adam Benedict. However, we believe the mind of Adam Benedict still inhabits this 'shell', along with the consciousness of an alien."

Baker was staring at the screen, an unreadable look on his face. Power was wide-eyed. There were muted mutterings and low voices around the room as people looked at each other in what I assumed was disbelief. Holland snapped a finger at a technician, and the screen changed to reveal a photograph of stars, in the centre of which were the hazy spiral arms of a galaxy. The technician moved some cursors around and the image zoomed in on a starless area in the middle of a torus of orange and yellow gas clouds. Holland waved a laser pointer at the centre of the void.

"This is from NASA's WISE space telescope. It's a false-colour mid-infrared image. Enhance, please. This is an optically dark point in space, an infrared bright galaxy that is seemingly bereft of stars. However, using computer algorithms designed to predict and detect the thermodynamic consequences of galactic-scale colonisation, we think this is what a massive cluster of Dyson spheres would look like."

Again with the rocket-scientist speak.

"Dyson spheres?" I asked, "like the vacuum cleaners?"

"Different Dyson," said Holland, sounding irritated that he had to explain things. "An idea from the '60s. A concept really, one which posits that an expanding, technologically advanced culture would ultimately be limited by access to energy and would be driven to harvest all the available light from their stars. Dismantling a planet or two in each solar system would give them the raw material to build star-enveloping sheets of solar energy collectors."

Hubert looked at him, ashen-faced. "How much more technologically advanced would such a culture be compared to our own?"

"There's a formula devised by Carl Sagan at NASA," said Holland. "He postulated that a civilisation capable of building a Dyson sphere would be approximately one thousand years more advanced than us. To build enough spheres to encase most of the galaxy's stars - well, that would take another millennium, or more." Holland took a deep breath. "Speculation, of course."

"But, that's what you think we're seeing?" I said, in a softer voice.

Holland nodded, his lips tight. There was a shuffling and murmuring around the table predominantly between the military contingents; the scientists had already been briefed by Holland and were less animated. He changed the picture and an image of a nuclear bomb test in the Nevada desert appeared, magnificent and frightening at the same time.

"This is a fifty megaton atomic weapon going off in the late 1950's just a few miles from here. It was part of a series of tests designed to produce small mobile atomic weapons from novel elements. The project, termed 'Trinity Deus', was canned after a disastrous failure that occurred right where we're standing. Disastrous, because it punched a hole in space-time and generated a wormhole. A tunnel through space-time. A tunnel connecting us to an alien galaxy at the furthest resolution of our most powerful telescopes. We're talking deep space and vast distances. Light takes millions of years to get there."

"So why haven't more aliens come through?" said Baker.

Holland smiled grimly. "The wormhole ain't tethered over there. I think it opens at completely random locations in their galaxy. They've no way of knowing where it's going to be."

I raised a hand. "So here, the wormhole appears for a few minutes each day as the Earth turns."

"That's correct."

"Trinity's legacy," I murmured. "Welcome to Earth."

Holland and Baker looked at me with annoyance. Holland puffed up his chest and affected a look of confidence, which I was sure he didn't feel.

"We've obtained the exact design and components of the nuclear device and my team are analysing it as we speak. The plan is to reverse-engineer the formula, and then, close the wormhole in this galaxy. End of problem."

He put down the laser pointer, leaned back against the wall, looked at me and gave an oily smirk. My hackles started to rise. "Well you'd better get started then," I said. "You're on the clock."

He shot me a thundery glance and looked around the room. "Dr Morgan here, is certain that the alien is already in possession of these data. She believes it'll try to transmit the formula to the other galaxy via the SETI transmitter thus enabling the other aliens to stabilise the wormhole and forge a permanent connection between our galaxies." He curled his lips and threw the laser pointer on the table. "I've told Dr Morgan that there's no way any signal from SETI could reach their galaxy. Not in a million years."

Baker held up a hand. "Seems pretty straightforward to me. We need to close down the wormhole, or destroy it."

I glanced at them both, incredulous. "Shouldn't you be figuring out how to communicate with Adam Benedict, and the alien inside his head? I mean, shouldn't that be the priority?"

Holland gave a little laugh, and asked the technician to change the picture again. The CT scans of Adam Benedict appeared.

"Adam Benedict? He's just a machine. All machines can be turned off. Shorted out. Unplugged."

I was pissed, so I stood up and grabbed the laser pointer from the table in front of him. I strode up to the screen and pointed it at the silhouette of Adam's body.

"This 'machine' has been shot at point blank range by a shotgun with little or no obvious damage. It can move very fast and is far stronger than it looks." I directed the red dot at the edges of the body outline. "There's a thin integument here which looks skin-like on the surface, but isn't. It's some form of artificial covering to make it look human. This covering heals itself - or maybe 'repairs' itself is a better description. Underneath this outer layer is a carapace or shell, which looks to be about half an inch thick and transparent to x-rays. The whole body weighs less than ninety pounds."

Baker looked up from his phone. "I'm no engineer, doctor, but this thing doesn't sound very robust at all. Shouldn't be difficult to put down."

I used the laser pointer to highlight the prickly-looking sphere in the chest cavity. "Maybe this has something to do with it. If only we knew what it was. And that other structure in the head area - my working theory is that the mind of Adam Benedict, and that of the alien, is housed in that structure. The sphere in the chest seems to be linked to everything else, so I think that's some sort of power source. But I could be wrong, guilty of anthropomorphic error, because on the outside it looks human-shaped. But then, so do you Dr Holland."

I put down the laser pointer and sat back in my seat, biting my lip. I tried to slow my breathing, and regain some control before I said something I might regret.

Holland was again on his feet and started pacing in front of the screen. "Human-shaped, but not human. Not anymore. We need to de-humanise this creature."

"You couldn't be more wrong." I said. "Adam – the human being inside this machine - I don't think we've seen the full extent of what he can do. I heard the alien talking to him, telling him that there were 'no limits'. That should worry us. I've seen him control electronic devices. He can access the energy-carrying waves of the electromagnetic spectrum. When I was linked to his mind, I could 'see' across the whole range of the EM spectrum - from infrared through visible light but also ultraviolet, x-rays and possibly even gamma rays."

The room was quiet, and even Baker had put down his phone and was looking at me. Holland had stopped pacing and looked flushed. Hubert had his hands steepled again. I appraised them all, fixing each and every one with a stare before moving on.

"Whatever you're planning to do, know this - he can get inside your head and read your thoughts. What you're calling a machine can project Adam Benedict's thoughts and those of the alien to us. We're dealing with a telepathic entity."

"Sounds like mind control," Baker laughed suddenly. "Like one of those 'B' movies from the 50's."

I gave him a dispassionate stare. "General, you might want to think about what I'm saying here. I've had him inside my head. He gets inside yours – you won't be laughing."

Baker snorted and returned to his cell phone. Hubert stood up and put a hand on my shoulder, gradually guiding me back into my seat. He picked up the laser, and flicked the monitor over to another image. I recognised the burning husk of an F-16 being hosed down by a couple of fire trucks and in the background was the Jet Ranger I'd been flying in.

"Dr Morgan's right," he said, addressing the room. "Adam Benedict brought down two fighter jets by taking control of their electronic systems at a distance of a mile or more. He made two sidewinder missiles explode by remotely arming their proximity fuses as they were approaching at supersonic velocity."

One of the scientists, a young man with a blonde wispy goatee and an eyebrow piercing put up a hand. "So there's a human in there. This Adam Benedict person. Why aren't we trying to communicate with him? And with the alien?"

Baker straightened his shoulders, and his lips curled downwards. "Seems to me we have a duty of self-protection first and foremost."

Holland nodded vigorously. "Indeed. Also, I don't understand how we can even communicate with them? They're alien, after all, evolving in a completely different way to us. We need a linguistics specialist brought in."

"They understand us perfectly well," I said. "It took them a matter of seconds to decode our neural pathways and learn our speech, our ways of thinking. We need to understand their behaviour. Their intentions. We need to change their perceptions of us."

Goatee became animated. "You said that Adam repeatedly stated 'you are all in danger'? They can't just want to wipe us out, just like that? Surely, with all that evolution comes a higher morality?"

"Same way you take into account the rights and feelings of ants when you wipe out a nest in your back yard?" I said.

"Finally something we agree about, doctor," said Baker. "We're now the ants. But even ants can overwhelm and defeat a much more powerful insect by sheer weight of numbers and co-operation. We need to put in place pro-active strategies and some offensive options." He looked across the table, "Major Powers, show these nice folks what we've been doing while they've been sleeping."

I looked across at the young Major who nervously stood up and pulled out a clipboard. It looked incongruous in the room of tablet computers and high definition screens. He consulted his notes and cleared his throat.

"The MAARS platform has been modified to be as impregnable to electronic incursion or sabotage as we can make it. Buffered with counter-jamming active EMR, it should be able to withstand any attempt to override its control functions. The same way Lindstrom's panic room seemed to work, for a time at least."

"Could you just explain for the rest of us non-military types what the MAARS is?" I asked, somewhat testily.

"Modular Advanced Armed Robotic System," said Powers. "The most advanced mobile weapons platform we have. It's fully loaded with sensors, and is armed with an M240B machine gun and four M203 grenade launcher tubes on a 360-degree rotating turret. It carries 450 rounds of machine gun ammo and four grenade rounds. We've situated ten of these around the site, driven wirelessly by offsite controllers."

I frowned. "What's to stop him just knocking out the controllers then?"

"Distance," said Baker, smugly. "They're a hundred miles away at Creech, way outside his range of influence."

"So if we can jam his ability to shut the MAARS down," continued Powers, "we can unload a lot of ordinance at him. In addition, we'll have a couple of Predators above the theatre of operations armed with non-smart munitions."

I looked at Hubert, horrified, but he stood up and did that shuffling of papers that newsreaders do at the end of their bulletin. "Well, let's hope it doesn't come to that. The next predicted opening of the wormhole is in four and a half hours. Let's get to work."

Baker and Powers nodded assent and there was a general scraping of chairs as people stood and made their way to the doors. Holland moved to the rear of the room, and out of the corner of my eye I saw him wave to the Goatee who wandered over, a puzzled look on his face. Holland put an arm around his shoulders and steered him over to a console.

I had a funny feeling, and started to walk over to them but then Hubert stepped right in front of me.

"You're correct of course," he said, "about needing to talk with the alien. Although all the information we've gathered to date suggests hostility, we haven't attempted direct communication."

I thought about that. "You know, Adam always suppressed the alien when he could. He never let me talk with it. Said it was to protect me."

Hubert looked grim. "I wish we could get into his head."

I was about to reply but then saw that Holland and Goatee were leaving together, heads down and deep in conversation. Holland was still guiding him with an arm around his shoulder.

"Kate," said Hubert, interrupting my reverie, "we'll leave for SETI in about sixty minutes. Be ready."

I nodded.

Then I took off after Holland.

CHAPTER TWENTY-THREE
Ground Zero, Nevada Test Site

Holland and Goatee hadn't gone far.

As I exited the building I saw Holland slide his passkey onto the lock of the adjacent office, which I remembered was the air-conditioned lab with all the computers and monitors. I wondered whether I should sneak a look through the window first, but they were all blacked out. There was no guard on the door and I remembered that I now had a pass, and access to all areas, being a 'civilian consultant' or something. I sidled up to the door and looked around. No one was taking any notice of me; the soldiers and FBI agents were continuing to shore up the fences and barriers and reinforcing the armaments around the site. I took the lanyard from my neck and pressed the card against the door. The light turned from red to green and there was a quiet click as it unlocked. I took a deep breath, pushed the door open and slipped inside. The room was as noisy as I remembered from the hum of generators and computer fans. It was dark, lit only by a strip of sunlight coming through the window blind and the twinkling light from the monitors and electronic switches. Once again my nose was assailed with ozone and my breath started to frost over.

The only occupants of the room, as far as I could see, were Holland and the Goatee, huddled together in front of a bank of video screens showing computer-generated graphs and digitalised representations of the wormhole when it had last opened. On the biggest screen was a blown up and enhanced image paused at the moment the sphere of light had contracted and the stars became visible. There was a coffee maker on the table next to them just out of their peripheral vision, and I edged over so that I could make out their conversation. Goatee was pointing at the screen and shaking his head.

"So, your theory is that while this is a kind of wormhole, the mechanism is some form of quantum teleportation?"

Holland nodded vigorously and put his pen behind his ear. "Has to be. That's the only explanation from these data."

Goatee sat back from the screen, rubbing his eyes. The chronometer read 07:05AM. He pushed back from the table, stood up and yawned. "In your scenario, physical objects aren't actually transferred between here and that other galaxy, but data or information are?"

"Yes, what we call 'quantum objects'. Transferred from one location to another, again without physically moving."

They still hadn't registered my presence, so I decided to noisily grab a cup and pour myself some stewed coffee from the pot. They both jumped, looking like naughty schoolboys.

I smiled at their discomfiture. "Very interesting, but how do you explain the fact that Adam Benedict did actually go through? I mean, he was taken in and came back, physically changed."

Holland was trying not to act annoyed at my intrusion, and peered at my lanyard as if to check I had appropriate clearance to be there. "You following us, Dr Morgan?"

"Absolutely," I replied. "But please, continue. We're all on the same side, aren't we?" I sat on the edge of the table, and crossed my legs. Goatee looked me up and down, but quickly averted his vision when I caught him doing it.

Holland sat back in his chair and folded his arms. "Well, Adam Benedict wasn't actually seen to go through the wormhole, was he Dr Morgan? I mean, according to the only eyewitness, Gabriel Connor, Adam was there one second, gone the next. We don't really know exactly what happened. The mechanism of passage to another galaxy is unknown."

I pursed my lips. "But what came back wasn't Adam any more - it was some kind of machine, right? So there's your evidence of an actual physical journey."

"Can't argue with that," said Goatee.

Holland's eyes were unsettlingly wide and he looked to be sweating despite the chill of the room. A film of moisture coated his upper lip and his armpits looked dark and damp.

"Adam's a good man," I continued. "He didn't ask for this. It wasn't exactly his choice to be humanity's 'representative'."

"Maybe not," said Holland. "But doesn't it worry you that he's got the alien's ear? I mean, he's not a scientist nor is he a diplomat, and he's certainly not trained in first contact."

I wasn't sure how to respond to that, so I climbed off the table and went to look out of the window. It was clear that the military preparations and fixed fortifications had been augmented throughout the night. An army Chinook was banking away from the site, having deposited another two dozen or so soldiers and their equipment on the one open lip of the crater. The rest of the structure was enclosed by scaffolding and topped off by the canopy. Aluminium ladders leading down into the cavern floor were guarded by MPs. Goatee joined me at the window as I watched all the activity with a feeling of foreboding. I got the distinct impression he was feeling the same disquiet.

"This is all wrong," I said, not looking at him. "The answer to the most important question - 'are we alone in the universe?' - is out there, and we're going to try and kill it."

"I guess the Army and political priorities are different to those of NASA," said Goatee quietly.

I thought about the priorities of the Army. To follow orders and to win, protect America, at all costs. But these days, in the age of the Internet and open access, surely recruits came with pre-existing notions of fairness and honour? Maybe each new campaign had to be 'sold' to the men as a heroic act no matter the true goals. I couldn't decide whether this was going to be any different.

"You know, there's another way of looking at the Fermi paradox," said Holland, arms folded and leaning on the wall. I arched an eyebrow, wondered where he was going with this, and whether I gave a shit. "Go on?"

"Well, the reason there are no advanced civilisations —"

"— Er, we now know of two," interrupted Goatee, slurping on his coffee.

"One, actually," continued Holland, holding up a finger. "Because I'm not counting us. Compared to these aliens, we wouldn't be classified as 'advanced'."

"All right, there's only one we *know* of…" I said.

"Yes, so the question is, why, in a universe with billions of galaxies each containing billions of stars, are there no more?"

"And you know the answer, I suppose?"

"There's a theory which posits a bottleneck in evolution preventing civilisations achieving interstellar travel."

"What sort of bottleneck?"

"One in which the incremental process of evolution generates intelligent life which is not quite intelligent enough to avoid its own destruction."

I nodded thoughtfully. "So what you're saying is that the development of intelligent life is fairly common, but always self-destructs before becoming spacefaring and able to spread beyond its planet of origin?"

"Exactly." Holland smiled like a schoolteacher complementing a backward pupil. "Consider the staggering number of near-misses we've had with our nuclear arsenal - and I'm not even including the weapon which blew a hole in space-time outside this window. We've accidentally lost nuclear warheads. One actually fell into a backyard in South Carolina by mistake. And, remember the near miss in 1960 because of the moon?"

I blew out my cheeks as I recalled the details. The North American Aerospace Defence Command (NORAD) had mis-identified the rising moon over Norway in 1960, and announced an almost hundred per cent certainty of an incoming nuclear attack. A snap decision had to be made in minutes by grossly misinformed personnel controlling the most fearsome power possessed by humanity.

"We were lucky," I said. "Somebody saw sense before pressing the red button."

Holland looked at me with fresh interest. "Any nuclear strike in 'retaliation', and humanity's adventure on Earth would be over. Think about all the nuclear weapons in the world, where they are and who controls them. Dictators, demagogues, madmen. People in positions of power who believe in the metaphysics of martyrdom and the afterlife now have the means to achieve it for all of us. It only takes one mistake. One idiot with his finger on the button."

I felt depressed. Outside, the Army's weapons of destruction were being zealously and eagerly assembled. "You think this is our bottleneck," I murmured.

"Yes. I think all emergent civilisations reach this bottleneck, and with one exception - the alien race we're now aware of - all fail to get through it. What makes humanity any different?"

"But what if the appearance of aliens on Earth changes all that," said Goatee, animatedly. "First contact, and all…"

Holland pulled a handkerchief from his pocket to wipe his brow. "How we handle the appearance of aliens is going to determine whether we continue and advance into the stars, or whether Homo sapiens' existence on this little planet is going to cease after, what, a hundred and fifty thousand years at most? Hell, the dinosaurs with their little brains had dominion over this planet for about a hundred and fifty million years!"

I was about to point out that it was Homo sapiens' big brains that had gotten us into this trouble in the first place, but Holland suddenly put his hand on my arm. His eyes flicked back and forward between Goatee and me, and then he dropped his bombshell.

"Someone else has to go through the wormhole to make contact. Someone more qualified. Talk to them, before it's too late."

I tried to hide my astonishment. "What? You've got to be kidding me."

Holland was nodding vigorously. "Yes. It's the only way."

He grabbed a keyboard and his fingers were a blur, the monitor scrolling through text and numbers to produce a graph that looked like a waveform with the heading 'spin correlation of entangled electrons'. I leaned down and got into his face.

"You can't be serious. You're not actually going to do this, are you?"

He looked up briefly, but kept on tapping commands into the keyboard. "Why not? If we wait for the politicians to approve it, it'll be too late. As soon as Adam Benedict makes an appearance the military are going to get first dibs."

He pointed at the chronometer on the screen. "Right. We've got thirty minutes before it opens again. Let's go."

"Don't be stupid," said Goatee. "If it isn't a quantum teleport, then it has to be a traversable wormhole and you'll end up there, dead, in the middle of space."

Holland folded his arms. "We'll never find out by sitting here with our thumbs up our asses."

"Send a probe through," I suggested.

"Then what? How do we get it back?" He shut down the screen and stood up. "I'm going in. If you're not going to help me, get the fuck out of my way."

I shook my head. "This is crazy. You're going to die."

"Or worse, you'll fuck things up even more," said Goatee.

Holland's eyes had a manic glare now. "You know I'm right. We don't have time to fucking debate this. If we lose - poof!" He made an expansive hand gesture. "Endgame for all humanity!"

"You can't," I said. "You don't have the authority."

"I believe I'm in charge of this research facility."

"And I believe you answer to Director Hubert," I said, with a coolness I didn't feel. "Let's give him a call."

I walked over to a satellite phone sitting on one of the other desks and picked up the receiver. I started to dial but out of the corner of my eye I noticed that Holland was pointing at me.

"Put the phone down," I heard him say in a strange voice.

I looked up and saw the gun in his hand. It was shaking a bit, but pointed at my head from a distance of two yards. Goatee had backed off against the wall and looked terrified, raising both hands in the air. I slowly lowered the receiver onto the cradle and raised my hands as well. "I've had guns pointed at me before," I said. "You're not going to shoot me". This didn't sound convincing when it left my mouth, which had suddenly dried up.

Holland actually gave a sneer. "This is bigger than me and you. So yes, I will shoot you if you try and stop me."

"You're out of your fucking mind," said Goatee.

Holland's lip twitched. Not much, but enough to show that Goatee's dig had hit the mark. "I'm the only one here in their right mind. Sit down on that chair and put your arms behind your back."

Goatee shook his head and looked back and forwards between Holland and me. He took another step forward, and held out his hand. "Give me the gun, Mike."

"Don't be a hero," I said to Goatee, fighting to keep my voice even. "Do as he says."

Holland's tone hardened. "Yes, do as I say or –"

Goatee rushed Holland, pushing me out of the way. I tumbled backwards and into the desk, just managing to stay upright. There was grunting as they took handfuls of each other's clothing and attempted to wrestle each other to the ground. Then Holland released a handhold and started jabbing Goatee in the ribs. Goatee released both hands and grabbed Holland's hair, bringing his face down sharply onto his bent knee. Blood flowed from Holland's nose and he staggered backwards, still holding the gun. Goatee rushed him again and now they were fighting over the gun, each had a hand on it, the other gripping the other's hand in a manic dance. Holland tried to kick Goatee but he jumped backwards out of range, letting go of the gun hand. As Holland raised the gun Goatee charged him, head down like a bull.

"No!" I screamed.

The gun went off, it's retort loud in the confined space. Goatee jerked to the side and fell to his knees. He made a hissing sound and grasped at his stomach where there was a rapidly spreading patch of blood. I ran over and caught him just as his body crumpled to the ground and before his head hit the linoleum. His eyes were staring, fearful, his face contorted in agony. A muted groan came from his lips, which were already turning blue. I pressed my hand to his stomach, but no matter the pressure I applied the blood still gushed between my fingers and oozed under my hand. It spread onto his pants, the bright red quickly darkening, taking on a brownish hue.

"Leave him, there's no time," urged Holland behind me.

I looked over my shoulder and saw that he was backed up against he desktop, still pointing the gun at me. I shook my head. "You can't be serious. He's going to die. We need to get help."

Holland wiped his face with the back of his hand where there was a bit of spittle mixing with the blood from his nose. "It's too late for that. I need to get to the wormhole when it opens. The future of humanity is at stake."

I ignored him and turned back to Goatee, who was now unconscious and breathing shallowly. A trickle of blood appeared at the edge of his mouth. I took his pulse, which was thready and irregular. Unbidden, a vision of my daughter popped into my head. Grey and lifeless on a slab. My heart took a jerky beat and my eyes filled with tears.

The gun boomed again, and the linoleum exploded next to me, showering me in splinters of wood and plastic.

"I said leave him," shouted Holland. He grabbed my hood and pulled me to my feet, and then thrust the gun in my face. "I'm going through the wormhole. I need you to witness what I've done. Tell the world. The needs of the many outweigh the needs of the few." He nodded towards Goatee. "Or the one."

In the back of my mind I knew he had just quoted a Star Trek movie, that scene where Spock sacrifices himself for the crew of the Enterprise. This, after Holland had just shot and probably killed one of his colleagues. I realised he was completely unhinged. I nodded dumbly, my mind churning through all the possibilities to form just one idea. One action. But I had no idea what it was yet.

Clutching my arm and with the gun firmly but discreetly placed in the small of my back, he guided me up the hill to the edge of the crater. The two MPs guarding the access staircase asked for his pass, and after a cursory inspection waved him through. As site Chief Scientist he'd made sure that the cavern was off limits to all personnel in the hour or so prior to the predicted wormhole opening, and had set up cameras and monitoring devices around the walls. Everyone was in the laboratories and mobile offices readying their equipment to record it's next appearance. I squinted up into the morning sun and rubbed at the perspiration on my forehead as I took a sneaky look around the facility as we walked. There were embankments surrounding the crater, in concentric circles down the slope to the access road. Every ten yards or so there were gun emplacements, machine guns, and the MARRS remote weapon system manned by more soldiers that I could count. No one was looking in our direction, all eyes were focused outwards. We started down the staircase, our feet making metallic noises with each rung. As we descended, I saw he'd positioned the CCTV cameras so that we wouldn't be visible on the staircase. When we reached the bottom he pushed me towards one of the large rock piles scattered the cavern floor. We crouched down out of sight and I surreptitiously glanced at my watch. I reckoned we had about three minutes before the wormhole appeared again.

"It won't be long before he's discovered, and the alarm raised." I said, trying to make him understand. "There's still time. You can go back. Get help. Think about what you're doing."

He looked at me in an off-base kind of way. "I can see the bigger picture. Why can't you, of all people?"

"What's that supposed to mean," I said.

He waved the gun towards the centre of the cavern. "You've spoken with him. Heard the alien's voice. There's nothing more important than this, nothing. I've dedicated my life to Astrobiology, the study of extra-terrestrial life. This is the holy grail for me. The gold at the end of the rainbow."

"What are you going to say to them? Have you got your speech prepared?"

To my surprise he nodded eagerly. "Yes, I certainly have. I'm going to make them understand that when humanity finds out we've made contact with an advanced alien culture, all our petty squabbles will disappear. I'll make them understand that we know that our survival depends on all peoples coming together as one species - the human race. That finally, we'll grow up and reject ancient and divisive belief systems that've been the cause of conflicts throughout our history."

I remembered the few occasions I had made contact with the alien mind. The 'alien-ness' and feeling of superiority had been overwhelming. I didn't think they would care about what Holland said about humanity.

I was about to say exactly that, but he continued. "I'll present humanity as being at a crossroads, where we'll need to divest ourselves of millennia of irrationality and break out of the bottleneck to move forward as a new member of the interstellar family."

I shook my head. The interstellar family. He'd definitely been watching too much Star Trek. His eyes glazed over, and he seemed to be speaking to himself now.

"I can do a better job speaking for humanity than Adam Benedict - a grieving widower with no scientific background or training in first contact. Yes, the fate of humanity rests on my shoulders now."

"You're fucking deluded," I said. "They won't be interested. This is a suicide mission. And you might just make things worse, have you thought about that?"

He blinked a few times and wiped a drop of sweat from his eyes again. "Maybe. Maybe not. Maybe you should come with me?" The gun was back in my face. "Your testimony not only as a doctor but also as a female could help. Like on the Pioneer plaque, showing them that we have two sexes, you know?"

I did know, and recalled seeing this in a documentary. The plaque showed nude figures of a human male and female. The man holding a hand up in greeting. The woman just standing meekly by his side.

"What, you want us to strip off and go naked together into the wormhole?"

He gave me a glassy stare, and gripped my arm even tighter. "No, but you're definitely coming with me."

"No, I'm fucking not," I said.

He jabbed the gun harder into my rib cage and continued to stare into my eyes, sweat dripping down into his glasses. "Don't you see? This'll work better. Ambassadors for the human race. You and me!"

I was thinking about my options, which included a straight knee into his groin, but then a diffuse light began to permeate the cavern and sparkling patterns started to appear on the walls. I peeked out from behind the rock to see a basketball-sized orb materialising in mid-air pulsing silently through the colours of spectrum.

"It's here," Holland hissed excitedly.

I sat back against the rock, realising that it was too late, despair chugging through my veins like concrete. I watched the orb contract and then expand into a glassy sphere a yard or more in diameter. The hairs on the back of my neck started to tingle, and I felt the temperature drop noticeably. My breath started to mist, and I felt a pressure on my chest to the extent that I suddenly had to physically concentrate on the act of breathing.

Holland pulled himself to his feet and with a grunt, jerked me upright. "You … coming … with … me…" he gasped, with each word yanking my arm and pulling me closer to what was now a roiling ball of fire. I felt my head spinning and pressure mounting behind my eyeballs, and I saw that he'd lowered the gun. With a supreme effort I pulled my arm free from his grip and made a grab for it. He resisted and after a few wrestles the gun flew out of his hand and bounced behind the rock. I dropped to my knees and crawled towards it, each inch feeling like a mile, the air thick like treacle. Twisting painfully to look over my shoulder, I could see Holland was torn with indecision whether to try to grab me again or to head towards the sphere.

"Holland, forget it! Get behind the rock!" I yelled, the words being sucked from my lungs as if someone had put a vacuum cleaner down my throat. He grimaced and shook his head, lurching forward one faltering step at a time, until he dropped to his knees directly underneath the sphere. He stared directly into it, and flinched as it contracted and expanded, its surface becoming inflamed, watery and glistening.

Then I saw the stars.

A galaxy appeared, a cartwheel with an outer rim of young stars and a core that resembled a bulls-eye. Spiral arms extruded from a massive black hole at its centre. Nebulae could be seen, gigantic clouds of gas and dust where new stars are born and created.

Holland reached out and touched the bright rim of the globe. His fingers became elongated, like rubber being stretched, morphing into shapeless liquid-like tubes. Then everything exploded in a convulsion of matter and energy and the inflating sphere engulfed him and expanded towards me. I dived behind the rock, hoping that it was sanctuary. In the split-second before I lost consciousness, I saw people running down the staircase, covering their eyes, their mouths opening and closing in silent screams.

Then darkness fell.

CHAPTER TWENTY-FOUR
Through the Wormhole

Like in my dream, there was a perception of being switched on, as if my consciousness was coming back online. There was no sense of physicality, no pull of gravity, and none of my external senses seemed to function. But I could think, and abstractedly I remembered Adam's use of the philosophical proposition *cogito ergo sum* by Rene Descartes.

I think, therefore I am.

I considered the very fact that I was thinking, presumably meant that I was still alive, an actual living entity.

But was I, in fact, alive?

Adam had died coming through this portal. Had I died as well? Was this what he experienced? I looked around, and at first the blackness appeared flawless and absolute, but then the twinkling of stars became apparent, like pins being pushed through a backlit velvet cushion. Billions and billions of pinpricks of light appeared, and then gas clouds and nebulae. The torturous, tattered band of the Milky Way was absent and none of the constellations were familiar.

In front of me, my arms and my hands seemed to emerge from no-where. I willed them to move and they did, and they seemed normal, with veins and tendons and nails. I abstractedly noted that I was still wearing my sweatshirt. I went to clasp my hands together, but they disappeared into each other, like hologram images, ghost hands, insubstantial and transparent. I reached up to touch my face but again I could feel nothing.

Looking down, I saw a silvery sandy beach, with ripples of water from tidal currents. Ahead the waves crashed as if they had real power, white and foamy but they died in just a few yards, nowhere near me. My feet were buried into the sand up to my ankles, but surreally I could still see them under the surface. I scrunched my toes, waiting to feel the softness of the sand, the dampness from the retreating tide - but there was nothing…

My vision faded in and out, like a television losing reception.

Was I a ghost?

Hanging in the sky I saw a giant star, ten times the diameter of the sun. A blazing yellow incandescent globe, with what looked like an appendage oozing out from it being sucked into a smaller, white companion. Beyond, there was a moving rim of pure night, a curtain of darkness, relentlessly extinguishing billions of stars from my view.

What was happening?

Then a voice – Holland's voice - echoed around the inside of my head.

Where am I?

A milky cloud appeared in front of me, like a fog bank on a cold autumnal morning. It assumed the shape of a human being, wispy puffs of gas forming and elongating into arms and legs. I don't know how, but I knew it was Holland. I could hear his voice in my head again, and it was now definitely his voice. Distant, yet near. The wispy form was semi-solidifying, but remained insubstantial and seemed to be drifting on a slight breeze. I could just make out a head, moving and turning and looking around, and the shape of two eyes and a mouth. The head turned to face me, but it's gaze looked through me and beyond me. He didn't seem able to see me, or feel my presence.

I sensed Holland's incredulity and amazement as he gazed on the celestial event occurring above us. Then I was in his mind, listening to his thoughts and watching as his scientific brain was trying to process what we were seeing - the death of a binary star system. The primary yellow G-type star was having material pulled into a secondary white dwarf star due to the latter's greater gravity well. When the core of the white dwarf reached a critical density, the fusion of carbon and oxygen would be unconstrained and result in the ejection of matter and energy into interstellar space.

A supernova.

I figured that it would be happening soon. Just behind the stars, the rim of blackness inexorably rolled into view having passed behind them. I stared with awe at the feat of interstellar engineering that was taking place. The black sphere - or whatever was being constructed - was almost one light-hour in diameter, ten times the distance from our sun to the surface of the Earth. It was consuming the sky in front of the stars at an unimaginable rate.

As I turned to follow the celestial curtain, a huge gas giant planet with multiple rings dipping below the far off horizon appeared, it's flaring turquoise hues melting into the sky and ocean like a divine painting. I realised that I was on the giant's moon. There was a multi-coloured cone of reflected light tracking outwards along the water to the horizon, where it merged with the planet, it's atmosphere furrowed with undulating inky blue and black lines from clouds and violent weather systems. The shadow of it's flimsy rings cast dark bands across the surface, and another moon could be seen traversing just above the equator, a mottled green and black sphere a thousandth the size of the planet.

I was getting lost in the beauty of this alien vista when Holland's thoughts and emotions re-appeared. I experienced his transit through the wormhole, and to my horror, I could feel the moment his physical body had died. The pain that once burned like fire faded away to an icy numbness. Holland had been ripped apart by unimaginable gravitational forces and frozen in the absolute zero of space. I wondered whether he was now aware that he had no corporeal existence, and was a free-floating mind of interconnected thoughts and emotions.

But what was I?

Blackness encroached the edges of my vision again, and the only thing I could hear was my own heartbeat and my ragged, shallow breathing. Then came a palpable sense of dread. The perception of a dark and terrible presence surrounding me and drawing closer. Anxiety permeated my mind like water through a sponge, and I was unable to shake the urge to look around and behind. There was evil here, hiding. Like a snake in the grass, covered by leaves, watching and waiting.

I could sense multiple alien consciousnesses, and the feeling of being suffocated as if a rubber mask were placed over my nose and mouth. I felt the aliens drifting away, their thoughts becoming indistinct and distant. Holland's wraith-like form came into existence in front of me, but more transparent and glassy.

"Holland. Can you hear me?" I ventured, softly but there was no reply, no feeling that he was aware of me. I sensed confusion and puzzlement, and he was subconsciously starting to cower, to mentally crawl into himself.

An unpleasant and intimidating awareness started to pervade my mind and I felt the aliens approaching again. I shivered, as an ancient evil surrounded me and wrapped me in icy sheets. I thought I could hear a low rumble of laughter. A taunting sound, arrogant and disdainful.

I realised what Holland's journey through the wormhole and into the alien's galaxy had achieved. The magnitude of the miscalculation he'd made. A mistake that in his hubris may have condemned humanity to destruction.

The aliens had accessed his memories, and had acquired the data on the Trinity Deus nuclear device. Adam didn't need to send the Lindstrom files through via the SETI transmitter, if that had even been possible.

There was a flickering to my left, and I turned to look at the ocean. In the light of the setting giant I saw a figure slowly rise out of the water as if on an elevator platform. I recognised it as a copy of Adam Benedict. Its eyes were closed, and it was naked, dripping with moisture and unguent. Another identical figure started to break the surface a few yards away, followed by another and then another, until the ocean was obscured almost to the horizon, with hundreds of thousands of human figures.

The Adam Benedict/machines were now lifting into the sky, one by one, and accelerating steadily and silently until they were all out of sight. The ripples in the water faded and soon there was no evidence that they'd ever been there. The sky was darkening and the rapidly approaching star-encompassing barrier, now occupying half the sky, was heading towards the gas giant. I put my hand up automatically to shield it from the light of the sun but it was even more transparent, glasslike and fading as I watched it. My thoughts were also becoming evanescent, and my vision was growing dimmer.

I heard Holland again, talking animatedly at the alien.

What about me?

His ghostly figure became less human-shaped and started to fragment. I could feel his pain, his despair. His horror and the terrifying realisation that he was going to die alone millions of light years from Earth.

I tried to reach out to him, to let him know I was there, that even at the end he wasn't alone and that I was here too. Another human being. But then, like a light bulb being extinguished, there was sudden and absolute blackness.

The pain began. A constricting band of pressure around my temples, which worsened as I opened my eyes. I was lying prone on a rock floor. Above me some fifty yards or so was the edge of the opening of the crater and a glimpse of a cobalt blue cloudless sky. Shafts of light played on the opposite rock wall, which was festooned with metal carabineers and pitons, a couple of ropes and a cavern ladder testament to Adam's and Gabriel's recent descent. Dust motes lazily and haphazardly floated on light beams, making their way down to the cavern floor.

I winced, and brought myself up onto my elbows, and when that seemed fairly easy, proceeded to sit up. Gingerly, I felt for any lumps on the back of my head, and then along my arms and legs, breathing a sigh of relief as nothing appeared to be broken or obviously damaged. I twisted my spine from side to side, and when I'd ascertained that this movement didn't produce any significant additional pain, I struggled to my feet. My vision blurred for a second and the cavern seemed to spin, causing me to reach out for a non-existent wall. I shook my head to clear it, which produced another surge of pain through my eyeballs, making me squeeze my eyelids closed and grasp my head in both hands.

There was no sign of the wormhole. The ladders tracking down the walls were twisted but intact, and I could see a few people pulling themselves up from where they had fallen onto the floor of the cavern, helping each other to stand. The lights and cameras and recording equipment were strewn around the floor, scattered like toys in a nursery, broken and eviscerated pieces of plastic and metal.

I saw Hubert limping towards me from one of the staircases. His hair was covered in dust and there was blood coming out of an ear. A bruise was starting to appear on his cheek.

"Kate? Are you OK?"

"I think so." Amazingly, I was.

"Unbelievable, wasn't it," he exclaimed. "Holland got sucked up into that thing like dust up a vacuum cleaner. You were lucky you didn't get dragged in as well."

I shook my head and got another surge of pain. "I did get dragged in. I was there. At the other end."

Hubert's eyebrows furrowed and he looked at me strangely. "Kate, you didn't go anywhere. You were just lying behind the rock. It looked to me like you blacked out."

"But I saw everything." I said.

"I don't see how," he said. "The edge of that thing seemed to stop right above you. I could see you all the time."

CHAPTER TWENTY-FIVE
Airborne

I stripped down and stepped into the narrow cubicle, turned the water on high and let it beat over my head in hot, steamy rivulets. I closed my eyes letting the heat soak into my skin as my legs threatened to buckle. I scrubbed lightly and was just starting to feel clean when the water supply shut off. My skin was tingling all over and I leaned back against the cool shower glass, staring at my reflection in the mirror. There were cuts and purple-yellow bruises all over my chest and arms, and bags under my eyes, but otherwise I looked not too bad for someone who'd travelled god knows how many light years to the other side of the universe and back.

The towel was thick and perfumed and I wrapped myself in it and slumped on the floor of the shower. There was a residual drip-drip of water from the faucet, and the soporific low hum of the Gulfstream's engines. I wanted to sleep, and wondered whether I could just drop off here and how long it would take Hubert or Stillman before they broke down the door to get me. I pulled myself to my feet and tried not to slip as I stepped out of the cubicle. There was a pile of clothes neatly arranged on the toilet seat, courtesy of Stillman. I pulled on sweatpants by Lululemon and a t-shirt and jogging top by Nike, followed by my own trainers. The clothes were a bit bright, and I thought they were some of Stillman's own, but they fit and looked good, certainly better than the jeans and sweatshirt I'd been living in.

I was in the process of tying my wet hair up, when there was a knock on the door and without waiting for a reply, Stillman poked her head round. She looked me up and down, nodding approval.

"Not bad, you look better in those than me," she said with a smile.

I returned the smile. "I don't think so, but thanks. I feel a bit more human now."

She stole a look behind her, back into the corridor of the jet. "Ready for your debrief?"

I sighed. No sleep then, not even a power nap. I followed her through to the main cabin, where Hubert and the two NASA scientists I recognised from the Golf Club were sitting. Hubert was looking at me concernedly, whereas the scientists were focussed on their laptops. He waved me into one of the leather recliners, where there was a drink waiting. I sank into the chair and lifted the glass to my nose. Kraken. I nodded approvingly at Hubert.

"How you feeling?" he asked, his eyes kind.

I took a sip of the Kraken, letting the rum trickle down my throat. I closed my eyes and took a deep breath, letting it out slowly, seeing if it would relax me. It didn't. "To be honest, not sure," I said. "Not everyday you travel through a wormhole and back."

One of the scientists looked up sharply. He was a thin, young African-American with an Afro straight out of Shaft. His fingers were still flying over his keyboard as he shook his head and gave me a strange look. "No, you definitely didn't go through," he said.

I looked at Hubert, who gave a little shrug as if to say, 'told you'. Stillman came back from the galley with a cup of something sweet smelling and hot. She sat down in the last recliner and swivelled to face me, saying nothing.

"I know what I saw," I said. "And what I heard."

The afro-sporting scientist stopped tapping on his keyboard and leaned forward. "Dr Morgan, we think you somehow got caught at the 'event horizon' of the wormhole. Rather than getting transported through like Dr Holland which would have led to your physical body being destroyed you were quantum teleported."

"Quantum teleported?"

Hubert leaned forwards. "Somehow, your mind but not your physical being was transmitted through the wormhole when it opened."

Stillman added, "Kate, you were never physically there, but it seems that you could experience what went on at the other end."

I thought about it. It kind of made sense. Neither Holland nor the aliens seemed to be aware of my presence. But I could see and hear everything they said. "How long was I unconscious?"

Hubert pursed his lips. "A minute, two max."

"That's not long enough," I said, shaking my head. "What I saw and experienced took much longer than that."

"Maybe the time-dilation effect?" interrupted the other scientist, a blonde Norwegian-looking woman wearing big bright red spectacles that offset her humourless affect. She glanced at Hubert. "She could have been there any length of time. We haven't been able to start processing the data from the recorders. Most were destroyed when the wormhole opened."

Hubert reached over and touched my knee. His voice was soft. "Kate, what happened to Mike Holland?"

I took another drink from the Kraken, and then stole a glance out of the window at the clear blue sky and clouds hurtling past. It all seemed so surreal again. "He's dead," I began. "Like Adam, he didn't survive the passage through the wormhole. His mind did though. He was trying to communicate with the aliens."

"You saw them?" asked Afro.

"No, but I sensed many of them. Their minds were so different... cold, dispassionate, arrogant ... alien minds." I closed my eyes again. "Holland wanted to tell them how wonderful humanity was, how we were worth saving. They weren't interested."

"What was their world like?" asked Stillman.

"I don't think we were on their world," I said.

I told them about the moon, the gas giant in the sky, the incredible feats of astro-engineering that I saw including the syphoning of energy from a star, and the construction of what I now assumed was a Dyson sphere around it. "This was just another sun, just another planet, being harvested for energy to them," I said. "The fact that the wormhole opened there was probably by chance. And yet…"

I stopped, and looked around the cabin, seeing that all eyes were on me. I thought again about what I had seen. The planet was not random at all. The machine hosts were being made there. Statistically, what were the chances of the portal opening there as well? I described what I had seen, the hundreds of thousands of Adam Benedict-shaped machines that had been manufactured by the aliens.

"Why do they need these machine bodies?" asked the Norwegian.

Hubert scratched his emergent beard. "Perhaps an organic physical structure isn't robust enough to travel through the wormhole? I mean, they sent Adam's consciousness and one of their own back in a machine, so that makes sense doesn't it?"

Stillman puckered her lips, "Do the aliens know Adam survived the return journey?"

"They know everything," I bit out, acid in my mouth. "They were able to access all Holland's thoughts. Everything he knows, they know."

Hubert looked back, aghast. "The Lindstrom formula."

I said nothing, my silence giving him his answer.

Stillman looked despondent. "Then we're royally fucked," she said.

"They're coming," I said. I downed the rest of my Kraken in one and looked out of the window again, watched us fly through a contrail. There was a little buffeting before the smooth air resumed.

Hubert made a show of looking at his watch. "We've got twenty hours or so before the wormhole opens again. We'll just have to put our efforts into protecting the crater site. Secure it with all our available forces."

I shook my head. "We've got no chance. A single machine host is one thing, but thousands coming through?"

Hubert's eyes narrowed. "I think we need to find Adam. Talk with him. Kate, you said that he thought he could prevent this?"

Stillman interrupted. "But won't Adam already know about Holland meeting the aliens? And therefore about the upcoming invasion?"

I didn't think so, but I wasn't sure. "I got no sense that they were in communication with Adam." I said. "So as far as the alien in his head knows, it'll still be looking to transmit the formula back home."

Stillman frowned. "I'm worried about Adam's state of mind, and the control that the alien has over him. If he's even survived the helicopter crash. We've heard nothing about his whereabouts, no sightings. What's he been doing? And why hasn't he gone to the crater? Or SETI?"

Afro nodded vigorously. "Exactly. He doesn't know that they've already gotten the formula, right? Shouldn't we still assume his plan would be to use the transmitter at SETI?"

I shrugged. "We've really no way to be sure. The emotions I'd felt from the alien were raw, uncultured and unhindered by morality. I got the impression that it was on a steep learning curve, and its excitement at the violence it had perpetrated was palpable. The pleasure and anticipation I'd sensed when it was telling Adam what the machine host was capable of doing was almost childlike. Maybe he's away somewhere, rebooting, enhancing, learning, whatever..." my voice tailed off.

I was exhausted, confused, and so far out of my comfort zone that I couldn't see it in my rear view mirror. Clear thinking was needed, and in my experience most of my sensible decisions were made when I was calm and happy. The erratic things I'd done, my life's fuck-ups and mistakes, were all driven by impulses when I was fearful and anxious.

Like now.

I had vowed never again to make choices that matter when I was out of control.

So much for that.

I closed my eyes and thought about Adam. What did I really feel about him? Was there really a 'him' any more? I supposed so... weren't we all ultimately our thoughts and feelings, our personalities, our consciousness - not our physical bodies? Isn't a quadriplegic still human if he or she can think and love and cry and experience life?

"Well, we're nearly there," said Hubert quietly. "There've been no reports of any unusual activity, so maybe we're ahead of the game."

I took a large swallow of the Kraken, and said nothing.

CHAPTER TWENTY-SIX
SETI Institute, Mountain View, CA

It was getting dark by the time we completed our breakneck drive in a convoy of blacked-out FBI vehicles from the small airport at Clear Mountain to the main gateway at SETI. We were waved through a gate that had been reinforced by barriers of concrete and fences of barbed wire manned by dozens of armour-clad FBI and US Army personnel. After a walking tour of the defences, we made our way through the fire stairs to the highest level of the main building and opened an access door to the roof. Hubert and I were handed UV-capable binoculars and we shuffled close to the edge of the roof and got down on our stomachs to survey the scene below.

There was an elevated knoll two hundred yards northeast of the ring of armour and police lines encompassing the main campus. The night vision glasses picked out SWAT teams with snipers strategically deployed in trees and on top of buildings. There were hastily built riot control fences manned by regular police officers with body armour and helmets. Dozens of FBI agents were positioned at each corner of the main building, accompanied by Army HUMVEEs with machine guns. Two FBI helicopters were visible behind another block of low set outbuildings, rotors spinning lazily but crouched and ready to leap into the air. On the main north-south drag leading in I could make out a road block with six or seven black and whites lined up, lights flashing, turning back traffic in a big loop across the six lane highway. I could see another helicopter approaching, searchlight sweeping metronomically left and right, police officers carrying rifles hanging out the windows.

My muscles gave an involuntary shiver despite the warm, balmy conditions. There was no wind, and the gentle thrum of the rotor blades in the background was the only thing I could hear. The trees looked like burnt, ominous versions of their daytime selves, and Hubert's face was aglow with the flickering orange and whites of the searchlight beams. In the far distance, the silhouette of the L.A. skyline pierced through the night canvas like a jagged ridge of concrete mountains. Millions of lights caused the dense mass of skyscrapers to glitter, and car taillights resembled blood cells flowing through the veins of the city. Despite the time, the hustle and bustle never came to a halt. I envied the city's residents, heading off for a movie or to chill out in a smoky jazz bar downtown.

I heard footsteps and Stillman joined us on the ledge dressed in her FBI vest and wearing a helmet. She crouched next to us and pulled out her firearm, checking the load.

"We don't know if he's coming here," she said without looking up. "What if he's somehow received a message already telling him just to sit tight and wait for his friends to come through?"

I felt my stomach tighten into a knot as I resumed my scan of the woods and trees around the main campus. The woods were simply too dark to see much at all, and the flickering searchlight beams merely increased the contrast. Black tree trunks against an almost black backdrop don't make for much to see and my imagination began to supply shapes and figures to fill the void.

Then Hubert took a deep intake of breath.

"Shit, I think he's here," he whispered, peering through his binoculars and pointing a finger towards the knoll just at the side of the denser tree line.

I brought my glasses up and looked to where he was indicating. As they focussed, I saw movement, a figure disappearing behind a tree, just as a searchlight swept over the spot where it'd been standing. I felt my jaw drop and my heart started thudding in my chest like a trip hammer. The tree, now fully illuminated by searchlights, started to sway with the downdraft from the approaching helicopters.

Hubert grabbed a walkie-talkie and started frantically yelling instructions into it. Stillman had her gun up and was pointing it at the knoll, seemingly oblivious to the distance involved.

I closed my eyes and concentrated. "Adam," I said softly, so no one around could hear. "It's Kate. Can you hear me?"

Instantly I felt a tickle behind my eyes, and the feeling you get when the hairs on the back of your neck stand up straight. I'd caught his attention. "I know you can hear me," I said, this time without speaking aloud. "Where've you been? Talk to me."

I waited, but while the feeling of insects crawling around my head continued, there was no response. Then, an explosion of sensory input suddenly overwhelmed me as I gained access to his thoughts. I rolled over onto my back clutching my head, and was vaguely aware of Hubert and Stillman's hands grabbing me. I could see their concerned faces, saw their mouths moving, but their voices were obscured by a shrieking white noise.

I was inside his head. Electronic and neurological pathways were being activated and overstimulated, all beyond Adam's control. He was a passenger, a driver in a race car careening towards a barrier with no steering or brakes. I could feel him concentrating hard, trying to attain a degree of control over his limbs, but the alien was running the show. I could hear it speaking with him, but the conversation was subliminal, and I couldn't get details, just impressions and vague thought bubbles. I concentrated hard but an undercurrent of malevolence, a dark pastel of evil, coloured everything. Then without warning, his mind closed and the white noise dissipated.

I was a bit shaky, and Hubert helped me to my feet. "He's still in there," I said, my voice unsteady. "I don't think that he's in control though."

Hubert's eyes bored into mine. "We could just let him through. Pull back. Let him use the transmitter and then talk with him. With it."

"The alien's not here to talk to us," I said, panic rising. "I think it wants to kill everyone."

Stillman had gone back to looking through her binoculars and we joined her to peer over the edge. Adam was running at full tilt towards barriers of plasticised alloy behind which were teams of police and FBI with guns pointing his way. Immediately, spotlights blazed with white light and swung round toward him, followed swiftly by gunfire as the police opened up. He traversed sideways quicker than the searchlight could keep up and took cover behind a low wall surrounding a laboratory outbuilding. Ricochets and impacts stitched holes in the plasterboard and concrete surrounding him. He took a step - back out into the line of fire - and raised a hand towards the searchlights. The bulbs exploded and darkness enveloped the SETI grounds. Gunfire ceased momentarily, and the helicopter reappeared, its light seeking him out. He reached out towards it and the rotor blades seemed to seize and whirl erratically. It started to spin out of control, tumbling over and over until it crashed into the trees on the knoll, blowing up and casting an orange glare over what was now a battlefield.

Adam walked slowly and directly toward the line of shooters who opened up with everything they had. However, none of their bullets reached him. As the rounds got to within a few yards they were deflected by an invisible barrier, ricocheting in all directions. The police were discharging automatic weapons as fast as the magazines would allow but he continued to walk forward, ignoring the fusillade, and to my eyes only vaguely aware of the deflected fire.

I could hear voices ordering retreat and regroup as he walked along the side of the laboratory towards the main building. Thirty yards away were two black armoured SWAT vehicles, lights burning brightly and guns swinging around. The police crouching behind started to flank him, firing sporadically as their SWAT trucks crunched gears and rolled forwards. Bullets were flying in from all sides as another group of police officers appeared from behind barricades parallel to the main building. Some were carrying large shoulder-held armaments. A couple of gas grenades were lobbed in his general direction, exploding noisily and producing yellow smoke that lazily drifted southwards on the breeze.

Adam stopped and raised both arms to the sky, almost in supplication, almost like surrender. Unfortunately, it was anything but surrender. There was a rippling in the air around him, like the blurring, pixilation effect you see on TV news. Huge gouts of gravel, soil, rocks and underground pipes and wiring exploded vertically from the earth and a tsunami of dirt and concrete spread outward and flipped the SWAT trucks. Soldiers and police officers were caught up in the wave and hurled into the air only to be crushed or mangled by flying debris. Then as suddenly as it had happened, vehicles and debris and bodies crashed to earth as if the flipping of a switch had restored gravity. Plumes of smoke and yellow-blue fires were starting as gasoline leaks were ignited. I could hear screaming and was aware that the gunfire had all but ceased. Then Adam stepped through the cloud, unscathed, and started walking towards the main SETI building. I thought he glanced up at me on the roof, but I couldn't be certain.

"What just happened?" shouted Stillman.

I didn't answer because I was inside his mind again. I could picture the earth beneath him consisting of a spiders-web of fault lines and micro-fractures secondary to decades of construction works. He had been able to see through the bedrock and through the layers of strata many hundreds of yards deep. Then these had been ripped apart and propelled upwards, without any explosives.

"Gravity," I said, wide-eyed. "He can control gravity."

Hubert was on the walkie-talkie again, issuing instructions for withdrawal. I pulled his arm down, and he looked at me, irritated. "We've got to get out of here," I shouted. "He's going to the transmitter, so let him."

The cries of the injured on the ground below could still be heard, and I took another peek over the ledge. Adam was ten yards away from the rear entrance of the SETI institute when a couple of soldiers emerged and spotted him. Well trained, they dropped into a crouch and raised their weapons. Before they could fire Adam merely raised a hand and the soldiers fell to the ground, unconscious or dead I had no idea. The doors crashed open disgorging dozens more troops, but Adam just spread his fingers like he was flicking water droplets and the soldiers were violently lifted into the air and thrown against the walls of the building. Taking one last look up at me, he entered the lobby, vanishing from sight.

"Shit, he's inside," said Stillman. "How are we going to get out now?"

Hubert pointed to the back wall, where a metal door was propped open with a brick. "There's a service elevator over there. It'll take us all the way down. Let's go."

He instructed the rest of the FBI agents on the roof to hold their positions, and the three of us ran across the roof to the door. It creaked open on a rusty hinge and we hustled through. Hubert called the elevator, which was already on our level, and as the doors inched open slowly we squeezed in. There was no light and the control panel was not illuminated so Hubert pulled out his phone and shone a light on it. There were only four floors marked, 1-4.

"Which floor is the exit on?" I said.

Hubert shrugged, and pressed '1'.

The doors closed with a lurch and the car started its wheezy descent. After what seemed like hours we jerked to a halt and the doors opened onto what looked like a version of hell. White and red lights were strobing through smoke and gas-filled corridors. There was a fire alarm going off, whoops and tones interrupted by a looped recorded message to leave the building by the fire exits. The public elevator doors were visible at the far end of the lobby, guarded by at least two dozen SWAT, semi-recumbent behind upside down reception desks and display cabinets.

We started to walk towards the SWAT team when the elevator doors swooshed open and Adam strode out. The SWAT and FBI agents didn't wait for instructions and opened fire through the smoke. Once again, the bullets were deflected and spun in random directions, stitching holes in the walls and ceiling. There was a sound like flies whizzing past my ear as a couple of rounds came our way. I dropped to the ground, as did Hubert and Stillman, hugging the wall.

"Adam!" I shouted. I saw him glance at me and through the smoke I could make out piercing green eyes.

Shit.

He looked away and made that supplicant gesture again. The floor in front of him began to ripple and undulate and melt as concrete and girders were ripped apart like paper tissues. He stepped forward through the debris and dust and disappeared through the hole. I pulled myself upright and ran to the edge of the hole which had melted through two floors. I could just see him walking into an office on the second basement level. He waved a hand at the wall which split and peeled outwards, sparks from sundered electrical wiring producing a firework display.

"The transmitter's down there," said Stillman as she joined us. "It's still online. There're still a bunch of technicians working on it."

Hubert had his hand over his mouth, trying to block out the dust that was everywhere, mingling with the gas. He coughed and looked at me. "It doesn't matter that it's irrelevant any more. We can't just leave them."

I nodded grimly, and we ran to the stairwell next to the elevator, and barrelled down two flights of stairs, Hubert huffing and puffing at the rear. Bursting out into the corridor, we encountered another group of police, guns locked and loaded, defending a large piece of equipment that I recognized as the SETI transmitter.

"Leave everything!" Shouted Hubert. "Back up the fire exit, cover the civilians!"

There was a low almost subsonic rumble and the wall down the corridor melted and Adam stepped through. He stood motionless as the police opened up, and a hailstorm of lead engulfed him and continued to be deflected away. I thought I could just make out a fuzzy layer of pixelated air surrounding his body, man-shaped and extending a couple of feet or so.

"He's projecting some kind of force field!" I shouted, and ducked around the side of the elevator as ricochet after ricochet whistled our way and punched holes into the walls and elevator doors.

Hubert started windmilling his arms and shouted to his troops, "Move! Get out! Retreat NOW!" and the police started to withdraw, firing rapidly and accurately, but as ineffectual as flies chewing on a rhinoceros.

I poked my head cagily round the corner. "Adam!" I yelled.

His back was to me and he was walking to the transmitter. He stopped briefly, but didn't turn. I was aware of Hubert frantically waving at me to get back into the elevator. He was yelling something, but I couldn't make it out over the noise of the alarms and the smoke obscuring his face. He was shouting into a walkie-talkie, and ushering his men into the elevator and the stairwell, Stillman doing the same.

Adam turned, and although the green light in his eyes was still visible, was it my imagination or was it less intense? I tried to concentrate my thoughts and my mind, but I still couldn't hear him in there. His face was impassive and he gave no sign he recognised me. I hesitatingly started to walk forward, when the six high explosive devices strapped around the transmitter detonated.

Reflexively I jerked back behind the wall as the nearest police and FBI were blown off their feet. I felt the pressure wave vibrate through the plaster that cracked and crumbled before me, pouring dust and detritus everywhere. A fist of orange flame punched its way out of the transmitter room, windows shattered, smoke poured along the ceiling and thousands of pieces of glass and steel showered down. More alarms - shrill and deafening - erupted. A huge bite had been taken out of the wall and the floor above. My head spun and I couldn't breathe and I tumbled to the ground. Dust was everywhere and all the lights went out. The fire alarm continued to blare, and sprinklers activated, spraying water in every direction. FBI agents lay on the ground, some in foetal positions trying to protect their ears and organs, others splayed like rag dolls covered in dust and plaster and glass. I groaned and managed to roll over on my side just in time to see Adam, unharmed, rise from the rubble like a phoenix from the ashes.

A few yards away one of the fallen SWAT lying awkwardly under a lintel brought his Glock up to bear with a speed his instructors at Quantico would have been proud. He squeezed the trigger rapidly and I watched all the rounds hit Adam centre mass at point blank range with no effect. Adam just pointed in his general direction and the gun was jerked away and sent skittering down the corridor. The agent crabbed backwards and put his body protectively over one of his fallen colleagues, a female officer with her neck at an awkward angle and blood trickling down her mouth. Adam walked slowly over to them and stopped, looking down, seemingly uncertain what to do next.

I could sense the alien talking with Adam; it's malevolence washing over him like a tidal wave. I could feel the conflict going on in his mind. The alien's control was being tested, but Adam was losing. Any moment now he would continue his killing spree and there was nothing I could do. I struggled to get to my feet, but my ears were still ringing and I had vertigo. My head started to throb, and my eyes felt dirty and gritty. I coughed grimy grey sputum on the ruined floor.

The fire alarms suddenly went quiet and the strobe lighting shut down, replaced by a dim red emergency light. I could hear the hoarse howling of injured people. I managed to get to my feet and as I was about four yards away I started shuffling towards him. Pain lanced up from my knee to my hip and I twisted into the wall, putting a hand out for support. There was a searing burst of agony when I put weight on my leg, and black mists swirled at the edges of my mind warning me that oblivion was near if I didn't take notice.

Adam looked at me, and his searing emerald eyes bored into mine. I could feel the crescendo of anger coming from the alien. Anger, and now hate. Uncontrolled hate, as if the alien had just learned a new emotion, and was trying it out. Adam's defences were folding, his mental walls collapsing, and his ability to hold off the alien failing fast.

I coughed into my sleeve, and a shower of blood appeared, along with a burning pain from my trachea. Adam still hadn't moved, but I was certain now that the phosphorescence was less intense. I was within a few feet of him so I tentatively reached out and touched his arm, then found his hand and curled my fingers around his and squeezed. He looked down at me and his eyes were now blue.

"Kate," he said. "Help me."

My vision blurred into his, and I saw him looking down at my dusty, blooded face. But then my face morphed into that of his wife, Cora Benedict. I could see her raven hair splayed over the floor, her once-beautiful face, scarred and bruised, lifeless and violated.

"What have I done?" he asked, in a plaintive voice that broke my heart.

I felt my eyes stinging and he reached out and touched my cheek. There was a vertiginous light-headedness, and I was back standing in the Chicago ER, the moment when my world collapsed. When light became darkness and endless pain followed like rolling waves on a beach. The howling I had made was so raw and desolate that patients in the other booths had flocked to me with eyes wet with tears. The months afterwards, in which I had cried myself to sleep so many times, crying as if the ferocity might bring her back, as if I could eradicate the memories by sheer grief. The vision cleared, and I was back staring into his eyes. I realised that it didn't bother me that this thing facing me, this shell, was not organic or human. Inside was the soul of a human being. A human denied the aspirations, dreams and challenges of life, denied a choice in who he was or what he was destined to do or be. A human who, in the depths of despair and hopelessness, was asking for help.

I indicated with my head down the corridor towards the elevator. "Come with me. I promise I'll help you. I won't let you down."

I could see Hubert watching me, his walkie-talkie still glued to his ear. There were a half dozen or so FBI agents flanking Hubert, guns trained on us, watching intently. My leg suddenly gave way, and Adam caught me and stopped me falling. He draped my arm around his waist and propped me up so that we could walk together. I looked up and gave him a watery smile. His lip twitched and I thought he nodded. We were almost halfway to the elevator when he stopped and cocked his head at an angle as if he was listening to something outside the range of human hearing.

"What is it?" I said. "We're nearly there."

Something is not right.

"What do you mean?"

But something was happening. Hubert was talking non-stop into his walkie-talkie, and the FBI agents were slowly backing off, taking cover in the elevator. A couple of them were looking upwards and around, and also listening to something. I couldn't make out anything over the sound of the sprinklers and my tinnitus from the bombs, but I was worried. Then all the FBI agents dived for the ground and covered their heads with their arms. Hubert threw down his radio and waved his hands at me, pointing at the ground in a gesture I took to understand as take cover. I glanced up at Adam, who continued to stare at the roof, head cocked, listening. Suddenly he grabbed my arms and without preamble pushed me to the ground. He pinned me with his body and lay on top, and I was again amazed by how light his frame was.

"What're you doing?" I stammered.

This is for your protection Kate. Close your eyes.

Then I could hear it, a high-pitched crescendo whine.

"What is it?" I demanded. "Tell me!"

He shook his head slowly.

Something different.

Then the ground shook and there was another earth shattering explosion and all the lights went out. I felt Adam's body pressing into mine, as a wave of pressure blasted through the corridor. I closed my eyes and felt my ears pop. A pulse, like a reverb or a subwoofer in a cinema, travelled through my muscles and bones as if through jelly. My heart jumped in my chest and fluttered irregularly.

As quickly as it had appeared, the feeling disappeared.

Adam collapsed against me, his limbs folding and crumpling. His head rested on my chest, and his eyes closed. I felt hands grabbing at me and I was unceremoniously pulled out from under him. He rolled over onto his side, flaccid, unmoving. FBI agents surrounded him like ants overwhelming an injured spider, quickly locking handcuffs and starting to wrap him in some sort of straightjacket.

I leaned against the wall, supported by a couple of agents. Hubert was suddenly in my face. "Time to go," he said, his expression grim.

I started to protest, but he shook his head and gave a look that brooked no dissent. I allowed myself to be led down the corridor and into the fire escape.

DAY 6

CHAPTER TWENTY-SEVEN
FBI Black Site, CA

I'd been hustled out of the destroyed SETI building and transported to a mobile hospital where I was soon given the all clear, medically speaking. Which was a bit counter-intuitive after being told I was apparently 'lucky to be alive'. My leg still hurt, but the Vicodin was helping, and my cuts and scrapes had been cleaned and dressed. After a few hours I was allowed to shower and change into another set of clothes, not as upscale as Stillman's, but I guess beggars can't be choosers.

Another motorcade later and I was back on the Gulfstream, which had wheeled up almost immediately. I dozed fitfully for the few hours of the flight, courtesy of the hypnotic thrum of the engines, the Vicodin, and the cabin crew who left me alone. I'd asked where we were going and was told that it was "classified" and that Hubert would meet me at the other end. Before sleep, and with some persistent prodding, the FBI agent babysitting me reluctantly let me know how they'd finally gotten Adam.

An *ebomb*.

Lying twenty miles off shore, the USS Ronald Reagan had fired a cruise missile with a payload of an 'explosively pumped flux compression generator'. The actual chemical explosive yield was minimal, but was focussed through a disc generator producing an intense magnetic field. The detonation compressed the magnetic flux and produced a shaped electromagnetic pulse. I'd questioned the agent about this, because I'd heard that EMP was a consequence of a nuclear explosion, but I was made to understand that Non-Nuclear EMPs (NNEMPs) were weapon-generated electromagnetic pulses without use of nuclear technology. The range was limited, but allowed finer target discrimination. The effective zone of the EMP delivered by the cruise missile was only two hundred yards so they'd targeted the missile at the front of the SETI building, limiting the structural damage, but blasting the immediate area with the EMP.

It had clearly worked. The EMP had disrupted all the electronic equipment in the immediate vicinity, and had shut down whatever electronica ran Adam's machine body. The agent also let me know that the EMP could damage physical objects such as buildings and aircraft structures due to the high energy levels.

He said this with a grin, followed up by, "Let's hope they killed the bastard."

I chewed my nail and looked out of the window.

We were descending fast, at a much steeper rate than normal commercial jets. Nevertheless, the landing was surprisingly soft and within a few minutes of the taxi we were being directed through the doors of a large aircraft hanger. The sun was coming up, the long early morning shadows spidering through the fields and trees onto the airstrip. The temperature was already in the high 60s and no clouds were visible in the sky. The spring grass shone like it had it's own gentle glow from within, and beyond the airstrip were fields of gold and green and rolling hills separated by run-down wooden fences and barbed wire. A couple of dilapidated flat-topped barns could be seen half a mile or so away, with similar barns on the nearest hills. I'd been told these appearances were calculated deceptions, and that inside each barn was a controller for state-of-the-art security equipment and electronic countermeasures.

With a hiss of hydraulics, the aircraft's door rotated and I was helped out of the plane. I limped down the short steps and met Hubert at the bottom.

"Is he here?" I asked, trying not to allow the excitement I felt be palpable in my voice.

Hubert nodded. "He's here. Under guard."

"Alive?"

"We don't know." He looked back over his shoulder. "The EMP worked. Knocked out his systems. I guess inside he's just a mass of circuit boards after all."

I hurried to keep up. "How did you get him here?"

"Well, we put him in a straightjacket, as many chains and cables that we could find, and airlifted him on the fastest jet I could requisition."

"But you don't know if he's alive or dead?" I persisted.

Hubert gave me a sideways glance. "That's right. The doctors have examined him, but they don't know what they're dealing with. Or what they're looking for."

We were walking towards an elevator door set against the far wall, a huge rectangular aperture twenty-four feet wide and eight feet high. The aircraft hanger was so large that inside it felt like it had its own climate. The cool morning breeze moved freely from front to back and the sunlight cascaded from windows onto endless concrete. There was a faint whiff of kerosene in the air, and smudged markings could be seen on the ground indicating where dozens of aircraft had once stood and been maintained.

"What's this place?" I said, looking around.

"This is an FBI Black Site. A place where certain types of research and evaluation of technology is done out of sight and away from the public eye. We've many of these dotted around the world." He abruptly stopped and turned to face me, his eyes probing mine. "Remember Kate, you've taken the oath. You're to regard yourself as a government employee. National Security binds you, and anything you see or hear is classified. Understand?"

I pulled a face. "You can't seriously keep him a secret for much longer. Didn't you hear what I said about there being thousands of copies? Hundreds of thousands?"

"We can keep it all a secret until I say otherwise," he replied stiffly.

An agent approached us and leaned to speak into Hubert's ear. He nodded after a few seconds. "Okay, then it's done."

"What's done?" I said.

His face was impassive, but there was frustration coming off him in waves. His lips curled downwards. "The President's coming. He wants to meet our friend."

"Well that's good isn't it?" I said. "Take me to your leader, and all that."

Hubert shook his head. "Definitely not. I've been trying to put the President off, stating security issues, but he's an asshole. He doesn't appreciate the danger. I explained that we know almost next to nothing about the alien, or the machine, and that all our experience confirms they're hostile. But he said he can 'negotiate with anyone'. And he is the President."

I bit back a reply as the elevator doors cranked sideways, opening like intertwined fingers, and we all got in. Hubert punched a keypad on the wall and the doors closed ponderously behind us. There was a momentary lurch as we started to descend.

"The portal will be opening again this morning," I said. "When's the asshole arriving?"

Hubert looked grim. "Very soon. We don't have a lot of prep time."

The elevator shuddered to a halt and we exited into a long grey corridor lit at five-yard intervals by yellowing halogen bulbs. Doors were present at regular intervals, sturdy windowless metal designs like you would find in a top security prison. We walked in silence and the corridor twisted right about thirty yards further ahead and opened directly into a brightly lit room containing a dozen or so desks with computer consoles and equipment, all manned by uniformed soldiers and FBI agents.

"Interagency co-operation," smirked Hubert. "Who'd've thought it?"

We approached a rectangular blacked-out window flanked by two metal doors that were themselves guarded by heavily armed soldiers. Hubert pointed to the window and one of the soldiers punched a keypad and the one-way electronic mirror pixelated into life.

Behind the screen was Adam Benedict, sitting upright in what looked like a dentist's chair but with his head slumped forward and eyes closed. He was wrapped in some kind of thick fabric and very solid-looking cables were attached to his hands and feet and bolted to the floor. Fussing around him were two white-coated figures with stethoscopes around their necks, so presumably medics. One was holding a syringe, the other a clipboard. Various pieces of medical equipment surrounded the chair and at the back of the room were six more soldiers holding serious-looking matt-black machine pistols.

Hubert gestured to the guard, who opened the door. We filed into the room, Hubert leading the way and me taking up the rear behind a couple of agents. We passed Stillman who was leaning on the wall by the door. She smiled at me but her eyes gave nothing away. The light was fairly dim and I could smell disinfectant. The two medics turned and stopped what they were doing. One of them, a tall bearded man with thinning grey hair and large round spectacles, introduced himself as Dr Stevens and shook hands all around. He nodded me a professional courtesy as I was introduced as a doctor. The other medic, a younger portly fellow ignored us all and went back to his equipment.

"Sit rep?" asked Hubert.

Stevens fetched a clipboard. He flicked through a couple of pages, settling on the current entry. "Unfortunately we've not learnt anything new yet. He's not regained consciousness - if that's actually what this neurological state is."

"Have you run an EEG?" I said. "We never had time to do that in Springs."

Stevens nodded. "Yes, but we just can't interpret it. There're no recognisable patterns of brainwave activity. We can't detect any electrical signals, but that doesn't mean anything."

"So the EMP could have killed him?" I said, a sinking feeling beginning in my stomach.

Stevens shrugged. 'Your guess is as good as mine."

Hubert was staring transfixed at Adam's face. He reached out and touched Adam's eyelid, gently pulling it up. "It looks human doesn't it, but there's something not quite right about the features. It's too perfect. I can't see any imperfections or even asymmetry."

Suddenly both of Adam's eyes opened and his head jerked up. Hubert took an involuntary step backwards, as did everyone else except the soldiers at the back of the room who moved forwards bringing their guns to bear. The noise of guns being made ready echoed around us, loud and clear. An unmistakeable hint of intent. Adam took in the group with a slow lateral movement of his head and when his gaze alighted on me, he smiled.

"Hello Kate, it is good to see you again. I am glad that you survived."

"Adam," I stammered, "Is that you."

There was a brief flicker of green phosphorescence before his eyes resumed their normal colour.

"Of course. Who were you expecting?"

CHAPTER TWENTY-EIGHT
FBI Black Site, CA

He'd spoken out loud, and not directly into my head. I wondered why, and I was about to try and send a non-verbal message when he looked away and addressed Hubert.

"Director Hubert, congratulations on setting up this facility. The electronic countermeasures are quite impressive. I am unable to overcome them at this time."

Hubert nodded solemnly. "I hope you understand that this is for our safety. And so that we can communicate without any, shall we say, unpleasantness?"

I winced. He sounded like a Bond villain.

Adam smiled while looking around the room, taking in the equipment, the soldiers, the medical personnel. "I have no intentions of harming anyone."

"You'll forgive me for finding that hard to believe," murmured Stillman, folding her hands and keeping her distance at the back of the room.

Adam looked over at her. "I could easily remove these restraints, but if it makes you feel better I will stay as I am."

"If you try to remove them," said Hubert, scowling, "these soldiers have orders to shoot to kill. And we have another EMP device underneath this room."

"You've shown your hand too early, Director Hubert."

"Try it and see."

Something didn't seem right. I put an arm out towards Hubert and without taking my eyes off Adam I said, "Stop it. Both of you."

Adam looked back at me, arched an eyebrow, and nodded. "You are correct, of course. I think this is called 'getting off on the wrong foot'."

Hubert took a step toward the chair. "Am I speaking with the alien?"

"Negative."

"May we speak with it?

"You can stop calling it, 'it' or 'the alien', Director Hubert. They are called Vu-Hak."

"Vu-Hak. Okay then," said Hubert, dryly. "Can I speak with the Vu-Hak in your head, please?"

Adam shook his head. "If I let it speak with you at this time, I will possibly lose the dominion I currently possess. However, I may be able to speak 'for them' if you wish? I do have certain insights."

I watched him talking and tried to read him. His mind was closed off and this worried me. Before, I was sure that he was trying to make me see that he was being coerced, that he was an unwilling participant in the destruction he had brought about. Now, I had nothing to go on and he was giving nothing back.

"Is there just one alien – sorry, one Vu-Hak - in there with you?" Hubert said, his face tight.

Adam nodded. "It is an individual, yes."

Hubert gestured to the guards to bring chairs and we formed a semi-circle facing him. Stevens remained off to one side perched on a stool which put him level with Adam's chair and next to a couple of monitors which had cables and wires snaking into the straightjacket. Up close I could see that dozens of thin wires had actually been embedded into the skin covering Adam's head, presumably attempting to record any brainwave activity. Adam looked impassively at Hubert, before letting his gaze drift around the room taking everything in.

"Where'd you go?" I said quietly, finding my voice, "It's been days. We've been worried."

His head swivelled to me and his lip twitched. "Worried for me, or worried about what the Vu-Hak might have been doing?"

I looked down. "About you," I said softly.

Hubert harrumphed, and interrupted. "Adam, we need you to tell us about these Vu-Hak. Who they are, what they want. Everything you know."

Adam shifted his gaze from me to Hubert. "The Vu-Hak are millions of years old, possibly the oldest species in the universe. They were once organic like us, and carbon-based. They spread throughout their solar system, converting rocky planets and asteroids to industrial use. They were rapacious users of energy and eventually enclosed their star in a Dyson Sphere to capture all stellar emissions. When they developed interstellar propulsion they uploaded their minds into machine bodies, similar in structure to the one you see here, and spread out at an exponential rate throughout the rest of their galaxy. They are what you would call a 'super-civilisation'. An alpha species. A species that colonises on a galactic-scale."

I fidgeted with my fingers, watching him. He seemed calm and collected, with no signs of belligerence or of being possessed by the alien. His eyes remained deep blue. I still wished he would let me into his mind, so that I could feel what was going on. I sensed I was missing something important.

Hubert said, "Did they encounter other intelligent species, or civilisations?"

"They encountered many other civilisations."

"And…?"

"They all died."

I heard Stillman take a sudden intake of air. "The Vu-Hak killed them all?"

"Not all of them," said Adam. "Almost every civilisation they encountered had already self-destructed. Wiped themselves out before they achieved intersystem spaceflight. But after they had discovered nuclear technology."

So there was the 'bottleneck' theory.

Holland was a smart guy.

Until, he wasn't.

"So, pretty much where humanity is right now," I said.

"Yes, just like humanity at this moment in the early 21st century. Most species that the Vu-Hak encountered which had not yet destroyed themselves were in the process of doing so. Escalating intra-species conflict and world wars led to their demise."

"Did the Vu-Hak come in peace though? I mean, if there were species that hadn't yet self-destructed."

"Initially, yes," said Adam, in a response that surprised me. "But first contact with a more advanced alien civilisation is almost always to the detriment of the less advanced culture."

"So they were all destroyed, I presume," said Hubert.

Adam shrugged under the straightjacket. "The Vu-Hak crushed any belligerent species and continued their expansion. They criss-crossed their galaxy, disassembling planets and smothering suns, until they could go no further."

"Then what, they just sat around in space playing scrabble or something?" I said, sarcastically.

Adam considered this more thoughtfully than it deserved. "The Vu-Hak had no equal, no competition. They looked around and asked 'is there nothing more'? And when they realised that there was not, they took the final step and divested themselves of physical structure, becoming one with the interstellar void. Entities of pure thought. A once-organic consciousness, now drifting aimlessly between the stars. Limitless, and immortal."

There was an uneasy silence in the room. The machines burbled electronically in the background, and the gentle hum of an air conditioner could be heard. Stevens fiddled absently with a couple of switches on the recording equipment.

"And you brought one of them here," said Stillman, her voice unsteady.

Adam looked up sharply. "I did not create the wormhole. That was humanity's folly."

Hubert stood up from his chair and started pacing, keeping his eyes on Adam. "What will happen when more Vu-Hak come through the wormhole?"

Adam looked at him, almost pityingly. "The Vu-Hak have been isolated to their own galaxy, millions of light years distant from any other. They have become bored. This galaxy provides them with new ... opportunities."

Hubert was shaking his head. "We can't let that happen."

"Do not worry," said Adam, "I will not transmit the Lindstrom data back to them. No more will arrive. The transient opening of the wormhole remains impossible to localize in their galaxy."

I looked up at Hubert, and he gave an imperceptible shake of his head. Adam still didn't know about Holland's passage through the wormhole into the Vu-Hak galaxy. Nor did he know that I'd seen the preparations being made there.

"What about the one sharing your head?" said Hubert.

"I believe I have achieved a measure of control."

"Well that's reassuring. For how long?"

"I do not know. When the wormhole opens on earth, controlling it becomes difficult. I am not sure why."

"But you know how to destroy the portal at this end? To close it permanently?"

"Yes, I believe I can do that."

"Then we don't have a minute to lose," I snapped. "The portal will open soon. Holland said…"

"Wait a minute," interrupted Hubert, shutting me down with a wave of his hand and glaring at Adam. "How can we trust you?"

"Because I am still Adam Benedict. I am human - despite what those monitors and your scans suggest. The passage of my organic body through the wormhole resulted in its death, which is true. But the Vu-Hak long ago discovered how to separate the living mind - the consciousness - from the body. What makes me - Adam Benedict, a human being - is still here." He glanced at me. "Dr Morgan knows this."

I gave a damp smile and my gaze shifted away, uncomfortably. I'd seen into his mind and encountered a tortured soul, akin to my own. Let down by the life he had taken for granted, broken by the lives he had lost. He'd experienced – and still was experiencing – unimaginable things. Things we couldn't start to understand let alone appreciate. And yet unbelievably he was fighting tooth and claw to retain his humanity, and wanted to help me, and protect us, despite no longer being fully human.

"Adam, why were *you* allowed to come back?" I said. "Why didn't the Vu-Hak just upload themselves into these machines?"

"Yes, and why is the machine needed at all?" Stillman interjected. "I mean, why couldn't they just come through the wormhole directly?"

"Fair questions," he replied. "Firstly, travelling through the wormhole requires a reinforced, non-organic repository. This is to prevent organic tissue or neural networks being ripped apart and dissociated by the massive forces within the wormhole."

"So they can't travel through without them," Stillman said, throwing a glance my way. "That explains all the other ones you saw, Kate."

Hubert scowled back at her and she reddened, realising what she had said. He stopped his pacing and put his hands on his waist. Adam was looking at Stillman, a curious look on his face.

"The 'other ones', Ms Stillman?" he asked, calmly.

Hubert stepped between them. "I'm still asking the questions Mr Benedict. Why did they send you back with one of their own? Do you have any thoughts on this?"

Adam paused for a few seconds, and I wondered if he was going to press Stillman on her faux pas, but then he closed his eyes and continued. "The Vu-Hak informed me that although they had learned about humanity by sifting through my memories, they wanted a human mind to interpret what they were seeing. I was to be a guide, a chaperone of sorts, assisting them as they evaluated our world and our capabilities. They did not believe that I could - or would - try and stop them."

Stillman sat back in her chair and blew out her cheeks. Hubert looked at me and sat down. I realised that the medics had stopped fiddling with the monitors and were hanging on to every word of the conversation now. The soldiers at the back of the room looked on impassively.

I shifted gears. "Adam, how does it feel to be you? To be no longer… physically human."

He gave what looked like a sad smile. "I derive no pleasure in what I have become. I am unique, an anomaly, a future research project to be discussed and analysed. I can never be who I was again, and that saddens me."

"But you look human from the outside," I said. "You can blend in, people would accept you."

He shook his head. "Acceptance. I think not. Once people found out what I was, I would be shunned."

I leaned forward toward him, holding his gaze. "No, it wouldn't necessarily work like that. We all look different, but inside, we have the same internal organs, blood groups, skeletal structure –"

"– And yet vast swathes of your world remain divided on the simple basis of skin colour," he interrupted. "Was that the point you were going to make?"

I was about to reply, when Stillman piped up again. "I've been wanting to ask. How is the machine body powered? We couldn't figure it out looking at the scans."

"At its core is a gravitational singularity - a black hole - measuring a few millimetres in diameter and constrained by localised curvatures in space-time."

Hubert's eyebrows hit the ceiling. "A black hole?! That's preposterous. Impossible."

Adam's mouth twitched. "Director Hubert, the Vu-Hak have capabilities you cannot even imagine. Recall that picture of me that you saw on the scans. My 'skin' is a thin carapace which only looks fragile, but it has a structural integrity analogous to that of the hardest diamond, and is in turn reinforced by focussed gravitational waves."

"Can you die?" Stillman asked. I looked at her sharply, but she ignored me. Adam let the inference pass.

"I do not truly know. I will certainly outlive friends, family, loved ones. In fact, everyone on this planet. This machine body is, by any definition that matters, immortal."

Family. Immortality. At the funeral of my beloved daughter, the minister said something that stuck with me, despite the hollowed out emotionless black hole that I'd become. She'd told me that 'one lifetime filled with great love was worth more than an eternity of nothing'. The triteness and bitter-sweetness had grated on me for a long time, until I had re-immersed myself in the memories of my daughter, my creation, and realised that the love I had for her would never diminish over the years.

My mouth was dry, but I said. "Adam, what about your daughter?"

"We were not close," he said softly. "We lost touch many years ago."

Stillman looked at me and then back to Adam, puzzled. "We'd understood that you'd reconnected recently? Gotten back in touch, and that things were going well?"

"No, that is not correct."

Stillman glanced over at Hubert who nodded for her to continue. "We've been talking with Amy," she said, "and in fact, we've brought her here to meet you."

She indicated for the guards to open the door. There was a clunk as the locks were disengaged and the door swung open silently to reveal Amy, flanked by Gabriel Connor and a female police officer. She shuffled slowly and hesitatingly into the room, eyes flicking side-to-side. She was clasping her bag tightly in front of her and Connor needed to guide her with a hand on her arm. Hubert and I stood up and moved our chairs out of the way so that she could approach Adam, who was looking at her with half closed eyes. She stopped a few feet away from the dentist chair and glanced sideways as if asking for instructions for what to do next. She looked at Hubert with knitted brows.

"What's he doing all tied up?"

Hubert ignored her. Connor took a few stops towards Adam, who slowly swivelled his head to look at him.

"Welcome back, buddy." said Connor. "How are you feeling?"

Adam looked at him and smiled, although his eyes didn't follow suit. "Hello Gabe. Have you missed me?"

Connor returned the smile. "Well, I sure never expected to see you again. What happened to you?"

Then Amy spoke up. "Hi, dad."

Adam looked over at her and tilted his head slightly to the left. He looked back at Connor and raised an eyebrow. "Where did you find her?"

He said it in such a detached way that Connor put his hands in his pockets and looked anxious and perplexed. I glanced at Amy, who was continuing to fidget and had started biting her nails.

"Amy lives in Vegas, don't you remember?" Connor said. "We thought it would be good for you to see her. Given everything that's happened, you know..."

I looked at Amy, and again a feeling of unease came over me. She'd pulled a piece of gum out of her bag, and was chewing away, mouth open, looking bored. Adam was now intently regarding his daughter, and I caught a flash of green fluorescence behind his eyes, and at the same time felt a pressure in my skull. I put a hand to my forehead and leaned on the chair back to support myself, and then became aware of another presence in my mind as Adam's voice floated up.

Kate, I have finally overcome the countermeasures in this room. It has coincided with the opening of the wormhole.

Amy also had her hands on her head and was rubbing her temples furiously. Hubert and Stillman were looking bewildered, while Connor and the soldiers were also appearing slightly discombobulated. Then I felt a wave of anger emanating from Adam. I felt him trying to suppress it, but then I sensed it wash over him. His eyes became solid blocks of green light, and he stood up, breaking the chains that had kept his arms and feet locked to the chair. The straightjacket shredded like the skin of a snake losing its winter coat, molecules separating and dispersing in a cloud of dust. He stepped out of the chair and reached over to grasp Amy by the throat. She cried out in pain as he lifted her up into the air, feet cycling away and struggling to break his grip.

"Adam, what are you doing?!" I shouted.

Stillman and I rushed forward and grabbed his wrists, trying to loosen the grip on his daughter's neck. It was like trying to separate welded iron bars. As he looked down at me his thoughts exploded into my consciousness and I realised the mistake we had made.

During Adam's last fateful trip overseas, Cora had answered a knock on the door and found Amy looking the worse for wear accompanied by two men. Tripping on a variety of drugs, Amy watched the men rape and beat Cora until she gave away the house's security code. After ransacking the contents of the safe, Amy watched passively as Cora fought for her life, and was left bleeding to death.

I saw all this through Amy's eyes, as Adam accessed her memories. He'd not been aware of any of this and hadn't had time to grieve for his wife, before he too was killed.

"Please," I said, "She's still your daughter. She needs you. Let her go."

But I saw Amy's life play fast forward through Adam's eyes. Amy had pleaded for help, had told Adam about her mother's death from cancer, her subsequent heroin addiction and her life in Vegas as a prostitute. Adam had offered to move her to San Francisco, and live with him and Cora, but everything fell through. He and Cora became wrapped up in their own lives, and Amy became a sideshow. Adam had stopped calling, and Amy had become an ex-person, an unnecessary complication. Regret washed over Adam like flat cold waves rolling up a shallow beach. I could sense he longed to turn back the clock, and take a different path, but now that was impossible. There was no way back. No way to make it right. Cora was dead, he was no longer human, and the remorse would eat him away for eternity. Finding out that

Amy was involved in Cora's death was almost unbearable. I saw his fractured, fragile emotional state and the precipice he was heading toward. The emotional tightrope that he was walking threatened to unbalance him once and for all.

And in the background – hidden like a shark in shallow waters watching unsuspecting bathers - was the Vu-Hak.

At that moment he spread his fingers, and Amy dropped lifeless to the floor, her head bouncing heavily on the linoleum. I saw that her lips had gone blue and she was not breathing so I grabbed her nose between my finger and thumb and took a breath before closing my mouth over Amy's and blowing. I leaned back and crossed my hands on her chest, and started CPR. I had delivered one compression when I was pulled away sharply by a steel grip on my arm and found myself being thrown into the now vacant dentist chair. Adam stood over me, his features flicking between anger and distress.

"What is done is done," he said.

I looked around for the others and saw that I was the only one still conscious. The soldiers, scientists, Hubert and Stillman, Stevens, all were lying motionless on the floor. I sensed the desperation washing over him and I reached out and grasped his hand.

"Let me help Amy. It's not too late."

"It is, Kate," he said, his voice weak and breaking. "I drove Amy to this. Me. I could have brought her in to my family. Made her welcome. Made sacrifices. She … she never had a chance. The drugs, the prostitution. It was all too hard for me. I had … other priorities. And now… you reap what you sow."

He let go of my hand and I saw his shoulders shuddering, as he attempted to stave off the anguish he was feeling. He looked down at the limp form of his daughter, limbs at awkward angles, like a discarded doll. Eyes open, pupils enlarging slowly. Dying. Then he took a step backwards, and shook his head.

"I cannot do this any more."

The blueness of his eyes was replaced by glaring green phosphorescence, and his countenance changed and stiffened as his mouth curled up in a rictus grin. I put my hands up to my mouth as I felt the alien mind burst through, its tendrils infiltrating into my head, accompanied by the fear and terror that my brain engaged in response. The Vu-Hak took control of my motor cortex, and I found myself dumped in the dentist chair again. Leather restraints rose up and encircled my arms and legs, tying knots so tight I felt my circulation would soon be compromised.

"Please," I managed, blinking away tears, "don't let it end like this."

There was a flicker of recognition, a candle in the dark, and then it was gone. The voice of the Vu-Hak boomed inside my head.

[He has gone. I am here. I am all there is.]

The Vu-Hak stared at a point on the ceiling, and a ripple appeared like an inverted drop of water on a pond. The tiles bent upwards and wires snapped and pipes twisted and groaned and everything was sucked into an enlarging ragged hole. With a last look in my direction, the alien disappeared, flying through the breach in a soundless blur of motion. A few seconds later there was a whistling sound followed by a low rumble as contents of the hole started to fall back down. I struggled with my restraints as slabs of earth and concrete and suffocating dust started to pour from the ceiling. Debris was bouncing off the floor and ricocheting around the laboratory, narrowly missing the sleeping soldiers and the rest of the group.

I coughed as the dust and grit started making its way into my lungs. I pulled at my restraints and to my surprise they had already loosened, falling away easily as the knots gave way. The metal buckles flopped to the ground so I jumped out of the chair and made for Amy who was still lying motionless. I thought I could feel a thready pulse in her neck and then I felt a hand on my shoulder and looked up to see Hubert, his face in a handkerchief and covered in dust, standing over me. He helped me take hold of Amy and carry her towards the door. Bigger pieces of earth and rocks continued to rebound and drop out of the still-expanding hole in the ceiling. Stillman had struggled to her feet and buried her face in her blouse, choking on the dust. Stevens appeared by her side and put an arm around her and they shuffled towards the door as well. The soldiers were slowly regaining consciousness and were attempting to gather their weapons on the other side of the room and staggering for the exit. A piece of concrete struck one of the soldiers full on his face and he went down awkwardly, blood pouring from his ruined nose. One of his colleagues tried to get to him but was also flattened by a huge gout of dust and debris as the ceiling split even further and metal pipes arrowed down, electrical sparks arcing around the gap from exposed wiring.

Hubert saw it too and shook his head in evident frustration. "The whole roof is going to come down. We've got to get out now!"

"But," I began...

"Those pipes are carrying oxygen!" he shouted over the crescendo. "If the sparks ignite ..."

"I get it!" I yelled back, and hobbled as fast as I could.

We reached the door and Stillman produced a key card and swiped it without effect across the keypad. She looked up, despair in her eyes. We laid Amy gently against the wall and Hubert pulled out his card and pressed it firmly against the keypad with the same result. Then the lights went off and we were in semi-darkness, flashes of illumination coming from the sparks produced by the ceiling wires shorting out. Two soldiers bumped into us, and one pulled out a small powerful torch that he ignited and shone on the door lock. The other pulled out his sidearm and pointed it at the keypad, firing six quick-fire rounds into it. I pushed on the door and it creaked open, the hinge mechanism destroyed. We fell out into the corridor, carried Amy through, and pulled the door closed just before a muffled explosion and a wave of pressure pushed it against us. More soldiers and agents had arrived on our side, and they all put shoulders against the door holding it closed as a wave of dust blew under the jam.

It held.

I slumped against the wall as Stillman came over and knelt down beside me. "Are you OK?" she asked.

I nodded. "You're hurt, though."

She looked down to see that her own blouse was ripped, and crimson ooze was making its way down to the belt line. She went pale and decided to sit down as well. "I'm fine," she said, and smiled tightly. "Just a scratch."

Hubert appeared looking worse for wear, his black suit greyed by dust and pockmarked by scratches and rips. He also had a cut on his head and a smear of blood was trickling past his ear. He squatted down on his haunches to check on Stillman and me, but then we all noticed Amy starting to move her head and twitching her neck. Her eyelids flickered and she gave a cough and proceeded to vomit up a large volume of yellow-green mucus and bile. I moved quickly and turned her head away but she pushed me away and hauled herself upright, flopping back against the wall. She winced and tentatively massaged her neck, which was angry and red with indentations where Adam's fingers had been. Her eyes flickered open and she looked around in a daze.

She caught my eye.

"What happened?" she said.

CHAPTER TWENTY-NINE
FBI Black Site, CA

"Well this is seriously fucked up."

Stillman was shaking her head as a nurse completed bandaging her abdomen after it had been cleaned and sutured. We were in a four-bedded hospital-type room with no windows, the walls creamy white and bereft of adornments. She was lying on top of one of the beds, which were arranged two facing two. On a panel behind her bed hung taps, oxygen hoses, switches and connectors. There was no decoration at all save a few limp curtains that could separate each bed from the others should privacy be required. The room smelled of bleach and the floor was shiny grey-green linoleum that wouldn't have looked out of place in a prison cell. There were unused stands for IV drips and monitors, dispensers for rubber gloves, sanitiser and soap.

The room was as devoid of beauty as I was of hope.

Amy occupied the bed opposite and was under the blankets, fast asleep, oxygen being fed via nasal prongs. She was hooked up to a monitor that was producing regular benign-sounding bleeps and pings. I was perched on an uncomfortable plastic-backed chair at the foot of Amy's bed, chewing another nail down to the quick. Sitting beside Stillman was a concerned-looking Hubert, patched up and wearing a new unblemished black suit. He glanced at his watch then stared at me with a concerned look on his face.

"Where's Adam gone?"

I didn't answer. I was going through the events of the last few hours, and trying to sift through the emotions and thoughts that had percolated through my mind as Adam and the Vu-Hak had fought for control.

"Kate?" said Stillman, a tremor in her voice. "Has Adam gone to the crater?"

I took a deep, shuddering breath. "It's not Adam in there anymore, it's the Vu-Hak. It's taken over. I don't know if he'll be able to come back. I don't know if he wants to."

"Why would you say that?" said Stillman. "We need him, don't we?" She looked at Hubert, eyes pleading, wet. "He's the key!"

I told them what I knew, what I'd learnt about Amy's betrayal and the murder of Cora Benedict. The guilt that Adam was feeling and the hopelessness I sensed as he finally let the Vu-Hak take control.

"I think learning about Amy has pushed him over the edge," I said morosely. "I got the feeling he's just given up."

"So without him, that alien is loose and unchecked." Stillman looked across the room at Amy. "It was a fucking mistake bringing her. What were we thinking?"

"We didn't know the truth," I said. "It was the right play, given what we thought we knew."

Stillman was looking angrily now at Amy, tears welling up in her eyes. I could see that she was on the verge of losing it and I started to get up but at that moment Amy stirred and reached up to pull her nasal prongs out. She stretched over to her bedside table and with tremulous hands managed to bring a glass of water to her lips. She looked around and blinked a few times while taking a couple of sizeable mouthfuls before realising that we were watching her.

"What?" she said.

I was still struck by the resemblance to Adam. Tall and willowy, with exquisite bone structure. It's no wonder she went down a treat in the underbelly of Vegas.

Stillman glared. "Have you any idea what you've done?"

Amy tried to return the stare, but averted her eyes after a few seconds. She took another drink and her shoulders started to move and the tears came.

"This is your fault," Stillman said.

Amy brushed a tear away from her cheek with the heel of her hand, "What do you mean?"

"You're an accessory to murder," said Stillman. "And not only that, because of you the whole fucking human race may be wiped out."

"Wait, Colleen," I began. "That's a stretch… she wasn't responsible for the wormhole."

Before I could continue, Stillman launched herself across the room and slapped Amy hard, the sound loud and brutal. The glass smashed into the wall, spilling water everywhere and spraying fragments onto the sheets. Stillman went to hit her again but was restrained by Hubert who grabbed her by the arms and dragged her away screaming, livid and inconsolable. Amy scrabbled back against the bed rest, pulling the sheets up around her and shaking her head from side to side and screaming obscenities. Hubert was shouting in Stillman's ear as she furiously tried to break free from his grip and launch another attack on Amy. The door crashed open and three FBI agents entered and helped Hubert manoeuvre Stillman to the other side of the room. The agents then flanked Amy's bed and stood there like sentries. Amy sobbed into her sheets and started rocking to and fro as Hubert sat down next to Stillman and brushed a hair out of her face, tucking it behind her ear. He gently lifted her chin upwards with a finger and looked into her eyes. It was a tender moment, and made me understand their relationship a bit better.

I took a deep breath and walked over to Amy who was rocking metronomically in her bed. Hubert and Stillman just stared at me as I perched on the edge and put my hand on her arm. She looked at me, her eyes wide and puffy, hair smeared over her face, her cheek reddening from Stillman's blow. I brushed her hair back and offered her a tissue from my pocket. She took it and I thought I detected a twitch of thanks from the corner of her mouth.

"It's not your fault Amy," I murmured.

She blinked up at me in surprise, and I heard Hubert starting to protest.

"It's not." I repeated firmly, giving them both a hard look. "Think about it. Think what we know. She's just a kid. Her mom died, her father was no longer a part of her life. She got into a bad situation. Drugs and all… that hardly makes it her fault."

"She brought those killers to Cora's home. She did nothing to stop it." Stillman objected.

"She was strung out and she was desperate," I pointed out. "She had no idea what was going on. What could she have done?"

To my surprise, Hubert nodded. "Alright," he said rising from the bed. "So we need to regroup and figure out our next move."

I swallowed hard. "There's something I need to tell you. Adam's been allowing me to eavesdrop on his thoughts and conversations with the Vu-Hak. I wondered why, but now it all makes sense. He was trying to warn me."

"About what?" asked Hubert, eyes narrowing.

"About how things will go down when they arrive."

"He told you as much?"

"He gave me access to their conversations. It would appear that when the Vu-Hak come through the wormhole they're going to remotely launch every nuclear weapon on the planet. Eradicate all human life."

"Won't that destroy them too?" asked Stillman, a horrified look on her face.

I shook my head. "I can't imagine they'd do it if there was any risk to themselves. I guess that as they don't have physical form, there's nothing to destroy."

"But they'll be coming as physical beings, won't they?" said Hubert. "They're needing to come through the wormhole in those machine bodies."

"Yes!" said Stillman, excitedly. "Adam was susceptible to EMP and nuclear weapons produce EMP as a by-product. Massively so!"

"I think they'll have adapted or developed a defence against it." I said. "Remember Adam's comment about 'showing your hand too early'? I'm pretty sure that was a big hint. In any case, that'll be it for humanity. There are fourteen thousand, nine hundred and twenty nuclear weapons capable of immediate launch on this planet. Oh, and let's not forget about maybe a couple of dozen lower yield weapons in North Korea. But all said and done, enough to vaporise the planet many times over."

Hubert and Stillman were staring at me so I continued. "That Vu-Hak didn't care that I'd found out the plan. Not only didn't it care, it teased me with images of nuclear fireballs burning and destroying everything in their path. I saw radiation fallout - fiery snowflakes from hell - then the nuclear winter obliterating the sun's rays for years. Permanent darkness followed by the extinction of every species on the planet. To them, we're just an organic life-form infesting this planet, a planet which they're going to destroy and use as raw material to construct one of those spheres around our sun."

Hubert's features darkened, and he looked at his watch. "It's eleven thirty. We've still got time to stop him. We just need to figure out how."

"What if everyone disarms all the weapons? Make them useless?" said Stillman, her gaze bouncing between us.

Hubert stood up and brushed the creases out of his suit. "There's no time. The rest of the world doesn't even know the Vu-Hak is here. There'd be widespread disbelief, committees would be formed, UN special sessions would be convened, you name it. Not gonna happen. No, Adam is still the key, if we can get to him. He controlled the Vu-Hak, and then gave up that control voluntarily. We need to get him back on our side."

"But how?" I said. "He's given up."

Hubert wagged a finger at me. "No. He's still got you. You might be able to get through to him. You might be our only chance."

Stillman eased her feet off the bed, and winced a little. She looked at me and smiled. The terror seemed to have gone from her eyes. "He's right. Like it or not, this is all on you now. No pressure."

I put my head in my hands and ran my fingers through my hair. Hubert came and sat down next to me. His grey hair was neatly combed and there were emerging crow's feet around his eyes, which were a warm, dark almond. "I don't know if I can," I said softly.

"You can. You must. You're stronger than you think. And you won't be alone."

I gave a watery smile, but then I looked over at Amy, who was still rocking backwards and forwards, her eyes a blackened mess from smeared mascara. I remembered the despair radiating out of Adam.

"What if Adam doesn't think humanity is worth saving?"

Hubert said nothing in reply, but that was enough.

There was a knock on the door, and an agent appeared. He motioned to Hubert, who patted me on the knee and got up to join him. They conferred for a couple of seconds, and then the agent left. Hubert gathered himself, and turned to face us.

"There's a video feed coming in from the crater. General Baker says that everything's in position, locked down tight. Wants to talk strategy."

I held my tongue. I knew the military strategy already. More of the same, only bigger guns.

"Just down the corridor," said Hubert. "Situation room."

CHAPTER THIRTY
Ground Zero, Nevada Test Site

Hubert led the way into a semi-darkened room lit by the glow coming from a bank of LCD monitors. There were a number of haphazardly arranged couches and a low centre table upon which sat a big multidirectional microphone looking like a black tarantula. Two technicians were huddled in one corner behind a desk containing banks of receivers and audio devices.

Stillman and I sat side-by-side on one of the couches at the back and Hubert took a seat by the table where he could talk into the microphone. There was a low crackle coming from hidden loudspeakers in the ceiling, and the room smelled of old cigarette smoke. On the screens were a variety of angles of the crater and what I guessed was the observation tower I'd seen being built yesterday on the uppermost level of the canopy. I could see the horizon, which from this elevated position was a long way away. The sky was a picture perfect blue behind the distant mountains, with just a hint of darkening as the afternoon wore on. The sun, a benign yellow ball, hung low in the sky, as the earth raced and spun towards another evening. The phrase 'the calm before the storm' drifted into my consciousness, and I wondered whether I was being prescient, or just pessimistic.

Hubert waved at the technicians, and another screen flicked to a view of Baker himself on the canopy, scanning the horizon through binoculars. He must have heard the connection activate, because he glanced in our direction and grabbed a headset, keying in the COM channel. "Director Hubert," his voice crackled. "Welcome to Ground Zero."

Hubert picked up the microphone. "See anything out there General?"

Baker looked at the camera and shook his head. "Nothing all day on visual. Captain Powers is back at Creech, controlling four Predator drones circling twenty thousand feet above us. There've been a couple of suspicious movements out in the valley, but we think probably wild cats, small deer, that sort of thing."

"Anything on radar?" I piped up.

Baker squinted into the camera, and gave a sour look when he saw me. "Nothing confirmed by radar or infrared. I've another four Predators coming on station in thirty minutes. I'll move them into a concentric pattern outside the inner ring, approximately ten miles distant. This should give us an early warning of anyone or anything approaching from a radius of fifty miles."

Hubert had told me that these drones were armed to the teeth with ballistic weapons, non-electronically controlled to prevent electromagnetic jamming and interference. I turned to him and whispered, "Could a single person get through on foot, like at SETI?"

Somehow the microphones picked up my question, and Baker leaned in. "Theoretically, yes. But our instruments are calibrated to detect and localise movement of objects smaller than a human being. We should see him coming."

"And when you do see him," I said tightly, "what's the grand plan?"

Baker blinked in surprise, then scoffed. "You've observed the cordon we've put up here. State of the art US military hardware. The best in the world. If he shows up, and is an aggressor, we'll take him down."

I raised my eyebrows. "Did you even watch the footage from SETI?"

Baker scowled, picked up his binoculars and pointedly started scanning the horizon. I was about to say something about the inflexibility of the military mind, when there was a familiar tickle behind my eyes and my legs wobbled.

"General," I said quietly, "Can you get the external cameras to pan around for us?"

He reached down out of shot and the screens switched to a view of the main road leading away from the crater snaking into the distance. As the camera moved along the road and passed a rock formation I saw a blur of motion, like a smudge on the screen.

"Back up. What was that?" I snapped.

The camera backtracked and brought the rocks into focus. There, standing silently on the top of the tallest boulder, was a figure. Details were indistinct, but there he was, standing tall and conspicuous, unconcerned about cover or stealth.

"Well I'll be damned," Hubert whispered. "How long d'you think he's been here?"

Baker had brought his binoculars up again and was scanning in the same direction. "Is it him?" he asked, and I thought I could hear a slight tremor in his voice.

I ground my teeth, jaw muscles bunching. "Yes it is …"

Baker flung the binoculars on the bench in front of him and picked up the field telephone, connecting him to the troop commanders around the crater. "Target in view, distance approximately three clicks south east, direct line of sight by the rock formation adjacent to the road. Nearest units, engage at will."

Two M1A2 Abrams tanks on station a mile up the road cranked their gears and brought their 120mm artillery to bear on the rock formation. Their guns blazed orange, the reports coming a few seconds later like distant thunderclaps. Their targeting systems were accurate and the rocks blew apart into a million pieces, orange desert dust and black smoke obscuring the result. Apache helicopter gunships were also now arrowing in from the south and unleashed Hellfire missiles into the expanding ball of smoke. They banked like fighter jets and opened up with their Gatling guns, sending tracer rounds and 30mm cannon shells into the target zone. The Abrams were now moving towards the rocks at high gear, their ten ton bulks eating up the ground at forty miles an hour, seemingly oblivious to the bumpy rock-strewn desert floor. They were firing continuously, their guns staying locked onto the target despite the high speed jumping and rolling. More huge explosions lit up the sky and the percussive forces were visible at the crater where General Baker was directing operations. Still firing, the tanks disappeared into the dust and smoke drifting up the road. The Apaches had stopped but remained hovering a hundred or so yards out, hugging the desert floor just high enough to have line of sight to the target area, and were still pumping high velocity rounds into the centre of the cloud. I assumed all the gunners were using IR or UV to see through the cloud and would be avoiding the tanks.

I heard Baker on the field telephone again, getting a line to the tank commanders. "This is Baker, report. Target situation?"

There was a crackle of interference, and static, and then; *"Approaching target now... completely destroyed... no signs of... wait ... what's that?"*

The line went dead.

Out of the cloud and tossed like a child's toy, a crushed Abrams tank bounced and rolled into view coming to rest upside down in the middle of the road. It was followed by the second tank, similarly crushed like an empty soda can, ripped into two pieces, gun and turret separated and spinning into the desert. The Apaches resumed shooting Hellfire missiles but suddenly their rotors lost all co-ordination and they jerked and twitched in the air like epileptic bats, spinning end to end and dropping to the ground, bursting into flames and setting off a fireworks display of residual ordinance.

"Shit, shit!" shouted Hubert at no one in particular.

I grabbed his arm. "Get Baker to pull them all back. Get the troops out of there!"

Hubert keyed the mic. "General, are you getting this?"

"Affirmative," came the reply. "But no visual on the target. Releasing ballistic packages into centre of cloud now."

I knew this meant the four Predators had been lining up like Stuka dive-bombers from World War Two, and had dropped their entire ordinance, which was now falling at terminal velocity from their release ceiling of five thousand yards. With no electronics, these bombs were lumps of metal and high explosives, arrowing in with huge kinetic energy and a thousand pounds of explosive. I could still see nothing moving within the cloud, but there was a light wind thinning it out and blowing it north towards the crater. As if reading my mind, Hubert flicked the camera back to IR, and I caught sight of a figure walking slowly through the cloud and then the bombs hit, and I had to look away as the IR flashed bright white. Prodigious plumes of smoke and dust and erupted as sequential impacts jettisoned rocks and debris into the air. There was a rippling effect at the edge of the smoke, like a stone had been skimmed across a lake. Adam emerged from its centre, unscathed, and broke into a run, heading directly up the road towards the crater.

Hubert's eyes were wide, and he seemed struck dumb.

Baker had already picked up the phone. "All units, target approaching on foot. Fire at will."

Hubert licked his lips and muttered, "Now we'll see if those MAARS units are worth a million bucks a pop."

The cameras switched to the fences and gun emplacements surrounding the crater and the massed troops occupying fortified positions down the slopes to the second line of fences where the automatic gun emplacements were bedded in. Another six Abrams tanks were racing around from the northern side of the crater to set up another perimeter higher up where the laboratories and gangways leading into the canopy were situated.

At that moment all the radar-controlled motion-sensitive MAARS emplacements facing south opened up at once. The subwoofer in the situation room began to shake with the noise, which was rattling my bones, and I stuck my fingers in my ears. M240B machine guns rained ordinance on the approaching figure, and grenade after grenade launched in a computerised orgy of destruction. The troops lining the slopes began firing their automatic weapons, machine guns on HUMVEEs opened up, and the Abrams joined in with their 120mm cannons. There was no break in the cacophony of noise and the figure of Adam Benedict was once again obliterated by smoke, fire, dust and hurtling debris. Then the dust cleared as a transparent bubble appeared with a human figure at its centre. Machine-gun rounds and grenades impacted harmlessly against the bubble, and the huge 120mm rounds from the Abrams tanks could be seen to disappear into the surface like water droplets onto a placid lake.

Another ripple appeared, bigger than before, pushing the smoke and flames away in concentric circles. Directly underneath the bubble, the desert floor started to liquefy producing a wave of earth and rocks that broke the surface and rolled up the hill tsunami-like towards the gun emplacements. Within seconds it had engulfed the guns and tanks, burying them completely, and continued to roll up the slope into the lines of troops already scattering and running for the cover of the crater. There was to be no escape, and no respite was being given. Within the bubble, Adam was gesturing right and left at remaining tanks and artillery pieces, which then crumpled as if they had been dropped to crush depth in the ocean. More Apache helicopters dropped like flies hit with bug spray, their power cut and systems fried. Predator drones were plucked from the sky, engines flaming, spinning into the sides of the crater and exploding in fireballs, which engulfed fleeing troops. Soldiers remaining at their posts were tossed aside, their bodies ruined and dead before they fell to earth.

Like an Angel of Death, Adam walked through the flaming wreck of a tank towards a group of soldiers with shoulder-held missiles. Their missiles streaked towards him at almost point-blank range but at the last minute careened off into the sky, wobbling and spluttering and exploding in the atmosphere. Soon, every piece of artillery, mobile or stationary, was either buried under rubble or in flames. The remaining soldiers fell back, supporting the injured and firing sporadically and uselessly at the unstoppable force bearing down on them.

"We've lost," I said, swallowing hard. "It's over."

Hubert was looking at the floor of the situation room, breathing heavily, head in hands. He turned to me, his eyes red. "No. We've one more play to make."

He picked up the handset and punched a single digit, and hung up. My eyes widened as the realisation struck home.

"You're not serious," I stammered.

He just looked at me and gave a slight shrug. "It's all we have. God forgive us."

On the monitor, Baker could be seen looking up into the sky, squinting, smiling. Wispy white clouds could be seen in the stratosphere, mixed with circling contrails.

B52 bombers.

There were fewer and fewer bursts of noise, all gunfire was spluttering out as the remainder of Baker's troops retreated down the hill. I could see Adam (or was it the Vu-Hak, and did it matter?), now on the edge of the crater, the bubble dissipating and evaporating as he climbed onto the gantry and disappeared down the sides into the crater itself.

On the monitor Baker looked directly into the camera, and gave us a salute. There was a faint crescendo whistling to be heard, just at the edges of perception but gradually increasing. The camera flicked skywards, and I thought I could see the bombs approaching, small black pinpricks against the powdery sky.

I looked back at Baker, and I caught a grim smile as he nodded at me. I put my hand up to my mouth, and then everything flared white as the nuclear fireball consumed the crater.

DAY 7

CHAPTER THIRTY-ONE
Ground Zero, Nevada Test Site

Like two bloated vultures, our Chinook helicopters warily approached the crater in ever-decreasing circles. The morning sun would not be making its appearance for an hour or so, but the sky was already softening to a blue behind the distant mountains, while clouds were blushed like a ripe mango. It was beautiful, the stars still twinkling in the charcoal of the firmament, but fading fast.

I looked out of the window, numb and beyond shock at what I was seeing. Next to me Hubert was craning his neck, grimacing and gurning as he tried to get a good look. I didn't recognise the crater from the previous photograph, which had shown a symmetrical pockmark on the desert floor, surrounded by gentle slopes, cactus plants and Joshua trees. The devastation from the four nuclear bombs was of an order of magnitude bigger than the explosion that had created it sixty years ago. The new crater was a ragged hole, having gouged out and flattened the slopes whilst scorching the earth. What I assumed were the remnants of military equipment and mobile laboratories were just tangled metal shapes, melted and flattened into the ground, blackened and smoking. Nothing was recognisable; there were no trees or plants and even the bitumen had melted away. Small fires were still burning from the remnants of larger buildings but the force of the blasts had incinerated everything and sucked the oxygen out of the air, leaving nothing behind to burn.

"It's not what I expected," I said to Hubert through the intercom.

"I know," he said, looking at me strangely. "It should be much worse."

I heard Stillman's voice through the headphones. "It's incredible. According to the readings taken from satellite, and now from the recorders on board, there's still no radioactivity from the crater."

The scientist in me couldn't accept this, despite all the data. We'd spent a good part of the evening pouring through the satellite uplinks and drone cameras, evaluating the effects of the first nuclear weapon used in anger on American soil. The first nuclear weapon to purposely kill American lives. In 'self defence'.

Hubert had assured me that nothing could have survived the sheer devastating power of hundreds of kilotons of TNT-equivalence and radiation delivered into a kill zone corralled by sheer rock walls. The focussing of any blast wave would have been amplified by the geography so that anything living within the crater would have been immediately vaporized.

It was a drone video that had started the head scratching. Despite the motion of the bird, the feed was steady and the picture sharp. The screen showed an orbital view of the crater taken just before the bombs impacted. There were burning tanks, destroyed buildings, and what looked like dead ants, which I knew, were human beings. Then the screen went white as the bombs exploded, rings of energy and fire rippling outward. But then a black circle appeared at the centre of the crater followed by a kaleidoscope of colours appearing to spiral concentrically into it. In disbelief I had watched the nuclear detonations being sucked in to the black heart of whatever had appeared in the crater.

"Down a plughole," I murmured aloud.

Hubert looked over at me, hearing my voice through the headphones. "Whatever that was, it sucked the radioactivity and all the heat out of the detonation."

Stillman said, "No radiation, so it's safe to go in."

"Safe?" I raised my eyebrows. "We've no idea what happened. Or what's waiting for us."

Hubert shrugged, and gave the command to the pilot who banked the huge machine around and descended nose up into the crater. There was a soft bump on landing and the rotors immediately started to power down. We unclipped and made our way to the stern of the Chinook, Hubert in the lead followed by Stillman. A couple of agents carrying Heckler and Koch submachine guns pushed past us and flanked the bottom of the ramp.

"Really?" I looked at Hubert. "More guns?"

The ramp opened to reveal the crater floor, which was now shiny and glasslike. As the Chinook shut off its engines, an eerie silence descended which felt almost like a purification after the deafening noise of the rotors. When my ears became more accustomed to the lack of sound I thought I could hear the creaks and ticks of the slowing blades and the hot motor starting to cool. Other than that only my rhythmic breathing brokered the air to my ears, and so I gingerly headed down the ramp and looked out. The crater had been flattened and now was three times the diameter I remembered. One half was in absolute darkness due to the angle of the rising sun, and ragged crevices and cracks climbed the walls like scars. A faint warm breeze drifted down from above and brought with it the smell of smouldering brush and scrubland. I stepped off the ramp and almost lost my footing as my shoe slipped on the glassy floor. Hubert steadied me with a hand from behind and pointed towards the darkened half of the crater. The agents fanned out either side and brought out pen torches.

I walked carefully to the wall and ran my hand over it, expecting a cool rock-like surface. What I felt was strangely warm and slimy, and some sort of unguent coated my palm and fingertips. I brought my fingers to my nose and sniffed, inhaling a weird odour that was oddly sweet and sharp. I pushed my finger in and the wall gave gently under the pressure, like a rubber mat, springing back slowly as I withdrew.

"What the fuck happened here?" said Stillman next to me, her voice tinged with awe. "Don't the laws of physics apply any more?"

I laughed out loud. The extraordinary, the exceptional, the sheer *unnaturalness* of the last week seemed to have come to a head, here in this crater. A week ago - shit, was it only a week? - I would have struggled to do my own taxes, now... I seemed to be the calmest person here.

"Something over there," shouted one of the agents, shining his torch into a larger opening further down the wall, hidden in the shadow. We crossed over to where he was standing, straining our eyes into the depths of a triangular-shaped cavity about six feet high. Hubert brought out a torch of his own, which he added to the agent's beam. The two lights fought for dominance, highlighting floating clouds of dust and what looked like small jets of steam venting from the floor. I peered around Hubert's shoulder, squinting into the rearmost corners, my eyes still not quite dark-adjusted.

"Oh my god, what's that?" whispered Stillman, putting a hand to her mouth.

The light beams had converged on a dust-covered human-sized figure, curled foetus-like against the wall. There were no distinguishing features apart from a head shape and an elongated body and legs, and in fact it bore a startling resemblance to one of the stone corpses found covered in volcanic lava at Pompeii.

"Is it him?" said Hubert, with a quick glance in my direction.

I tentatively reached out and touched the shape. It was solid, almost rock-like, and dust sloughed off where my finger traced a line. I took a sniff, and pulled my nose back at the sharp, acridness of the odour.

"Cocooned, maybe?" offered Stillman.

Hubert squatted down next to me. "Is he alive?"

I didn't answer. In the far recesses of my mind, I could sense something... subtle, non-specific, like white noise in between radio channels. Gradually, a strange warmth spread throughout my body, slowing my heart and relaxing me. I turned to Hubert, my heart pounding. I couldn't hear Adam's voice, or access his thoughts. But, there was something ...

"I think so... maybe."

I tightened my lips and reached out to touch what I assumed was the head. The shape suddenly moved away from the wall, rolling towards me. I jumped back and fell on my ass, knocking over Stillman as well. Hubert and the FBI agents had also stepped away nervously, but had kept it together and still had their weapons and torches pointed at the shape.

It pulled itself into a sitting position, arms, legs and torso becoming defined and separated from what had previously been a homogenous lump of rock. It leaned back against the wall and raised its head. There were no distinguishing features, no eyes, no nose, nothing, it was like it had been moulded out of play-doh. There was a crunching sound, like what you hear when a packet of chips is scrunched, and the outer layer began to crack, micro fractures spreading exponentially from the head downwards. Jagged pieces of stone chips and dust started to fall off, slowly at first, and then with increasing frequency until the outer layer was gone. Underneath, and seemingly completely unharmed, was a cerulean-coloured face, and a similarly hued body that could have been sculpted by Michelangelo. The face was still recognisable as Adam Benedict, although tufts of black hair were hanging off the skull and what was left of his skin. The eyes were burning green, without a hint of blue. He regarded everyone with a slow turn of his head and his eyes stopped on me.

Kate.

The voice in my head was weak as if coming from a great distance, accompanied by an echo. He gently shook his head as if trying to clear it. I reached over and stroked his face, marvelling at the warm yet metallic-like texture. He took hold of my hand and pressed it against his cheek.

I am sorry.

I felt him sweeping around my head, sucking up the images and experiences of the last few hours. He saw the nuclear explosion, and the violent deaths he had inflicted on the troops. I felt his wave of sadness and guilt wash over me.

"It's okay," I said. "It wasn't you."

It is not okay.

"It wasn't your fault," I said, firmly.

Hubert squatted down next to us and leaned in so that his face was level with Adam's. He continued to point the torch directly at his face, and I pushed it away irritably. Adam slowly brought his hands up and stared at them, turning them over and over as if seeing them for the first time. He clenched his fists, and spread the fingers wide. For a brief instant they seemed to pixelate as the air blurred and they became momentarily transparent. I took one of his hands in mine, felt a slight electric shock on contact and then a not-unpleasant tingling and numbness.

"Adam," I said slowly. "Is the alien still here?"

He looked around at us all, and his voice was, stronger, clearer. "No. The Vu-Hak is dead."

Hubert looked at him, disbelief tattooed across his face. "How did you survive, and it didn't?"

Adam didn't reply straight away, but looked at everyone again, starting with me and slowly taking in his surroundings. He sighed, a very human sound, and shook his head.

"It does not matter," he said

"What do you mean," asked Stillman.

Adam didn't look up. His voice was soft, and we had to strain to hear him. But what he said chilled my soul.

"The portal is intact. They will be here soon. All of them."

CHAPTER THIRTY-TWO
Ground Zero, Nevada Test Site

Hubert stood up, stared at his watch and tapped it with his forefinger as if that would change the time. It didn't. We had twenty minutes before the portal would appear again and the wormhole open. I bleakly looked up the sides of the crater to the opalescent cloudless sky above. The jagged edges of the walls pointed and indented upwards, their clefts in shadows as dark and discouraging as my mood. I watched Hubert reach out and absently run a hand over the shiny burnished rocks, lustrous as a gemstone. I could almost make out his reflection in the mirror-like surface. A gentle breeze wafted down, and I felt it ruffle my hair, cooling and pleasant, bringing with it promises of a balmy, temperate morning. I shook my head at the surrealism of it all, the hypnagogic quality of what we were experiencing.

Hubert looked back at Adam, a haunted look on his face.

"So, that's it then? Game over?"

Adam didn't answer, his green eyes giving nothing away. He creakily stood up and leaned against the wall for support. I went to assist him, and he seemed to gratefully accept my help. He still weighed almost nothing, and it was like picking up a papier-mâché mannequin. Most of the skin covering his body had fallen away, and he was barely visible in the dark recess, a navy-indigo silhouette.

"Is there nothing we can do?" Hubert pressed, voice taut.

Stillman walked over to Adam, and blinking away tears, said, "We'll survive. We're here for a greater purpose."

Adam straightened up to his full height and stared calmly down at her. "Does humanity deserve to survive? There is no purpose to the universe. The universe owes humanity absolutely nothing."

Stillman was shaking her head. "Humanity – us – we're God's creation. We're more than just the sum of our molecules. There's a greater meaning to our lives. More than we're aware of –"

"– Humanity is doomed," Adam interrupted. "Greed and the acquisition of power still dominate the thinking of our leaders. This flawed thinking, and the possession of nuclear weaponry, is the impediment to humanity's survival. Humans kill each other for power, territory, money, and sometimes for no reason other than being born in a different place, with a different skin colour. Or for believing in the 'wrong' god. And shall we discuss the destruction of this planet's climate and ecosystem? Or the fact that the wealth of its citizenry is disproportionately held by a privileged 1% who generally do everything in their power to keep it that way while at the same time millions of humans die every day in starvation and of treatable diseases?" Stillman looked like she was about to burst, but Adam stopped her with a raised hand. "The Vu-Hak showed me remnants of the civilisations they had encountered. Civilisations, which had either destroyed themselves, or were on the verge of doing so. There are no other spacefaring civilisations. They never make it."

"We can change," said Stillman. "Complete disarmament. It could happen."

"You cannot put the genie back in the bottle. Humanity is not sufficiently mature to control such technology. This is the way of the universe."

"And the Vu-Hak are?" said Stillman, angrily.

Adam pushed himself off the wall and walked slowly out of the shadows and into the sunlight. The rays reflected off his cerulean body, highlighting the grooves and muscles, making him shine like a new car. He looked like a god, a comic-book caricature made real. He turned and faced us and I thought there was definitely sadness to his voice, instead of his usual emotionless tone.

"You do not understand the nature of things. The way the universe is set up. Each galaxy acquires an apex predator. A super-predator if you like. The Vu-Hak occupies this position in their galaxy. All worlds fell under its dominion. None were allowed to survive, or to challenge them. None."

"But they shouldn't be here, in our galaxy!" insisted Hubert. "It's a mistake. Humanity should be allowed to learn from its mistakes... this can't be our legacy!"

Adam walked away from the wall and looked upwards, taking in the sunlight. "Ninety per cent of humanity believes in an afterlife. Many of your leaders believe that death brings everlasting life. These people possess the means to pull the nuclear trigger and bring human history to an end. It will happen very soon, Vu-Hak or not."

Hubert snorted. "So, because humanity is on the verge of self destruction, what difference does it make if we go out a couple of years early? Is that what you're saying?"

Adam blinked slowly in that reptilian way I'd seen him do many times. "There is another reason. Something that I have slowly come to realise. An extrapolation, if you like, from what I have said and observed. The nature of humanity, and what it has exhibited behaviourally thus far, make us an ideal candidate for this galaxy's superpredator. We are little different from the Vu-Hak, at least in the early millennia of their evolution. If allowed to proceed unchecked through this bottleneck, humanity will spread its destruction, its wanton disinterest in other species, beyond its home world. To the detriment of all other emergent species."

Stillman stood stiffly against the wall. "So you don't care anymore about your fellow humans?"

"I am no longer human. I will survive, as my world crumbles around me. I will live a million lifetimes in this shell. How can I care about humanity any more?"

"No," I said, standing up. "I refuse to accept that you don't care any more about humanity. You saved my life. Why did you bother if you don't care?"

Adam shook his head and his green eyes turned towards me. I felt his emotions push through, fragments of happiness and affection bobbing about on the surface of a deep ocean of melancholia.

My daughter watched as Cora was murdered. Now I have killed my daughter in cold blood. I wanted to do it; I wanted to end her life. This is what humans are. There is no hope for any of us.

I looked up aghast, realising he didn't know. I grabbed both his hands in mine. "Amy isn't dead. You didn't kill her. She's in the hospital. She's going to be okay."

Adam looked at me and uncertainty played across his features, His eyes flicked right and left.

I did not kill her? I tried to...

I gripped his hands tighter, and was rewarded by a responding squeeze. I realised I had to build on this.

"After what you learned today, your anger was inevitable. What you did was understandable. It was ...a human response. But, you have another chance. Forgiveness. It's what makes us better than animals. And it's what will get humanity through these dark times."

He pulled back and I felt his anguish pour over me, cold and heavy like a wet blanket.

I... Amy and I, how can we get past this? And even if we could, how could she accept me? I am always going to be different. I can never fit back in to human society.

I closed my eyes, squeezing back the tears. Memories flooded in again. I remembered the immense and inconsolable sense of loss when my daughter had died. When my estranged father had died soon afterwards, I'd moved to Creech just to re-establish some connection with him. Something to give me a sense of belonging, a sense of family. When Adam revealed the truth about my father and mother's relationship, it mattered less than I thought it would.

"We can help Amy, together," I said. "You and I. She needs you. She needs her father back in her life."

He shifted his gaze downwards. "Look at me, Kate. What can I give her?'

"You can give her love. Your daughter will always love you. Under the surface, there is always that bond that cannot be broken. Your wife gave you a precious gift, a daughter. A daughter who has made mistakes, yes, but mistakes that can be forgiven. And she will forgive you your mistakes as well. Just give yourself a chance …"

I stopped, a sob lodging in my throat as I saw my daughter's face again. The bloodstain on her forehead, the chalkiness of her skin, her closed eyes. I understood what he was feeling. Why he was disconnected. When my daughter died, nothing made sense anymore. Any direction and meaning my life possessed was gone, blown away by a hurricane of grief.

I pictured Adam walking the seafront of San Francisco, gazing out at the breakers as the fog came in and the bridge faded behind the grey drizzle. The wind blew and the waves bumped against the rocks but for him the world had stopped existing. Passers-by, nearby traffic, were irrelevant, like photographs in an album belonging to someone else. He'd read her letters, listened to their special songs, and lay on her side of the bed with the pillow in his arms, staring out of the window unable to sleep. His despondency was washing over me, drowning me. A murdered wife, a broken daughter from a failed marriage, his own death and resurrection as a tin man; all in the face of the coming apocalypse. It slowly dawned on me that it might never have been a realistic hope. He was too far-gone, had experienced too much trauma, and worst of all, knew that there was no end to it for him.

When everyone is dead, I will be alone again…

As he spoke to me I had visions of the beautiful green fields of earth being reduced to ash and charcoal, with the smell of burnt flesh and wood smoke hanging in a haze obscuring a blood red sun. The heart and flesh ripped out of cities, now standing like skeletons, broken and serrated edges puncturing the sky. Oceans no longer moving, semi-stagnant pools of corpses, human and wildlife. Empty skies darkening as the nuclear winter approached. I pulled at his hand, making him look down at me. There were no tears, his face expressionless and vacant, despite the profusion of emotion going on behind his eyes.

"You don't have to be alone," I said quietly. "I'll be there for you. I promise. We'll help Amy – you and me, together."

His eyes seemed to narrow, and I thought there was a twitch at the corner of his mouth. Then I felt a faint breeze on the back of my neck as the temperature in the cavern dropped rapidly. A pungent ozone-like smell of assailed my nostrils, and the temperature dropped further. The hairs on the back of my neck stood up and the whole atmosphere became charged, like a thunderstorm was about to strike.

I realised we were too late.

A small sphere of light was materialising in the middle of the cavern, no bigger than a golf ball, but as incandescent as a small sun. A pressure started to build up in my head, and a visceral growling reverberated in my ears. I watched Stillman walk slowly over to Hubert and I wasn't surprised when he hugged her tightly, closing his eyes. I saw him whispering to her, but I couldn't make out what he was saying. The fight went out of me and I fell to my knees, tears flowing freely. I looked up at Adam, who was staring into the sphere as dazzling strobe-like beams danced around the cavern's walls, spinning and whirling with prismatic iridescence. The sphere spasmed and grew into a tumescent ball of silvery liquid. A deep matt blackness appeared as a pinpoint at the very centre, soon pulsing and expanding within the sphere itself. As it grew, stars and novae became visible as the portal opened and the passageway to the other galaxy was unlocked.

Then I heard Adam laughing.

I felt the melancholia drain away from him, to be replaced by a sense of contentment, and of purpose. The green phosphorescence exploded more brightly behind his eyes, and I waited for the voice of the Vu-Hak to burst through. Instead I heard Adam's voice in my head, clear, sonorous, gentle, calming.

You promise?

He walked towards the portal and I reached out to grab him but he smiled and gently pushed me to the side. I felt my knees give way and I dropped to the ground, sliding down the wall. I tried to get up but couldn't move.

"Adam," I managed to get out. "Please don't go."

He looked over his shoulder at me and smiled. The portal was right above him and he didn't appear to be affected by it at all. I could see it turn watery and his reflection appeared in its surface. I waited for it to expand for the final time and for the Vu-Hak to emerge. Adam held out a hand to me and waved. I felt his mind opening and a flood of thoughts, organised and coherent, speared my brain like a syringe.

"Please, Adam…" I couldn't complete the sentence. My head was spinning and spots were dancing in front of my eyes.

Then the portal consumed him and the world went dark.

CHAPTER THIRTY-THREE
One week later
Arlington National Cemetery, Washington, DC

Standing by the Tomb of the Unknowns, I pulled the collar of my jacket around my neck, and put my sunglasses back on. It was cool, the air was fresh, and there was some early morning dew on the grass. Three hundred and twenty soldiers had just been put to rest, and America had again said its farewell to another cohort of young men and women that had lost their lives in the service of their nation. A lone guard slowly marched across the front of the white marble monument, his rifle topped off with a bayonet, the thick yellow stripe down his crisp blue uniform pants flicking metronomically in time with each step.

The side of the monument facing me depicted three Greek figures symbolising 'Peace', 'Victory' and 'Valor'. I walked around to the western side, past the three wreaths lying limply on the ground, and waited for the guard to pass before stopping. The inscription on this side read: *'HERE RESTS IN HONORED GLORY AN AMERICAN SOLDIER KNOWN BUT TO GOD'.*

This only made me angrier.

I watched the presidential motorcade pull past the visitor centre and turn onto Route 110, accelerating smoothly away as the phalanx of motorcyclists flashed red and blue lights and cut through the traffic. Quiet crowds still lined the grasses and hillocks around the Kennedy grave and visitor centre, waving American flags in a sombre and generally respectful way. Already, people were making their way home, snaking through the pathways to the car parks where tour buses and taxicabs were waiting. The smell of gun smoke lingered, the sound of the 21-gun salute still echoing around the fields containing the thousands of identical white tombstones.

I had always liked visiting here, in another life. Seeing the brave men laid to rest, the stones giving a promise of not being forgotten, collectively reminding a population brought up on video games and rap music what sacrifices bought their freedom.

I was about to go but felt a tug on my sleeve. I turned and there was Colleen Stillman, wearing a square black hat, a charcoal suit and gloves. She gave me a forced smile. "Hi Kate, how're you doing?"

I frowned, and looked behind her at the dispersing crowds. I identified at least two FBI agents standing silently, hands at their sides, watching. I sighed and gave her a withering look. "Where's Hubert?"

She shook her head. "Busy. You know how things are. It's only been a week."

"A week of lies and denials. Hubert won't return any of my calls."

"Kate, you know that we can't tell the real story. Not yet. The public just isn't ready."

This angered me more than I thought it would. I folded my arms and stared down at her. "When will they be ready Colleen? I read the *Post* this morning. 'Terrorist attack at SETI foiled by heroic local police' and what was the other one, oh yes an 'unexploded Cold War bomb detonated in Nevada'. Is that the best we can come up with?"

Stillman looked away, watching the departing crowds. "Everyone agrees that this is for the best. Even the folks at SETI think that this could set back the search for extra-terrestrial life. Scare away donations, that kind of thing. Remember, the public have always been suspicious about 'mad' scientists being 'out of control', doing things without government approval, all that."

"It's a whitewash, and a disgrace," I said, my voice becoming strident. "People have a right to know what happened. Hundreds died because we fucked up our 'first contact' with an alien race. This is a turning point in humanity's history and we're just going to pretend it didn't happen? What about taking this on the chin and looking outward for once? Thinking about a more grown-up posture for humanity in the future? Maybe trying to keep a lid on our basest instincts, maybe destroying all our fucking nuclear arsenals …"

Stillman took a deep breath and took hold of my arm, walking me over to the side of the monument away from the guard and facing one of the cemetery fields. "It is what it is, Kate. The president's approved this story. There're no aliens. The portal, wormhole or whatever it is - or was - hasn't opened since Adam went through over a week ago. He stopped them."

I stared out at the parallel lines of tombstones arrowing into the distance, broken up by trees and pathways. I'd heard that they were arranged like this to represent soldiers marching in a straight line. Some of the graves had flags by their sides; a few had small bouquets of fresh flowers. Just visible in the distance was the white-capped Potomac river and the Washington Monument.

I shrugged out of Stillman's grip and gave her an angry look. "I'm not going to keep quiet."

Stillman folded her arms and returned my stare. "No-one will listen to you Kate. It's over."

I rubbed at my eyes, irritated and frustrated again. "What about Adam? Does his sacrifice get recognised at all? He saved you, he saved me, and in fact he saved everyone on this fucking planet. Doesn't he deserve recognition for that?"

"He will, in time. Just not yet."

I shook my head, and gave an exasperated laugh. "And what happens to Amy?"

Stillman finally couldn't hold my stare and looked out over the fields of tombstones. "Amy's in a secure psychiatric unit, and is getting the best help for her addictions. She'll be told the truth about her father at some point, but not until she's better. She's too messed up at the moment."

"Can I see her?"

"I don't think that's a good idea, Kate."

"No, I guess not."

We were silent for a minute or two, and then Stillman reached out and touched my elbow. "Kate, we really don't know what happened down there, do we?"

"What do you mean?" I asked.

She looked away, watching the guard continue his vigil. There was a chill to the wind, and I wished I'd brought a scarf or something. "Adam said the Vu-Hak that came with him was dead, but he didn't explain how that happened. That worries me. What if he was lying? I mean, Adam survived, that machine body survived, but the alien somehow conveniently is dead…?"

I closed my eyes. I hadn't sensed the presence of the Vu-Hak when we found Adam in the crater or just before he entered the portal. Previously it'd always been there, a persistent subliminal sensation. I looked at Stillman and saw a frightened woman, not unlike me, a woman trying to make sense out of the non-sensical.

"I don't think the alien was there," I began. "I think either the nuke or Adam somehow killed it. But even if he didn't kill it, he took it with him through the portal."

I looked away, feeling the tears pricking the surface of my eyes. I felt her arm on mine again, a reassuring touch, a gentle squeeze. I nodded a silent acknowledgment. "We're safe," she said, smiling up at me. "The portal is no more. The Vu-Hak haven't come back. Humanity can develop in its own own time. Evolve. Everything's changed behind the scenes. Even the president …"

One of the agents approached soundlessly, like a ghost. Stillman glanced at him, nodded, and let go of my arm. "Kate, I need to head back. Lots to do." She pulled a card out of her pocket, and handed it over. "My private number is on there, call me anytime. If I don't hear from you in a week or so I'll get in touch and we'll meet up, yes?"

I took the card without looking and put it in my bag. Stillman reached out and we shook hands. She turned to go, but then stopped. "I heard you're going back to Chicago?"

"Yes, I've reapplied for my old position in the ER."

"Well, anything we can do for you, foot in the door and all that, just let me know? Change of career ... Special Agent. Think about it?" Stillman winked at me and disappeared into the crowd

I put my hands in my pockets and shivered in the cold morning air. The guard continued to drill silently in front of the marble tomb, all rigidity and perfected movements. I pulled a handkerchief out of my handbag and wiped my eyes underneath my shades. No one noticed me, just another mourner at a funeral.

The wind was picking up and I felt a tingling under my scalp and a little electric shock-type jolt down my neck. The hairs on my neck stood up despite my high collar, and I could see goose pimples on my wrists. I looked around and behind and through the wall of people, but nothing caught my eye. No one was looking at me; everything seemed normal. People were leaving, slowly shuffling down the walkway and slopes past the manicured lawns and rows of neatly trimmed bushes and trees. But the temperature was dropping abnormally fast, and I blew out a breath that frosted instantly in the air.

My eyes blurred and I felt a pressure behind them as if someone was squeezing me at my temples.

Someone *was* watching me.

My reptilian brain was screaming 'flight' and adrenaline was being pumped around my body in preparation. But for what? I looked around me and behind me but there was nothing there. There was no sound at all; no wind noise, chatter, bird song. It was as if the atmosphere had been sucked off into space and my ears had been stuffed with cotton wool.

Then I caught movement just at the edge of my vision, fast and surreal, out of place with the ebb and flow of the crowd. I saw a tall dark figure, very pale with jet-black hair, wearing sunglasses and a dark suit. He looked straight at me and his mouth twitched in a half smile. He removed his sunglasses, to reveal perfect blue irises and deep black pupils. I could feel my facial muscles loosening, and my tongue moved in my mouth, oversized, like it didn't belong there. I blinked, and tried to smile in return.

EPILOGUE

I picked up a rock, slate-grey and worn smooth by millions of years of tidal erosion, and with a flick of the wrist sent it spinning into the sea just as the waves started to recede. Bouncing and skipping, each impact seemed to add energy and sending it higher until it struck a wave and disappeared. I counted twelve individual skips and abstractly wondered what the world record number of bounces for skimming stones was. Immediately, the answer came. Fifty-two. Impossible, I thought. But then I thought about it some more. The stone generates lift in the same manner as a flying disc, by pushing water down as it moves across the water at an angle. The stone's rotation acts to stabilize it against the torque of lift being applied to the back. An angle of about 20° between the stone and the water's surface is optimal. If horizontal speed can be maintained, skipping can continue indefinitely.

I rummaged around the rocks at my feet, selecting and discarding a dozen or so until I found the one I wanted. Placing it in my hand, I assessed its weight at 257grams and ran my fingers across its surface, noting the smoothness and the absence of significant pockmarks. I wedged it firmly between my finger and thumb, bracing its underside with my other fingers and after taking a quick look at the surface of the water, cast the stone horizontally with a whip-like action. This time I had aimed down the beach, catching the smooth water of the tide as it lapped up on the flat sand. The stone accelerated out of sight, skipping and bouncing with little regard for the laws of physics. I counted sixty-five bounces.

"Gee, how'd you do that?" came a voice.

I turned to find a small boy descending the wooden stairs built into the cliff at the edge of the beach. He was wearing board-shorts, scuffed Converse trainers and a dirty white t-shirt. His hair was bleached blonde and flapping around his ears as the onshore breeze played with it. A scrappy little cattle dog, red-brown with pelt like a worn carpet, had also scuttled down the stairs and was now sniffing around my legs and wagging his small tail. I bent down and ruffled the fur between his ears, and he sat back on the sand and seemed to smile up at me. I glanced back at the boy, who looked eight or nine years old, and was now standing at the foot of the stairs nervously watching.

"It's all in the wrists," I said, and tried a smile.

The boy nodded slowly, but did not approach.

"Where are your parents?" I asked.

He indicated back up the stairs with a flick of his head. "Not far. They'll be along soon."

I looked up the cliff, tracked the winding wooden staircase as far as it would go before it disappeared a few hundred yards into the scrubland of the Park. I caught a glimpse of another, less well maintained section higher up the slope as it meandered its way around the cliff. Beyond, just above the tree line, the sky was a blood red orange with wispy smoke plumes oozing into the atmosphere, diffusing and mingling as they rose. Eastward, back along the beach, the rainforest canopy was broken up by the skeletal remains of holiday apartments, previously millionaire's weekend retreats with ocean views to die for. Now they were deserted and broken, their burnt-out rafters and beams obscenely silhouetted charcoal against the darkening sky.

I closed my eyes, immersing myself in the roar of crashing waves and the hissing of the water being pulled back over finely ground sand and gravel. I registered a mixture of odors; the charcoal of burning timber, putrid and decaying animal carcasses, sharp petroleum fuel, all clinging to the onshore breeze.

"Are you one of them?" the boy asked, his blue eyes as wide as dinner-plates.

I regarded him silently, considering how to reply.

"My dad said you'd all left."

His dog pulled loose and galloped excitedly into the surf as a wave rolled in. The wave crashed over him, causing him to yelp in canine bliss, and shake furiously in that corkscrew motion patented by all furry animals. He splashed out of the waves and approached me again. I dropped to my haunches, and he licked my hand with a raspy, sandpapery tongue.

I marveled at how real it felt.

Turning my hand over, I regarded my long fingers, the homogenous skin pigmentation, and the absence of any defects. I made a fist and the neural feedback felt totally normal, muscles and tendons flexing and skin tightening in synchronicity. I could see moisture from the dog's tongue evaporate from my fingertips, my afferent neurological pathway signaling a sensation of cooling as expected. I wondered why I had no fingerprints. I shook my head, sighed, and rose to my feet.

The boy took a step back, and I realized how strange I must appear to him. I was dressed in a white one-piece garment that covered me from shoulders to mid thigh without any seams, creases or pockets. I was barefoot. My hair was cut just above my ears, and despite the breeze, remained perfectly in place. A single horizontal strip of shadow crossed my nose like an Apache Indian and obscured my phosphorescent green eyes. My skin was almost as white as my clothing and hair.

I sat down on the rocks and let the tide lazily lap around my toes. Out over the Coral Sea, the sky was showing signs of the coming evening, but was still a glorious cloudless powder blue, and the water below the ocean's white-capped waves was picture-postcard azure. The crescent moon was just visible, craters, mountains and plains appearing in ivory bas-relief.

I looked sideways at the boy, and tapped the rock next to me. "Come, sit with me?"

His dog had flounced back into the waves, and had started a game of chase with a stick he had found floating in off the tide. The boy looked up and shook his head, staring at his dog, wondering whether to call him in.

"It's okay," I said. "What's your name?"

He looked back up the staircase, and shrugged. "David."

"Hello David. Nice to meet you."

I tried another smile, and it helped that the dog was caught up in another wave and rolled over and over like a log caught in a rapids, yelping and barking in delight. The boy sidled over and slowly sat down next to me. Up close his skin was pale and patchy, with broken veins over his temple. He looked thin and unhealthy, and his bare arms were covered with scratches and bruises. His knees were a mottled purple, faded like a patchwork quilt.

I reached over and put an arm around his shoulders, and in silence, we watched the dog playing in the surf. He had found a jellyfish, all pale and translucent with long stringy blue tendrils, and was starting to eat it. Abruptly, the boy leaned forward, clutched his stomach and vomited into the pool of seawater at his feet. I held him until he had stopped retching, and washed his mouth and face with seawater from another puddle. I could feel his ribs moving under his shirt and the tremor of his muscles as he tried to control the nausea.

I closed my eyes and allowed his emotions and thoughts to flow into mine. I sensed his fatigue, his loneliness and his terror. He was finding some comfort in my presence, despite the fact that he knew what I was. I coaxed his liver cells to manufacture anxiolytic proteins, which I then released into his blood stream and through the blood-brain barrier. I could sense them washing through his cerebral cortex, taking away the fear and anxiety. He looked up at me, eyes filled with tears.

"Thank-you," he said.

Then he glanced over my shoulder, and his eyes widened once more. He pointed a shaky finger towards the sky but I took hold of his hand and lowered it to his lap. I sensed a subliminal rumbling, like the passage of an underground subway train, and concentric ripples appeared in the surrounding rock pools. Sand started to trickle down from cracks higher up the cliff, and the tremors began to loosen the compact sand at my feet. Following his gaze, I saw a bright moon-sized blot in the sky, enlarging fast. The grumbling noise became more visceral and the waves stopped their progress and now just sloshed around my feet like oil being swirled in a frying pan.

The boy put his fingers in his ears, closed his eyes and started to scream. I elevated the level of anxiolytic chemicals coursing through his body, and immediately his eyes closed, consciousness fading. I caught him as he slid off the rock and lowered him gently to the wet sand.

His dog had stopped playing, and was looking out to sea, barking steadily and in puzzlement. I stood and watched, as the shimmering sphere became an enlarging obsidian whirlpool bereft of lights or color. As it grew, the ocean hollowed out in a concave arc, the seabed underneath becoming exposed to air for the first time in many eons. The atmosphere pulsed and surged as waves of unidentified energy charged the air with static.

A human figure appeared, and slowly glided down towards me. He touched down softly on the sand, ripples and tremors appearing under his feet. Like me, he was dressed in white, but with black hair, sharp, angular features and an aquiline nose. He looked around at the beach, then up the cliff-face at the staircase, then at the boy, sleeping peacefully by the rock. He lifted his head, as if sniffing the air, and closed his eyes.

"It's time to leave," he said. "We can't delay any longer. Finding you took too long."

I shook my head. "I need to make sure he'll be alright."

His eyes blinked lazily, green phosphorescence flashing. "There's nothing you can do for them. You must know that."

I ignored him, and bent over the boy who was making quiet breathing noises. I put a hand on his chest, receiving physiological feedback from his cardiovascular and neural systems. I turned him slightly, pulling his top leg over the other one and laying him in the recovery position. I felt irritation being directed at me, and I looked up at the figure watching.

"I won't let him suffer," I said.

The man walked over, knelt down next to me, and placed a hand on the sleeping boy's forehead. He gave an unexpectedly gentle caress of his brow, brushing a lock of hair away.

"He is suffering. It'll be better if he dies in his sleep."

The man stood up and put his hand out, palm up. I sighed, knowing it would come to this. I was now putting us all at risk, jeopardizing our future, whatever that was.

"We should go."

The dog ambled over and licked his hand, tail wagging. He pulled it back, as if scalded. His mouth turned downwards and he blinked once. The dog shivered and its legs gave way. It slumped to the ground, unmoving.

I heard a noise, and saw that the boy was stirring, twisting his neck and making soft groaning sounds. The man blinked once again, and the boy's head drooped forward until his mouth and nose disappeared into the seawater pool.

I closed my eyes and waited for the tears to come. When they didn't, I looked up at the swirling anomaly, floating above the sea.

"It's done then?"

"Yes."

"Are there many left alive?"

There was a brief pause, then: "Does it matter?"

I shook my head sadly. "Not any more."

ABOUT THE AUTHOR

P.A. Vasey is a Cancer Physician, born in Newcastle, UK. He moved to Brisbane, Australia in 2004. His professional writing credits include over 200 publications including peer-reviewed journals, book chapters, conference contributions and electronic outputs in the field of cancer research.

'TRINITY'S LEGACY' is his first novel. It was an official semi-finalist for the 2018 CYGNUS Book Awards for Science Fiction, a division of the Chanticleer International Book Awards.

The second novel in the trilogy, **'TRINITY'S FALL'**, was released in December 2019 and became a #1 Amazon Best Seller in multiple categories.

The third and final novel, **'TRINITY EVOLUTION'**, will be released in 2021.

At the author's website http://www.pavasey.com you can get a free no-obligation download of a short story entitled **'I AM TRINITY'**.

Made in the USA
Coppell, TX
01 October 2025